# CONQUEROR'S KISS

A soft murmur of pleasure escaped Jennet, and she rubbed her cheek against Hacon's warm chest. She shook free of sleep's hold only to be caught in passion's grip. The way Hacon moved his hands over her back, lightly cupping her derriere and pressing her tightly against his hardness, made her ache. She gave a soft gasp of delighted surprise when he smoothed his hands up her sides.

Hacon took quick advantage of her parted lips, covering her mouth with his and plunging his tongue deep inside. He groaned softly when she wrapped her limbs around his body and eagerly welcomed his fierce kiss. It took every ounce of his willpower not to take her there and then, but they were far from private. He could hear the rest of the army camped all around them beginning to stir. He ended the kiss, grit his teeth against his strong reluctance to do so, and gently broke free of the embrace. Before his aching hunger for her made him change his mind, he hurriedly rose to his feet. The way she looked at him, her beautiful eyes warm and inviting, made it the hardest thing he had ever done.. . .

## Books by Hannah Howell

ONLY FOR YOU

MY VALIANT KNIGHT

UNCONQUERED

WILD ROSES

A TASTE OF FIRE

HIGHLAND DESTINY

HIGHLAND HONOR

HIGHLAND PROMISE

A STOCKINGFUL OF JOY

HIGHLAND VOW

HIGHLAND KNIGHT

HIGHLAND HEARTS

HIGHLAND BRIDE

HIGHLAND ANGEL

HIGHLAND GROOM

HIGHLAND WARRIOR

RECKLESS

HIGHLAND CONQUEROR

HIGHLAND CHAMPION

HIGHLAND LOVER

CONQUEROR'S KISS

HIGHLAND BARBARIAN

Published by Zebra Books

# HANNAH HOWELL

# CONQUEROR'S KISS

ZEBRA BOOKS
Kensington Publishing Corp.
www.kensingtonbooks.com

ZEBRA BOOKS are published by

Kensington Publishing Corp.
850 Third Avenue
New York, NY 10022

All Kensington titles, imprints and distributed lines are available at special quantity discounts for bulk purchases for sales promotion, premiums, fund-raising, educational or institutional use.

Special book excerpts or customized printings can also be created to fit specific needs. For details, write or phone the office of the Kensington Special Sales Manager: Kensington Publishing Corp., 850 Third Avenue, New York, NY 10022. Attn. Special Sales Department. Phone: 1-800-221-2647.

Zebra and the Z logo Reg. U.S. Pat. & TM Off.

First Zebra Printing: November 2006
10 9 8 7 6 5 4 3 2 1

Printed in the United States of America

# Chapter 1

*April 2, 1318—Berwick, Scotland*

Quiet humming did little to stifle the grumbling of Jennet's stomach. Her constant hunger was somewhat easier to bear in the convent, where each woman within the thick, gray walls suffered equally. Unlike the greedy Lady de Tournay and her swinish family, Jennet mused, then hurriedly began her morning ablutions, hoping the icy water would push such uncharitable thoughts from her mind. She had fled to the convent to find peace. That would remain elusive if she did not shake free of her bitterness, born of six years in servitude to the ill-tempered de Tournays.

Again her stomach loudly protested its emptiness. She cursed, then swiftly begged the Lord's pardon. It was such lapses that kept her from succumbing to the abbess's constant urgings to take vows and begin working toward becoming a nun. Jennet was not sure she had the character to be a nun. She had too much bitterness, was too cynical, too angry and unforgiving. A year in the seclusion of the convent had done little to ease those feelings.

"And," she muttered as she donned her plain brown gown, "I dinnae rush to prayer each morn."

She shook her head, then began to braid her long raven hair. The abbess must have seen how tossled she was, proof that she had rushed to prayers straight from bed early that morning. As she donned her headdress she frowned, listening carefully. It was difficult to be certain, but there did seem to be a dull but rising roar of many loud male voices.

"Mayhaps the Scots have finally given up their siege," she murmured as she sat on her cot to begin the mending she had been given to do. "They have certainly been harrying the town for months. Or"—she froze, needle in hand, and felt a swift rush of terror—"they have scaled the protective walls and finally retaken the border fortress from the English."

Jennet forced herself to remain calm, to ignore the muffled sounds. She was safe. Despite the tales the abbess told, Jennet could not believe the Scots would defile a convent. Even eighteen years of war under the Bruce could not have made her people so ungodly. A battle might well rage outside, but here she was free of that at last. This time she would not have to face the violence and destruction directly.

The wimple she mended was barely done when she realized the sounds she sought to ignore were much closer now. Even as she wondered if she should chance a look into the hall, the door to her tiny room burst open, splintering slightly as it slammed against the stone wall. The sight that filled the doorway caused her to drive her needle into her hand. Only partly aware of that self-inflicted wound, she extracted the needle, absently put her wounded palm to her mouth to ease the sting, and stared at the man who had invaded her refuge.

He leaned indolently against the door frame, his strong arms encased in greaves and crossed over his broad mail-covered chest. His helmet, with its noseguard, hid so much of his face that she could see little but his smile. That indolent grin turned her shock and fear to rage. She was facing certain death, and he was laughing at her. Hissing a curse, she pulled her dagger from a hidden pocket in her skirts. Her fury was reinforced by the terrified cries of the nuns that began to echo through the halls.

"And what do ye mean to do with that wee needle, lass?" he drawled in a soft, deep voice.

"Cut ye a new smile, ye godless heathen," she cried, and lunged at him.

He caught her with ease, one large gauntleted hand curled tightly around her thin wrist, the mail cutting into her skin. "So fierce for a nun." As they struggled, he turned slightly so that her back faced the hallway.

There was no way she could break his grip, but the amusement in his voice kept her struggling to push her dagger down until it might pierce his flesh. "I am no nun," she cried, "but a seeker of refuge, and I mean to send ye straight into hell's fires for defiling this holy place!"

"'Tis a petty threat to hurl at a mon who is already excommunicated."

"So the abbess spoke true. The Bruce's men are naught but the devil's minions, cast off by the Pope." She saw a look of cool amusement on what was visible of his hard face, then, without warning, a blinding pain filled the back of her head.

Hacon caught the too-slim girl as she collapsed, rendered unconscious by his comrade's blow to her head. "I wondered if ye meant to act, Dugald, or stand by and watch me being slaughtered."

Dugald grunted. He frowned down at the heavy silver chalice with which he had struck the girl, then dropped it back into the sack he held. "She had no chance. 'Twill be a woeful shame to kill her. The wee lass has spirit."

"Kill her? Now, why should I kill her?"

"We were told to show as little mercy as the English king did when he took this place in Baliol's Rebellion. Kill all we can and plunder the place."

"And this"—Hacon neatly tossed the unconscious girl over his shoulder—"is plunder."

"Aye? Looks like a wee lass to me. And what need have we of a nun, forsaken by the Pope as we are?"

"She isnae a nun. Are ye so eager to spill her blood?"

"Nay. I have no stomach for killing a lass, and weel ye ken it. I have no stomach for angering the Black Douglas either. The Bruce chose a fierce, hard mon as his lieutenant, and 'tis unwise to cross him. Douglas doesnae mean to halt here but to go on. What will ye do with your plunder then? Ye cannae hide her from him."

"I willnae hide her. She is mine, and there is an end to it. Now, grab hold of her blanket and help me tie her onto my back." He nodded toward her cot.

Even as he did as he was told, Dugald grumbled, "And how do ye expect to fight with such a burden?"

"This slight lass is no burden, and I doubt much fighting will be done. The townsfolk flee if they are able. We but need to fill our coffers with plunder."

"If we dinnae get to the doing of it, the plunder will be all gone."

Hacon winked at his scowling cousin. "Dinnae wear yourself thin worrying. I ken weel where to look. Have I not given us a good beginning?" He nodded at the sack Dugald carried.

Dugald nodded grimly as he strode down the hall of the nunnery toward the main entrance. Hacon adjusted the weight of his captive more comfortably against his back and followed. He winced and increased his pace as a woman's high-pitched scream echoed through the dim hallways. He preferred the chaotic battle out in the streets between the victory-drunk Scots and the panicked, fleeing English to the rape and slaughter of the defenseless nuns going on in here.

For ten years he had been with Robert the Bruce, ever since the beard on his face had been but the light fluff of a boy. When the Bruce returned from exile in Arran, Scotland had been demoralized, the devastation widespread. Bruce's victory against the English at Loudon Hill had renewed the people's hope, and Hacon had joined many others in racing to aid the claimant to the Scottish throne.

But now he ached to go home to Dubheilrig. Instead, he found himself on yet another raid into England, another bloody foray over land that had been deeply scarred by war.

"Ye cannae stop fighting for the Bruce now," Dugald said as he started through the gates leading to the narrow, winding streets of Berwick.

"How do ye ken I was thinking about that?" Hacon asked as he strode beside his kinsman into the heart of the walled town.

"That black look upon your face. I have seen it before. Ye cannae walk away from it yet. Aye, ye got your knighthood at Bannockburn, but ye havenae won a square foot of land yet."

"Did my father send ye to be my conscience?"

"Nay. He trusts ye to do as ye ought. Aye, as ye must. 'Tis just that I feel I must speak the truth. The Bruce holds our lands. Only he can return them to us. 'Twas our weakness which lost them to the de Umfravilles. Weel, after being honed in this war we willnae be weak. 'Tis some comfort, kenning the de Umfravilles lost those lands to the Bruce, but even that comfort will wane if the Bruce gifts our lands elsewhere."

"That will ne'er happen," Hacon muttered as he stepped ahead of his cousin. "Come along. If I cannae win back our lands through faithful service and the strength of my sword, then I mean to have enough plunder to buy them back." He strode off into town, confident Dugald would watch his back, just as he had done for ten long, bloody years.

Hacon slouched in a rough, heavy chair before the fire, heartily approving of the new-style fireplace and chimney set in the wall. It was far better than the usual, a hearth in the center of the room with an inadequate venting hole in the roof. He wondered how Dugald always managed to find such fine quarters for them. This had to be one of the few houses in Berwick that still had an intact thatched roof, one untouched by the fires that even now scorched the town. After glancing at the plunder scattered on the table in the center of the room, he fixed his gaze upon the female plunder sprawled unconscious at his feet.

Twice the girl had come awake while strapped to his back. Twice she had wrapped her lovely slim hands about his throat. Twice Dugald had had to strike her unconscious again to save his cousin. Hacon grinned. She had spirit. Dugald could well be right—she was the devil's child, even though she had been hidden away in a convent. He would be sure to keep all weapons out of her reach. She could prove to be a very troublesome bounty.

But a bonnie one, he mused, leaning forward. She looked very tempting sprawled on the sheepskin with her thick raven hair splayed out around her. Her headdress had been an early victim of the battle in the streets. While he suspected her too-thin build was a result of the famine that had ravaged the area over the last two years, he found no fault in it. There were curves enough to please him. Her skin was the soft white of ivory touched with all the warmth of good health. He easily recalled her magnificent eyes, their vivid green enhanced by sparks of fury and defiance as she had faced him in the convent.

"Do ye think I have harmed her?"

Glancing up at Dugald, who stood on the other side of the girl, Hacon shook his head. "She breathes easily and there is a growing flickering in her eyelids. She will wake soon."

"Then ye had best guard your throat."

The way Dugald eyed the girl, as if she were as great a threat as any well-armed Englishman, made Hacon laugh softly. "She has more spirit than many another in this place."

"Aye, which will make her a muckle lot of trouble. Wouldnae it be wiser to leave her behind?"

"Much wiser, but I willnae do it."

"Why? She is naught but a skinny wee lass."

"Ah, now there is a puzzle." Hacon shrugged. "I just willnae."

Jennet had grasped consciousness in time to hear the one man's disparaging description of her and the other's response. Her head ached and she knew it was their fault. She had made no move to reveal that she was now awake; her captor's answer had interested her since it might reveal her fate.

Now, however, deciding their talk was of little help, Jennet released the groan she had held back. She propped herself up on one elbow and tentatively touched the back of her head. The man had clearly curbed the strength of his blows, for she could find no serious injury, but her head was pounding. Slowly she gazed up at her captor.

He still looked big, a tall, lean, battle-hardened man. Now that his helmet and mail hood were gone, she saw that he had thick blond hair reaching to his broad shoulders. She doubted it would lessen the breadth of his chest by much if he took off his padded jupon and the snug, bloodstained leather jerkin he wore. He had long muscular legs encased in a better quality hose and cuarans of excellent waxed rawhide tied closely about his calves. She remembered the flint of armor on his forearms earlier, but suspected that had long been discarded. His clothes gave her little hint as to his station. Even the armor she recalled could simply be pieces he had stolen from dead knights upon the battlefield.

As she carefully sat up, she lifted her gaze to his face. He had the finest pair of eyes she had ever seen on a man, a clear rich blue. His lean face, high cheekbones, and a long straight nose bespoke a better birth. In fact, his looks reminded her very strongly of a Dane or a Norseman, and she frowned.

"Ye are a Scot?" she demanded. "We havenae got the twice-cursed Danes rampaging about to add to our grief, have we?" The man smiled too much, she thought crossly as he grinned at her.

"Aye, I am a Scot. I have my mother's looks, and she is a distant cousin to the king of Norway, so I should watch how

I speak of those people." He thrust his hand toward her. "I am Hacon Gillard of Dubheilrig."

She took his hand and found herself firmly propelled to her feet. "Jennet."

"Jennet? No other name, no kinsmen? Ye are no one's daughter and from no place?"

"Of course I am someone's daughter." She sighed and rubbed her forehead with her left hand since Hacon was slow to release her right one. "I am Jennet, daughter of Artair, a Graeme, who wed Moira, an Armstrong. I can be from Liddesdale, for those are my mother's lands. More often than not, I am from no place in particular, dragged hither and yon by my father."

"Neither name is connected with much wealth."

She glared at him. "Aye, so ye will gain no ransom for me. The Bruce's fine soldiers have already slaughtered my mother. Aye and mayhaps my father as weel. I have naught left. Best to let me slip free. I can only be a trouble to you."

"Of that I have little doubt." He stood up, placed his hands on his trim hips, and looked down at her. "Howbeit, I will keep you with me."

"Now, why should ye wish to do that?" She had a very good idea of why but wondered if he would tell her the truth.

Reaching out, Hacon took a thick lock of her hair in his hand, idly caressing it with his long fingers. "Ye Jennet, who can be from Liddesdale, are my plunder."

That was an answer in itself, she supposed. She told herself that anger would gain her nothing; nevertheless she clenched her hands into tight fists at her sides. Escape was still possible if she did not act too rashly, did not give in to the fear that threatened to conquer her anger. From the corner of her eye she saw the other man stealthily move to flank her. She had to be certain the move she finally made was unexpected.

"I am plunder, am I?"

"Aye—my plunder."

"Wee and skinny though I am?"

"Och, weel, one cannae always have the pick of the litter."

There was a tone in his voice that told her he thought he was being funny. He was grinning, and a soft chuckle came from his companion. A guffaw from behind them told her that other men were enjoying her predicament as well. That knowledge sent her temper soaring. The rape of Berwick and her own undoubtedly impending ravishment were not laughing matters.

Muttering a curse on all men, she struck out with both fists, neatly and forcefully hitting each man who flanked her square in the groin. Both howled with pain and cursed roundly as they bent over, clutching themselves. She raced for the door—and ran straight into a tall, armored man who blocked the long, narrow opening.

Staggering backward, she was roughly grasped at the shoulder by Hacon, who had stumbled after her. Still dazed, rubbing her nose, which had collided with the man's mail-clad chest, she found herself swiftly yanked behind Hacon. Curious as to why, she took a good look at the man who had ended her attempt to escape, and tensed, fear gripping her. It could be none other than Sir James Douglas, the one some called "the Good Sir James" but many another called "the Black Douglas."

And not simply because of his swarthy coloring, she thought with a shiver, her gaze fixed upon the bloodied sword in his hand. The nuns had told her many a chilling tale about this man whom they had dubbed "the Bruce's godless lieutenant." There was something about the colors he and his men wore that added to her fear, but that flicker of a memory was doused when Douglas spoke. As the words came from his mouth, she hid herself more completely behind Hacon, terrified that she would reveal her astonishment. The Black Douglas, the scourge of the North, the man who made many an English soldier tremble, spoke with a lisp.

"You are having some difficulty, Sir Gillard?" asked Douglas.

"Nay, only a brief quarrel."

"She is for ransoming?"

"Nay. She is my plunder."

"You and your men choose strange plunder." Douglas signaled to someone behind him, and a young soldier was roughly shoved into the room. "I hold the belief that the only live plunder worth taking is that which can be ransomed."

Accustomed to the man's speech impediment now and curious as to why Hacon had grown so tense, Jennet dared to glance around him again. The youth in question had obviously been cruelly handled. His beardless face was bruised and scraped. He looked ready to collapse, swaying slightly as he stood clutching a bundle of cloth protectively against his chest.

"Has the boy caused some trouble, sir?" Hacon asked.

"Some. He nearly killed one of my men and was nearly killed for it. He would be dead now had I not arrived to pull him free."

"And now?"

"And now I give him back to you. Talk some sense into the lad. I have no doubt you and your men are loyal. You have stood for the cause for ten long years. Howbeit, I believe you may carry a softness of heart. Mercy, Sir Gillard, has no place in this fight."

As abruptly as he had appeared, the Black Douglas left. Jennet breathed a sigh of relief and was startled to hear it echoed by the others in the room. Hacon shoved her toward Dugald, who grabbed her arm none too gently. Ignoring her glaring human shackle, she watched the youth as Hacon approached him.

"Your first battle, Ranald," said Hacon, "and ye try to kill one of Douglas's own men? Are ye that set upon dying, laddie?"

"I didnae ken they were his men," the youth replied, his voice hoarse and unsteady.

"They are weel marked. I weel recall pointing them out to you."

"Aye, uncle, ye did. I wasnae thinking clear."

Uncle, Jennet mused and inwardly nodded. There was a strong resemblance, although the boy's hair was not as light as Hacon's.

"Ye are lucky Douglas was in a good humor or that thoughtless head of yours would be rolling about in the street now."

"I ken it."

Jennet could see how weak the youth was and, driven by compassion, finally spoke. "If ye wish him to hear all ye say, ye had best let him sit down." She forced herself not to flinch under the glare Hacon sent her before he helped Ranald to a bench at the table, where four other men sat.

"What was so important," Hacon asked his nephew, "that ye put your own life at risk?"

"A bairn."

Although she tried not to, Jennet gaped, as did the men, as Ranald unwrapped the bundle he held. Within its folds lay a baby, a child she guessed to be about a year old. Briefly she feared for the child's life, then pushed that fear aside. Ranald would not have saved the infant if he thought his own kinsmen would kill it.

Hacon crouched beside his nephew, yet again cursing his sister for not chaining the boy safely at home. "A bairn, laddie? What can ye do with a bairn?"

"I dinnae ken. I just couldnae let them kill the wee thing. They meant to stick it on a pike. The mother . . ." Ranald stared down at the wide-eyed child and smoothed an unsteady hand over the babe's red-brown curls. "I couldnae save the poor woman. Will I always hear her cries for mercy?" he whispered.

"Mayhaps," Hacon replied with an equally soft voice, then sighed. "Ranald, we stop here but to loot Berwick, then move on to fight more battles. What can ye do with the bairn?"

"Ye willnae tow the loot into every battle. I could set the bairn down with it."

"Most of the plunder will be sent back, deeper into Scotland, with men to guard it, men who willnae want the care of a wee babe."

"I could leave it here with someone when we leave."

"Aye, mayhaps, if we find someone. Most are now dead or hiding. And we may have to leave on the run. Berwick is the last stronghold the English have in Scotland. I cannae believe they will give it up so easily."

Jennet tugged free of Donald's hold. "Weel, ye can discuss all of that later."

"I can, can I?" Hacon drawled.

The touch of scorn in her beautiful eyes stung him. He wondered fleetingly if it was born of her anger of the moment or from a fury for all men that had been set deeply. Recalling what she had said of her parents' fate, he knew it could be directed at all who fought for the Bruce.

Then she looked at young Ranald. Her expression softened, and Hacon felt the distinct pinch of jealousy. She was lovely in her anger, but with her heart-shaped face transformed by a gentler emotion she was breathtaking. A glance at his nephew told him Ranald was equally aware of her beauty.

"Aye," she said as she walked toward Ranald, "for the boy needs these injuries tended to or ye will soon be talking to the air. Get me a bowl of water and a clean cloth."

Hacon started to obey her before he realized what he was doing. When he glared at her, she met his look calmly. Muttering a curse, he fetched what she had asked for. Ranald did need his wounds seen to. Now was not the time to draw the line as to who was the captor and who was the plunder. After pushing some of the stolen goods aside, he set what she had requested on the table. He watched her closely, not truly afraid she would harm Ranald but not ready to trust her completely either.

Jennet gently took the baby from Ranald and placed the child in the arms of the man seated next to him. The man stared at the babe with such horror that she almost grinned.

He held it correctly, however, so she turned her attention back to the battered boy.

At close inspection she realized that Ranald's resemblance to Hacon was stronger than she had thought. But there was a look of gentleness, a hint of innocence, in Ranald's face that could not be found in his uncle's. The blue of Ranald's eyes was not as rich, but he held the promise of being a fine-looking man.

"Strip him to the waist," she ordered Hacon. "The way he moves tells me this jupon hides more bruises and injuries.

Even as he did so, Hacon recalled how she had nearly escaped. He would have to make her see what a mistake that would be. All the while he lent his assistance to her skillful nursing of Ranald, he puzzled over the problem. Her presence would serve him well but would also keep her alive. He had to make her see that, although he was her captor, he was also her best source of protection.

Seeing the way Ranald kept glancing toward the child, Jennet murmured, "The babe is fine. If the child has survived dire famine gripping the land, 'tis strong and will endure."

"Aye. I but wish I could have saved its mother. I heard her cries but . . ."

She stopped his tortured speech by dabbing at his cut mouth with the wet cloth. "If ye mean to tear your soul apart over the death of innocents, best ye leave swiftly for the nearest monastery." She almost smiled at his startled reaction to her harsh words.

"I w-wish to be a knight," he stuttered, flicking a nervous glance toward his watchful uncle, who stood at Jennet's side.

"Then ye will have to stop up your ears and harden your heart. If ye mean to live by the sword, ye will ever be seeing the havoc it can wreak. When men are seized by the bloodlust of a battle, they cut down all that falls in their path. The best ye can do is learn to stop that madness from seizing you or whatever men ye might lead."

"'Tisane right. She carried no sword."

"Neither did the ones the English king's men cut down when Edward took this place, nor the ones Robert the Bruce slaughtered at Perth seven years ago." She stood up, finished with the binding and washing of his injuries. "Aye, when armed men run over the land, the innocent and unarmed best hide or they will fall alongside the warrior."

"Since ye ken that," said Hacon, "what were ye about when the Black Douglas arrived at our door?"

"Trying to get away," she answered, thinking it a particularly stupid question.

With unexpected fury, he grabbed her by the arm and dragged her to the door. He yanked it open and pushed her out a step or two, keeping a firm hold on her. Night had fallen, but the sack of Berwick continued. The stink of death and fire stung her eyes. The guards he had set outside their door watched him with open curiosity.

The light cast by torch and moon was somewhat meager, but she was glad of that. Dead littered the street. The invaders roamed the town searching for others to kill and for more plunder. What sounds she could hear were those of pain, fear, and lingering bloodlust. The Scots claimed Berwick belonged to Scotland, yet they were no kinder in the taking of it than the English had been years before. Berwick would be bled dry yet again. It could easily go on for days. She felt close to weeping.

"Ye meant to run away? Away to where?" Hacon demanded. "Out into this? Even the nunnery is no longer safe. Ye wouldnae survive it long, I think."

She agreed but did not say so. "I have escaped such harried places before," she said. If Hacon had meant to scare her by showing her how his allies behaved, he had succeeded, but she would never let him know it.

"Ye speak as one who has some sense. Use it, woman. Ye may not like where ye are now, but 'tis better than most other choices before you. Even those who are your friends will most likely cut ye down first, then grieve over the error later.

The ones not dead or captured tonight huddle together in fear and will strike out at all who approach. It will be like that until we leave this place.

"Aye, and *when* we leave this place," he continued, "'twould be wise for ye to still think twice about fleeing from me. Ye will be marching with the enemy, lass. Do ye really believe ye will be asked the why of that first? The Black Douglas isnae the only one who believes mercy has no place in this war."

"Mercy has not visited this accursed land in years," she muttered as he tugged her back inside, then barred the door.

"Best ye remember that."

"With the stink of death so heavy in the air, 'tisnae likely I shall forget it." Her hands on her hips, she frowned up at him. "And such a fine speech ye make." She ignored his small, mocking bow. "Ye use the horror out there to hold me here without troubling yourself to bind me. Aye, ye but try to make me stand firm for your own purposes."

"Ye dinnae ken what my purposes are."

"Nay?" She gave a soft, scornful laugh. "I am not one ye can ransom, so there can be but one reason for ye to hold me." She leaned toward him, speaking softly to keep their words private. "If ye think showing me how poor my choices are will make me welcome rape, ye had best think again."

"Now, lass, I but showed ye the truth of your situation. It would make your road smoother if ye would see me not as an enemy but as a benefactor."

"Benefactor?" She did not think he could have chosen another word better suited to keeping her anger stronger than her fear. Her cruel mistress, Lady de Tournay, had favored the word. "'Tis a wonder to me how many abusers favor calling themselves benefactors. Weel, dinnae think ye can change yourself from foe to friend simply because ye havenae cut my throat as ye did with the nuns."

"I ne'er touched the nuns. I but stole what I wished to."

She suspected he spoke the truth, but ignored the interruption. "I will ne'er see ye as my *benefactor*."

"Ah, that ye will do." He gently rubbed her anger-flushed cheek with the back of his hand. "Aye, that ye will do. And the gift of life deserves adequate reward, do ye not agree?" When she just stared at him, wide-eyed, he asked, "What? Naught to say?"

"I think," she said very carefully, "ye have been knocked about the head once too often." His soft laugh was threateningly attractive. "And," she added with a touch of anger, still disguising her fear, "if ye wait to hear me thank ye for my life, ye will take root first." Turning sharply, she walked away from him, deciding to see what she could do for the orphan babe Ranald had risked his life to save.

Hacon smiled as he watched her. Her every movement was graceful, sensuous. The warmth of desire tautened his body. It was not going to be easy to gain the prize he sought. However, he mused, as he returned to his seat by the fire, instinct told it would be well worth the effort required.

# Chapter 2

Now that they were all settled into the purloined house and had eaten, Hacon sprawled in his chair before the fire and turned his full attention to his lovely captive.

Looking up from the linen sheet she was cutting into nappies for the baby, she warily eyed Hacon. He had allowed her the brief use of a knife to score out squares in the sheet, but he had watched her closely and constantly. He did not trust her. She did not trust his amiable interest. He probably sought to make her relax her guard, to seduce her into thinking they could be more than captive and captor, only to try to lessen the strength of her resistance when he finally took her.

But then, she mused, the quiet companionship in the usurped house had already eased some of her fears, foolish though she knew that was. She sat at Hacon's feet performing a very domestic chore. Dugald sat on a stool to her left, diligently cleaning his and Hacon's armor. The five others occupying the large main room did much the same. Having chosen where they would bed down for the night, they wiled away the evening with chores and soft talk until they felt the need for sleep. Wrapped in this safe quiet, Jennet found it easy to forget that these men were the enemy, that they had arrived just hours ago with swords in hand to kill and loot. She had to be careful to remember that and remember it well.

"Why are ye here, Jennet of Liddesdale?" Hacon asked.

She looked back at him, watched his finely drawn brow arc slightly in a question, and sighed. It would probably not hurt to tell her story. Revealing how she had already suffered at the hands of the Bruce's army might soften him toward her and allow her to escape or to talk him into setting aside his plans for her. The chance was slim, but he might feel sufficient mercy to decide she had suffered enough in her life.

"I have been here for many years."

"But you are a Scot. Why are ye in an English stronghold?"

"Many here are Scots. 'Tis in Scotland after all. I lived here with an English couple ere I went to the nunnery a year ago."

"The daughter of a Graeme and an Armstrong abiding with the English?"

"I was the maid of the lady of the house, her handmaiden." And all else, she mused with a touch of resentment.

"Did none of your kin take you in? Couldnae they find some Scottish lady for ye to serve?"

Those were hard questions. Under certain circumstances answering them could be very hurtful to her. She could not, however, see any evil intention in his expression, and sighed. In this war treachery stood at every turn. Not every Scot welcomed Bruce as his king or wished an end to England's rule. Hacon was probably testing to see if she was just as she appeared—a victim, someone swept up in the war, or a traitor. Any Scot caught in an English stronghold was suspect. She had seen the grisly proof of that merciless attitude when her mother was murdered, then later when Scots brutally massacred fellow Scotsmen at Perth.

"My parents never meant for me to be some lady's servant," she explained. "I was but nine when the Bruce's soldiers raided my mother's village and murdered her. Later, I was at Perth when the Bruce took it from the English. My father had brought us there. He guessed how it would be if Perth fell. He paid the de Tournays to claim me as theirs. I was allowed to leave with them when the Bruce declared all wellborn Scots in Perth traitors and put them to the sword."

"And your father?"

Hacon felt a twinge of guilt, for he too had been at Perth. It was yet another part of the war he had disagreed with but had been unable to stop. Denouncing one of the Bruce's actions openly was a swift way to mark oneself a traitor. He was his family's only hope to regain all that they had lost. He could not afford to throw his life away fruitlessly protesting injustices.

Jennet shrugged. "I didnae see my father killed, nor have I ever gotten word that he was amongst those slain. Howbeit, I have seen naught of him since that day. I can only assume he fell at Perth."

Leaning forward, Hacon murmured, "If he fought for the English, took their side against the Bruce . . ."

She smiled crookedly. "My father ne'er took sides. He fought for whomever paid him the highest sum." She shook her head. "He thought me safe with the de Tournays. I thought myself safe with the holy sisters. Now I am hostage to thieves."

"Thieves, are we?"

"Weel, I didnae see ye buy that pile of bounty upon the table. Aye, ye are thieves."

"Ye are a fair one to toss that name about so scornfully. The Graemes are well known as thieves, leastwise, those who wander the hard land between the Esk and Sark rivers. Aye, and the Armstrongs of Liddesdale can claim that name as weel, becoming cursed reivers. There are many who say the whole town should be hanged. Ye carry the blood of both."

Every word of that was true. Over the years she had found that fact increasingly hard to bear. In the de Tournay household she had always been the first one suspected if anything went missing. She had her excuses and arguments ready, well honed from years of use.

"And what else may my people do to survive when nearly every year some army tramples o'er their lands, burning and looting? Their lands are a constant battlefield. If it isnae the English, 'tis the Scots. They see more blackened fields than harvests. They feed more armies than their own people.

"Aye, they were thieves, both my father and mother," she continued. "Aye, and their kin still are. Howbeit, they dinnae try to dress it in pretty words such as 'freeing Scotland from the English yoke,' and they dinnae call themselves knights or lords of the realm. They dinnae wave some king's banner or carry holy relics. Nay, nor do they call it 'rightful plunder.' They are reivers, pure and simple. 'Tis all the chivalrous and the knightly have left them."

Hacon sat back and stared at her. A quick glance around showed him that all his men were listening to her as intently as he was. The girl spoke some hard truths. She had a skill for stealing the glory out of battle. However, except for young Ranald, Hacon and the others had been riding beneath Robert the Bruce's banner long enough to have seen the hard truth for themselves. Although the cause of uniting Scotland beneath a Scots king, instead of some English puppet, was a good one, it was costly and not every step taken to achieve it had been an honorable one. It was strange, nonetheless, to hear a young girl speak so openly. He found this hint of a keen intelligence intriguing.

"Ah, but we steal only from the enemy," he said.

"And who declares these people the enemy?" she countered. "Ye do. Ye decide who will lead you, then that mon picks one whom he feels threatens him, and ye ride over all and sundry to cut him down. To be an enemy one need only to be caught between two forces. As my mother was. As I have been. As those poor innocent sisters were. Here I sit, and yet though God above kens I have been given reason enough, I am no mon's enemy."

"Nay?" He grinned. "So speaks the lass who tried to cut my throat and twice tried to throttle me."

"Being taken as plunder is apt to sore try my temper," she drawled, then turned her attention to making some clothes for the baby out of a soft piece of homespun she had found. "I will need some milk for this bairn."

"Oh, aye? And how am I to get that? Do ye think I can call up a nurse on your whim?"

"'Tisnae my whim." The baby beside her was starting to fuss, and she used the infant's need to bolster her courage. "'Tis the wee laddie's."

"Where am I to find milk in the midst of a town being pillaged?"

"If there was a cow or two about, I am certain some Scot has grabbed it as plunder. Aye, mayhaps even a goat. 'Tis true there wasnae much about to be taken. The famine was bad. Some were reduced to eating their dogs or horses. Howbeit, there were a few goats about before some traitor let ye in the gates. I ken weel there were some at the convent. Ye will just have to find them."

Ranald stumbled to his feet. "I will go, uncle. I brought the bairn here."

"Aye, ye did, but ye are in no condition to stumble though the streets finding milk for it. And 'tis best if ye stand clear of Douglas's men for a while. Sit down." Ranald obeyed and Hacon stood up. "I will go, though I dinnae think 'twill do much good."

"Ye might try the house where he was found," Jennet suggested as Hacon belted on his sword, Dugald hastening to do the same. "There may be a goat or cow hidden there. Such was the hunger gripping the land that people dared not leave any animal unguarded. A goat could even be hidden in the house."

Since Dugald was already getting directions to the house from Ranald, Hacon looked at her. "'Twas that bad?"

"Aye. 'Tis said some men in prison even ate their weaker cellmates." Seeing the look of horror on his handsome face, she shrugged. "Ye burn the fields and steal cattle often enough and there is nothing left. Ye keep killing the men and soon there is no one left to plant or harvest. If there is naught to harvest and naught to slaughter for meat, then there is naught to eat. 'Tis quite simple."

Muttering a curse, Hacon strode out of the house, Dugald at his heels. He wanted to scorn her words, but it was impossible. They were the simple, cold truth. His shame lay in realizing how little thought he had given to the innocents. He did not wish to think on how many head of cattle he had driven to Dubheilrig, for now he saw that he had helped foster such starvation.

"Ye shouldnae listen to the lass," Dugald murmured as he fell into step at Hacon's side.

"Why not? She speaks the truth."

"Aye, but what good is it to let it gnaw at you? Ye cannae change it. 'Tis the way of it. If ye dinnae take the cattle, another would and think ye a great fool for leaving it behind. Aye, and every mon here would take from us given half the chance. 'Tis the way of it."

"Being 'the way of it' doesnae make it right."

"Nay, but ye cannae end it. Ye are but one mon, though some who have fought against ye may claim otherwise." Dugald smiled faintly, then grew serious again. "Ye have ne'er set the torch to a cottage or a field nor do ye set about cutting down all and sundry, crazed with the scent of blood. Neither do the men riding with you. 'Tis enough. Unless ye can get every mon who ever lifted a sword against another to stop plundering, burning, or killing innocents, it will go on. I dinnae think e'en the Bruce has that power."

Hacon sighed and nodded. "And so 'twill remain 'the way of it.' She hates what I am." Even as he spoke the words he wondered why that should trouble him so deeply.

"She carries a lot of hard, bitter feelings for a wee lass. Still, that willnae stop ye from wanting to lie with her."

"Nay, it willnae." Hacon turned to look at Dugald and was comforted by the sympathy on his cousin's dour face. "Yet it troubles me. It troubles me to think that, while her flesh may yet warm to my touch, and aye, her heart too, in her mind I am naught but a butcher. In her thoughts I am naught but a mon soaked in blood and stinking of death."

"Then ye must change her mind, though I dinnae understand why it matters."

"Neither do I," murmured Hacon as he started on his way again. "Neither do I; but it does, curse her beautiful eyes."

They walked on in silence for a little longer until Dugald pointed out the house where Ranald had found the child. The woman's body still lay sprawled in front of it. A man's body blocked the doorway. The babe Ranald had risked so much for was clearly an orphan now. Yet as Hacon tugged the man's body out of his way, he thought that the last thing he needed was to add a babe to the ever growing clan of people he was responsible for.

Once inside, he and Dugald made a thorough search of the ransacked house. It was evident in what little remained that the couple had not been poor, but they did not find what they needed. Hacon dutifully gathered up some baby clothes to take back with them. He was resigning himself to having to appeal to the Black Douglas himself when a faint noise caught his and Dugald's attention.

After listening intently for a moment they agreed the sound came from beneath the house. A search of the floor revealed a trapdoor. Hacon had to stand and wait as Dugald went down, for the opening was too small for him. Once the three goats hidden down there were pulled and prodded out of their underground shelter, Hacon stood and stared at them, Dugald at his side.

"The lass guessed right," he finally murmured.

"Aye, she seems a clever wee thing. But then she has lived here for seven years."

"Weel, with that English family at least. I think that, despite how her words can trouble a mon, I will still listen to what she says. It may be that she has a useful insight."

Dugald nodded. "She does have wit."

"Ye sound surprised." Hacon grinned at his cousin as he espied three lengths of rope near the door. The ropes had obviously been used as tethers for leading the goats, and he moved to collect them. "I didnae ken ye had begun to doubt that a woman could possess some wit." He handed two ropes to Dugald and began to tie one to the simple leather collar on one of the goats.

His smile a little sad, Dugald followed suit. "I havenae seen many women of late who werenae screaming or wailing with grief. This war has been so long and so constant, a mon doesnae get much time to dally with a lass."

"Nay? And here I thought ye had an eye for the fair Margaret back in Dubheilrig." He laughed softly when his cousin flushed slightly and scowled. "Come on, we had best get these back. I havenae had a muckle lot to do with bairns, but I do ken they can make a fair noise when they feel the bite of hunger." He started out of the house, tugging one goat behind him, listening to Dugald softly curse the two he dragged along.

"A bairn, a wee lass, and now three accursed goats," muttered Dugald. "Do ye really think we can tow these o'er hill and dale?"

"I ken it willnae be easy, but we cannae send them back to Dubheilrig or with whatever plunder is driven back."

"So we drag the lot behind us as we raid? That is madness."

Hacon grimaced, fully agreeing, then shrugged. "What else can I do?"

"Leave them here."

"Dugald, ye heard what I told the girl. 'Twas the full truth. If we are driven from here by the English or their supporters, she will be seen as the enemy. After what we have done here, that will mean a sure death for her. Aye, and mayhaps not a verra merciful one. If we hold the town and gain the castle, Douglas will leave some of our men here. They will also consider her as plunder and will use her as such."

"Ye could make your claim to her clear."

"I could, but not every mon would honor it. The moment I am gone, my claim to her will weaken. 'Tis something that must be strengthened by my presence, by my sword. Nay, she stays with me. There are always some men left at camp who sit with the wounded and newly gathered plunder. She can stay with them."

"Her and the bairn."

"Aye, and the bairn."

"And the goats."

"Aye, and the goats," Hacon snapped, glaring at his cousin. "Weel? Say it."

"Say what?"

"That ye think me a fool."

"Nay, not a fool. She is a fair lass, as fair as I can ever recall setting eyes on. I would wonder what ailed ye if ye didnae want her. Aye, I might even consider ye a fool if ye tossed away the chance to lie in her arms."

"Then why do ye keep harping at me?"

"I just wanted to be sure that what is dangling between your legs wasnae dulling your mind. I wanted to be sure ye saw each and every problem. Ye do, and so I willnae worry on it. There is one thing I will ask of ye though."

When Dugald paused, Hacon frowned. He pressed, "What is it?"

"Leave Ranald to guard her and the bairn." He grimaced. "And these rank beasts. Aye, ye are right in saying that there are always some on a raid who hold back to make a small camp. Make Ranald be the one, or one of the ones to watch our goods."

Hacon sighed and ran a hand through his hair. "Ye think him a poor fighter."

"Nay, ye set that laddie to guard the woman and the bairn, and he will do as weel as any other. Aye, better than most. That would be something he could put his heart into. But he cannae stomach this butchering, Hacon. He will get himself killed. Mayhaps take one or more of us with him. He is one who needs to feel he has a just cause to strike out at another. A threat to his home, his own land . . ."

"Or a wee bonnie lass and a helpless bairn."

"Aye." Dugald nodded. "He isnae one for raiding. He is one ye leave behind to protect your family. He isnae a coward. I'm not saying that, but . . ." He grimaced.

Lightly clapping Dugald on the back, Hacon smiled. "I see what you mean. Ye are right." Starting on his way again, Hacon added, "I but pray I can do what must be done without cutting the lad's pride. But do ye think he has the stomach to hold the lass for me, to stop her from trying to flee?"

Keeping pace with Hacon, Dugald replied, "Aye, especially if ye remind him that she could get her fool self killed. 'Twould also be best if he isnae too close to a Douglas mon. I dinnae ken who he faced, but there are some cold, hard men in Douglas's band. If they feel the lad gave them some insult . . ."

"'Twill not be an English sword Ranald best keep the closest watch for. They would use the guise of battle, hide in its confusion, and murder the boy. To the rear he will stay. I but need to find the words to ensure he sees no insult or criticism in the order."

Jennet exclaimed with delight when they dragged the goats into the house. She wasted no time in feeding the fretful baby. Hacon turned his attention to Ranald, helping the youth get comfortable on a pallet on the floor. The lad would be sore for a day or two, but Hacon was heartily relieved to see that he would suffer no lasting damage.

It was late when Hacon finally sought his bed, a sheepskin laid before the fire. Although he had not told Jennet outright that they would share that bed, he saw no surprise on her face, only annoyance, when he gestured for her to lie down. At least she showed no fear, he told himself as he unwrapped the thongs holding his cuarans in place and removed the rawhide boots. He was eager to feel her slender body curled up against him. Stripping down to his braies, he cynically eyed the sleeping child she had set between them.

"That game willnae work, lass," he said, and decided her look of puzzled innocence was very well feigned.

"And what game is that, Sir Gillard?" She had not held out much hope of success in using the baby to keep him at a distance but was still annoyed that her ruse had failed so completely.

"Using this innocent bairn to keep me away. Put him on the other side of you."

"Then he would be between me and the fire. That would be too dangerous."

"Ah, is that the difficulty? Weel, 'tis easily solved. We will just change places. Slide over, lass."

She inwardly cursed as she did as he commanded. Then the fear she had more or less kept at bay began to break the bonds she had placed upon it. She concentrated harder on quelling it. There was no way she could fight him. Not allowing him to see her fear was her only hope of retaining some shred of pride.

Closing her eyes tightly, she tried not to look at him. To her great self-disgust and consternation the man's image was already etched clearly in her mind. It was impossible to understand, but she felt a hint of fascination mingled with her fear.

He was far too easy to look at, too pleasing to the eye. When he had started to take his clothes off, she should have looked away, but she had not been able to. He was all lean, hard muscle. A light triangle of blond curls, a shade darker than his pale hair, adorned his smooth, broad chest. It tapered into a thin line which disappeared into the top of his linen loincloth. His legs, lightly coated with hair, were long, attractively muscular, and excellently formed. His skin was a light golden tone, not as pale as she would have guessed. He was also remarkably free of the scars that men of battle tended to collect. There was one on his right thigh and one over the left half of his rib cage, but neither was very big or ugly.

A flaw would have been helpful, she thought as she felt him settle down beside her. She should be disgusted by the thought of lying with him, yet she was not, not really. A perverse part of her whispered that if rape was unavoidable, at least her abuser was not ugly or still carrying the stench of battle. It hinted an acceptance of her fate that chilled her.

She supposed the fact that he had not yet raped her, had not even struck her, made the threat too tenuous to seem real. It could be the only explanation for why she found herself wondering what Hacon would be like as a lover. She knew few women who got the chance to hold such a fine-looking man in their arms. She would not be a woman if she did not at least ponder what it would feel like. However, such complacency and curiosity could prove very dangerous in her situation. The man did not offer lovemaking but rape, not desire but defilement. She must not forget that.

When he curled up against her back, slipping his arm around her waist, she tensed. That was a liberty she should immediately and sharply rebuff, but she made no move to do so. What good would it do? It could anger him, which would only add to the brutality of what was to come. Worse, she found the weight of his arm upon her pleasing, comforting. Still, when he nuzzled her hair, she instinctively tensed and hunched her shoulders in rejection to the caress, then waited for his violent reaction. None came. Confusion began to crowd out her fear.

"Do ye always come to bed fully dressed?" he asked, ignoring her scrunched-up shoulders and touching his lips to the outer curve of her ear.

"Of course not, but I willnae shed my clothes before a roomful of men." She struggled to remain stiff, rejecting his touch, but the warmth of his mouth softened her, heating her blood in a way she strove to deny.

"I wouldnae let them look. I would cover us with my plaid."

"Ye dinnae have a plaid. I didnae see one."

"Weel, I dinnae wear it all the time. I would use it to hide ye from their eyes, and I would hold ye close beneath it."

"If ye held me any closer, ye would find yourself between me and the bairn."

"'Twould sore grieve me," he murmured, ignoring her tart comment, "to cover ye up so. I should wish to see your beauty with my own eyes."

"Ere that happens, your eyes will have gone blind from aging."

She was certain he was grinning. She could almost feel it, then wondered how that could be. Part of her acknowledged that he was a man she could trust. But that was pure madness. The man had come into Berwick sword in hand, desecrated a nunnery, then yanked her into his life, giving her no choice in the matter. He would now make her his whore. He meant to use her body to sate his lust as the Bruce's soldiers had used her mother before cutting her throat. Every feeling she had toward the man ought to be a bad one, but that was not the case at all.

The way he moved his hand over her stomach was beginning to make her feel odd. Beneath his slow, idle caress stirred a heat that was curling up through her body. She wanted to make him stop but feared what he might do if she slapped his hand away. Her mother had fought her abusers and gained only more brutality. She must show a complete lack of interest, act as cold as the midwinter sun. She found herself wishing he would just take her and be done with it, then decided confusion was stealing her wits.

"Leave be," she finally said, trying to wriggle free of his hold. "I want to go to sleep."

"Do ye ken what I want, Jennet?" he whispered against her ear.

"Nay, and I dinnae care either." She began to wonder how far she could push him, or if it was even wise to test those limits.

Ignoring that, he continued. "I want you—naked and warm in my arms. I want to feel the heat of you wrapped around me." Propping himself up on his elbow he leaned over her and kissed her cheek. "I want to see this tempting mouth"—he slowly trailed his fingers over her lips—"soft and wet from my kisses. I want to see this sweet face flushed with desire—desire for me."

"Weel . . ." She silently cursed, for her voice was higher than usual and revealingly unsteady. "I hope ye are a mon who has learned to accept failure with grace, for I dinnae intend to answer a single one of your wants."

He settled back down on the sheepskin, still holding her close. "Not tonight leastwise."

"Not ever," she muttered.

Briefly she felt weak with relief, realizing that, for tonight at least, she was safe. What troubled her was the hint of softer feelings that stirred beneath her fear and relief. She had never had a man speak to her like that. There had been one or two who had expressed a wish to bed her, but always in much cruder terms. She did not know how to deal with Hacon's soft, heated words. They put ideas into her head—tempting, sinful ideas.

Sin, she repeated in her mind. Rape. She would have to hold tight to those words and to the memory of her mother's cruel fate. Even if by some miracle he had decided to seduce instead of rape her, what Hacon Gillard wanted was a sin. A sin that would cost *her* a great deal more than it would *him*.

# Chapter 3

Hacon swore and struggled to get a firm hold upon a thrashing Jennet. He had barely gotten to sleep, finding the urge to possess his pretty captive difficult to subdue, when the nightmare had seized her. Her cries had brought his men to their feet, alert and ready to do battle. By the time he got Jennet securely enfolded in his arms, they had realized what had alarmed them and returned to their beds.

He scowled as her tears dampened his chest. This was not the loving embrace he had envisioned. Hacon sternly pushed aside his lust, stirred by the way she clung so tightly to him. It was too soon. They had barely passed one night in each other's company. And now she was caught in the tight grip of a nightmare.

"Maman! Maman! Stop, please stop. Dinnae hurt her."

"Sssh, lass. Hush now." He dared to give her a slight shake. "Wake now, dearling."

Jennet slowly fought her way free of her terrifying memories. It took her a moment to realize who she was clinging to, and then she feigned a continued confusion, needing to remain within his arms. Hacon felt warm, strong, and safe. The way he moved his large, callused hands over her hair and back eased her trembling. She wished he could as easily smooth away the painful, blood-soaked memories that haunted her.

"Sometimes I can even smell the blood," she whispered, and made no complaint when he tightened his hold.

"Ye were recalling the time your mother was murdered?"

"I have seen hundreds murdered."

She realized the man she clung to was one of those responsible for all the bloodshed. Jennet sighed and eased free of his hold. He did not let her move far, keeping one arm wrapped snugly around her waist as she turned her back to him. Her eyes widened when he tucked her up against his body. Pressed against her back was proof that he was feeling far more than mere sympathy for her troubled dreams. The man's lusts were stirring. Fear battled her curiosity. The memory of her mother's brutal death was still fresh in her mind, and a fear of rape quickly banished all else.

"Be at ease," he murmured, and pressed a kiss against her hair. "Go to sleep, my wee plunder. Nothing more will trouble your slumber this night."

What immense arrogance, she mused as she closed her eyes. Surely even he could not be so cocksure as to think he could fend off nightmares. Therefore he had to be assuring her that he was not going to press his attentions on her—this time. She viciously cursed the tickle of disappointment that rippled through her.

"There, ye sleep," he whispered, and kissed her shoulder when he felt her begin to relax. "There is a lot of work to be done in the morning."

Although she was curious as to what work he meant, Jennet did not ask. She was feeling too pleasantly sleepy to continue the conversation. She would know soon enough.

It took every ounce of willpower Jennet possessed to stop herself from hurling the tin plates she was washing out into the muddy streets. Hacon and his men had eaten a hearty meal and promptly left. It was clear that she was expected to clean up after them. Her annoyance with the assumption had led her to leave the plates unwashed. Now she was paying for that fit of pique, since the porridge they had eaten had dried and each plate needed a great deal of scrubbing before it came clean.

"'Tisnae rape I must fear but being worked to death," she muttered as she finished the last plate and slammed it down upon the table.

"Did ye say something?" Ranald asked from where he sat sprawled in the open doorway.

"Me—speak? Would a poor, lowly slave dare to utter a sound? Nay, I think not."

She grabbed the bucket of water she had been using and strode toward the door. It did not particularly please her that Ranald had the wit to scramble out of her way. Her foul mood might have been eased some if she could have doused him with the murky water.

She stood on the threshold and surveyed the town. Berwick did not look much better than it had last night. It appeared battered and bruised, many homes now roofless, doors flung open or shattered by the Scots' battle-axes, and the streets were littered by the household goods that had been cast aside by the plunderers as unworthy of their attention. A large number of men roamed the streets, and it was not easy to tell the common man-at-arms from a knight or a laird. Scots did not have the coin to indulge in the finery which would denote their position in life, as many of the English did. She wondered if the Scots' readiness to plunder their English neighbors was born partly from a wish to lessen that disparity in wealth.

"We will soon repair the town," Ranald promised as he moved to stand beside her.

"How kind of you. It might have been kinder not to have destroyed it in the first place."

Ranald shrugged. "'Tis war."

Jennet fought a strong urge to spit. "Men are pigs. Put a

sword in their hands and they give no thought to the poor folk who have no quarrel with them."

"If the English want peace, then they should cease trying to put *their* king on *our* throne."

There was some truth to that, but she felt no inclination to say so. She was diverted by Hacon's approach. He strode up the market street with Dugald at his side. His jupon and hose were of a slightly better quality than those of the more common soldiers, but it was mostly his stature, his bearing, which proclaimed him as more than some mere man-at-arms. Jennet was briefly annoyed at how much pleasure she derived from the sight of him, then decided she was being foolish. He was a fine figure of a man, and any woman with eyes in her head would appreciate him. She must simply make sure that he did not see that *she* did. She frowned when his gaze met hers.

Hacon ceased listening to Dugald when he caught sight of Jennet in the doorway. Despite the cross look on her face, he thrilled to the sight of her. She was a tiny, slender lass, but he hungered for every inch of her. He walked up to her and abruptly placed a swift, light kiss on her frowning mouth, then quickly caught her by the wrist to halt her attempt to swing the bucket at his head.

"Is that any way to greet your mon, lassie?" He smiled down at her, aroused anew by her rich green eyes, ivory skin, and raven black hair.

"Ye are *not* my *mon*." She wriggled free of his grasp and strode back into the house.

She tossed the bucket into a corner. That small act of violence did not ease her ill humor at all. Jennet scowled at Hacon as he crouched by the baby, who lay on a blanket near the cold fireplace. Hacon was playing with the child's toes, causing the tiny boy to giggle happily. Jennet found the sight disturbing. She did not wish to see the man acting in a way that made him less of a threat to her.

"The laddie thrives," Hacon said as he stood up and turned back toward her.

"Aye, the good supply of goat's milk has kept him from suffering from the hunger gnawing at so many others."

Dugald walked over to where Hacon had stored most of their supplies in a far corner of the room. He rummaged around in the saddle packs before returning to Hacon's side. Jennet tried to see the papers that Dugald handed to Hacon, but it was impossible.

"Are those the warrants for your hanging?" she asked.

"Nay, my impertinent wench. They are maps." He tucked the papers inside his jupon.

"Maps of what?"

"England, Mistress Curiosity. The Douglas has called for them." He started back out the door, Dugald at his heels.

"He wishes to find new places to raze and plunder, does he?" she called.

Hacon paused in the doorway to smile at her, then pointed toward a large mound of clothing at the far end of the main room. "Now, lass, ye shouldnae be so concerned with a soldier's business when there is so much woman's work to attend to."

"And what am I to do with all that?" she demanded.

"Wash them, what else?" He quickly slipped out the door.

Dugald hesitated. "And dinnae let that Satan-kissed goat near them. I caught the blighted beast gnawing on my shirt this morning." He hurried out after Hacon, flashing a quick grin at a chuckling Ranald, who still stood guard at the door.

Jennet cautiously approached the pile of clothes. Using only two fingers she gingerly picked up one of the soiled shirts and grimaced, holding it out at arm's length. The aroma wafting up from the heap told her that each piece there was probably in as sad a state as the one she held.

"Even that greedy goat wouldnae be able to stomach these," she grumbled.

She heard Ranald laugh but ignored him. After dropping

the shirt back into the pile, she went to collect the bucket. It
would require a lot of water to clean those clothes, and would
take most of the day. She wondered if servitude in Hacon's
bed could possibly be worse that what he had consigned her
to do. Jennet cursed. She doubted Hacon would relieve her of
one duty simply because she had accepted the other. Captiv-
ity could prove to be a long and exhausting business.


As subtly she could, Jennet opened one eye to surrepti-
tiously watch Hacon. It had not been easy to feign sleep when
she woke up wrapped securely in his strong arms. She
doubted he had been fooled by her act. He had chuckled
softly, touched a light, gently arousing kiss on the side of her
neck, and then risen. For one brief moment she had been
tempted to hold him at her side. Her attempts to quell her at-
traction to the man were failing miserably. It was only the
third night that they had spent together, and she was already
weakening to his touch. She quickly closed her eyes when he
glanced at her over his broad shoulder.

Hacon kept his back to her as he dressed. His arousal was all
too easy to see. It was difficult to ignore the knowing grins of his
men, but he preferred them to taking any chance of alarming
Jennet. He inwardly grimaced. The uncomfortable state he was
in was probably one he should become accustomed to. Some of
Jennet's wariness had eased, but he doubted she would be prepared to sate the hunger gnawing at him for quite a while yet.

"Ye may as weel rise, lass," he said as he finished lacing up his
jupon. "There are many womanly chores for you to attend to."

Jennet gave up all pretense of sleeping and glared at his
back as he moved toward the table where his men were already helping themselves to a large kettle of porridge. "I
thought I was plunder, not a slave."

"All plunder should be put to good use." He winked at her
before sitting down at the table. "Ye havenae been much use

at night so ye might as weel be set to work during the day."
He grinned when his men laughed.

"Ye have the manners of a goat! Although"—she glanced
toward the three animals tethered near the door—"mayhaps I
should apologize to those poor beasts for belittling them so."

"Mayhaps ye should cease lolling about and tend the bairn,
who's beginning to fuss. And if ye wait too long, there will be
naught left for you to eat."

She cursed and hurried to fetch the baby, pausing only to
quickly wash up. Once the infant's nappie was changed, she
carried him to the table. She sat next to Hacon, settled the
baby on her lap, and handed him the wineskin of goat's milk
to nurse from. Hacon set a steaming plateful of oatmeal in
front of her. It was not easy to eat with the child in her lap, but,
picking up the roughly craved wooden spoon, Jennet realized
she was growing adept at it.

"What are ye doing?" she demanded when, finished with
her own meal, she looked down at the baby to find Hacon
holding a finger covered with porridge before the child's
mouth.

"He looks a big lad. I thought he might wish more hearty
fare." Hacon smiled faintly when the child warily put his
mouth around Hacon's finger and began to suckle.

"That doesnae mean he is ready for it."

"We willnae give him verra much," he said as he fed the
baby yet another fingerful.

At that moment Jennet's attention was diverted from Hacon.
One of the goats had chewed through its tether and was standing behind Dugald, who was too busy watching Hacon and the
baby to pay heed to the animal. The goat began to chew on
Dugald's jupon. Jennet knew there was no way to stop it without alerting Dugald. She hoped there would not be too much
trouble even as she had the sinking feeling that it was the same
goat that had feasted upon Dugald's shirt earlier.

Just as she opened her mouth to warn Dugald, he realized

what was happening. With a bellow of rage he swatted at the goat, who neatly danced out of reach. Jennet cried out a protest when Dugald leapt to his feet and reached for his sword. A grinning Hacon caught Dugald's wrist, halting the man's move to draw his sword.

"Nay, Dugald." Hacon struggled to hide his amusement even as the rest of the men hooted with laughter. "We need the beast. Besides, he only had a wee taste."

"'Tis the same hell-begotten beast that chewed up my shirt. Soon I will be forced to go naked."

"We would ne'er let it come to that, cousin." Hacon pushed the goat toward Jennet, who grabbed what was left of the gnawed rope about the animal's neck. "Now, my fellows, we have work to do."

The men quickly left the table. Hacon ushered his complaining cousin out the door, all the while assuring Dugald that his jupon was not badly damaged. Within moments Jennet was alone. Even Ranald had hurriedly left to take up his post outside the door. She sighed and looked at the goat, who appeared as pleased with itself as any animal could.

"Ye will be turned into a fine stew if ye arenae more careful."

She settled the baby on a blanket near the table, then re-tethered the goat. After staring at the table, littered with the remains of their morning meal, she sighed and got the bucket. She doubted the men were working as hard as they expected her to.

Jennet paused in scrubbing the plank floor and rubbed the small of her back. It was probably a waste of time to clean the floor, but she felt a real need for some hard, exhausting labor. If she wore herself to the bone, she would not have the strength to think about Hacon. The man was hard to ignore or forget. Instead of getting better at it after almost a week, she was utterly failing. She could no longer tense with rejection when he held her close throughout the night. The way he played with the baby, the way he teased and laughed, and the way he treated his men all worked to make her forget that he was the enemy, the man who had taken her as plunder.

She was puzzling over how to battle the softening she felt toward him when a sound diverted her. A man was swearing, his deep voice hoarse with pain, and the sound was drawing nearer. She scrambled to her feet even as Hacon and Dugald entered supporting a pale, cursing man between them. Something was clearly wrong with the man, whom she recognized as William, the oldest of Hacon's small band. The gray-haired man had somehow injured his arm. Jennet quickly moved to the table as Hacon and Dugald helped William lie down on it and began to take off his jupon.

"What has happened to him?" she asked, as the rest of the men arrived and encircled the table. "I see no blood."

"We think his arm has been broken," Hacon replied, then looked toward Ranald, who stood in the doorway. "The Douglas has a physician with his men. Find Sir Leslie. He would ken where the mon is and help ye find him."

"Is it now safe for Ranald to approach the Douglasses?" Jennet stared at William's now bared arm, trying to determine if it was truly broken.

Hacon cursed. "Nay." He looked at another man. "Ye must go, Padriac."

"Wait just a moment." Jennet was sure she knew what ailed William, and it was not a broken arm. "Let me look at him first." She moved closer to William and began to move her hands over his thick-muscled arm.

"Now, lassie, this is more serious than Ranald's scratches and bruises. William needs more than a wash and soft words."

Although Hacon's words were sharp, even mildly insulting, he did not stop her from looking over William's arm. "I do realize that." Jennet nodded when she found exactly what she had expected at William's shoulder. "My skills go beyond that. Papa always said I had a healing touch. O'er the years I easily and quickly learned a great deal. The nuns also noticed that I was adept at healing and taught me even more. William hasnae broken his arm."

"Nay? Then why does it hurt him so? Why cannae he move it without pain?"

"The mon has pulled it away from his shoulder. Feel. But, gently," she advised as Hacon touched William's shoulder joint. "'Tis something easily mended, although he will find it painful. I am not certain I have the strength to do it swiftly and neatly, but I can easily tell you what needs to be done. We must yank it back into its rightful place."

All the men looked wary, even Hacon, but none suggested that she might be wrong. Jennet carefully instructed the men to hold William steady, then explained to Hacon what to do. She winced when Hacon snapped the arm back into place, for she knew it was hurting William. A quick check of the man's shoulder told her it had been done correctly. The way all the men were now looking at her in some surprise and with new respect made her a little uncomfortable.

"'Twill ache rather badly for a while," she told William as his companions helped him down off the table.

"Thank ye, mistress," William said.

"'Twas nothing verra grand."

"'Tis my sword arm ye have saved, mistress."

She sighed and shook her head as William and the others left. "Mayhaps I should have left it alone."

Hacon leaned back against the table. "That would leave him helpless."

"It would also have stopped him from killing anyone."

"Aye, but made it verra easy for someone to kill him."

Jennet had no answer for that. She crossed her arms beneath her breasts and slumped against the table. Her gaze fell upon her newly scrubbed floor. Tracks of mud now crisscrossed it. All her hard work had been wasted. Besides, the fact that she was deeply aware of the man at her side proved that scrubbing floors would not kill the feelings he stirred within her, feelings that ate away at her ability to hold him at a safe distance.

"Then he should put himself out of harm's way by staying home with his family," she finally said.

"His family was murdered when Edward the First entered Scotland and drove the Bruce into exile."

"Did ye go into exile too?"

"Nay, though what we had to endure was nearly as bad. Our lands were given to a supporter of the English, a family called de Umfraville. We became but serfs upon our lands. 'Tis little better now. True, our land is held by the Bruce himself now, but until he gifts us with the return of Dubheilrig, we cannae really call it home."

"Instead of but part of your gains going to the king, all is his to claim."

"Aye, all is his." He looked at her with an expression of curiosity. "Do ye truly have a healing touch?"

"I cannae cure anyone simply by laying hands upon them, if that is what ye ask. The abbess said I had an understanding, a God-given skill. When choices need to be made, I seem able to make the right ones. I learn whate'er I can, and do so easily, yet I am not bound by that learning. I am able to make use of new ideas when the need arises." She shrugged. "'Tisnae such a grand gift."

"'Twill be most useful when we finally set out from here."

"How will it be useful? Do ye not mean to return to your home now? Ye have regained Berwick for Scotland."

"Aye, but we will soon plunge deep into England."

"Why?"

"To harry the enemy, lass. We need time to secure this place, to strengthen our hold upon it. Sir Walter has been named the steward of Berwick, and he is a good mon. Howbeit, even he might falter if the English make a unified attack upon the town too soon. By harrying their lands south of here, we can divert them."

"Ah, I see. When they hear that their fields and homes are threatened, many English lords and knights will rush to protect them." She thought it a cruel battle tactic, yet could see its military advantage. "Now I see where my skill at healing may be of some worth. One or two of your men may be bruised a wee bit whilst cutting down the English serfs and merchants."

"Ye have a harsh view of the world, wee Jennet." Hacon moved to stand in front of her.

Jennet tensed when he put his hands on her shoulders, for although his touch was gentle, his expression revealed his deep displeasure at her words. "'Tis a harsh world," she said.

"Aye, if that is all one tries to see." He slid his hands up and down her slim arms. "To see mercy and honor sometimes requires a closer look." Hacon ached to pull her into his arms, but she was still too wary of him.

"They should not be so weel hidden that one must sort through all else to find them." Jennet told herself to pull away from him, but his tender caress of her arms held her in place.

"Mayhaps."

Hacon succumbed to the need to kiss her. But as he slowly lowered his mouth to hers, her eyes grew wider and she drew her head back. He sighed and redirected his kiss to her forehead. It was a poor substitute for what he craved, but he was certain it was the wisest move to make. Her kiss would be all the sweeter if there was some willingness on her part. As he stepped away from her, he mused that he would probably have to take her by surprise and steal that first kiss. This time she had had a chance to rally her defenses.

"I must return to the meeting the Douglas is holding," he said. "William's injury diverted me."

"Just how did William hurt himself?" She was a little dismayed to hear the hint of breathlessness in her voice and prayed he did not notice it.

"He was holding the reins of a pair of horses when something caused them to bolt. The poor mon was dragged a ways before he could free himself."

"Then he must be sadly bruised and battered. He should be here, resting."

"Aye, he should rest, and I believe he will do so—at the inn, where a buxom wench he has his eye on can soothe his brow." He winked and smiled. "I will try and find us something to sup on besides porridge. We will eat little else once we set out into England in a week's time," he said as he strode out of the house before he forgot all of his good intentions of moving slowly with Jennet.

The moment he was gone, Jennet slumped against the table. He had been meaning to kiss her and she had been alarmingly slow to resist. Things were not going at all well. Resistance to Hacon was growing more and more elusive. They were not going to leave Berwick and go north, deeper into Scotland and nearer her home, but south on one of those infamous, swift raids. She would have no chance of eluding Hacon for weeks, even months. If she had difficulty keeping him at arm's length after only a week, she knew she could never hold him back for the length of a raid. Wondering what she had ever done to deserve such torment, she returned to scrubbing the floor, hoping that the strength to remain cold to the man would be aided by her complete exhaustion.

# Chapter 4

With a soft cry, Jennet sat bolt upright on her pallet. She wondered dazedly why she had not been hindered by the man who had slept curled around her every night for over a week. An instant later she knew why, knew what had so abruptly awakened her. Hacon and his men were silently, hastily arming themselves. An alarm must have been sounded. She was about to find herself in the midst of another battle.

A tingle of fear seeped through her veins as she moved to help the men. As she laced up jupons, assisted in tugging on mail, and helped a man buckle on his sword, she wondered if it was wrong of her to be so helpful. Shaking her head, she decided she had no choice. In the midst of a counterattack by the English and their allies, she would be seen as one of the enemy. Right now she needed the protection these men offered. And, she mused with an inner sigh, after spending so many days with them, she truly did not wish them harm. If nothing else, she had come to realize that these men could bring her back home, back to Liddesdale.

"Nay, Ranald." Hacon stopped his nephew from running into the streets with the others. "Ye are to stay here."

"Here? But I can fight too, Uncle."

"Aye, and where I wish ye to use that fine sword is right

here, protecting all we have gathered, protecting that wee bairn and"—he grasped Jennet by the arm and tugged her close—"this wee bonnie plunder."

"Ye wish me out of the battle. After what happened before, ye fear I shall fail you," Ranald accused.

"Dinnae be a fool. What ye did before wasnae failure. 'Tis that which makes me choose you to stand guard here. I ken ye will stand firm no matter what happens. I ken ye will remember why ye have been set here and let naught distract you. Now, dinnae let this fool lass try to flee—"

"Fool lass?" Jennet muttered.

"—because," Hacon continued without pause, "there will be no safety out there for her. She will find no friend now."

"I do possess the wit to ken that much," Jennet snapped.

"Good. Then ye will be here waiting for me when I return."

"Ye are so sure of winning, are ye?"

"But one kiss from your sweet mouth, my lovely plunder, and I can be naught else but victorious."

She opened her mouth to tell him just how little his chances were of getting a kiss, only to discover she had given him the opportunity he waited for. His arm came about her waist and he hefted her up against his chest, then thoroughly kissed her. His hunger, which he made no secret of, was fully evident in the embrace. She felt her own desire for him, a desire she had been unable to vanquish, flare to life. Still reeling from that deep kiss when he set her on her feet, she silently watched him leave, Dugald at his heels. When she finally turned to look at Ranald, the youth was grinning at her. She glared at him.

"When I first saw your uncle," she drawled, "he was grinning just like that. I tried to cut his throat."

"Oh." Ranald's grin vanished. "Um, the bairn awakes."

"The bairn now has a name," she murmured as she moved to pick up the child. "I have called him Murdoc."

"Why Murdoc?" Ranald sat at the end of the table facing the doorway, dividing his attention between it and her.

"Weel, when he was playing so happily the other day, I sat by him and started saying names. I felt he ought to have one, since he as been with us for eight days. Murdoc was the one he smiled at. He crawled toward me when I said it." She started to change Murdoc's linen.

For a while, as she dressed and fed the baby, neither she nor Ranald spoke. The din of battle coming from outside was broken only by Murdoc's happy gurgling. It was a distressing combination of sounds.

Sitting on the sheepskin, watching Murdoc play, Jennet tried not to wonder on the identity of each person she heard scream. When she realized most of her fear was over Hacon's fate in battle, she decided she needed some diversion. Although Ranald was unquestionably alert, there was an expression of despondency on his face.

"Is something wrong, Ranald?" She felt a quick thrill of panic, wondering if he knew something about the battle she had missed while tending to Murdoc.

"Weel, I cannae be sure. Ye ken my uncle. I mean, ye have been with him for over a week now."

"Curse my wretched luck—aye. Why do ye mention it?"

He smiled briefly, then grew serious again. "Do ye think he meant all he said about his reasons for setting me here, to keep me back from the battle going on out there?"

"Someone must stay behind when there is such as that lying about the place." She nodded toward the booty, now neatly stacked in a corner.

"Aye, and ye and the bairn."

"Mayhaps. Did ye think he was just mouthing some pretty words?"

Ranald shrugged. "I cannae help wondering on it. My first time fighting with him and I set myself against the Douglas men instead of saving all my strength for the enemy. I cannae but wonder if this is a punishment for doing such a foolish thing."

"'Tisnae foolish to stop men trying to kill a wee, helpless bairn. Ranald, it but showed your uncle where your strength lies—in protecting, not attacking. 'Tis the way of it for some. Mayhaps ye just need more to fight for than some mon who declares himself king and calls enemies all who dinnae cry aye loud and clear. Ye are the one set to guard home, family, and fortune. 'Tis hardly a dishonor to be given such a job. After all, it doesnae do a knight much good to come home victorious, only to find all he has stolen and all he cares for slaughtered."

"Nay, it certainly doesnae." Ranald laughed softly, then tensed. "The battle edges this way."

"Aye," she murmured, and held out her hand. "Give me my dagger. Ye ken where it is." She sighed when he eyed her warily. "I dinnae mean to use it on you."

"Weel, ye did try to cut my uncle's throat."

"I thought he meant to kill me." She softly cursed his expression of disbelief. "I was content in my wee room at the convent, mending clothes. Then the war I sought to hide from was within the nunnery itself. Even the holy sanctuary wasnae safe. My door burst open and there stood your uncle, grinning like a fool. I thought I was for dying and that was why he grinned." She shrugged. "I decided that if I was to be murdered, I would at least take that cursed grin from his face first. I swear on Murdoc's life, I will return the dagger to you when this is all over."

Ranald hesitated another moment, then moved to get her dagger from where it had been stored with the other booty. He handed it to her and returned to his post. Jennet was just about to slip it into the hidden pocket of her gown when a man burst into the house. She rushed to pick up Murdoc. The man was huge and his dress marked him as English, one of the enemy. His surcoat and sword were dabbed with blood.

Jennet swallowed hard, tasting the bitter tang of fear. Ranald was but sixteen and, by his own admission, still new to battle. This was a formidable opponent for a novice.

"By all the saints," growled the Englishman, "you bring your whores and bastards with you." The look he sent Jennet was filled with scorn and loathing.

Standing to face the man, Ranald said, "By what I can glimpse behind you, through the open door, ye are on the wrong side of the battle line. Flee while ye can, Englishmon."

"Flee? From a beardless boy with mother's milk still drying on his mouth?" He spat on the floor.

Despite her fear, Jennet cursed men and their ways. The Englishman stood there goading Ranald instead of grasping the chance to run and save his own life. As was intended, Ranald bristled, infuriated by this slur upon his manhood.

"This *boy* will make ye regret that insult," cried Ranald. "Ye will die here, Englishmon."

"Nay, *laddie*—you will. And then, after I take my fill of your whore, I will cut her white throat. Aye, and then the babe's too. 'Tis always best to clean out a nest of vermin."

"Jennet, take the bairn and set yourself on the stairs to the loft," ordered Ranald, never taking his gaze from his opponent. "I wouldnae want ye soiled by the pus that will ooze from this maggot when I cut him down."

With a roar of fury the Englishman attacked. Jennet bolted for the steep steps. Halfway up she stopped and sat down to watch the fight with horrified fascination. Holding the baby firmly with one arm, she clutched her dagger in the other hand. The Englishman had more height, more bulk, and more protective armor than Ranald. Even as she prayed for Ranald's survival she could not feel certain he would win.

Ranald neatly parried the man's first blow, then retaliated. Jennet realized that if Ranald could get in a telling blow quickly he could win. The Englishman had more size and strength than skill. But, if the battle lasted any length of time,

Ranald's skill would be less of an advantage and his lithe build would become a deadly weakness. The Englishman would be able to endure longer. She began to pray, even harder, a little horrified that she was asking God for a victory which would bring about a man's death, yet wanting that victory to be Ranald's.

Both men were drenched in sweat before any change occurred in their steady thrust and parry. Ranald was forced into the dangerous position of stepping backward each time the Englishman pressed him. Stumbling over a short stool, Ranald fell, his sword tumbling from his hands. The Englishman faltered as well, turning awkwardly to avoid the rolling stool and the loose weapon. This gave Ranald the chance to recover from his fall and avoid the man's down-swinging sword.

As he rolled, Ranald grabbed for his great sword, reaching behind to pull it from its sheath upon his back. He then rose to a crouching position, his weapon held out in front of him. Jennet had considered the *claidheamh mōr* too much sword for the slim youth. It required strong arms and two hands to wield it. Now, however, the large claymore proved its worth.

Enraged, the Englishman swung toward Ranald. His next lunge at the youth proved to be his last. Ranald's great sword pierced the man's chest. The Englishman dropped his sword, bellowing as the claymore cut through his mail and padded undercoat straight into his heart. Jennet wanted to look away yet could not. She felt an uncomfortable mix of revulsion and relief as the man's blood flowed.

When the lifeless body crumbled to the ground, it took Ranald with it. She began to fear Ranald had not escaped the fight unscathed when he stumbled to his feet, one hand still gripping the sword. He stood, swaying slightly, staring down at the man still impaled upon his sword. Jennet realized Ranald was more upset than she was.

She slipped her dagger into her pocket and slowly edged

down the stairs. She spoke in a calm, firm voice. "Ranald, 'tis time to take your sword out."

"Aye, aye." Ranald yanked it free, then with unsteady hands, wiped it clean on the Englishman's surcoat.

"Now, close the mon's eyes." He nodded and did so. "Good. Now, come sit back here, where ye were ere he thundered in here."

When Ranald stiffly obeyed, she hurried to pour him a tankard of strong ale. She handed it to him, watching closely as he drank. By the time he was done, setting the tankard aside, she thought he looked much better, some color having returned to his cheeks. She leaned against the table, Murdoc set on her hip, and wondered what she should do next.

"I will ne'er be a knight," Ranald said finally, his voice hoarse and uneven.

"Now, why do ye think that?"

"My first true fight, the first mon I have slain, and I shake like one with the fever. In a battle I must be ready to turn and fight again, with no hesitation. Nay, I shall ne'er be a knight. I shall ne'er live past my first true test in battle."

"First! Didnae ye come into Berwick with Hacon and the rest?"

He nodded. "But we surprised them, so the real fight was a short one. Then I met up with Douglas's men."

Jennet wanted to tell him that he should put aside his sword. The world did not need another knight. However, he was so despondent over what he saw as his failure, she felt a rush of sympathy for him. She knew that most of what she was about to say contradicted all her beliefs, but she wanted to cheer the youth.

"Ranald, ye cannae think this is the end to all your hopes. I am certain that, if another mon came after ye, ye would have met that attack as weel as ye did this one. To be a knight takes a hardening of body and heart. Ye just need more . . . weel, hardening."

"Do ye really think so?"

"I cannae believe every mon is born with the skill to fight and the stomach to do it. Do ye think your uncle or Dugald or any of the others are cold-blooded murderers?"

"Nay, they are good men."

Although not sure she could agree, she knew it was not the time to argue the point. "Then, at some time, back at the start of their fighting days, they too had to deal with your feeling of uneasiness. Mayhaps ye should ask them how they harden themselves."

Sitting up a little straighter, Ranald stared at the door. "Aye, I may just do that. And soon I will have the chance."

As he spoke she heard an achingly familiar laugh. Hacon appeared in the doorway, grinning at something Dugald said, and she had to grip the edge of the table to keep from running to him and flinging herself into his arms out of pure relief to see him alive. Her feelings for the man were growing treacherously strong.

Those emotions faded abruptly as she took a closer look at him. His sword was sheathed, but it had clearly been put to use. The blood tainting his armor attested to that. He wore his helmet and mail hood, his face nearly obscured except for that grin. Suddenly, he seemed a threat to her again, a man who could smile while others died. She felt light-headed with confusion.

The grin on Hacon's face was abruptly erased when he espied the dead man on the floor. In a few quick strides he was at Jennet's side, studying her intently. Once assured she was unhurt, he turned his attention to Ranald, at the same time draping his arm about Jennet's shoulders and holding her close. He ignored her muttered protest over the familiar handling, tightening his grip to still her when she tried to pull away.

"Any trouble besides that, lad?" Hacon nodded toward the dead man, whom his own men were efficiently stripping of armor.

"Nay, he was all of it."

"And ye are unhurt?"

Ranald nodded.

"Ye have no pain from your old wounds either?"

"Nay, no pains." Ranald looked at Jennet and held out his hand for her dagger. "'Tis over. Remember?"

She sighed and handed it to him. "Aye, I remember. I was just hoping ye wouldnae."

Looking at the dagger with raised eyebrows, Hacon then fixed his gaze upon Ranald. "Ye gave the lass a weapon?"

"Only while your throat was out of reach, uncle." Ranald smiled a little weakly, then moved to put Jennet's dagger back amongst their supplies.

Frowning after his nephew, as he discarded his helmet and mail hood, Hacon asked Jennet, "Are ye certain the lad suffered no hurt? 'Tis a braw Englishmon he had to face."

Staring at him, she wondered which man was the true Hacon—the one who revealed honest concern for his young nephew or the one who smiled while the blood of others dried on his clothes. She concentrated on the matter of Ranald, hating her confusion and glad to put it aside.

"Aye, but he did so with skill and without flinching. What ails him is . . . weel, 'twas his first killing."

"Nay, he fought in the battle to take this town," Hacon said, and Dugald, back at his side, nodded.

"Aye, but he didnae really get a chance to fight ere he met up with the Douglas's men. Ranald took the killing hard, though he never faltered in doing what was necessary." She briefly described the confrontation as Hacon's men quietly removed the corpse. "I fear I havenae talked him out of what troubled him. Because of how he felt once the deed was done, he thinks he will ne'er be a knight."

"I will have a talk with the lad. I thought he had passed that mark and taken it weel. But now"—he grinned down at

Jennet—"where is the warm kiss of welcome for the victor in this battle?"

She held up Murdoc, who dutifully pressed an inept wet kiss on Hacon's cheek. To her surprise and amusement, Hacon gave the baby a loud smacking kiss on his soft cheek, making Murdoc giggle. As she returned the child to his seat on her hip, Hacon eyed her with a half smile.

"That wasnae exactly what I had in mind," he drawled. "I was thinking of a kiss that would put fire in a man's loins, not the smell of goat's milk on his face."

"Ye think on what is in your braies far too much."

"I cannae help it when I am set upon the rack every night, stirred to hunger yet coldly rebuffed."

"I dinnae even touch you," she said, feeling the need to defend herself against what sounded like an accusation.

"I ken it. There is the real pity of it all."

He pulled such a doleful face she was unable to suppress a giggle. There was the real danger of the man. He teased, he smiled and laughed, and he made her want to do the same. She wondered if he knew how easily he was seducing her simply by revealing that part of his nature, then tensed. Could that be his deliberate intention?

"'Tis a torture ye bring upon yourself," she said, "and one ye can end at any time."

"Aye, though ye seem to forget that."

She decided it would be wise to retreat. "I had best see if Ranald needs any help."

"He said he had no injuries."

"I ken what he said. Whether it was the truth or not, weel, that is another matter entirely."

Hacon watched her join Ranald, then with Dugald's help began to shed the clothes he had worn to battle. "I almost have her," he said, keeping his voice low so that only Dugald could hear. "Weel, I do," he muttered when Dugald made a scornful noise of disbelief.

"Oh, aye, I can see it clear. She fair wastes away for the wanting of you."

Deciding he would ignore Dugald's snide remarks, Hacon confessed, "I kissed her ere I went off to battle."

"Such great progress after eight long days."

"She wants me. 'Twas there to feel in her kiss."

"Weel, ye may see it or feel it, but I cannae. If 'tis there, she does a fine job of keeping it to herself."

"Aye, but that she would do. I have learned that much about her nature. Then, too, her being a virgin keeps her fighting it."

"She is a virgin?" Dugald straightened up from helping Hacon out of his hose. "Are ye sure of that?"

"As sure as any mon can be without bedding her. Didnae ye think she was?"

Dugald shrugged. "I dinnae give it much thought but, nay, I guess I didnae, despite where we found her. 'Tis not a suspicion born of how she acts or the like. 'Tis just that from what little I ken of her, she has often been near or at some battle or raid. She is a woman and not hard to look on. And she was a Scottish maid in an English house. I just assumed she would have lost that maidenhead by now. I will get ye some water to clean off with."

Watching as his cousin saw to that small chore, Hacon frowned. There had been a distinct change in Dugald's manner when Jennet's maiden state had been revealed. When Dugald returned, he stood there staring and frowning as Hacon washed himself.

"Weel?" demanded Hacon, unable to tolerate any more of Dugald's staring. "Say it."

"Say what?"

"Whatever it is that has ye standing there staring at me."

"Mayhaps ye ought to leave the lass be, give up your plan of bedding her."

"And just why should I do that when I have thought of little else since first setting eyes on her?"

"Because she is a virgin. She doesnae come from the finest stock. She was but a handmaiden. If she was but seeking refuge with the nuns and didnae mean to join them, then her only chance to make a good marriage is to stay a maiden. Ye plan to take that dower away. I cannae feel 'tis right for ye to use her as ye please, then toss her aside. Ye would be stealing her future."

"And who says I mean to cast her aside?"

"Weel, ye have ne'er said otherwise. What *do* ye plan, then?"

Hacon shrugged, then pulled on a clean shirt. "All I have been able to think on this last week is how badly I want the lass."

Jennet sat before the low-burning fire brushing out her hair before bedding down. She was weary of going to bed fully dressed. Her only consolation was that she now had a number of good, serviceable gowns to wear. She had almost completely smothered her guilt over making use of stolen goods.

Despite her increased wardrobe she still wished she could crawl into bed attired as she always had been before—naked or in a thin chemise. Unfortunately, living in such close quarters with so many men left her no privacy. And then there was Hacon. It was disturbing enough to sleep in his arms while fully dressed. She dared not consider the temptation of sleeping with him flesh-to-flesh.

As if conjured up by her wayward thoughts, he sat down beside her. Please, God, she silently prayed, couldnae ye make him a wee bit ugly? 'Twould give me some strength, and I sorely need some. Inwardly sighing, knowing that even a loss of his looks might not help her now, she met his steady gaze.

"I talked to Ranald," he said, draping an arm about her shoulders when she set down her hairbrush and ignoring the way she tensed. "The other men mean to speak to him too, to let him ken he isnae alone in how he feels now that the first mon has fallen to his sword."

"So he will find the strength to fight again."

"Ye dinnae approve. Nay, dinnae try to deny it," he said when she started to speak. "Do ye really think we enjoy the killing?"

"Nay, I wouldnae say that. Nor do I think it. 'Tis just that it ne'er stops. Even those who seek holy orders arenae safe. Why must men do it? 'Tis a bloody harvest and all one reaps is sorrow. Year after blood-soaked year of pain, grief, and hunger."

He sighed. "There are many reasons for it. We dinnae want English rule, dinnae wish to be a conquered people. Some fight for plunder, some for revenge, some out of pure hate." He shrugged.

"What are your reasons then?"

"I support the Bruce, but that isnae all of it. As I have told you, my father lost his lands. They went to a family who supported the English. Now the Bruce holds our lands. He could give them back to me if I fight weel for his cause. He has given many another land. Aye, and titles. I believe I am close now. Then Dùbheilrig will belong to a Gillard again. We would be masters of our own lands once more and not simple tenants."

She sensed he felt strongly about it, so said nothing. It was as good a reason as any for fighting. Hastily covering a yawn, she slid free of Hacon's light hold and prepared to lie down. She gave a soft gasp of surprise when he clasped her shoulders and turned her to face him.

There was an intent look in his fine eyes that made her feel warm yet frightened. The man really did want her. She heartily wished she did not find that idea so attractive. When he brushed his lips over hers, she resisted an immediate rush of warmth. Was he meaning to take her now? Would she fight him much if he did? If the blind, hot need his kiss had stirred within her before was any example, she might forget how to say nay. It wiped the tethering word *sin* right out of her mind. Rape no longer seemed a fitting description either, though he could yet prove her wrong.

"I was ready to go to sleep," she whispered, telling herself she was not accepting his soft, nibbling kisses, just remaining still so as to not anger him while he forced his attentions upon her.

"Without giving the mon who protects ye a goodnight kiss?"

"I think Ranald is asleep already."

"Ah, ye sore try a mon's temper, lass. Torment him past all clear thinking."

"I dinnae do a thing. Not a thing."

"I ken it. Mayhaps 'tis past time for me to cease being so agreeable. Aye, I will have a kiss ere ye lie down to turn a cold back to me for another long night." He wrapped one arm about her, cupping the back of her head in his hand. "Dinnae look so afraid, lass. 'Tis but a kiss. Naught to worry about."

Little did he know, she thought even as he kissed her. It did frighten her some, in the way it made her feel. All resistance left her, heat and hunger flowing in to take its place. She wanted to cling to him, then realized that she already was. Her arms were tightly wrapped about his neck, and she was pressing herself as close to him as possible. As his tongue stroked the inside of her mouth, she wanted even more. Suddenly she knew exactly what he meant when he spoke of aching for her. There did not seem to be an inch of her that did not cry out with need.

As he ended the kiss, she struggled to regain some composure. Her eyes still closed, she eased her body away from his. She could sense his gaze upon her. There was some comfort in hearing that his breathing came as hard and fast as her own.

"I am going to open my eyes now," she said carefully, once she had regained the power of speech.

"Ah, good. I had worried that ye had swooned from the pleasure of it."

She ignored him. "And if ye are grinning, even a tiny wee grin, ye will be sorely regretting it."

Very slowly, she opened her eyes. He was pressing his lips together very tightly. It was no good. The grin was not visible from his mouth, but it gleamed from his eyes. He knew. Knew how he made her feel, knew how hard she had to fight to say nay, and how much she ached to say aye.

"There will be no more kisses." She moved to her side of the sheepskin and laid down.

He too laid down, then tucked her up against him. "Oh, aye, my pretty plunder, there will be more kisses. And, if I can ever find us a private place, there will be more—much, much more."

She decided to ignore him. Argument was impossible. Perhaps her brief suspicion had been right—he did not plan rape but seduction. If that was the way of it, she was in a great deal of trouble.

# Chapter 5

"I will kill the beast. I will cut his bleating hairy throat."

Jennet struggled to contain her laughter. Poor Dugald looked murderous as he stumbled to his feet, rubbing his backside where one of the goats had butted him. That it had happened in front of his many compatriots gathering on the common grazing fields outside of Berwick's walls added to his embarrassment. The men's hoots of laughter heightened his sense of injury. Although she understood his anger, she could not let him kill one of the goats. She quickly placed herself between him and the animals.

"Step aside, lass," Dugald muttered as he approached, dagger in hand.

"Now, ye cannae kill the beast. Murdoc needs the milk. Ye wouldnae steal the food from the bairn's mouth, would you?"

Dugald stopped and scowled at her. "He doesnae need the milk of all three."

"Aye—not now. Howbeit, we are headed into England, into battle. Some of these animals may die. At least, by starting with three, we will have a good chance of keeping one alive for Murdoc."

Dugald muttered a curse and stalked across the common, not hesitating to cuff any chuckling man within reach. Jennet allowed herself a brief laugh before she turned to scold the goat. She was struggling to get the stubborn animals attached to one main lead rope when Hacon, leading a horse and a shaggy Highland pony, emerged from the milling crowd of soldiers. Jennet eyed the animals warily. She had done little riding in her life. Clearly, that reprieve was about to end.

"Ye wish me to add the wee one to the lead?" she asked with ill-concealed hope.

"Nay, the wee one is for your wee backside, and weel ye ken it. Hey, laddie." Hacon reached around her to Murdoc, resting comfortably on her back in a rawhide sling that one of the men had made. "Ye look hale and cheery." He ruffled the babe's curls.

"Ye expect me to get on that beast and trot after ye?" Jennet asked.

"Aye. I put a blanket o'er the saddle so ye willnae find it so hard."

"Such chivalry. I am rendered speechless."

"Aye, I thought it was verra chivalrous myself."

"Weel, think again. I have decided I willnae go." She crossed her arms under her breasts and waited to see what he had to say to that.

Hacon rubbed his chin with one hand and studied her in silence. "Ye have decided to be difficult, have ye?"

She nodded. "I will be naught but trouble for you, so I have decided to relieve ye of that burden in advance."

"How kind. Do ye mean to stay here then? Douglas's men will be glad of some pretty lass's company."

"I could return to the convent." But even as she spoke she knew that choice was lost to her.

"Lass, ye ken weel there is naught left at the convent."

Silently cursing, she scowled at him. She did not like his reminders of her precarious circumstances. Of course she could not stay in Berwick. She doubted she would get two steps inside the gate before one of the men there seized her. Clearly, there was no refuge for her anywhere.

"Then I will go north to Liddesdale, to my mother's people."

"Through the land the Bruce's army has just crossed?" he asked, and shrugged. "Weel, hie to it then. I am sure ye will get a warm welcome from the folk ye meet. Aye, they willnae have forgotten us so quickly and will be awaiting any Scot they dinnae ken."

Unable to resist, she glanced toward the north. Even if she could elude harm from the people she chanced to meet, she would have to cross the bleak heights of Coldingham Moor alone. It galled her to admit it, but she was safer with Hacon and his men, even if they were about to embark upon a raid. She tensed when he stepped close to her, cupping her face in his big, strong hands. There was a look of sympathy in his startlingly blue eyes which she was not sure she appreciated.

"Now, ye are a clever lass, though I think ye may speak your mind more than is wise in such troubled times. I ken it must be hard to admit it, but staying with me is the wisest choice."

The way he lightly stroked her face at the corners of her eyes had an odd effect on her. He moved his thumbs in a gentle circular motion. She had the strongest urge to close her eyes, could feel them growing heavy-lidded. The way his gaze caressed her face, lingering on her mouth, did not help her gain the strength to pull out of his hold. She was distressingly interested in his firm, well-shaped mouth. Jennet tried to push the word *sin* to the forefront of her mind, but the word that lodged there instead was *kiss*.

"In Berwick, lass," he continued in a low voice, "ye will find rape, mayhaps even death. Ye have seen that in the near fortnight we have lodged here. To travel anywhere else could weel mean the same. At least by staying with me, the swords ye see willnae be aimed your way."

"But ye mean to drag me along on a raid." She inwardly grimaced at how husky and soft her voice had grown.

"Aye, and I am sorry for that, but I will do it all the same. Ye will be set back with Ranald, at a safer distance from whatever fighting takes place."

The assurance did little to make her feel better. She would be stuck on the back of that pony for every hour of the day. Her only respite from the swift, hard ride deep into England's northern counties would come when they paused to plunder some poor village or fight the English. She would have the hard, often damp ground as her bed, little more than porridge to eat day in and day out, and no shelter from the weather. The Scots did not carry the luxuries the English did. There were no tents, no servants, no train of wagons laden with supplies. The Scots packed little more than their weapons, a sack of oats, a tin plate, and a blanket or two. The gentry had horses and the men-at-arms had their hardy Highland ponies, which gave them a speed and elusiveness that had once driven Edward the Second to tears.

She suspected she would be moved to tears a few times herself. A raid took weeks, even months, of hard riding interrupted by theft and bloodshed. It was exhausting, hazardous, and filthy. It was not something she wished to experience, but she was being given no choice. She was almost glad of the way Hacon was stirring her desire, for it kept her from thinking too much about the ordeal she was about to face.

He brushed soft kisses over her forehead and cheeks. "Ye will be weel protected."

"I said, no more kissing," she whispered in an unsteady voice.

"Now, lass, what is the use of a mon taking a wee bit of plunder if he cannae enjoy it now and again?"

Before she could respond, his mouth was on hers. She tried to fight how it made her feel, tried to think of disgusting things such as slugs and leeches. She even tried to invoke the painful memories of her mother's brutal death. As ploys to halt how his kiss heated her blood, they all failed miserably.

Instead, all she became aware of was how good he tasted and how each stroke of his tongue increased the heat of desire curling through her body.

"If it pleases you, Sir Gillard, we thought we might start upon our way now."

The deep, lisping voice cut through the fog with which Hacon's kiss filled her head. Jennet needed little time to recover her composure when Hacon abruptly ended the kiss. She watched Sir James Douglas as Hacon turned to face the man. There was something about him that chilled her soul, and it was not only because of the bloodthirsty tales told about him. At the moment, she was heartily glad that Hacon stood firm at her side.

"I am ready to ride, sir," Hacon replied.

"Ye still mean to take her with you?"

"Aye, sir. She will stay to the rear with the extra ponies, with the plunder we may gather, and mayhaps with the wounded."

"See that she does."

When Douglas and his grinning companions had ridden away, Jennet breathed a hearty sigh of relief. "I cannae like that mon."

"Good." Hacon grasped her arm and tugged her over to the pony he had brought for her. "Then ye will stay far away from him and his men." He hefted her up into the saddle and idly helped her fix her skirts over her legs. "Ye may have heard a tale or two about the mon."

"Aye, dark tales."

"Believe them, lass. I have ridden with him for ten long years." Holding the pommel of her saddle with one hand, he held her gaze with his eyes. "Have ye ever heard of 'Douglas's larder'?" She shook her head. "The English held his castle. He sneaked into the place and slew most of the garrison while they were at mass. He killed those who remained while they supped in the castle. He threw the bodies, the food, the wine, and aye, even the live prisoners and the wounded into the pits of his castle and burned the place down o'er them. Remember that, lass. It tells ye a great deal about the mon Sir James is."

"At mass?" she whispered, shocked by such sacrilege.

"Aye, at mass."

"Weel, it fits what else I ken."

"Which is?"

"'Twas Douglas's men who murdered my mother. I recognize the colors now."

"My regrets for your mother's death come late, but trust in their sincerity. And learn from that tragedy. Dinnae forget those colors." He went and gathered up the goats, and was tugging them back to her just as Ranald rode up. "Good lad," he murmured as he tied the goats' lead rope to the pommel of Jennet's saddle. "Stay close by her, Ranald, and try not to lag too far behind. Even the lowest, most timid of serfs will set upon you if ye are caught alone." He grinned at Jennet. "Now, how about a wee kiss ere I ride off into danger?"

He reached toward her chin, but she slapped his hand away. "I think not, sir knight."

"Ye are a hard-hearted lass, Jennet of Liddesdale," he said as he mounted his horse, then winked at her before riding off.

Glaring at his broad back, Jennet muttered every curse she could think of. If rape and death did not lurk at every turn, she would be gone before he could blink. Instead she had to stay with him despite knowing, after only a few kisses, that his plan to seduce her was rapidly drawing to a successful conclusion.

"Jennet?" Ranald nudged his mount alongside her pony. "We must ride now."

"Aye, I ken it." She gently kicked her pony to start it on its way. "Into England so I can see more fields burned."

"'Tis war," said Ranald as he kept pace with her. "We must harry the English and try to stop them from gathering their army and assaulting Berwick in force. The English would do the same."

She shook her head. They all said that, sounding like sullen little children. As far as she could see, it was a thin excuse for wanton destruction. She had seen little else in her life and was heartily sick of it.

And yet, she mused with self-disgust, my blood heats for a knight who lives by all I find so abhorrent. It was a dilemma she had no answer to. She knew Hacon would continue to take full advantage of their enforced proximity. Getting out of his reach was the only way to avoid succumbing to his wooing and her own weakness, but that was not yet possible. She could only pray that a chance came before Hacon won the game.

Trying to hide a wince, Jennet eased herself down to sit on the ground and watched as the Scots' army set their plain, rough camp amongst a scrub forest of hawthorn and birch. The pace of the advance had been grueling. Jennet was sure they had covered at least forty miles in their first day of riding. She had barely snatched enough time to see to Murdoc's needs. It had been hard on the poor child. It had been even harder on her. She did not think there was a part of her that did not ache, but one part in particular was in agony. Despite Hacon's efforts to soften her seat on the pony, her backside throbbed. She did not want, even, to look to see what her thighs had suffered.

Hacon arrived with their meal, sitting next to her and handing her the metal plate and a rough wooden spoon. She almost threw the food in his face. Hunger won out over anger, however. Wearily she ate, barely tasting it. Since it was only porridge again, Jennet decided it was no real tragedy.

"Ye havenae done much riding in your life, have ye, lass?" Hacon asked as he handed her his wineskin.

She took a small drink and shook her head. "Nay, and if God is kind, I willnae have to do any more."

"Weel, I fear God isnae going to help you this time. We are weel into England now, and this is the pace we will set for most of our stay here."

"Then I shall pray for a plague to befall every horse and pony in the land."

"Ah, but then we would have to run back to Scotland. Are ye prepared to trot a hundred miles or more with the English on your heels?"

"I have seen little of the English. From what is said, Edward couldnae command his army to a brothel."

"It doesnae have to be the army." He set their empty plates aside and regarded her with keen interest. "Have ye heard a lot about the English army and about Edward's troubles?"

"I doubt I have heard any more than ye have."

"Nay? I havenae spent the last few years living with the English."

"And I was but a lady's maid, not one of the court."

"Ye must have some reason to speak so disparagingly of the English king and his army."

"Ye mean to keep nudging at me until I tell ye what little I ken about it, aye?"

"Aye." He met her cross look with a faint smile.

She sighed. "Ye would ask me, mayhaps, to help ye kill even more people?"

"Lass, I willnae use whate'er ye might tell me for that purpose. I but look to keep my men alive."

"Weel, Edward isnae as strong as his father was. He cannae hold his men together. From what I hear, his lieutenants are more interested in their own private squabbles than in fighting the Scots. The ones he needs to help lead the men are disordered and unable to move one way or another. Rumor has it that his army is mutinous. 'Tis said they havenae been paid, as was promised." She shook her head. "It worried the English soldiers in Berwick as weel as their supporters, for they feared there would be no help for them if they came under attack. 'Tis clear they were right to worry."

"There does appear to be little resistance. Howbeit, we havenae gone verra far yet."

"If I were to make a wager, I would say there willnae be much resistance. There was a strong feeling in Berwick that this land was to be left to care for itself. We couldnae even get help to put down the bandits. And I dinnae mean just poor folk stealing to survive. Nay, many an embittered English knight came back from their bloody defeat at Bannockburn and turned to banditry. The famine these last two years only encouraged that." She looked at him. "Were ye at Bannockburn?"

"Aye. I was knighted there."

"I was there too. The de Tournays made their way to Stirling after the Bruce took Perth. I watched the battle from the castle walls," she whispered, "until a mon-at-arms sent me away. He said it wasnae a sight for a wee lass's eyes. I was but newly turned fourteen. Then, after de Mowbray surrendered the castle's defenses to the Bruce, we made our way to Berwick, riding out over the battlefield."

For a moment Hacon could make no reply. The memory of that momentous battle before Stirling Castle filled his mind. The Scots had been outnumbered, only seven thousand of them against an English force of twenty thousand or more, yet they had defeated the English in a bloody rout. The English knights had become impaled upon the Scots' schiltrons, those lethally massed groups of men with their twelve-foot spears held pointing in every direction and standing firm against every onslaught. The six-pointed calthrops thrown upon the ground to maim the English horses, and rows of hidden pits, had also taken a heavy toll on Edward's fine cavalry. When the English cavalry had been broken and the wounded and riderless horses had raced back upon the main body of Edward's forces, the English army had been thrown into confusion. Hacon inwardly shuddered as he recalled what Jennet must have witnessed.

Although hard-pressed, the English had fought bravely. Arrows, sword, and battle-axes had left dead piled up on both sides. The English commanders had chosen a poor fighting position, however. Caught on the narrow, boggy strip of land between the Scottish army and the River Forth, the English army had been trapped. When Edward the Second fled the battle, pursued by Sir James Douglas all the way to Dunbar, his army finally broke. The whole center of the English host fled toward the Forth and were destroyed. The English left flank was forced into the muddy gorge of the tidal River Bannockburn. Those not killed by the Scots drowned when the high tides arrived. The river became so choked with drowned men and horses it was said a man could pass over it without wetting his feet. The battlefield had also been covered with dead. Nearly ten thousand English knights, archers, and foot soldiers had lain where they had fallen, left to rot in the hot June sun.

Hacon silently cursed. Even now, four years later, he could still see it, still hear the deadly cacophony and still smell the stench of gore. The man-at-arms had been right—that slaughter had been no sight for a young girl, yet Jennet had not been spared it. *And I just admitted to being there,* he thought with a grimace. It was becoming clear why she spoke so bitterly about knights.

"Ye seem to have been on the English side at the wrong time," he finally murmured.

"Aye, but before then I was on the Scottish side at the wrong time. 'Twas the Bruce's men who raped and slew my mother while I cowered in hiding, yet the village supported the Bruce. They had the misfortune to have the enemy, the Comyns, as their lords. It really doesnae matter which side ye find yourself on. Neither kens what mercy is. What I want to find is a place where war can ne'er reach me." She looked down at Murdoc who lay on his back happily playing with his toes. "And ne'er reach the bairns. I have seen enough of battle."

"Too much, I think. It haunts your dreams."

"Weel, aye, I have been wakened by a nightmare or two."

Taking her thick braid in his hand, he idly caressed its length. "Some just make ye cry out or weep but dinnae wake ye."

When he slipped his arm about her shoulders, tugging her close to his side, she only briefly thought of resisting. She was simply too tired. Promising herself she would move out of reach if he got too familiar, she relaxed against him. There was a growing chill to the air and he was warm, she mused as she yawned.

"Lass, it hasnae been a war twixt Scotland and England alone. 'Tis also a war between the Scots. Now we hold Berwick, which has the last English stronghold in Scotland. Scotland is free of the English. Mayhaps now there will be some peace."

She glanced up at him and was surprised to find he was not looking at her. He always looked at her, usually straight in the eye, when he spoke. Her eyes widening, she realized something important about her captor's character. He usually looked her in the eye because he spoke the truth, or the truth as he saw it. Sir Hacon Gillard was an honest man. The reason he stared off into the night now, his face slightly averted, was because he did not believe what he was saying any more than she did. It was a fact about his nature that might prove helpful. She hastily swallowed the words she was about to say, words that would have revealed her thoughts. Instead, she chose to argue with him.

"Aye, there will be no war if Edward or his son doesnae have another king he wishes to place on the throne of Scotland. Or, if the Scots who have become disinherited by the Bruce no longer feel like fighting for their lands. Or if the

Bruce doesnae make any new enemies. There are many more ifs, but I willnae trouble ye with them."

"Ye have a poor view of the world, lass." He rested his cheek on the top of her head.

"Not of the world, just of men with swords in their hands and an eye for glory and fortune."

"Now, wee Jennet . . ."

"Nay, dinnae waste your words. The ideas I hold have been set hard. I was born on a battlefield."

"During what battle?"

"I dinnae ken. My mother, father, and his wounded friend crouched in a muddy ditch as mother labored to bring me into the world. Father's chosen side had lost, and the victors were roaming the land for miles about, cutting down all who tried to flee."

"But your parents escaped?"

"Aye, my father has a true skill for staying alive. Although"—she sighed—"I dinnae think he slipped away from Perth. The Bruce considered every Scot there the worst of traitors for holding with the English. I cannae see how my father could have talked his way out of that situation. He was clearly wellborn, clearly a Scot, and clearly fighting for the English. I wanted to stay to be certain of his fate, but I couldnae." She sat up and looked at him. "Were ye at . . ."

"Nay, I wasnae at Perth." He heartily prayed that God would help him spit out that lie convincingly. "I left the army just before that. Word had come that my mother was ill. With my men, I returned to Dubheilrig. Fortunately, her condition was not as serious as was thought." When she could not fully hide a huge yawn, he smiled faintly. "Time for ye to get some rest."

The speed with which he spread a blanket over a soft, moss-covered patch of ground, then got her and Murdoc bedded down, surprised her. He tucked a second blanket over them with more haste than gentleness. It was almost as if he wanted to flee her presence. She told herself not to be such a fool. Until now, the man had been as hard to shake as any burr.

Nor only had he set her down in the midst of his men but, she realized, they were all set slightly apart from the main force. Several yards beyond she could see the first of the many small campfires of Douglas's large force. When she caught herself on the point of asking Hacon when he would join her, she quickly closed her eyes. Not only did she cringe to think what he would reply, but she dreaded what he might read behind the words. The very last thing she wanted him to know was that she was becoming pleasantly accustomed to him being by her side all night. When she heard him walk away, she breathed a soft sigh of relief. If luck was with her for once, she would be sound asleep and blissfully impervious to temptation by the time he rejoined her.

Hacon made his way to where Dugald and Ranald still sat by a low campfire. Sitting down, he took a long drink from his wineskin. For a while he remained silent, trying to sort out his thoughts about Jennet.

Dugald, his voice low, cautiously broke the silence. "Ye and the lass looked friendly."

"Appearances can be deceiving, cousin," Hacon murmured.

"Aye? She didnae look angry at you. Not this time."

"She is angry with all of us."

Ranald frowned. "What do ye mean, uncle?"

"The lass has breathed the stench of war since the moment she was born." He briefly related some of what Jennet had told him. "She sees every mon who wields a sword as no more than a murderer."

"Nay," Ranald protested. "She must see the rightness of this cause—to rid Scotland of the English. Do ye think she is on the side of Edward and England then?"

"Jennet is on neither side."

"As a true Scot, she *must* be on the Bruce's side."

"There is many a *true* Scot who isnae, laddie. In truth, the lass has cause to loathe the Bruce and all who support him. 'Twas the Douglas's men who raped and killed her mother. Aye, and may have killed her father. Howbeit, the side the lass wishes to be on is that of peace." Hacon picked up his sword and laid it across his lap, staring at it. "She sees this, and those who carry one, as the curse of mankind. I dinnae think I can convince her that there can be differences in the men who wield such weapons."

"Her father wields one. She herself said he fights for whoever pays the most."

"Ah, but that is her father, her blood kin." Hacon shrugged. "A father can do a great many wrongs e'er a child will turn from him. 'Tis a strong bond of love that doesnae break easily."

"Aye," agreed Dugald, watching Hacon closely. "But ye dinnae look for love. Ye just seek a passing warmth."

"So ye keep reminding me. I wonder why."

"Weel, I cannae be sure ye would be wise to look for more."

"And why not?" Hacon knew he already wanted more than lust from Jennet, a lot more, but he kept that to himself.

"She is born of poor folk with no lands or coin."

"So was my mother."

"Ah, but your mother wasnae the bairn of two thieving clans. Jennet is bred of an Armstrong and a Graeme—two lots of reivers' blood in her veins."

"She has been with us for near to a fortnight and not stolen one wee thing. Aye, and ye have heard her speak out against our taking of plunder. Ye cannae think her a thief."

Dugald shrugged. "I but say what others will."

"They willnae say it more than once," Hacon said in a cold, flat voice.

"And what of her father?"

"What of the mon?"

"She says she believes he died at Perth. Ye were there."

"She doesnae ken it."

"Not now, mayhaps, but she is sure to ask ye where ye were that bloody day."

"She already has. I lied." The shock on Dugald's and Ranald's faces was oddly comforting. "I looked her in the eye and said I had been called to my sick mother's side. I just couldnae tell her I had been there and been witness to that murder."

"But, uncle"—Ranald ran a hand through his hair—"I cannae see how that lie can hold. Too many ken that ye *were* there. Ye cannac stop every mouth. Besides, I dinnae understand why ye told the lie at all."

Shaking his head, Dugald muttered, "'Tis hard to seduce a lass if she thinks the blood of her own father stains your sword." He looked at Hacon. "Weel, I see that your feelings have already passed that of an itch in your groin."

"And ye would object to that would ye?" Hacon saw no reason to deny what was probably all too obvious to others.

"Nay, what I was just saying was what I felt certain others will say. In birth and fortune ye could do better. For myself, I like the lass, though she does have a sharp and too free tongue. Ye might try to curb that."

"I think I could do better trying to hold back the tide." Hacon smiled and Ranald chuckled.

"Aye, 'tis true," Dugald continued, "but ye might try all the same. Such free speaking can lead to trouble. There is as little trust as mercy to be depended on these days. The Bruce is always looking for traitors, and there are plenty about. The Bruce hasnae set his backside on a quiet throne, and years of fighting to hold it have made the mon verra suspicious. Aye, and ye have an enemy or two who would like to see ye fall. They could try to turn her words into a dagger with which to cut ye down."

"Why would they heed what a lass says?" asked Ranald.

Hacon had to bite back a smile at the youth's scornful attitude. "A lass can work a strong influence o'er a mon. Then there are those who cannae believe a lass can speak her own mind, they think that her words must be an echo of her mon's." He looked at Dugald. "I will try to soften her words. At best I shall work to keep them private, unheard save by me. Aye, 'twould be safer to get her to be quiet, but I willnae force her to it. I enjoy hearing how she thinks."

"Just be sure ye are the *only* one who hears it," Dugald muttered.

When Hacon finally sought his bed, he realized he had not eased any of his concerns, only added to them. Gently curling his arm about Jennet's small waist, he smiled faintly when she murmured in her sleep and cuddled up against him. It was a sweet torture. Her softly curved backside was pressed to his groin, causing him to immediately tighten with arousal. He liked the way she snuggled up close, innocently inviting him in her sleep, and he ached to make love to her. It would be a while yet, however, before she allowed him to satisfy his growing hunger for her. If nothing else, he needed to find them a private place.

As he nuzzled her sweet-smelling hair, then rested his cheek against it, he decided to set aside his concerns. It did little good to prey upon them, would not bring the answers he needed any faster. What he would set his mind on, solely, was keeping Jennet safe and savoring the passion she struggled so hard to hide. He promised himself that by the time they returned to Scotland she would be his.

# Chapter 6

The body beneath her needle suddenly went limp. Jennet glanced at the man's face. He had fainted at last. She had begun to fear he never would. Returning her attention to the dagger wound in his side, she finished stitching it closed and bandaged it, then sat back on her heels, studying her work and deciding it was the cleanest spot on the man's body.

As she went to wash up, two more men arrived. One man's jupon was bloodied and he nearly carried a barely conscious youth who still bled freely from the wounds at his waist and leg. They made their way through the clutter of the camp straight toward her. She had become the leech for the whole army it seemed. No one had asked it of her, it had just happened. For nearly five weeks she had been forced to see the gory results of the raid deep into English territory. They had marched south through Richmond and burned Northallerton. Now Boroughbridge was being set alight. She was tired of cleaning the blood off men, tired of mending torn flesh.

While doing what she could for the two newest arrivals, she glanced toward a group of women who were captives like herself. There were only five now, but she knew there would soon be more, for women were considered acceptable plunder by both sides. The poor souls did not have as kind a captor as she did. Fearful and bruised, they huddled together beneath some alder trees. Jennet could use their help but did not know how to gain it. None of them would hold any love for a Scot or wish to keep one alive. Nevertheless, she knew she had to try.

"I could use some help," she called out to them.

"Help?" the short, bosomy brunette nearly screeched. "Why should we wish to help these beasts live? I have been trying to understand why *you* work so hard. 'Tis said you are a captive too."

"Aye, I was taken at Berwick." She began to bathe the wound of the more seriously injured man. "I am more fortunate than you. My captor doesnae beat or rape me."

"Then why does he keep you?" snapped a thin-faced redhead.

"To seduce me," she replied. "What is your name?" she asked of the less wounded man who crouched on the other side of her patient.

"'Tis Robert," he replied in a hoarse voice.

"Weel, Robert, ye will have to hold him still." She carefully threaded her needle. "Now, ye women," she continued as she began to stitch yet another large wound, guessing this one could well prove fatal, "I understand why ye would wish these men ill—"

The brunette gave a scornful laugh. "Ill? I wish them to rot and burn in a thousand hells."

"Fair enough. Of course, helping these men could help you."

"How? How could doing even the smallest good for our abusers aid us?"

"I said *could*, just mayhaps, not for certain. If ye turn a hand to aiding them—only in mending their hurts and the likes—ye could soften their feelings toward you. Ye would-nae just be captives but one of those who helped bind that mon's wounds or bathed that mon's fevered brow. And there is their selfishness to think on. Ye might be seen as more use in aiding the wounded than in being one mon's plunder. The others may begin to object to your being abused. After all, if ye are treated too harshly, ye might not be able to help them. 'Tis but a thought."

"Aye, but it holds some sense," murmured the brunette, even as she walked to Jennet's side. The redhead quickly followed. "If naught else, 'twill keep me busy, too busy to become sunk in self-pity and sorrow."

Jennet glanced at the three women who remained huddled together, making no move toward her, not even acknowledging that they had heard her request. "They dinnae agree?"

"Who can say? I think they have grown sick in their minds. I am Elizabeth and that is Mary." Elizabeth nodded toward the redhead at her side. "We have the misfortune to belong to Gordon Frazer and his faithful cur, Mad Morgan."

"I am Jennet."

As she briefly shook each woman's hand she tried to hide her pity. Both men were well known to be rough and brutish. They were short, squarely built, and indisputably ugly. Whereas some men were reluctantly caught up in the bloodlust, Frazer and Morgan thrived on the killing.

Afraid she had been quiet too long and revealed her horror to the women, Jennet quickly said, "Help me bandage this boy."

"So young," muttered Elizabeth as she lent a hand. "Too young to die."

"He willnae die," declared Robert.

"Nay? 'Tis no mere scoring of the skin here. 'Tis best if you face the truth about your friend's fate."

"He is my brother," Robert whispered, then tugged away from Jennet and Mary when they moved to help him. "I dinnae need coddling. I mean to set here by my brother."

"Fine. Set there," Jennet snapped as she tugged off his battered helmet. "Ye willnae serve the lad weel if ye faint from your wounds and fall on top of him." Once his jupon and shirt were removed, Jennet nearly gasped, for he had an open bleeding wound that covered the full breadth of his chest.

"It has been said that Sir Hacon grabbed himself a sharp-tongued wench," Robert muttered. "I see 'tis true."

"So my fame spreads out before me, does it?" As she bathed the sword cut across his hairy chest, she shook her head. "Ye should have spoken up. I would have seen to this sooner had I kenned it was so bad."

"'Tis but a scratch."

"A scratch, ye say? If this 'scratch' was but a hair deeper, ye would have parts of you dropping out that ye would sore grieved to lose. Mary, there is a fair lot of blood matting that red hair of his. See if he has lost more than his wits."

When she began to stitch his wound, everyone fell silent. Out of the corner of her eye, Jennet saw Elizabeth gently cover the man's young brother with a blanket and begin to bathe his face. Clearly, Elizabeth would not turn the hate and anger she felt for her brutal captor against everyone. Jennet wondered if there was a way to free the woman before Gordon Frazer's harsh treatment of her killed all the softness in her.

"What were ye doing in Berwick? Were you with the English?" Robert asked, his voice ragged with pain as she bound his wounds.

Deciding there was no reason to keep it a secret, Jennet told her story as she efficiently tended to his lesser injuries. "'Twould be nice to learn my father's fate, but . . ." She finished with a shrug, trying to appear resigned.

"Weel, ye should ask your mon."

"He isnae my mon."

"He might ken, for he was there."

"Sir Gillard was at Perth?"

"Aye. 'Tis said he aided the Bruce in seeing the city's weakness and in finding a way inside."

Jennet stared blindly at the rag she was rinsing out. Hacon had lied. Worse, he had lied just moments after she had decided that he was a deeply honest man, that he could not successfully tell a falsehood. He had looked her straight in the eye and told a very big lie indeed.

A sick mother, she inwardly scoffed. How could she have been so stupid? What knight walked away from an important battle for a sick mother? How could he have gotten word of her illness anyway? Now that Jennet knew it was a lie, she could see just how thin it was. Yet, fool that she was, she had accepted it without question.

Yet why would he even tell it? Unless he knew her father was dead because he himself had struck the fatal blow. She quickly pushed aside that horrifying thought. Hacon did not know her father. She had never even told him what her father looked like. Despite that logic, fury and painful disappointment knotted her insides. Then she realized Robert was still talking to her. She forced her attention back to the stout redhead.

"I am verra sorry. I didnae hear what ye just said." She forced her mouth into a faint smile. "Talk of Perth can set my mind spinning with memory."

Robert nodded his understanding as Mary helped him redon his shirt. "I was just saying that Sir Gillard willnae ken much about Perth after the taking of it. He didnae stay for the killing of all the poor souls who were declared traitors."

"What do ye mean—he didnae stay?"

"Weel, when he was what was about to happen, he wanted no part of it. A brave mon, Sir Gillard. He and his small band withdrew. If it wasnae for his aid in the capturing of Perth, Sir Gillard could have been cried as a traitor too. 'Tis an easy brand to be marked with these days."

Shaking his head, Robert sighed. "Would that I could have been so bold. I stayed. 'Tis true that I didnae get that blood on my hands and wouldnae aid in the killing, but I stayed. 'Tis as bad."

"Not truly. I dinnae think it could have been stopped." She frowned. "But ye saw it?"

"Aye. Stood there silent and shocked."

Although fear of the truth she might hear chilled her, she asked, "Can ye recall any of the faces of those who were slain. 'Twas a long time ago."

"Aye, but I can recall them clearly. Too clearly."

Swallowing hard, she asked, "Did ye see a mon with hair the color of a deer's hide? A verra lean mon, nearly too lean. Rather tall as weel, and with skin as soft as a bairn's and as pale as mine?"

"He sounds an easy mon to recall but"—Robert frowned— "nay, I dinnae think I saw him there. Yet"—Robert ran a hand through his sweat-darkened hair—"I *can* recall seeing a mon like that."

She leaned closer to him. "With eyes as green as mine?"

"Aye." Robert's dark eyes grew wider. "Aye, but not with the poor souls killed that black day." He frowned. "He wasnae a Scot now that I think on it. He cannae be the one ye mean."

"Mayhaps not, but tell me more and let me decide upon it."

"Weel, he was in the tavern, serving ale to the soldiers. He was dressed poorly but spoke weel, as if he had once had coin. Said he had come here from France, a poor younger son with no chance to gain there. He hoped to make his fortune here but found himself in the midst of our war." He grimaced. "I had a wee bit too much of the ale and talked too freely. Aye, and he was a mon ye felt ye *could* talk to. He fixed those eyes on a mon and words just tumbled out. His voice . . . weel, how can I describe it?"

"Made ye feel he was a confidant, one ye could trust." Jennet knew it well, knew it was her father's greatest weapon as well as his strongest shield.

"Aye, that is it. Mayhaps I told him more than I should have, but he was a Frenchmon, an ally. It couldnae hurt."

"And his name? Was it, mayhaps, Artos de Nullepart or the like?"

Robert gaped at her. "'Twas that exactly. How could ye ken it?"

"Because the mon was my father." She could barely contain her joy for—rascal and thief though he was—she dearly loved him. "He has used the name before or one similar to it. It but means 'Artair of Nowhere.' Suits him well."

"Nay, ye are a Scot, and he was from France. Are ye sure?"

"As sure as I can be without having seen it with my own eyes." She impulsively kissed his dirt-smudged cheek. "'Tis a good thing ye are a poor mon, Robert, or your meeting with my father could have left your purse a great deal lighter."

"Here," muttered Elizabeth, "you should not be calling your own father a thief. That is what you just did, is it not?"

"Aye, I did." Despite the hint of smoke in the air that told her yet more cottages and fields were burning, Jennet smiled in the near certainty that her father had escaped death yet again. "'Tis what he is. He has said it himself. Weel, in truth, he says he but allows for a more even sharing of the wealth. Ye see, he ne'er takes from a poor mon." She frowned. "Howbeit, since it appears he lived after Perth, why havenae I seen him?"

"Weel, you have been moving about, aye?" When Jennet nodded, Elizabeth continued. "'Twould take time for him to find you with all the fighting going on. He may have had to join in it here and there. With all the turmoil about, 'tis not so strange he has not found you."

"Of course." Jennet began to clean up. "While a part of me thrills with hope, another does not. What ye have told me, Robert, can only mean Papa lived through the slaughter at Perth. Howbeit, he has had to continue to elude death throughout the years since then, and that may have required more luck than he had. So, I willnae declare him alive and weel just yet. I but have a wee bit more hope, 'tis all."

"When and if ye do see the mon," Robert said, "I hope he is fighting on the right side."

"Oh, Papa will see it as the right one. No doubt 'twill be the side he has ever chosen—his own." She smiled a little when Robert gave a tired laugh.

"If ye think ye can tear your eyes from that mud-splattered serf, ye might aid one who is bleeding like a gutted pig," drawled a deep voice.

Jennet turned with the others to look at the man who spoke. He was vaguely familiar to her. She had seen him talking to Hacon a time or two. From the look she had seen on Hacon's face during and after those brief meetings, this was not a friend. She was glad when Mary started to respond to the man's terse demand.

"Not you," he snapped. "Ye." He pointed at Jennet. "Ye will see to my wounds."

Biting back the suggestion that he could stand there and bleed to death, Jennet collected the medical supplies she needed and wended her way toward him, past the wounded and exhausted men who were scattered over the clearing. She was not sure if the man could cause trouble for Hacon but decided not to chance it. All personal feelings aside, Hacon was her shield, all that kept her from being beaten, raped, and possibly even driven mad.

"Sit down," she ordered when she reached him and pointed to a large rock.

"Ye are the pert wench they all say ye are, eh?" He sat down. "Mayhaps ye need more mon than Hacon to tame you."

"And ye ken who that would be, do ye?" She eased off his helmet to look more closely at the sword slash over his brow.

"Aye, myself—Sir Niall Chisholm."

"Weel, I am surprised." She began to wash his wound, a shallow cut that came down from his forehead and ran very close to his right eye. "I think I will stay with the mon I have, thank ye kindly. Better the devil ye ken and all that."

"Hacon Gillard is too soft with you."

"Ah, ye feel I ought to be treated as those poor souls have been." She nodded toward the three bruised, slack-faced women still huddled together under the tree.

He frowned. Jennet could not be sure if it was a sign of distaste, which would indicate some better side to his character than he was revealing, or if he was frowning in anticipation of pain from her ministrations. At a young age she had learned to go slowly in judging people.

But as she leaned over him to secure a bandage about his head, he reached up and cupped his hand over her right breast. She met his steady, insolent gaze. There was no hint of lust in his gray eyes, just an intended insult. Although she felt some shock and distaste, she was mostly annoyed.

"Remove your hand, Sir Chisholm, or ye shall be verra sorry."

"Going to call your mon to aid you?"

"I need no mon to fight my battles for me." She tied off his bandage with more force than was necessary, but he only winced.

"'Tis no battle, lass. Just a wee fondle."

"'Tis impertinence and disrespect. Move your hand—now."

"Wheesht, how I tremble before such a fierce adversary."

It would be wiser to simply move out of his grasp, she mused, even as she brought her right fist up to connect soundly with his jaw. The look of utter stupefaction on his face as he tumbled backward off his seat gave her a great deal of satisfaction. But his expression rapidly changed to one of fury. As he stumbled to his feet and drew his sword, she frantically sought the best defensive action to take. Just as she was about to bolt out of range of the sword he raised, another sword came into view, noisily clashing with Niall's mid-swing. Jennet felt momentarily weak with relief when she saw Hacon. The look on his face, however, made her realize that relief was the last thing she should feel. There was more trouble to come.

"A good blow, lass," murmured Dugald as he moved to stand beside her.

A glance at Dugald caused Jennet to be briefly diverted, for his sword arm was clearly wounded. "Ye have been hurt."

"'Tisnae fatal."

"Nay, but this may be," she muttered, frowning at Hacon and Niall, who moved to face each other squarely while wounded men scrambled and clawed to get out of their way.

The first crash of their swords made her wince. Hacon was grimly determined to kill or maim Niall, and Niall was grimly determined to survive. They moved as if performing some macabre dance, constrained in a tight circle with Niall consistently stepping back as Hacon advanced. Niall could do no more than desperately block each swing and thrust of Hacon's sword.

Jennet watched the battle, as silent as the combatants, then knew she had to find a way to stop it. It was not only her distaste for such things that prompted her decision. The fight was not a fair one. Niall was unsteady, still troubled by the wound on his head. He staggered beneath each blow of Hacon's sword, barely fending off each deadly strike. Instinctively, she knew that Hacon's distinct advantage would trouble him later. However, if she did not stop the fight soon, it would be too late to save Hacon from slaying a man who was in no condition to fight for his life.

She slipped her arm about Dugald's waist and whispered in his ear, "Ye will swoon now."

"I dinnae think so," Dugald said with a strong hint of outrage. "'Tis but a wee wound I have. 'Twould take more than this mere scratch to make me swoon like some fair maid."

She whispered a curse between gritted teeth—men could be such idiots!—and was about to lambaste Dugald when the fight took a desperate turn. Hacon knocked the sword from a rapidly weakening Niall's hands, and Niall fell sprawled on the ground. Hacon pinned him there, one booted foot on the panting man's chest, then placed his sword against Niall's right wrist.

"Jennet, 'twas this hand the mon touched ye with, was it not?"

"What matter if it was?" She had the sick feeling she knew

what Hacon planned to do, and it was clear he was in no state of mind to see the consequences.

Hacon looked down at a gray-complexioned, sweating Niall. "I wouldnae want to cut off the wrong piece of this dog."

"Dugald," she whispered. "Ye will feign a swoon right now or I shall cease to keep that goat ye are so fond of away from you." After one brief horrified glance her way, Dugald went limp, his sudden weight in her hold making her stagger and sit down hard. "Hacon! Dugald has swooned."

Frowning at her, yet keeping a close watch on Niall, Hacon muttered, "He wasnae badly wounded."

"Nay? Would a strong mon like Dugald swoon over naught, like some weak lass? Hacon," she said with a touch of desperation, "I need help. Isnae Dugald more important than this quarrel with Sir Chisholm?"

Cursing softly, Hacon sheathed his sword and strode over to her side. "Where is Ranald?" he demanded, helping her arrange Dugald more comfortably on the ground.

"He is keeping a watch on Murdoc." With Hacon's assistance, she took off Dugald's jupon and folded it beneath his head. "I needed that more than I needed another guard. He is o'er there, just beyond those three cowering women. Now, I shall need some clean water." After tipping out the water she had used to tend Niall, she thrust the shallow pan into Hacon's hands.

"He still doesnae look badly wounded," Hacon mumbled even as he moved to get her the water.

"Can I cease this game now?" Dugald whispered when Hacon had walked away.

Seeing Niall making a hasty if unsteady retreat, she replied, "Aye, ye can wake up now."

"Weel, I dinnae see why ye asked it of me. Hah! Asked? Ye blackmailed me, ye did."

"Sir Chisholm had just had a head wound cleaned and stitched. Couldnae ye see how unfit he was to do any fighting? But then, mayhaps I judge your cousin wrong. Mayhaps it wouldnae trouble him later, when his anger eased, that he had fought and maimed a mon who could barely stand. I but thought he was one to prefer a fair fight." She met Dugald's sour look with one of utter innocence.

"Your father didnae beat you often enough. Nay, Hacon wouldnae like it, but ye didnae need to threaten me with that goat of Satan. Ye could have just explained yourself." He finished in a whisper as Hacon returned.

"So, ye have recovered," Hacon murmured as he crouched at Dugald's side and handed Jennet the water.

"Aye." Dugald hissed a curse as Jennet began to bathe the wound on his sword arm.

"'Twas but the loss of blood," she said. "It can often make a mon suffer a moment of weakness. 'Tis naught."

She frowned when a man's shadow fell over them. Dugald and Hacon grew very still, tense and wary. Their full attention was on the man who had just stepped up to them. Finally, Jennet looked too and frowned.

There appeared to be little about him to cause such a reaction. He was, she mused, an ordinary man, eminently forgettable. His height and stature were average, his hair thinning and dull brown, his features neither fair nor ugly. Then she saw how he stared at Hacon and inwardly shivered. This man loathed Hacon. The emotion added chilling life to his otherwise unremarkable hazel eyes.

Suddenly she tensed as dreaded memories crowded her mind. She had looked into those eyes before—nine years ago. As clearly as if it was all happening again, she became that terrified child tucked away in a hidden niche of the cottage, staring into those eyes. The man held a knife to her mother's throat and laughed along with his companions. Jennet could hear that small, boyish voice deriding her mother for giving him and his friends little pleasure. It was that voice which had condemned her mother to death for that failure. The knife had moved, her mother had jerked once, and then the man had stood up, the bloodied knife still clutched in his mailed fist. It was then that he had looked her way, had held her gaze for a full minute before strolling out of the cottage, his boisterous companions at his heels.

This man was one of those who had so brutally murdered her mother. Jennet struggled against revealing her knowledge, against the urge to scream "Murderer."

"So, your mon was but scratched," drawled the man, his voice that of an immature boy despite the heavy brown beard on his face.

"Aye," replied Hacon. "The lack of assistance didnae cost him his life this time, Sir Balreaves."

"Nay, but it appears it nearly cost him his sword arm."

"'Twill heal."

"True, but ye will be without your faithful shield for some days, Gillard. Ye will need to be verra alert. Verra alert indeed."

"Do ye threaten me?" Hacon slowly reached for his sword.

"What reason would I have to do that?"

"Ye think ye have."

"Ye misjudge me, sir. I but remind you of the dangers of battle."

"Not all of which come from the enemy."

"Aye, sadly true. The confusion of battle can lead to many a tragic error," Sir Balreaves murmured, and smiled faintly before he walked away.

That clear threat to Hacon forced Jennet's thoughts to the matter at hand. It was evident that Sir Balreaves was still fond of killing. She decided not to mention Balreaves's part in her mother's death and set her mind fully on the danger of the present.

As Jennet began to stitch up Dugald's wound, she asked Hacon, "What have ye done to that mon?"

"Naught. Why?"

"Why? Because he hates you, hates you with every drop of blood in his veins. Did ye bed his wife?"

"Nay. I dinnae bed other men's women. Never have."

"How noble." She knew the sarcasm she had aimed for was not really there, for she did think it a rather fine constraint for a man to place upon himself. "Ye most have done something."

"Aye," Dugald said, his voice hoarse. "He breathes."

Jennet frowned as she carefully bandaged Dugald's arm. "'Tis all?"

Hacon shrugged. "'Tisnae quite that simple. He wants Dubheilrig and believes I try to steal his place at the court. Then there is the insult he thinks the Gillards have dealt him.

"He wished to wed Katherine, my sister and Ranald's mother," Hacon continued. "Howbeit, she wed another. 'Twas Katherine's choice. When she was widowed, Balreaves again sought her hand and again he failed. She left him at the altar, changing her mind at the verra last moment. That too was her choice. Howbeit, I believe he thinks that I, and my family, forced her to refuse him. As the years pass, his hatred deepens."

"To the point where he will stand idly by and watch ye and yours slain and ne'er lift a hand to help you?" Jennet asked.

"There has been a time or two when that seemed the way of it."

"Seemed? Ha! Ye ken it and ken it weel." Finished with Dugald, Jennet stood up and collected her nursing supplies. "Men. 'Tis not enough to make an enemy of the English or those who dinnae support the Scots king. Nay, ye must also have a few of your own holding swords at your back." She looked at Hacon, knowing that her fear for him ate at her, a realization that only added to her anger. "And ye will continue to set yourself in his path."

"I willnae cower in some corner, nor can I accuse him. He is higher born than I and has a firm place in the Bruce's court. I havenae enough proof yet to accuse a mon like that."

"Dugald nearly losing his sword arm as the mon idly watched isnae proof enough?"

"Dugald's arm still looks weel attached to me."

"So ye will continue to stand firm and wait for his treacherous strike."

"I havenae much choice, lass."

She softly cursed. "With the rule of the world in the hands of such idiots, 'tis little wonder that it crumbles to ruin about us." Still shaking her head in disgust, she walked away.

Hacon grinned as he watched her leave. "The lass is softening, Dugald."

"Oh? I think your mind rots. I didnae see any softening; I saw anger. And she called ye an idiot."

"Ah, but 'tis concern for me that stirs her anger." Looking at the scowling Dugald, Hacon laughed quietly. "Ye dinnae see it."

"What I see is that the lass may weel be right when she says ye have been knocked offside the head too often. Ye see things with the twisted clarity of a madmon."

"Aye, mayhaps, but 'tis a verra sweet madness, Dugald," he drawled as he rose to follow Jennet.

# Chapter 7

A soft murmur of pleasure escaped Jennet, and she rubbed her cheek against Hacon's warm chest. She shook free of sleep's hold only to be caught in passion's grip. The way Hacon moved his hands over her back, lightly cupping her derriere and pressing her tightly against his hardness, made her ache. She gave a soft gasp of delighted surprise when he smoothed his hands up her sides and cupped her breasts, rubbing the tips to hardness with his thumbs.

Hacon took quick advantage of her parted lips, covering her mouth with his and plunging his tongue deep inside. He groaned softly when she wrapped her limbs around his body and eagerly welcomed his fierce kiss. It took every ounce of his willpower not to take her there and then, but they were far from private. He could hear the rest of the army camped all around them beginning to stir. Soon, too many eyes would see their heated embrace. He ended the kiss, grit his teeth against his strong reluctance to do so, and gently broke free of the embrace. Before his aching hunger for her made him change his mind, he hurriedly rose to his feet. The way she looked at him, her beautiful eyes warm and inviting, made it the hardest thing he had ever done.

"Time to wake, Jennet," he said as he quickly put on his hose. "'Tis morning, loving."

"Morning?" The heat of her desire faded swiftly as she looked around and saw all the men preparing for another day of riding. "Oh, sweet God." She felt her cheeks burn with a deep blush.

"Aye, ye do choose some poor times to assault my person."

"*I* assault *you?*" she cried, glaring at Hacon as she scrambled to her feet.

He brushed a kiss over her forehead. "'Tis all right, dearling. I forgive you." Still lacing his jupon, he hurried away. "Dinnae tarry. We should see the walls of Ripon by noon."

Jennet cursed viciously as she packed up her blankets. He had caught her at a weak moment, she told herself, but she found no conviction there. Her weak moments were coming all too often. If the Douglas's army did not turn back toward Scotland soon, did not head north toward Liddesdale and allow her a chance to flee to her family, she knew she would be lost to Hacon's seduction.


Smoke curled up from the burning houses within Ripon's walls. Just as at Boroughbridge two weeks before, a few thatched roofs had been fired in the initial attack. Now, however, the swift raid had slowed to a siege. The summer breeze brought the stench of death to Jennet where she stood on a small rise just north of the town. The people who had survived the first onslaught of the Scots were now barricaded in the holy minster. Although there was an occasional clash of swords as those Englishmen not safe within Ripon's sturdy minster engaged their enemy, Jennet suspected that confrontation had become negotiation.

She feared she was growing hardened, that she was beginning to consider the raid as merely tedious. They had ridden south from Berwick in early April. April had become May and now May was at an end. One day blended into the next—long days of riding, short nights spent in the sleep of the exhausted, and brief interludes of raping, looting, and battle. She had been horrified to find herself viewing the siege of Ripon with something close to pleasure since it meant that she could stay in one place for a little while.

"Why do ye stand here and watch it if ye hate it so?" asked Ranald, standing next to her.

Jennet sighed. "I truly dinnae ken why. Mayhaps I but try to understand. 'Tis hopeless. I try to grasp at some sense of right, but isnae there."

"We fight for the Bruce. There is the right of it. He is our king."

"Why? Because he murdered one of the contenders to the Scots throne on a church altar? It doesnae seem such a firm claim to the crown to me."

"Ye shouldnae say such things, Jennet," murmured Ranald, glancing nervously around. "There are too many ears about to catch the words, words that many would consider treasonous."

She too glanced around and grimaced. A number of men were standing nearby watching the siege upon Ripon and resting a moment before retuning to the skirmishing that had continued for nearly three days. The only man who really interested her, however, was Sir Balreaves, who was standing close enough to have overheard if he had bothered to listen carefully. That he was smiling at her in a way that made her shiver suggested that he had been listening. Jennet decided it might be wise to heed Ranald's warning. The last thing she needed was more trouble in her life, trouble that could be avoided by simply putting a rein on her tongue.

Looking back toward Ripon, she wished the problem of Hacon was simple to solve. She recalled how just that morning she had come awake to find herself in his arms. She had not halted his kisses or sweet, intimate caresses. Hacon, not she, had become aware of the waking men all around them. She had been blind to everything but the delicious heat he had stirred within her. Even now she could feel it, suffered the ache his departure had left in her. Scowling toward Ripon, knowing he was down there somewhere hidden by the smoke and dust of battle, she hoped he suffered an equal discomfort.

"Come, Jennet," Ranald murmured, gently taking her arm. "I see some wounded making their way toward camp."

She sighed and allowed herself to be drawn back toward that muddy, stinking spot crowded by men, horses, and a growing train of stolen goods. In truth she had not been doing much thinking or deciding about the right or wrong of war. To her disgust she had been looking for Hacon, trying to see if he was still hale. Ever since she had looked into Balreaves's eyes, she had been unable to stop worrying. Somehow it seemed more menacing, more dangerous, that one of Hacon's own allies wanted him dead. Knowing that Balreaves was a cold, heartless murderer only added to her fears. She was pulled from her thoughts when Elizabeth hurried over to her.

"I am glad you have returned," she said, and towed her toward Robert's younger brother, Donald, who had thus far defied the odds by living, though he had been slow to recover. "I am certain his fever has finally broken, but you are more learned in such matters than I."

After sending Ranald to check on Murdoc, Jennet knelt by Donald and felt his forehead and cheeks. "Aye, he is cooler. And fair soaked in sweat. Ye have done weel with the lad. I was certain he would die, but he has clung to life despite being dragged along on this accursed raid. We had best wash him down. We shall be busy soon. Ranald saw wounded being brought this way."

Helping Jennet undress the youth, Elizabeth said, "I could not let my man's own brother die, could I."

"Your mon? Oh, thank ye," she murmured when Ranald brought her some fresh water. "What do ye mean? I thought ye belonged to that brute Frazer."

"I did, and Mary belonged to his friend, Mad Morgan, but no longer. It seems Robert tosses the dice very well. He had to play many a time, but he finally won us last eve. Now we are free of those animals."

"I am so verra pleased for you. At least Robert willnae beat ye."

"Robert will do naught at all. He has said so. If 'twas possible, he would send us home. Mayhaps when the army turns back toward Scotland, there may come a chance for that. Mary may go, but I will not."

"I hadnae realized Robert had the wealth to buy your freedom."

"Nay, he has little. 'Twas your man who gave him the coin."

"Sir Gillard?"

"Aye. Robert said Sir Gillard tried to buy us, but Frazer and Morgan would have none of it. Robert and your man talked it over and had the idea of winning us. It was very good of Sir Gillard."

"Aye. Verra good," Jennet murmured, deciding she would have to think on the matter later, when she had time to really understand what it said about Hacon.

Elizabeth shook her head as she and Jennet washed Donald. "Poor boy. He is too thin."

"Ah, weel, it willnae take long to put some meat on him. Elizabeth, why will ye stay?"

"Why, to be with Robert."

"He wants ye, does he?"

"He will. I mean to see to that." She smiled when Jennet laughed.

"Ye have no home or family to return to?"

"None worth the trouble. My cottage was burned. I did have a husband for near to a year. A mean brute of a man. He was hanged for killing three men whilst in one of his rages. Near killed me a time or two as well. You look so shocked."

"Weel, 'tis a tale worthy of such a feeling."

"Ah, Jennet, for all you have been though, you are still so innocent. 'Tis good fate that set you in Sir Gillard's hands.

Well, I mean to put myself in Robert's hands. He is the first good man I have ever met in my life. Not perfect, but good. If that man gets back to Scotland alive, I mean to be at his side."

She glanced over her shoulder. "Here come those wounded you spoke of. We best hurry and see to the fools." Elizabeth tucked the blanket around Donald and stood up. "You were right, you know."

"Right about what?" Jennet asked as she and Elizabeth started toward the wounded men.

"About nursing the men. Mary and I have found with each day that passes we are treated more fairly. In truth, I find I rather like the work."

"And I wish there wasnae such need of it."

"There will always be a need."

Jennet moved to kneel by a man whose leg was soaked with blood as Elizabeth went toward another. Mary was struggling with one whose arm appeared to have been broken. As Jennet set to work, she feared Elizabeth was right about fate being kind to have put her in Hacon's hands. But she found the thought very distressing.

Needing water, she called to Ranald and Dugald. She needed to call Dugald twice before he turned from the constant sword practice he indulged in to regain the strength in his healing arm. Once the two men began carting the supply of water she would need, she turned her full attention to the wounded.


Hacon cursed as he was slowly encircled by four armed Englishmen. Douglas had ordered Balreaves to watch his back, but just as Hacon had feared, the man was doing nothing to help him. Instead of rushing to Hacon's aid, Balreaves loitered just out of harm's way. There was no need for Balreaves to fear that his failure to do as Douglas had commanded would be discovered. Hacon doubted he would survive this confrontation with the enemy.

His battle sword in one hand, his shield on his arm, and his dagger in his other hand, Hacon cautiously pivoted as he vainly tried to keep each of his foes in view. Out of the corner of his eye he saw Balreaves. The man sat on a rock at a safe distance, a faint smile on his face. Calmly he waited for the English to commit murder for him.

The Englishmen tightened their circle around Hacon. He bellowed his fury over Balreaves's desertion and lunged at the Englishman directly in front of him. As he had hoped, the sudden charge caught his enemy off guard. Their brief confusion allowed him the chance to engage his chosen opponent unhindered. Hacon quickly cut the man down, then whirled to face the other three as they began to close in on him again.

"Are ye so eager to lie dead beside your friend?" Hacon taunted them.

"You are the one who will die," answered the Englishman in the middle.

"Mayhaps, but taking down this Scotsman will cost ye dearly."

All three bellowed their scorn at his boast and came after him. Hacon could fend off only two at a time. He eluded the third twice before his luck failed and the man got behind him. The man's sword cut cleanly across his back. Hacon staggered as the sword point slashed through his protective clothing and cut through his flesh. Before he could recover his footing, he took a second wound in his upper thigh. The pain was followed by a sudden weakness that brought him to his knees. Hacon waited for the death blow . . . but it did not come.

As he collapsed onto his side, Hacon saw the reason. Two of his countrymen had arrived to help him. Suddenly, Balreaves was also there to wield his sword against the enemy. The three Englishmen were quickly dispatched, having been caught by surprise just as they had thought themselves victorious. Balreaves moved to stand at Hacon's feet as the other two Scots knelt by his side to inspect the wounds.

"That battle was nearly your last, Gillard," Balreaves said.

"I was caught with my back unprotected." Hacon glared at the man and wished he was not wounded for he ached to fight Balreaves.

"Do ye accuse me of neglecting my duty? I shall forgive ye that slur, for ye are in pain and not thinking clearly. These two men saw me come to your aid."

"Aye, he did help some," murmured the man on Hacon's right.

It was not only the pain he felt as the two men helped him to his feet that made Hacon grind his teeth. Frustration and anger knotted his stomach. He could not accuse Balreaves of leaving him to die. There were witnesses who would have to say that Balreaves had lent a hand in saving him. Neither man could have seen how Balreaves had stood aside until he was forced to either fight or risk revealing that he'd disobeyed Douglas's orders.

"Ye had best take Sir Gillard back to camp," Balreaves ordered the two men supporting Hacon.

"Aye, get me back to camp." Hacon tried not to lean too heavily on his companions, but the loss of blood was rapidly weakening him.

"Aye. We would not wish our gallant knight to bleed to death," Balreaves said as he idly wiped his sword clean on the jupon of one of the dead Englishmen.

Hacon found the strength to send Balreaves a parting glare. "Have no fear of that, Balreaves. We will fight again." He could see that Balreaves understood what he meant, and ignoring the curious glances of the two men helping him, Hacon turned all of his attention to the difficult task of remaining conscious until he reached the camp.

"Hacon!" Dugald called in a shocked voice.

A chill went through Jennet as Dugald scrambled to his feet, leaving her to finish bandaging a man's arm. She doubted a small and easily mended wound would put that fear in Dugald's voice. As she completed her work, she caught sight of a pale Ranald loping in the direction Dugald had gone, and she grew even colder. She did not want to see what was wrong, but she knew she had to.

Feeling stiff with fear, she stood up, took a deep breath to steady herself, and turned to get her first good look at Hacon. It sent her reeling. For a moment she feared she would do something completely useless, like swoon, but she fought for a thread of composure, firmly telling herself not to be such a weakling.

Hacon's jupon was soaked with blood. Logic told her that not all of it was his own blood, but she found logic a little hard to hold on to. As she forced herself to collect the supplies she would need to help him, Ranald and Dugald took him from the men who had brought him back to camp. That Hacon had been nearly carried off the field did nothing to lessen her fear. He was pale, too pale, and appeared frighteningly weak as Ranald and Dugald sought a place that was neither too crowded nor too muddy, then helped him to lie down. She reached Hacon's side just as the two men finished stripping him to his braies.

"'Tisnae as bad as it looks, lass," Hacon whispered in a strained voice as she knelt by his side.

"Oh? Do ye also mean to tell me 'tis but a scratch? I swear, if I hear that said but one more time, I shall scream." When Ranald helped Hacon get comfortable on his side, she realized that the more serious wound was on his back, a deep gash that ran diagonally from his right shoulder nearly to his left hip.

Dugald cursed. "If ye hadnae been wearing such fine protection, ye would have been cut in twain."

She thought the same but forced the sickening image from her mind. "Had ye no one guarding your back?"

"Aye—Balreaves."

"Balreaves?" Jennet's fear for Hacon flared to anger over what she saw as reckless stupidity. "What ails you? Did ye think there were not enough swords pointed at you? Did ye feel the need of one more?"

"The Douglas set him there."

"So? Ye do have a voice. Ye could say naught?"

"Dearling, ye dinnae argue with the Douglas. And what should I have said? 'Dinnae put Balreaves there for the mon means to murder me?' 'Tisnae an accusation ye toss out lightly. Ye need proof, and I have naught."

"So ye just stood there and let him choose his time to strike."

"He didnae strike. He had no need to bloody his own sword, did he? He but stood back and waited for an English-mon to do the killing for him."

"He stood verra far back," she confirmed. "I saw him, not so long ago, standing on the hillside swilling wine."

"Ah, weel, when this happened he was on the field, close enough to aid me, but he did nothing. The two men who brought me here came to my aid. Balreaves quickly took up the fight then, didnae he, so none could say for certain that he allowed me to be cut down by our enemy."

Although she knew he spoke the truth, her anger lingered. She used that fury to force herself to stitch Hacon's wounds. It helped only a little. Her ministrations were as great an agony for her as she knew they were for him. Her stomach churned and her eyes continually stung as she fought back tears. Only the knowledge that neither would aid Hacon helped her fight her hatred of the grisly chore. There would be two new scars on his fine body since the slash across his upper thigh needed a few stitches as well.

By the time she finished, all she wanted was to get away from the man. Seeing Hacon so badly hurt had made her face what she had fought so hard to keep locked away in her heart, denied and suppressed. Now that it was free, she knew she could no longer hide from herself that she loved him. She feared she might do something foolish—like declare her love and swear to do anything he wished if he would just stay off

the battlefield. But it was a poor time to make such a decla-
ration. She did not want Hacon to know it. And in her present
state she did not feel confident of her ability to hide it.

He doesnae want my heart anyway, just the flesh which
holds it, she mused as she helped make Hacon comfortable,
placing a rolled blanket behind him to keep from inadver-
tently rolling onto his back. Weel, I ken I will soon let him
have that, but *I* will pick the time and the place. And I willnae let him ken that he has won more than my passion. Aye,
he will see victory, but I refuse to let him guess how complete
it is. After Ranald and Dugald left, she moved to kneel in
front of Hacon and carefully tucked another blanket over him.

"'Tis summer, lass. I dinnae think I need to be kept so
warm," he murmured.

"It grows damp and chill in the night, which draws verra
near, if ye hadnae noticed."

"Aye, true enough." He watched her as she knelt by him,
frowning. "Ye shouldnae be so cross with a mon when he is
suffering so," he said.

"I was but thinking on how, if the sword that cut your leg
had finished its upward swing, ye would no longer be mon
enough to play your games with me."

"Here now, do ye not think these wounds are enough to
trouble my sleep and keep me from you?"

She was almost able to smile. "'Twas but a thought. I best
see to Murdoc. Do ye need anything ere I leave?"

"I wouldnae refuse a wee drink of water."

After raising the waterskin to his lips, she idly adjusted the
folded jupon beneath his head. "That all? Naught else?"

"Weel, a wee kiss would do much to ease the pain I am in."

A vast array of tart responses came to mind, but she said
none of them. Instead, she cupped his face in her hands, put
her mouth on his, and gave him a slow, deep kiss. The look
of utter astonishment she briefly glimpsed on his face gave
her nearly as much satisfaction as the kiss. After she slowly

pulled away, she gave him a sweet smile and left him alone. That ought to keep him confused, she thought with a soft laugh.

Then she sighed, her amusement fleeing. Perhaps she ought to let her heart dictate her actions, say what she now ached to say, and take her chances. She hastily pushed that idea aside. It was a bad one for a number of reasons. She would not hand her heart to a man who had expressed only the desire to seduce her. That man was also a knight, a man who lived by the sword, the sort of man she had learned to scorn. She could not separate Hacon the man from Hacon the knight.

And then, she recalled with a frown, there was his lie about not being at Perth. She had not confronted him with it, but she could not forget it either. It was not a complete lie, for he had not taken part in the murders that might have claimed her father's life, but it was still not the truth. She had to question her short-lived judgment of him as an honest man. That left her wondering how well she could trust her other judgments about him.

Once at Murdoc's side, she shooed Ranald away and picked up the smiling baby. "Ah, weel, laddie, 'tis a fine knot I have gotten myself into. That long blond knight is about to win the game of seduction. Howbeit, I mean to take full advantage of these next few days. Aye," she added when Murdoc babbled at her, "I shall tease and torment that mon until he sweats. Aye, he has won, but he will walk o'er a few hot coals ere he gets the prize."

She glanced toward Hacon, saw him trying to resettle the blanket over his groin, and quickly turned away, hiding her grin against Murdoc's soft curls. "Aye, my wee bonnie mon, hot coals indeed. And since I mean to pick the time and place for conceding, I had best set about it. Once Hacon is healed, the poor mon will be after me like wolves after the weakling of the herd."

\* \* \*

"Here now," Dugald said as he stepped up to Hacon, who had finally stopped angrily tugging at his blanket. "Ye should be still. What ails you?"

"That cursed lass," muttered Hacon as he tried to relax.

"Cursed?" Dugald sat down, frowning. "And here I was thinking ye may not be the madmon I thought. She kissed you. I saw it. Or mayhaps I saw it wrong and she bit you."

"Nay. She kissed me."

"Ah, I see. And that angers you." He shook his head and gave an exaggerated sigh. "Ye *are* mad."

"Dugald, *she* kissed *me*. 'Tis the first time she has done so of her own free will. Can I do aught about it? Nay. I am stuck here." When Dugald slowly grinned, then chuckled, Hacon snapped, "Ye think that funny?"

"Wretched wee lass," Dugald murmured, then chuckled again. "She has turned your own game back on you."

"What?"

"Weel, these past two months ye have been doing all ye can to make the lass want what she shouldnae be wanting and do what she kens she shouldnae do. She couldnae get away, could she? Now *ye* are the captive. Now *ye* cannae get away. Aye, I said she was a spirited lass."

"Ye show a marked lack of sympathy for a friend and kinsmon."

"Ye began this. Ye wish to take her only dower away. Aye, and ye left her fearing rape for many a day, though she had the wit to guess your game. I cannae blame her for wanting to make you suffer a wee bit in return."

"A wee bit?" Hacon muttered. Then, looking toward Jennet, who was engrossed in feeding Murdoc, he grew thoughtful. "'Tis strange though," he mused aloud. "Strange that she would pull me toward her even for the reasons ye give. She has the wit to ken I willnae be helpless for verra long and that I will be coming after her. Unless . . ." he frowned and rubbed his chin.

"Unless"—Hacon smiled—"she means to honor that unspoken aye. She just intends to make me pay dearly for it." When Dugald grew solemn, Hacon drawled, "I see. Your pleasure lies only in seeing me being tormented."

"Ye mean to steal her only dower. I cannae feel that is a good thing."

"And I have told you that I dinnae mean to toss the lass aside with no thought to her future. Do ye not trust me on that?"

"Aye, aye, I trust you. Howbeit, ye may be wrong. She kens weel that ye arenae one to toss her down and have at her whether she is willing or not. So, cousin, she could still say nay when ye are weel enough to set after her."

"I dinnae see it that way. So, since I am soon to gain my prize, I shall need a private place. Ye must keep watch for one."

"*I* must watch, must I?"

"Weel, I cannae."

Muttering a curse, Dugald stood up. "If ye are right and she means to give you the loving ye have been after so long, there is one thing ye had best be sure of."

"And what is that?"

"That ye are weel and truly healed. Ye have kept a rein on this lusting of yours for so long, 'twill be fierce when ye let go. Considering how heartily ye will be indulging yourself, ye best be certain those wounds are closed tight or ye will end up bleeding all o'er the wee lass." With a chuckle he abruptly left.

Hacon laughed too, then grimaced as even that slight movement added to his pain. He hoped Jennet did not intend to tempt him too arduously. Feeding his sexual hunger for her would be much akin to rubbing salt in his wounds. He did not really think he deserved that. After all, if she did not feel some passion for him, then his pursuit of her would not have troubled her so and she would not be feeling a need to exact vengeance.

He closed his eyes. He did feel weak. Despite his pain, he knew he could sleep. He also knew he would be wise to grasp whatever rest he could. If he and Dugald were right about what Jennet planned, he doubted he would get much healing sleep whenever she was around.


Jennet eased beneath the blanket, trying hard not to disturb Hacon. While she fully intended to give him back some of what he had been handing out to her for so long, she did not think it fair to wake him up to do so. He was, after all, wounded and in pain. In fact, perhaps she should not be near him at all. But just as she started to get up, intending to sleep alone, he slipped an arm around her waist and held her in place.

"I tried not to wake you," she murmured.

"Ye didnae. I wasnae asleep, merely resting. The pain is still too strong to allow me to sleep often or easy." He nuzzled his face in her hair. "Where is Murdoc?"

"With Ranald. Your nephew felt that if there was trouble, ye would be in no shape to protect two people. As he said— at least I can run away. And I can do that even faster without Murdoc. Poor Ranald seems to have the care of the bairn more and more often. I pray it willnae cause him trouble amongst the men."

"Nay. They all see the bairn as another piece of my plunder that he must protect. They might wonder why I should trouble myself with the babe, but, since I do, they see it as sensible to keep him safe."

"Are ye sure of that? 'Tis the truth?" She inwardly cursed the moment the words left her mouth, for his one lie did not really give her the right to question everything he said. It occurred to her that her hurt and disappointment over the lie might well go a lot deeper than she had realized or wished to admit.

"Aye, 'tis the truth." He frowned at the back of her head. "Why should I lie?"

"Why, indeed. I but thought ye might be trying to ease my worry o'er Ranald."

"Ye need not worry. There are few who question his skill

with a sword. I made certain his battle and victory o'er that muckle great Englishmon was heard far and wide."

Nodding, she nestled closer to him, bringing her backside up against his groin. His arousal was immediate and very evident. She had to fight to hide her grin.

Such quick results were not only amusing but also exciting. Hacon was wounded and in pain, yet he still wanted her. She could not help finding that thought flattering, even seductive.

"Weel." Hacon cleared his throat, but it did little to take the huskiness from his voice. "We will be leaving here soon."

"The battle is over?" She turned to look at him, moving carefully and deliberately so that her body gently rubbed against his. "Ripon has surrendered?"

"Most of the townspeople were sheltered within the minster. They didnae surrender, they simply bought a year's truce."

"Bought a truce?" She placed one hand upon his chest, and was surprised to realize how rapidly his heart was beating. "Ye mean a fee to hold back slaughter for a while."

"'Tis a fair deal and done more often than ye might suspect. We move on farther south, toward Knaresborough, soon. I think we willnae go much deeper into England but turn toward home after that. While 'tis true we havenae seen the English army, there is no reason to keep tempting fate."

She kept her gaze upon his face while idly smoothing her hand over his chest. His look of desire was not consistent with his calm description of the fall of Ripon. He was fully aware of the game she played. Within that expression of awareness was the hint of amusement and annoyance. Jennet discovered she really did not care that he had guessed her ploy. She only wondered how much he would tolerate before he actually spoke out.

"If we are to set out again, I had best get some sleep," she murmured, feigning a yawn. "Is there anything ye wish ere I seek the rest I will need?" She found it a real challenge not to laugh at the look he gave her. "Your bandages arenae too tight?" She slowly, lightly traced the one on his thigh with her fingertips and watched the clear blue of his eyes grow darker with desire.

"Just a wee kiss ere ye seek your rest," he drawled. "'Tis the least ye can do for a poor, tormented mon."

Cupping his face in her hands, she placed her lips close to his. "Do your wounds pain ye a great deal?"

"'Twasnae my wounds I was thinking on," he muttered.

"Nay? And ye *so* close to death and all." She nearly gasped, more with delight than surprise, when he slowly, enticingly rubbed his groin against hers.

"I feel exceedingly alive, my troublesome booty. Aye, fair throbbing with it."

Deciding that was enough of that, she kissed him. Using all the knowledge she had gained from him since being dragged from Berwick, she gave him a seductive, inviting kiss, one that promised all she had so far denied him. When she ended the embrace she was pleased to see how heavily he was breathing. She quickly turned away from him to hide that she suffered the same affliction.

As she cuddled up to him, he softly groaned. She was inclined to do the same when he eased his arm about her waist and cupped her breast in his hand. Carefully, she removed the hand, but a moment later he slipped it back. She gave a mock sigh of exasperation.

Jennet realized she was playing with a two-edged sword, but she would not quit. She had been continuously tempted for two months, had continuously refused the enticing delights he offered. Now he would learn how that felt. Now, with her actions, she would say aye, but wounded as he was, he would be unable to accept the blatant invitation. However, she mused as she tried to ignore the desire tautening her body, when he was healed and able she would not make him chase her very far before she let him catch her.

# Chapter Eight

Jennet bit back a smile when she heard Hacon softly groan, then curse. In reply she gave a sleepy murmur and wriggled her backside against his groin. The hard evidence of his arousal excited her. Ever since Ripon she had played this game and now, nearly two weeks later, she knew Hacon would soon be answering her blatant invitation. His stitches would be taken out today. That thought only added to her enjoyment. All the while she had teased him she had fed her own desires. She was more than ready to give him what he wanted.

When he began to slide his hand up her rib cage toward her breasts, she turned onto her stomach. His muttered imprecations made her grin. For a moment she allowed him to caress her back and derriere, then feigned waking up. She sat up, yawned, and stretched, purposely arching her back so that her breasts were thrust outward. Hacon reached out for her and, pretending she did not see his hand, she stood up. Her hands on her hips, she smiled sweetly at him.

"Ye look hale and hearty this morning," she said.

"Oh, aye, lass. As hearty as any stallion with a paddock full of mares."

"A colorful description," she murmured, and bent over to lift his blanket.

"Like what ye see?"

She trailed her fingers along the now healed wound on his thigh. He trembled faintly beneath the light caress. Jennet was sorely tempted to touch that part of him which boldly shaped the front of his braies. She dropped the blanket and straightened up before she gave in to that inclination.

"Your stitching will be removed today."

"Fetch what is needed then and set about it."

"Me? Ye dinnae need me to do it. Any fool can pluck out stitches." She started to walk away.

"Where are ye going?" Hacon demanded.

"To fetch Dugald. He can tend to you when he has the time."

"And what will ye be doing?"

"Oh, there is work aplenty to keep me busy."

"Jennet!"

Her back to him, Jennet grinned as she pretended not to hear him. She found Dugald and told him what to do, then went in search of Elizabeth. Once those stitches were removed, Hacon would hunt her down. Jennet wanted to have a bath before he found her.

"I dinnae see her in camp," Hacon said.

Dugald swore and lightly cuffed his fidgeting friend offside the head. "Sit still, ye great fool, or these stitches willnae come out neatly. God save us all, ye are worse than any stallion scenting a mare in season." Dugald concentrated on carefully plucking out the tidy stitching across Hacon's broad back.

"There—I am sitting as still as any rock. Now, tell me, where has the lass gone?"

"Am I her mother? I dinnae ken where she is."

"Ye were supposed to keep a close watch upon her." Hacon shifted slightly on his stone seat.

"I thought yc gave that chore to Ranald."

"I dinnae see him either. Ye must have espied the lass some time today."

"Aye, but a wee while ago, in truth. With Ranald and that mon Robert, she and the woman Elizabeth walked off through the trees just o'er to your right. I didnae take the time to ask what they were about. I would wager they went to bathe."

"Weel, Elizabeth has returned, as has Robert." Hacon scowled across the crowded clearing in the direction of the trees. "So what can the lass and Ranald be doing? Ye dinnae think she will trick the lad and flee, do ye?"

"Flee to where? We are still in England and we havenae spent all these weeks inspiring folk to love a Scot."

"True, may God forgive us. Then what is the lass doing?"

"She may simply like a longer bath than Elizabeth. If ye would just set still, ye can see for yourself in a moment. Beleaguering me with your questions doesnae do much good."

"When I set after the lass, I mean to catch her and hold firm. Ye had best ensure that we are left alone."

"Oh? And mayhaps the lass will prove a verra fast runner."

"*I* believe she doesnae mean to run at all."


Jennet hummed softly to herself as she rubbed her hair dry with a soft rag. It felt good to stand there in only her chemise, her damp hair cooling her fevered flesh. Wearing all her clothes, day and night, in the June heat was growing intolerable. It also felt good to be clean all over. The pace of the raid had made cleanliness a luxury. So too had the constant mud and dust churned up by the swiftly moving force. This day of rest was heartily welcome and long overdue.

She glanced back toward camp and shrugged. Dugald could not be taking so long to pluck out those stitches. It was beginning to look as if Hacon was not coming.

She was distressed to think that Hacon would ignore the blatant invitation with which she had been torturing him for so many days. Yet, she knew that if he did ignore her, it would be the simplest solution to her inner torment.

Her quandary was twofold. She knew that lying with a man who was not her husband was considered a sin. She also knew that she was not yet reconciled to what Hacon was or to the life he led. She certainly was not sure she would gain anything from him aside from passion.

"But it doesnae matter," she said, then glanced around to be sure no one had heard her talking to herself. "I want this," she murmured, testing the confession aloud.

Hearing the words brought a sense of affirmation. Hacon made her feel good—very, very good. It had been so long since anything or anyone had done so. Since the very first time she had opened her eyes outside of her mother's womb she had been shown how quickly life could be cut short. It was possible she might yet find a peace-loving man who would offer her the sanctity of marriage and make her feel as good, but she was not confident that she would be allowed the chance. She would take what she could now, while she was hale and alive, and pray that God would understand and forgive her sin.

"And now that I have made this decision," she muttered, "Hacon might at least have the courtesy to appear. If he doesnae, I shall have to return to camp feeling the greatest fool in Christendom."

"And what do ye have to feel the fool about?"

Although she immediately recognized that deep, rich voice, she gave a cry of surprise. Clutching her drying cloth to her chest, she turned to Hacon. It puzzled her that such a large man could approach with such stealth, especially through the thick, overgrown scrub forest that separated her from camp.

"Where is Ranald?" she asked, a little surprised that the stalwart guardian of her privacy had made no sound.

"I sent him away."

"Ah, the master speaks," she murmured, wondering why,

when she had firmly decided to become his lover, she was feeling shy and just a little bit nervous. "And why am I granted the pleasure of your company?" She was curious to see if he would speak bluntly.

"I am here to answer the invitation with which ye have tormented me since Ripon."

"I? *I* have tormented you?" She could tell by the way he looked at her that her act of innocence failed to fool him. "Your wits have gone abegging, Sir Gillard."

"Aye, they must have, or instead of waiting for you, I would have taken ye, as was my right."

"Your right?"

Before she could begin the argument which he knew she wanted to make, Hacon pointed to the rags she clutched. "Do ye truly believe that hides aught, lass?"

Glancing down, Jennet muttered a curse. She was holding the rag in one fist between her breasts. It hid nothing, simply looked foolish dangling from her hand. A rush of blood tingled in her cheeks as she saw that her thin shift also hid very little, particularly where it had been dampened by her dripping hair. She kept her gaze cast downward until she forced her embarrassment aside and looked up, only to discover Hacon had moved closer—a lot closer. If either of them took a deep breath, their bodies would brush together.

The last time she had seen him he was wearing only his braies and Dugald was plucking out his stitches. Now he wore his belted plaid. His strong, bare legs showed beneath the skirt, and his equally bare torso was hardly hidden by the length of cloth brought over one shoulder. There was enough dampness to his long hair to tell her he had paused for a thorough wash before seeking her out.

"What I have on hides nearly as much as what ye are wearing," she murmured.

"In but a moment I mean to have us wearing even less."

"Aye? Do ye forget that ye have more stitching in you than in your jupon?"

"My stitches are gone. I am hale—and eager."

That was clear to read in the darkening warmth of his eyes. "And what of the enemy? Should ye not stay alert for them?"

"Even the English wouldnae be so cruel as to disturb me on this day."

"I shouldnae wager my sword on it, Sir Gillard." She gave a start of surprise when he suddenly cupped her face in his hands. Clearly, he was weary of talk.

"Do ye mean to take back the invitation ye have offered these last days, an invitation plain in all but words?"

"Nay."

"Are ye certain ye ken what I ask of you?"

"I was in the nunnery but one year," she said. "Ere I fled to its confines, I wasnae blind to life's ways. Aye, I ken weel what ye want of me."

His response was a kiss. It was a slow, deep kiss with a hint of ferocity. Her desire for him swiftly rose, warming her. Passion pushed away all thought of war, of man's brutal grasp for power, of the innocents hurt and the dead forgotten. She let the passion possess her fully, gave herself over to it, craving its sweet oblivion.

She clung to him as he covered her face and neck with warm kisses. Then he softly cursed. Slowly she opened her eyes. Hacon was glaring down at her shift. Following his gaze, she saw how he fumbled with the laces. Gently, she placed her hands over his, stilling them.

"Nay, ye might tear it. I will do it."

Allowing her to take over that chore, he ran a hand through his hair. "I tremble like some green lad."

"Ah, and ye so weel versed in these matters," she teased as she unlaced her shift but did not remove it.

"Though I am no innocent, neither would any call me a

lecherous dog." He attempted to loose his plaid, then cursed again. "'Twill be winter ere I am shed of this."

She pushed his hands aside. His difficulty did a great deal to soothe her own trepidation. There were any number of possible reasons for his sudden awkwardness, and each was rather flattering.

"I am but too eager to be rid of our clothing," he said as he took off his plaid and spread it upon the ground.

He sat down on the large cloth, then held his hand out to her. Feeling only a slight uncertainty, Jennet placed her hand in his and allowed him to lightly tug her down beside him. He wore only his braies, and one thorough look at his virile form told her why her passion for him could be so strong, while she remained so confused in her heart and mind. Despite her doubts about him, she instinctively knew he could show her all the rich beauty to be found in fleshly pleasure. She desperately wanted to taste a little joy, even if it might prove fleeting.

When he silently urged her to lie down, she offered no resistance. She trembled slightly when he eased her shift over her head. It was the first time she had been naked with a man. The way he stared at her made her all too conscious of her inexperience. She started to cover herself with her hands, but he swiftly stopped her. Gently clasping her wrists, he held her hands to her sides as he crouched over her.

"I am too thin," she murmured, his silent gaze prompting her into nervous speech.

"Nay." He brushed his lips over hers. "Even when the bite of hunger sharpened your looks ye were lovely. Now, even that has gone."

"Ye feed me weel."

"Tug my braies off, lass. I need to feel our flesh meet."

The moment he freed her hands, she did as he asked. Despite her efforts not to, she looked as she took away the last piece of his clothing.

A man's naked form was not strange to her. Through the giving of courtesy baths, nursing the sick and wounded, and even seeing the stripped dead upon the battlefield, she had viewed variations of that form. None, however, had been erect with wanting, a wanting inspired by her. Nor, she mused as she met his gaze and tossed aside his braies, had she ever contemplated joining her body with any other. She was suddenly not sure if the experience would be pleasurable. Hacon looked to be far larger than she could accommodate. She feared that her uncertainty showed in her face.

"Dinnae fear, my sweet plunder." He slowly lowered his body onto hers. "This sword will ne'er hurt you. Though, if ye be virgin, 'twill draw some blood, I mean to make it a pleasurable bloodletting."

For a moment all she could think of was how good it felt to be skin to skin with him. Then his words registered on her mind. "*If* I be virgin?"

"Nay." He quickly kissed her. "I speak no insult nor impugn your morals. Ye have told me of a life spent upon battlefields and in servitude. A maidenhead is often stolen in such situations. Aye, and ye have been alone, unprotected, for many a year now."

Since his reasoning was sound and she could detect no insult in his gaze or voice, her anger eased. "Weel, my maidenhead hasnae been stolen. Howbeit, I will confess it would have been had I not fled to the convent when I did."

Supporting some of his weight on his forearms and elbows, placed on either side of her, he cupped her face in his hands. "So, I shall be your first mon." He slowly tangled his fingers in her thick hair.

"Aye—my first." And last, a small voice whispered in her head, but she ignored it for it hinted at promises she did not wish to make, not to a man of battle. Nor did she believe Hacon desired such promises.

Still cupping her face in his hands, he gave her another

slow, deep kiss. She wrapped her arms around him, holding him close and loving the feel of his hard, warm body pressed against hers. The way he gently rubbed his groin against hers set her to trembling. The depth of her desire, the speed with which it possessed her, was in itself a little frightening. That hint of trepidation was lost, however, when he began to caress her, his callused hands skimming lightly over her.

When he moved his heated kisses from her face to her throat, she began to stroke his body, as he did hers. The words he muttered against her collarbone were husky and indecipherable, but she heard his approval of daring. She gave a soft cry of pure delight when he filled his hand with her breast, then brushed his lips over the tip.

The desire that ripped through her at that gentle touch paled beside what followed when he first lathed her aching nipple with his tongue, then began to slowly suckle. She squirmed beneath him, burrowed her fingers into his thick, soft hair, and held him there. So strong were the feelings tearing through her that she found it impossible to be still. She lost all sense of time and place, knew only Hacon and the pleasure he was giving her.

A brief flicker of sanity returned, inspired by shock when his caresses reached the curls between her thighs. She tensed as he moved his hand over her groin. He stopped her from closing her legs in an instinctive response to such an intrusion by holding her thighs apart with his legs.

"Dinnae grow cold and afraid now, my sweet plunder," he whispered, kissing her ear.

She gasped as his intimate stroking increased the knotting want growing inside of her. "Ye shouldnae touch me there, should ye?"

"Oh, aye, lassie. Aye. 'Tis the seat of all your pleasure. 'Tis the sweet haven of delight in which I will soon bury myself."

"Should I touch ye there too?"

"Aye, but not now." He pressed his face in the curve of her

neck, his breath coming hot and fast against her skin. "I hold back by only a wee thin thread as it is. Ye touch me now and I will be done ere ye are even readied."

She was not sure what he meant by "readied," but could not form the words to ask. All she could do was cling to him as he continued his seductive caresses, adding to the pleasure of his touch with soft yet feverish kisses upon her breasts. She immersed herself in the heated glory of all he made her feel. Then, when she thought she could tolerate no more, when the need grew nearly painful, she called out to him and tried to pull away.

Instead of allowing her to flee, he crouched over her, his body holding hers in place. She opened her eyes as she felt him begin to join their bodies, but quickly closed them again, unable to hold his intense gaze. The realization that her maidenhead was about to be lost forever had barely set in her passion-dulled mind when Hacon broke through it. She cried out softly at the sharp pain, yet was not truly concerned about it. The delicious sensation of their bodies united at last held all her interest. It was a moment before she realized that Hacon had gone very still.

Cautiously, she looked at him. The lines of his face were taut, his expression one of both pleasure and pain. Slipping her arms about his neck, she tugged his mouth nearer to her own.

"Is there not more to this?" she whispered, answering an urge deep within her and moving her body against his.

"Aye." He tried vainly to catch his breath. "But I didnae want to begin until I was certain your pain had ebbed."

"'Twas but a wee pain, quickly gone." It was not the full truth, but she did not know how to explain that she felt the pain yet did not, that she could ignore it with ease.

"Are ye certain, lass? Ah, Jennet, ye are so small, so slim."

"Aye, but it seems I can hold one verra large knight."

He groaned and kissed her even as he started to move. She soon matched his rhythm, each of her senses caught up in that erotic thrust and parry. Her taut hunger intensified until she felt blindly driven. When it finally crested, she cried out his name, swept into a realm of mindless delight. Only faintly was she aware of how his movements grew briefly frantic, of his huskily muttered words of love. Then he clutched her hips, pushing himself as deeply within her as her body would allow. He stilled, calling out her name as he shuddered. She wrapped her limbs around him more thoroughly when he collapsed atop her. Jennet found his weight easy to bear, enjoyed the sense of lethargy that gripped her, the lingering thrills of sated passion.

She murmured a weak protest as he finally eased free of her hold. He rose and left her, but she paid little heed. Tugging part of the plaid over her, she clung to the sumptuous feelings with which their lovemaking had left her.

One glance at him when he returned told her he had been to the small rivelet in which she had bathed. She blushed as he washed between her legs with a dampened cloth, then held it against her for a while. It was soothing, but she found such personal attendance a little embarrassing. She breathed a small inner sigh of relief when he tossed the cloth aside and tugged her into his arms.

"Is the soreness verra great?" he asked, idly moving his hands over her slim curves.

"Nay. Hacon? Why did ye wait? Why did ye not simply steal my maidenhead long ago, as many another mon would have?"

"And what would be the pleasure in that?"

"Enough to suit many another mon."

"Weel, there is none for me in such a mating." He nuzzled her neck and watched her closely. "I have a question for you. Why did ye give in? Why, after keeping me at a distance for so many weeks, did ye decide to say aye?"

"Ye make me feel good."

"'Tis all?"

It was not *all*, but she had no intention of telling him more, especially when she found her emotions such a puzzle to herself. "I dinnae play for pity when I say my life hasnae been a joyous one. It has been soaked in war, death, grief, and all else that a people mired in fighting can suffer. When I wasnae caught up in some battle, I was trapped in the meanest servitude. The gray world of the convent was a change for the better. There have been few times in my life when I have felt good, when I truly found pleasure in living. When I say ye make me feel good, 'tis no small accolade."

"Mayhaps not, but . . . to give up your maidenhead? Dugald has oft told me it could be your only dowry."

"If my father is dead—aye—it could be." She shrugged. "It may be a sin . . ."

"Nay, there is no sin here."

"Then ye disagree with all the leaders of the Church," she countered. "Dinnae worry upon that. I dinnae. For once, I wished to feel pleasure, to experience the joy that can be found in living. For a wee while I wished to forget all the dark, sad things all about me."

"And lying with me does that?"

"Aye. I could see that quite early in the game. I didnae really fight *you* but rather the temptation of that pleasure, the urge to grasp at it with both hands. Weel, I finally decided I *would* grasp it. If that be a sin, I cannae see it as a verra big one."

"Nay, a wee penance is all." He frowned down at her. "I understand what ye are saying but, weel, it doesnae seem such a grand reason for lying with a mon."

"Nay? Mayhaps ye are hardened to seeing death 'round every corner. I am not." She slowly rubbed her foot up and down his strong calf. "Mayhaps ye have ceased to worry that the next time death may wait there for you. I havenae. Ye make me feel alive, verra alive, and I can ignore the nearness of the Grim Reaper for a wee while. I think 'tis a verra grand reason indeed." She lightly trailed her fingers over his chest.

"What are your reasons? Why did ye want me? There is many another lass about."

"Aye, but I wanted you from the moment I set eyes on you. There ye sat, quiet, peaceful . . ."

"'Twasnae so verra quiet and peaceful after ye arrived."

He grimaced. "Nay. I tried to stop the men, but the blood-lust blinded them."

"Ye tried to stop them?" While she had believed he had taken no part in the rape and murder at the convent, she had never thought he had come there with any intention except to steal. "Is that true?"

"Aye." He frowned at her before continuing. "As ye said, 'twas a place of sanctuary, a holy place. Howbeit, there was no way I could stop them. So Dugald and I took all we could set our hands on. At least we willnae drink and whore the booty away. Then I found you." He traced the delicate shape of her face with one finger. "There was such sweetness in your face, whilst ye busied yourself with women's work. I soon discovered there was spirit and spice beneath that sweetness, and they only added to the wanting. I ached for you from the very first."

"Because I was sewing a wimple?" She found most of his speech highly flattering, but thought it puzzling that a man of war would be so moved by such a common sight.

"Mayhaps I have been from home too long," he murmured, and began to brush kisses over her cheeks. "Ye made me think on Dubheilrig ere it was taken from us. 'Tis as good a reason to make love as yours."

"Is it? I must think on that." She was not sure she would be able to do much thinking at all if he continued to kiss and stroke her. "Should we not return to camp and the others?"

"We shall be with the others soon enough. Aye, and with them more than we may wish. Let us savor this time alone, this moment of stolen privacy."

"Are ye sure we are private?"

"Aye, my sweet plunder. Verra private. Dugald stands twixt us and any intruders." Once again he cupped her face in his hands and brushed his lips across hers. "Are ye sore, loving? Has your first taste of passion left ye hurting much?"

Realizing why he asked such questions again, she quickly decided she was more than able to savor a second taste of lovemaking. "Nay. 'Tis but a wee pain, like a stinging itch." She slipped her arms about his neck. "I believe ye can make me forget it, my braw Scottish knight."

"As I make ye forget the war?" He stroked her breast, lightly brushing his thumb over the tip.

It took a moment for Jennet to catch her breath. She was surprised at how swiftly her desire returned, how easily he could rekindle the fires within her.

"Aye, make me forget the war, the death, the weeping of grief stricken lasses and bairns. Aye, even the hunger that has gnawed at my innards for two long years. Steal all thought and black memory from my mind with your loving. Do ye think ill of me for seeking that?"

"Nay, lassie, though 'tis not the reason I wished ye to have. Howbieit, 'twill serve for now. Aye, 'twill serve. I am a patient mon."

She opened her mouth to ask him what he meant, but he kissed her instead. Soon she was lost in the sweet oblivion of desire, her question forgotten.

# Chapter 9

Jennet huddled by the goats behind a snarled hedgerow of holly bushes, struggling to ignore the vicious plundering of Skipton that was going on only yards away. The townspeople and serfs were no match for the Bruce's battle-hardened men. Those who were able had fled to the nearby hilltop castle, which the Scots had wisely bypassed.

The morning after she and Hacon had made love, Douglas had turned the army west toward Otley and expressed the intention of marching back to Scotland soon. She had been delighted, certain that the killing would shortly end. Now, only a week later, she knew it had been a foolish hope. Instead of being nearer to Scotland, they were but twenty miles northwest of Leeds, and the destruction continued, unrelenting.

She prayed the battle would end soon, then cursed herself for bothering. She had done little else but pray, yet the looting, the burning, and the killing continued. Glancing down at Murdoc, who slept peacefully on the ground beside her, she thanked God that the child was too young to understand what raged about him.

Memories, painful and horrifying, assaulted her, stirred to life by this new blood being shed. It was all too similar to the day her mother had died. Her old hatred of the Bruce's forces burned within her. She struggled to fight it, if only because it was a treasonous feeling, one that could easily cost her her life.

"Jennet?"

Quickly stifling a screech of surprise, Jennet placed her hand over her heart and glared at Elizabeth. "Ye just stole ten years of my life," she complained as the woman scrambled to sit on the other side of Murdoc.

"I beg your pardon. I did not mean to afright you, yet I could not approach too boldly. Others might have seen me. Where is your faithful guard Ranald?"

"But a few yards away, on the other side of these bushes."

"Good. 'Tis one reason I sought you out instead of cowering with the other women. I knew you would be protected."

"Aye. We are too close to the fighting this time."

Elizabeth nodded. "Much too close." She regarded Jennet with concern. "Are ye ailing? You look very pale."

"I am always verra pale," Jennet murmured.

"Not like this. 'Tis a sickly cast. Are you fevered?" She reached out to feel Jennet's forehead and cheeks.

"Nay. 'Tis that my mother died in such a raid by Bruce's men. Being so close has brought back those memories."

"Poor child. Yet you stay with these men. Why? They fight for the same man, for the Bruce."

"Where would I go, Elizabeth? Aye, I could set out for Liddesdale and my mother's kinsmen, but I dinnae think I would get there alive. We are nearly two hundred miles inside of England. And most times I dinnae blame the Scots or the English, the Bruce or Edward. 'Tis war that killed my mother and mayhaps my father. War and men, with their mad lust for battle."

"Aye, great fools that they are. Well, there is no changing the beast." Elizabeth suddenly winked at Jennet and faintly smiled. "And mayhaps you stay because of your fine, stalwart lover."

Jennet opened her mouth to immediately deny that, then grimaced. "Weel, mayhaps—sin-filled creature that I am."

"Sin-filled?" Elizabeth laughed. "Child, you have few if any marks upon your soul."

"The Church teaches that lying with Hacon is a sin."

"I was taught the same, but I cannot believe it a sin worthy of hell's fires. If it is, then hell must be full to bursting by now." She smiled faintly when Jennet gave a brief laugh. "'Tis a hard world God has set us in. Aye, He set down rules, 'tis true, but I cannot believe He would condemn such a kind-hearted girl as yourself for seeking some happiness amidst all this slaughter and destruction."

"That is what I tell myself—again and again." She tensed. "Hold, did ye hear that?"

Before Elizabeth could reply, their safe enclave was invaded by a large, disheveled man who charged out of the bushes. It was not only the bloodstained sword and heavily padded jupon that made him look threatening. There was a look of pure murderous hatred upon his face. Jennet knew that, at least at this moment, no mercy for women or a helpless babe would be found in his heart. She quickly drew her dagger, which Ranald habitually gave her now whenever the men left to fight.

"Protect Murdoc," she ordered Elizabeth as she rose slowly to a fighting stance.

"Where is Ranald?" Elizabeth demanded fearfully as she picked up Murdoc, sheltering him in her arms.

"Do ye mean that beardless boy left to guard you?" The man laughed. "Sent to hell by my companion."

Pain tore through Jennet, for she feared the man might speak the truth. She forced herself to push aside all emotion, to fix her mind upon her attacker. If she was fortunate to escape the confrontation alive, there would be time to grieve for young Ranald later.

Her survey of the situation told her she would require a

great deal of luck. All she had was a dagger. The man held a sword. That, combined with his longer arms, meant he could probably take her head from her shoulders before she even had the chance to scratch him. Her only hope lay in making him act so rashly, so foolishly, that some of his many great advantages were lessened.

"That boy shall ne'er see hell," she said, "but ye soon shall. He was stalwart and brave. Ye creep about like a craven dog, striking down the weak and defenseless." She would not have thought it possible, but his expression became even more twisted with hatred.

"It can be no sin to cut down the vermin that trails after these murderous Scots."

"Most men wait until the *real* battle has ended first. Howbeit, since ye have no stomach for fighting men . . ."

He howled with fury and lunged at her. Jennet easily evaded his mindless attack. When he tried to turn in the midst of his blind charge, he stumbled to his knees. She took quick advantage of his clumsiness. Racing over to him before he could get to his feet, she plunged her dagger into his back.

The man howled again, a sound full of rage and pain. He swung back at her with his free hand and sent her sprawling. Jennet barely kept enough presence of mind to cling to her dagger, pulling it free as she fell back.

"Bitch! Whore!" the man bellowed as he stood and faced her.

She rose quickly to her feet. "And weel should ye ken such as those, born of the breed as ye were."

She inwardly cursed the weakness of that taunt and was surprised when he foolishly lunged at her again. The man was either blind with hatred or very stupid. This time she managed to cut him in the side before he knocked her down and turned on her.

She scrambled to her feet and cried out in pain. In her fall she had turned her ankle. She did not think it was a serious injury, but it would hinder her movements. Her agility and speed were her best weapons, and now she might have lost both.

"So, whore," he snarled. "You begin to tire."

"I am not the one who stands panting like a dog."

"I shall cut your insulting tongue out."

"Oh, aye? I have nary a scratch so far, whilst ye bleed like a stuck pig."

This time he did not rush her quite so blindly. She barely managed to elude the deadly swing of his sword. The arm of her gown was torn by the blade and her skin stung by the brush of its sharp edge. A stick hurled by a terrified Elizabeth tripped the man, but Jennet's sore ankle made her too slow to take advantage of that aid. She cut the man but not too seriously. As she tried to flee, he grasped her leg.

Jennet hit the ground, face first and hard. The wind was knocked from her body and she was unable to do more than turn over, gasping for breath. Before she could even try to rise and flee, the man was standing over her.

He smiled as he raised his sword. Jennet knew she faced certain death. Fear was not the emotion which gripped her but a chilling resignation. It held her in place, kept her staring almost calmly at the sword as she waited for the killing blow.

Suddenly, the sword was no longer there, nor was most of the arm that held it. She saw his look of stunned horror, felt the warm blood on her face. Another sword came into view, piercing her attacker's chest and pushing him back. She heard his strangled cry as he fell. Her next clear sight was of Ranald's worried expression as he knelt by her side.

"He said you were dead," she whispered, glancing only briefly at Elizabeth, who, clutching Murdoc in her plump arms, knelt on the other side.

"'Twas a near thing. Are ye hurt, Jennet?" he asked.

"Winded and verra sore. Is he dead?"

"Aye. Ye were right. When the need arose I could turn

swiftly from one battle to another. I dinnae feel exultant, but I dinnae feel too poorly either. 'Twas them or us, aye?"

"Aye." She smiled weakly at Elizabeth when the woman began to wipe her face clean with a scrap of cloth.

"Are ye certain ye arenae injured? Ye can move, can ye not?"

"I can, but I dinnae seem to wish to." She sighed. "Ranald, I dinnae really wish to view the body."

"Ah, I see. Set there then." He scrambled to his feet. "I will pull the mon to the other side of the bushes."

"Are ye and Murdoc unhurt?" Jennet asked Elizabeth as Ranald set to work.

"Hale but shaken. You fight as weel as any man, lass."

"That doesnae make me verra happy," Jennet mumbled as, with a little help from Elizabeth, she sat up. "I aided in the death of a mon, Elizabeth. I can see no cause for pride in it."

Setting a sleepy Murdoc at her side, Elizabeth took Jennet's dagger and wiped it clean. "That man you feel pity for felt none for us. He meant to kill two women and a helpless child. If you had not fought him, had not kept him at bay until Ranald could come to our aid, we would be dead now. You fought for your life, our lives—the same as any soldier fights for his."

"The same? Nay, I think not. They choose their bloody work."

"Choose it?" Elizabeth laughed shortly and shook her head. "Some do—mayhaps. Most have near as little choice as you did just now. Not all men are their own masters. And in this sad war a man who chooses not to fight could easily be called a traitor."

Before Jennet could respond, Hacon strode toward her, not once taking his gaze from her. Behind him followed Ranald and Dugald. She felt the last of her fear ease away. That annoyed her a little, for she did not like to think she was so dependent upon Hacon for her peace and security. When he knelt by her side to allow her a closer look at him, she frowned up at him.

Here was Hacon the knight, the man of battle. His helmet hid his expression, making him seem remote. Even though his armor and jupon were dulled by the dirt and blood of battle, he looked imposing, almost threatening.

"Did Ranald fetch you from the field?" she asked.

"Nay, I was already on my way back. The true fighting is o'er. Are ye certain ye are unhurt? There is blood upon your gown."

She looked down, then quickly averted her gaze. "'Tisnae mine. I have but a wee scratch upon my arm and many a bruise. Ye have blood upon you. Are ye hurt?"

"Nay." He briefly touched her hair and stood up. "I shall quickly rid myself of the stench of battle, then we shall find a quieter place to make camp. Elizabeth, would ye tend to her wound?"

Elizabeth nodded and watched Hacon and Dugald walk away before turning to Jennet. "Such a fine man," she murmured as she started to attend to Jennet's small cut. "You would be a great fool to let that one slip free," she added after Ranald picked up Murdoc and moved away.

Gritting her teeth against the stinging pain as Elizabeth washed her injury, Jennet said, "Ye think I have more to say about my fate than I do. Hacon will stay or go as he pleases."

"Then mayhaps you should work harder to try and gain what pleases *you*."

"And ye think that binding myself to a knight, to a mon of war, would please me? I seek peace. I wish a mon of peace."

"Bah. You want him. And where, might I ask, would you find a man of peace? Even the monks and bishops take to the battlefield from time to time. Men are not bred to be creatures of peace."

"Then 'tis past time they saw the error of their ways," Jennet snapped.

"Nay, child. 'Tis past time you opened your eyes and looked about you. Aye, 'twould be wondrous fine if men would cease their fighting, but that will not happen soon. 'Twould be wise to try and grasp the best while you can."

Jennet stared down at her clenched hands and remained silent while Elizabeth finished binding up her arm. She did not like to think that she asked for too much. Neither did she want to consider Hacon leaving her. Her heart urged her to hold tightly to Hacon, but her mind clung to the dream of a peaceful life, a life without the clash of swords or the fear of battle. Hacon did not fit into that dream. At times the battle between her heart and her mind raged so fiercely that she felt torn apart. She did not think the two could ever be reconciled. It was painful to think that soon she would have to make a choice between the needs of her heart and her flesh and the sweet allure of her dream. Or, she mused as she looked up to see Hacon returning, he would make the choice for her.

"Something ails her," muttered Hacon that night as he glanced toward where Jennet slept, then looked back at Ranald and Dugald, who lingered around the small fire with him. "Weel? Dinnae say I see what isnae there."

"Nay." Dugald frowned toward Jennet. "Mayhaps the battle she had to fight today troubles her."

"She didnae kill the mon," Ranald said. "I did that."

"But she drew blood, laddie, and we all ken how she hates that." Dugald smiled faintly. "She makes no secret of that. She had a hand in the fighting she scorns. That cannae set weel with the lass."

Hacon rubbed his chin and nodded. "Aye, I think ye have guessed it aright, my friend."

"But she *had* to fight," Ranald muttered. "The mon meant to kill her, Elizabeth, and the bairn."

"The lass will see the truth about that," agreed Hacon, "but it may take her a wee while. It may do her some good to have had a wee taste of it. She can be a bit harsh in her judgments on us all. Aye"—he held up his hand to halt Dugald's response—"I ken she has tasted the bitter cost of war, that her judgments are born of those losses. Howbeit, I think she has ne'er faced the cold choice of kill or be killed. Mayhaps, now that she has, she will soften a wee bit."

"Mayhaps." Dugald shrugged. "I wouldnae look for too great a softening."

"Nay, I willnae." Hacon smiled faintly as he rose to his feet. "And if she continues to mope about, I will speak some sense to her."

"Oh, aye," mocked Dugald. "That should settle it all."

Chuckling softly, Hacon strode over to the rough bed he had laid out for Jennet earlier, briefly but fiercely regretting their lack of privacy. He had not been able to make love to her since that first night outside of Knaresborough, and suspected it would be several days more before any chance arose. Stripping down to his braies, he knew tonight the loss would be easier to bear, for she was bruised and weary. Even if they had privacy, he would not have expected any passion from her.

"Hacon?" she murmured as he crawled beneath the blanket and gently tugged her into his arms.

"Nay, 'tis the King Edward himself."

"Hah." She snuggled closer to his warmth. "Ye cannae fool me. Ye speak the language better than he."

"Ah, so 'tis true he cannae even speak the tongue of the people he would rule—English or Scots."

"Weel, I have heard he can curse in English."

"Those ground beneath his heel probably expect naught else." He nuzzled her hair, then rested his cheek on top of her head. "How do ye feel, lass?"

"I ache, but I ken that will pass. 'Tis but a few bruises."

"Aye, ye were knocked about some, but Ranald says ye fought bravely."

"Am I to take pride in that?" She did not wish to

remember the incident or how close she had come to
taking another's life.

"And why not? Would ye rather have stood lamblike and
been cut down along with Elizabeth and wee Murdoc?"

"Nay." She grimaced. "Why, Hacon? Why should he have
wished to kill us?"

"War breeds hatred. Aye, and it brings out all those who
lust for blood and enjoy the killing." He kissed her cheek. "Ye
did what ye had to, dearling. There is no shame in that."

"The Lord says, 'Thou shalt not kill.'"

"He meant murder without provocation, loving. I am sure
of it. Come, would ye not have fought to save your mother,
had ye been bigger and held a weapon?"

Sighing, she nodded. "I would have cut their throats. I have
often thought of it, but I was too young, too weak. I could do
no more than cower in hiding and watch her die."

He stared at her in horror. "Ye saw what was done to your
mother?"

"Nay, not all. She set me in a niche, out of sight, when the
battle began. 'Ye stay right here, child,' she commanded. 'No
matter what ye see or hear, dinnae move. Dinnae make a sound.'
So I did. When the men came I closed my eyes. I did peek once,
mayhaps twice, but I didnae move. I didnae make a sound. Even
after the men left. I stayed where I had been put until one of
the few men who had survived came and found me."

Muttering a curse, Hacon held her close. "Did ye see the men
who did it, lass? Do ye ken which of Douglas's men it was?"

"Nay. 'Twas but a quick glance. All I ken is that there were
three of them."

Jennet found it difficult to lie to him, but she knew she had
to. She could not tell him that Balreaves was one of those
three men, the one who had delivered the death strike. There
was already enough trouble between Balreaves and Hacon.
She would not add to it. Her mother was dead, and although
revenge would be sweet, it would never bring her mother

back. Jennet told herself to leave Balreaves's punishment to God and be satisfied with that.

Unless, she mused, Balreaves remembered her. Inwardly she shook away that thought. It had all happened years ago. The man would never recall one brief, locked glance with a small, terrified child. So long as she kept quiet about the man's part in her mother's murder, Hacon would never know.

"Ye have gone verra quiet. Have ye recalled something?" he asked in a near whisper.

As if conjured up by her thoughts, Balreaves's cold, familiar voice said, "So, your sharp-tongued little whore still lives."

Jennet grasped Hacon's arms to halt his grab for his sword. She gazed up at Balreaves. He looked calm, unwearied, almost untouched by the battle. Jennet began to think he did as little fighting as he could. He wore the odd, faint, and chilling smile she had begun to recognize as peculiarly his. Even in the shadows she could see the coldness of his eyes. She wondered why God continued to let the man live.

"Aye, I still exist," she replied. "'Tis so verra kind of you to inquire after my health."

"And in the future ye would be wise to do so with a more courteous tongue," snapped Hacon.

"Do ye threaten me, Sir Gillard?" Balreaves demanded, smiling faintly. "Or mayhaps ye hurl out a challenge?"

"Would ye meet it if I did?"

"Nay, I think not. Why should I bloody my hands when there are so many about who can do the deed for me?" He stared down at Jennet. "Have we met before? I sense something familiar about you."

"Do you?" Jennet was surprised she could speak so calmly while her heart raced with fear. "Ye have confused me with another, I think, for we have ne'er met."

"I am not usually wrong," he muttered.

Hacon made a soft, scornful noise. "There are many who would argue that."

"Are there?" Balreaves turned his cold smile upon Hacon again.

"I doubt there are many men who would consider murder right."

"More than you might think. But murder? Do ye accuse me of trying to murder you, Gillard?" When Hacon said nothing, Balreaves shrugged. "Mayhaps what ye see as murder is naught but a rightful vengeance."

"Ye have no claim to a rightful vengeance."

"Nay? There are many who would argue with that. The insults the Gillards have dealt me would have another mon screaming for your blood."

"Then scream for mine," Hacon snarled, and raised himself up on one elbow. "Face me squarely and let us have done with this."

"When the Bruce himself has asked that we Scots cease to fight each other and turn our swords only upon the English? Nay, I think not. I am a mon of great patience. I can wait. Ye *will* pay for those insults ye heaped upon me." He frowned at Jennet again. "I am certain we have met before, but the memory remains elusive. 'Twill come to me," he murmured, then started to walk away.

Heartily praying that the memory would not come, Jennet watched the man disappear into the shadows. The hint that he might recall that short exchange in the cottage nine years ago left her terrified.

Even if it did not complicate the already deadly tension between Hacon and Balreaves, it would still cause trouble. Balreaves would not want his actions of that day to be widely known. In her time of traveling with the Bruce's army Jennet had come to see that not every man indulged in brutality. Even those who saw rape as rightful plunder due the victors, would frown upon the murder of an unarmed woman. Her mother had also been a lady, wellborn if not rich, and the unspoken law was that such women were sacrosanct. Balreaves was not one to want any blackening of his name. If he recalled that day, recalled her, he would want her silenced. That would put Hacon in the precarious position of trying to protect her even as he watched out for himself. She would have to try harder to keep out of Balreaves's sight. Perhaps, if the man did not often see her, he would fail to remember.

"What did he mean?" demanded Hacon, abruptly breaking into her thoughts.

She turned to frown at him. "What did he mean about what?"

"About recognizing you. He said he sensed something familiar about you. Do ye ken that man from some other time?"

"Nay, I have ne'er met the mon before." She told herself that it was not a full lie, for she had not met Balreaves, merely exchanged a look with the man.

"Then why does he frighten you so?" He placed his hand upon her chest. "Your heart races like a cornered deer's."

"He would frighten anyone. The mon's eyes are cold, so verra cold. Only hatred and cruelty enliven their depths."

Enfolding her in his arms, Hacon murmured, "Aye, if there was ever any good in the mon, it has been eaten away. I think he is one of those who glories in bloodletting, eager to cut down the innocent as weel as the soldiers. He hides it weel though."

"Why should he hide it? Would it matter if all knew his ways?"

"Aye, it would. Not all those in power are as cruel as the Douglas." He stroked her hair as he stared off into the dark. "I dinnae like his interest in you. Best ye stay clear of the mon."

"Ye need not tell me to do that. He isnae one I wish to meet with often."

"Good. Now lass, why did ye stop me from taking up my sword? Do ye like to hear his slurs and insults?"

"Of course not. I but thought it a poor time for ye to come to blows with the mon. Aye, ye had your sword but no armor, and ye needed to get to your feet. 'Tis also dark and the shadows can hide much treachery. I didnae trust the mon to face you fairly, thought he might have goaded you on purpose."

"Ah, and had a companion or two lurking close at hand to aid him in cutting me down. 'Tis possible." He touched his lips to her forehead and rested his cheek against her head. "Ye had best get some sleep, dearling. Our pace will increase now as we turn north and draw nearer to Scotland. Our moments of rest will grow shorter, and rest is what ye need to heal."

"I wasnae hurt badly," she murmured, then quickly smothered a yawn.

"Ye will be stiff on the morrow, and I fear there can be no respite from travel."

After giving a sleepy nod, she snuggled up more comfortably against him. He was big and strong, his skin beautifully taut and warm. She already felt stiff and achy but made no complaint. She would simply have to endure and hope her recovery was swift. The way Hacon lightly massaged her helped a great deal, and she murmured her appreciation.

As sleep gained a grip on her, she thought of Balreaves again. She wished she could forget the man but knew that would be unwise. He was a threat that needed careful watching, both for Hacon's sake and her own. Balreaves was a murderer, his hands stained with the blood of her mother. Trying to press even closer to Hacon, she prayed the man would not spill Hacon's blood. If Balreaves killed Hacon, it would leave as many scars upon her heart as her mother's death.

# Chapter 10

"To Liddesdale?" Jennet gaped at Hacon as he helped her off her pony.

"Aye, to Liddesdale." Hacon handed the reins to Dugald, who led his hose and Jennet's pony away.

All the pleasure Jennet felt over being back in Scotland began to fade. They had finally turned north after Skipton. It had taken nearly two long, hard months to get home, two months of swift travel broken by periods of bloodletting and plunder. Now they were back in Scotland and the horror would soon end. Her heart had lightened when they crossed the border that morning, but Hacon's talk of Liddesdale ended that. Why did he want to take her to her family?

"But why? What is in Liddesdale?"

Clasping her hand, Hacon began looking for the best place to site their camp amongst the thick tangle of bracken. "Did ye not tell me your mother's kinsmen live there? Ah, this place will do. Iain," he called to one of his men. "Start our fire here." His hands on his hips, Hacon frowned at Jennet. "Ye dinnae look pleased with the news. Do ye not wish to see your kinsmen?"

"Weel, aye, yet I cannae see why ye wish to take me there. 'Tis not on the way to Dubheilrig, and ye were verra eager to return to your home. I thought that was why ye had decided to leave the army come the morning."

"Aye. There is no sense in riding all the way to Stirling or wherever the king is holding his court, just to be formally disbanded. We will part from the army by midday. And 'tisnae so out of the way either. Your kinsman may have news of your father."

"Aye, they may have."

"Come, lass." He lightly kissed her mouth. "Dinnae look so woeful. They may have good news."

"True. If he survived Perth, they would be certain to ken it."

Hacon nodded, then quickly moved away to get their blankets. The men were doing fine on their own, but he felt a need to slip away from Jennet the moment Perth was mentioned. Instead of finding comfort in his lie, he grew more afraid of it with each day that had passed. He could not believe his luck had held, that she had yet to hear the truth. Yet, at other times, he had the feeling she already knew. It was one reason he wanted to go to Liddesdale. If there was good news about her father, he could rid himself of the lie that now stood between them.

Jennet frowned after Hacon. The chance to visit Liddesdale should please her, but it did not. She was certain Hacon meant to leave her there and that thought stole all the joy from the prospect of seeing her family again.

"Jennet."

Starting, she turned to see Elizabeth behind her. "Ye are still with us then. Robert didnae make ye remain in England."

"Nay, only Mary stayed. Robert left her with a farmer and his family who said they would help her return to her family. Now . . ." She linked her arm with Jennet's, but stumbled over an exposed tree root when she started to walk. "Curse it. Why do these fools nest amongst the trees like birds? Are there no flat places in this land?"

"Aye, enough when the rivers and lochs havenae overrun their banks. Howbeit, from what I understand, they avoid the open places because they dinnae wish to be caught out in the open by the English."

"Do you think the English are after us?"

"Who can say? If they are, we are safest right here. In the open they can encircle us, use the land itself to trap us. They could push us into the mud, corner us so that we have them to our fore and some river or loch at our backs. 'Tis what we did to them at Bannockburn and they were slaughtered."

"I have suddenly grown very fond of these forests and thickets," Elizabeth muttered, and smiled when Jennet laughed.

"Where are we going?" Jennet asked as Elizabeth pulled her along.

"There is clean, fresh water near at hand. While the men are busy making camp, we will slip away and bathe."

"How I would love that, but I must tell Ranald first. I cannae wander off without leaving word."

"Or with him following close at hand. We are in luck, for here comes your guard with your babe."

Smiling faintly, Jennet took Murdoc from Ranald and hugged the child close. Most everyone called Murdoc her child now. She did not mind at all, did indeed feel as if he were her own.

As soon as she told Ranald what she and Elizabeth wished to do, he agreed. He took Murdoc while she quickly gathered what she would need. On the way to the brook, Ranald paused only to tell another of Hacon's men where they would be. Jennet realized she had grown accustomed to the constant watch kept on her. She no longer saw it as part of her bondage but as a necessary precaution.

This time Ranald did not take up his watch out of sight but remained close by, keeping his back turned to them to allow them some privacy. Since the time the Englishman had nearly killed her outside of Otley, the youth never left her side. She suspected Hacon had insisted upon it.

"Ah, this is wondrous," Jennet murmured as, wearing

only her chemise, she joined a naked Elizabeth in the slow-moving brook.

"Such modesty." Elizabeth laughed softly, gave a teasing tug at Jennet's chemise and began to wash.

"Aye." Jennet grimaced. "Ah, weel, it needs a wash as much as I do." Frowning at her sliver of soap, Jennet added, "This wee piece willnae last much longer. Mayhaps my aunt will have some I may use."

"So, you travel to your family?"

"Aye. Hacon means to take me to Liddesdale."

"You do not sound pleased." Elizabeth frowned at Jennet as she began to soap her hair.

"I am a verra contrary lass." Jennet shook her head, annoyed by her continued confusion.

"Well, 'tis true you can be sharp at times . . ."

"Nay, I mean contrary in how I feel. I should want to see my kinsmen. Howbeit, I dinnae like Hacon taking me to them."

"Ah, you fear that he means to leave you there, that your time with him will end when you reach Liddesdale and your family."

"Aye, that is my quandary." She slowly began to soap her hair. "When he told me of his plans, I grew all cold inside."

"You have a few days left to change his mind." Elizabeth ducked beneath the water to rinse off the soap.

"But do I wish to?" Jennet asked as soon as Elizabeth stood up again. She ignored her friend's soft curse of exasperation. "'Tis true that my heart and—aye, I must confess—my flesh crave the mon, but"—she tapped her forehead with one finger—"in here lurks naught but criticism of that craving. 'Tis in here that I am recalled to what he is—a mon whose living rests upon the death of others." She saw the cross look upon Elizabeth's face and quickly ducked beneath the water to avoid the lecture. But Elizabeth was waiting, undeterred, when she emerged again. "Ye mean to scold me."

"I mean to try and make you see some hard truths, child. Sir Gillard is a good man." She nodded toward Ranald, who was idly playing with Murdoc. "He protects you well. He gifts you with clothes."

"Stolen."

Ignoring that muttered interruption, Elizabeth pressed on. "He has ne'er raised a hand against you. He does not indulge in the wanton destruction and rapine the others do. Aye, and you cannot tell me he is not the first mon you have shared a blanket with."

"He is the *only* mon I have shared a blanket with."

"But you know in your heart you will find none better. 'Tis hard for me to argue this, for I cannot understand your hesitancy."

"Nay? What if the mon does keep me? What do I face in the years God grants me? Hacon will rush off to battle from time to time, leaving me to wait. Aye, to wait and pray that he returns alive and unmaimed. I shall spend my days praying that he can kill others with success, with no harm to himself. The thought is a chilling one. As he stains his hands with blood so shall I stain my soul, for I shall have asked God to spare him."

Before Elizabeth could respond, a cool, deep voice drawled, "Such an abundance of beauty."

Giving a squeak of surprise, Jennet quickly submerged her body. Out of the corner of her eye she saw her friend do the same, but Elizabeth looked more annoyed than embarrassed. Ranald stumbled to his feet, protesting Sir Niall's intrusion but hindered from fighting the man by Murdoc's presence.

"Sir Niall, I told you to leave," Ranald snapped. "The women must be allowed their privacy."

"Such concern o'er the modesty of a pair of camp fodder." Niall chuckled when Ranald's hand went to the short sword he wore strapped to his hip. "Do ye mean to fight me with your sword in one hand and the bairn in the other?"

"Ranald," Jennet said, knowing that Ranald, a mere man-at-arms, could not challenge a belted knight withought bringing a great deal of trouble upon himself. "There is no need to spill blood o'er petty words."

"He shouldnae be here. I asked him to halt."

Looking back at the women, Sir Niall drawled, "And deprive my eyes of such a lovely vision? I think not. In truth, this beauty begins to inspire me to seek the touch of cleanliness myself."

"If ye try to enter the water, sir, I shall have to stop you," warned Ranald.

"Such a valiant defense of Sir Gillard's refuse," murmured Sir Niall.

Suddenly, behind Sir Niall and Ranald, Jennet saw Hacon approach. He drew his sword even as he stepped up to the pair. The look on Hacon's face was one of hard, cold fury. Jennet feared there would be bloodshed this time, but there was no way she could stop it.

"First ye beg me to deprive you of your hand, Niall. Now ye offer me your eyes." Hacon pointed his sword at Niall.

The man paled as he turned to face Hacon. "I but came to fetch some water."

"In what?" Hacon looked the man over. "Ye carry naught that could hold it."

"Nay?" Niall backed away from Hacon, then began to edge around the man. "I had best return to camp for a vessel then."

"Ye had best cease to plague me, Niall. One day my anger may win out o'er my mercy." He watched the man hurry away, then turned to Jennet. "Ye are clean enough now."

"Aye," she answered.

The moment Hacon and Ranald turned their backs, Jennet hurried out of the water, Elizabeth quickly following her. With the soft rags she had brought she tried to sop up the water from her chemise and hair. Hacon stepped over to her and took the rag from her hands. She gasped and hastily looked around. Ranald, Murdoc, and Elizabeth had already left. For the first time in several days she and Hacon were alone.

"Elizabeth dresses quickly," she murmured.

"She had no need to dry her clothes first. Nor was she concerned about her wet hair." He gently rubbed her hair dry, then, after a moment of silence, said, "He wants you."

"Who does? Sir Niall?"

"Aye, Niall. He wants you—badly. The mon fair stinks of lust for you."

"Such foolishness." She gave a soft cry of surprise when Hacon grasped her arms and turned her to face him.

"Do ye doubt my desire? My hunger for you?" He slowly smoothed his hands up and down her bare arms.

"Nay. I have had proof of that."

"Then why do you think it foolishness that another mon may feel that same hunger? Niall feels it. I can see it in the way he watches you, in the way he tries to catch you when I am not near at hand—as he did this time. Aye, Niall hungers for you."

"He but tries to goad you," she protested, not sure she liked the idea of some other man lusting after her.

"Aye, but mayhaps 'tis only the reason why he makes no secret of his lust. He acts upon it because he doesnae like me, but his wanting you is real enough."

"Doesnae like you? Dinnae say ye have another mon set upon killing you." Even as she spoke the fear aloud she doubted it, for she had seen none of the lethal hatred in Niall that she did in Balreaves.

"Nay, he would ne'er go so far as to murder me. He doesnae ache for my blood upon his hands, only to pull my woman into his bed."

"*Your* woman, am I?" She was pleased by the hint of possessiveness in his tone yet nettled as well, not wishing to be seen as some mere object.

"Aye." He tugged her into his arms, holding her close as he slowly caressed her back. "*My* woman. Ye dinnae like that?"

"I dinnae wish to be seen as no more than some doe in season that two rutting bucks are squabbling o'er." It was not easy to maintain her sense of outrage when his touch stirred her passion completely.

"Oh, ye are more than that, my sweet Jennet. Aye, more than that." He kissed her mouth, then began to cover her face with soft, hot kisses. "Niall kens it. That is why he acts upon his lust for you." He nibbled the lobe of her right ear before tracing its shape with his tongue. "That is why he wants to put his mark upon you, mayhaps even take you from me."

It was very hard to keep her mind on the subject. Her interest in Niall's plans for her was ebbing swiftly as Hacon continued to touch her. She gasped softly with pleasure when he slid his hands beneath the hem of her chemise to caress her rump and the backs of her thighs. "Niall cannae take me without rousing some outcry," she managed to say. "'Twould be called theft, for I am seen as part of your plunder."

"Nay, no longer. I havenae treated you as some mere captive; I've allowed you the full freedom of my camp. Ye are seen as my woman. If ye went with Sir Niall willingly, 'twould be considered fair. I might weel draw condemnation if I sought to fight Niall o'er the matter." He began to unlace her chemise.

She placed her hands over his, halting him. "Nay, someone could come."

"Ranald and Dugald will see that no one breaches our privacy." He tugged her arms back around his neck and resumed unlacing her chemise. "I saw a chance for us to be alone and have made verra certain we dinnae lose it."

"Are ye certain 'tis safe for us to be alone, to be away from camp?" She closed her eyes and tilted her head back as he tongued the hollow of her throat.

"Aye, mayhaps safer, for we have the camp between us and Scotland's border." He eased the straps of her chemise from her slim shoulders. "The enemy we need watch for willnae come from Scotland. They would have to ride over Douglas's army to get to us. So, loving, we may gift ourselves with the time to savor the pleasure ye seek of me."

Jennet opened her mouth to say she sought a great deal more than pleasure, but just then he touched his lips to her breast and delight stole her words. She threaded her fingers through his thick hair to hold him close as he lathed and suck- led at her breasts. It had been too long since she had enjoyed the desire they shared. She gave herself over to it completely, allowing it to clear all thought from her mind and all painful confusion from her heart.

She trembled with the strength of her need as he slowly eased her chemise down her body, following its descent with soft, tantalizing kisses. The blind euphoria she was sinking into was briefly disrupted when he knelt before her, cupped her backside in his strong hands, and placed a kiss upon the soft tangle of curls that masked her womanhood. She stepped back, shocked over such intimacy, but he did not allow her to retreat. With but a few strokes of his tongue, he banished her concern. The delight he gifted her with soon had her brazenly welcoming his intimate kisses.

When she felt the culmination of her passion at hand, she cried out, expressing her need to have their bodies joined. He ignored her request, taking her to the heights with his searing tongue. She buckled slightly as her release shuddered through her but he held her in place. Even as her passion ebbed he was stirring it to life again. When her need was fully renewed, she barely whispered his name, then gasped with surprise and pure ecstasy as, still kneeling before her, he lowered her body onto his.

The new position caused her to hesitate for only an instant. Her need for him was too pressing. When she cried out, seized by her release, he was with her. He held her down, burying himself deep within her quickening body as his seed flowed into her. It was a while before she realized that the man she clung to was still dressed.

"Ye didnae take your clothes off," she murmured as he slightly eased their intimate embrace and settled himself more comfortably on the mossy ground.

"Weel, I freed what was needed."

"Clever mon." She began to feel a little embarrassed as the memory of what they had just done settled in her mind. "Is that allowed by the Church?" she asked in a somewhat meek voice, then grimaced as she felt his chest tremble with silent laughter beneath her cheek. "I but wished to ken how big a penance I may have to pay."

"I dinnae think 'twill be a verra big one. Then, too, ye could do as I do."

"Aye? And what is that?"

"Dinnae confess it. Keep it twixt ye and God. S'truth, I dinnae think the priests really care to hear about it." He set her aside and stood up. "Now, ye wait here. I will be back in but a few moments." After adjusting his attire, he strode off.

Jennet slipped her chemise back on. Shrugging, she tugged on the rest of her clothes, then sat down to wait for him. As she combed her hair with her fingers, she thought about the brief conversation she had had with Elizabeth, struggling yet again to set some firm, clear course for herself.

She envied Elizabeth's certainty. Then again, Elizabeth's path was much smoother than her own. Robert was a poor man who could choose any wife he pleased. All Elizabeth had to do was make certain she was the one he chose.

Hacon was not so free. He had responsibilities to his family and to the people who now gathered into a clan under his leadership. When Hacon chose a wife, he must consider far more than his own wants. He needed to look for alliances, a gain of power and protection, a fortune. She had none of those things to offer and never would. Although her bloodline was good, her birth of sufficient quality to suit a man of

Hacon's breeding, she had nothing else to give him. Making him want her as his mate was not enough. In truth, she could not help but wonder if it would be somewhat unfair to him. She knew the torment of wanting what one could not have, and she did not wish to inflict that torment on him.

Sitting down, she plucked viciously at the mossy carpet beneath her. There was the still-unanswered question of whether she could truly find happiness with a knight. Each time she decided that Hacon was not a bad man, she saw him return from battle, the blood of others upon his sword and armor.

She cursed. "Give it up, Jennet, ye great fool. There is no answer. Best ye sit and let the fates take you where they will."

"Do ye often talk to yourself?"

She jumped in surprise, then scowled at Hacon, who calmly sat down beside her. "Ye shouldnae creep about so," she admonished.

"I didnae realize I was," he murmured as he set their food out. "Does something trouble you?"

"Nay." She helped herself to some lamb and tried not to recall that it was stolen. "'Tis naught."

"I wondered if ye might be worried o'er seeing your kinsmen. Ye didnae seem as pleased about visiting them as I thought ye would be." He watched her closely as he began to eat.

"Mayhaps I dinnae truly wish to ken the truth about my father's fate. Sometimes 'tis best not kenning." She took a drink from his wineskin. "A shame ye werenae at Perth," she murmured, studying him surrepititiously. "Ye might have seen enough to either give me hope or take it away. 'Twould ease this uncertainty."

"Aye, but if I had been there, ye could weel blame me if your father was murdered."

"Nay, I ken the mon ye are weel enough to feel certain ye would ne'er take part in such a slaughter."

Hacon looked away, unable to hold her gaze. Here was the chance to confess his lie, but he lacked the courage. It was easy to speak of forgiveness when one did not believe there was anything to forgive. Would she feel so confident in her judgment of him if he admitted to being there? He dared not take that chance, not when the one they wondered about was her father. Before he confessed, he needed to know exactly what had befallen the man.

"Ye flatter me, lass," he murmured.

"And that is why ye cannae look at me?"

Regaining his composure, he turned to smile at her. "Aye. I am unused to such kind words."

"Ho, such accolades flow your way constantly."

"Ah, but ne'er from such a sweet, lovely mouth." He reached out to cup her chin in his hand.

Before she could declare that a lie, he kissed her. She knew he was trying to divert her, as he always did when she mentioned Perth. It worked. His slow, deep, inviting kisses soon had her thinking of far more pleasant matters. With a sigh which was a mixture of resignation and desire she went into his arms.

Hacon was halfway to his feet, his sword in his hand, before he realized it was only Dugald who had disturbed his sleep. After a quick check to be sure a slowly waking Jennet was modestly covered, he sat and glared at his cousin. He and Jennet had only just fallen asleep after their lengthy lovemaking. If he was going to be awake, Hacon did not want it to be because of some problem but to savor another taste of the passion he shared with Jennet. His annoyance was tempered by the look of worry on Dugald's face.

"This had best be verra important," Hacon muttered.

"Aye." Dugald grimaced. "Ye were to stand watch tonight?"

"Ye already ken that. I asked Lachlan Macintyre to stand in my place. He owed me." Hacon felt Jennet, who was now resting against his back and watching Dugald, grow tense.

"Weel, poor Lachlan has paid that debt in full."

"What do ye mean, Dugald? Dinnae dance about the truth."

"We found Laclan with his throat cut. He was murdered, set upon from behind."

"By the English?" Jennet asked, despite her strong suspicion otherwise.

"Nay, though there is no proof that it wasnae." Dugald ran a hand through his dark, unruly hair. "No other guard was killed or even approached. No attack was made. That doesnae make sense. If the English, even one of them, drew so near to camp unseen and slew one of our number so easily, 'tis certain more killing would have followed."

Hacon muttered a brief string of hearty curses, then hissed, "So, Lachlan took the blade meant for my throat."

"I cannae believe otherwise," Dugald agreed. "From what little could be read upon the soft ground, he was set upon from behind while his back was to our camp. Aye, as it should have been, for he had no cause to expect such an attack from anyone in the camp."

"Balreaves," Jennet whispered, instinctively slipping her arms about Hacon's waist and pressing closer to him.

Hacon patted her hands where they rested upon his bare stomach. "Aye, it must have been. Poor Lachlan. Weel, I will ask no other to take my place, to set his back to a murderer who seeks me out."

"We should return to camp." Jennet suddenly sensed danger lurking in every shadow.

"Nay, lass." Hacon shook his head. "I willnae cower amongst my men, risking their lives to shield mine. Nay, nor will I deprive myself of what few moments of pleasure I might steal."

"I could say," drawled Dugald, "that 'tisnae only yourself at risk in this spot, but I willnae."

After another bout of cursing, realizing he had forgotten for the moment the danger Jennet could face, Hacon grumbled, "Why be so diplomatic?"

"Because I dinnae think Balreaves will strike again. Not this night. Lachlan's murder had the whole camp alerted. Too alert for the sly killing Balreaves prefers. Aye, enjoy your time alone. 'Twill be your last for many a day."

"Until we are certain Balreaves isnae close at hand."

"Mayhaps. I would prefer the mon dead myself. Sleep weel," Dugald said, adding as he walked away, "but not *too* weel."

Sighing, Hacon laid down on his back and tugged Jennet into his arms. "Balreaves will pay for Lachlan's murder."

"How? Ye wait for proof, yet the mon is clever enough to give you none." Jennet huddled closer to Hacon, more afraid for him now than when he had marched off to battle, for his enemy had no intention of facing him squarely.

"My chance will come." He pressed a kiss to the top of her head. "Dinnae fret o'er it. Not tonight."

Jennet lifted her head to scowl at him. "And when should I, and ye, frct o'er it? When the mon's dagger rests in your back?"

"Now, lass . . ."

"Dinnae 'now, lass' me. Ye cannae ignore this."

"I willnae. Come the morrow I shall set my mind fully on the matter." He placed his hand against her cheek and brushed a kiss over her mouth. "Not now. I dinnae wish to lose one brief minute of this night. 'Tis ours."

She sighed, then gave herself over to the rich delight of his kisses. It was not very easy to banish her fear, but she knew Hacon's sweet loving would soon do just that. For once she would not argue. It could be their last night together for a long time. Or, if he left her behind in Liddesdale, it could be their last night together ever. That thought caused her to tighten her grip on him, adding desperation to her kiss.

As he nibbled her ear, he murmured, "Set aside your fears for now, loving."

"If that is your wish." She smoothed her hands down his side, pausing to lightly caress his taut, smooth hips.

"My command," he muttered in an absent tone as he traced the pulse in her throat with his tongue.

"Ah, a command. I recall another command ye made when we first lay together. Then again, mayhaps 'twas more of a request."

"Aye? What was that?" He turned his seductive attentions to her breasts.

"Not to touch ye here." She slowly curled her fingers around his erection. "Have ye changed your mind?"

"Aye."

She smiled faintly, for his voice was a mere rasp and he trembled as she caressed him. "Mayhaps it will help ye to forget Balreaves."

"Balreaves? Ne'er heard of the mon."

Jennet wished that was true, then shook aside the thought and concentrated on giving Hacon a night he would not soon forget.

# Chapter 11

As Hacon rode forward to speak to Douglas, Jennet, mounted on her pony, looked around her. Spread out through the scrub forest of pine was the army she had traveled with for so long. Last night, when they had stopped to camp and Hacon had confirmed that they would head for Liddesdale by midday, she had not given much thought to the army. She realized that, in some ways, she would miss it.

Their arms and armor glinted as a rare late summer sun touched upon them. With them marched the captives of war, who were forced to herd the stolen livestock. Women plodded along, walking away from their homes and families and into a life Jennet did not care to contemplate. She felt guilty, for she had done little to improve their lot, either through halting their abuse or setting them free. Then she shook the regret away. There was nothing she could do. She had to soothe her conscience with the knowledge that she had aided Mary and Elizabeth in a small way. Mary was now headed back to her family and Elizabeth was where she wished to be—with Robert.

Hearing Murdoc make his usual babble of greeting from his sling draped on her back, Jennet turned slightly in her saddle to see who approached her. Elizabeth stood there, one hand full of thistle blooms, the other ruffling Murdoc's thick curls. The woman looked so happy that Jennet could not help but smile at her.

"I shall warn you, Elizabeth," Jennet said. "Days as fine as these are rare indeed in this land."

Elizabeth laughed softly. "'Tis rare that the sun shines so warm and bright in England as well."

"So, ye are in Scotland proper now."

"Aye, and now there is no doubt that I shall be staying."

"Robert has asked to wed you?"

"He has."

"Oh, Elizabeth." Jennet reached out and briefly clasped her friend's hand. "I am so verra pleased for you."

"So am I." She exchanged a grin with Jennet. "'Twas a moment of great romance and emotion. We gazed into each other's eyes and my Robert said, 'Ye have stuck with me like a burr and ye mean to keep sticking, dinnae ye woman?' I said, 'Aye, I do.' He said, 'Weel then, we may as weel say them vows.' 'Done,' says I, 'as soon as I catch sight of a priest.'"

When Jennet started to laugh, Elizabeth joined in.

"Such levity," Hacon said as he walked over. In deference to the heat, he wore no armor, simply a dark blue overtunic and matching hose. "May I share in the jest?"

"'Tis no jest, Sir Gillard," Elizabeth said.

"Nay." Jennet smiled at Hacon. "Elizabeth and Robert are to be wed. We but shared a moment of happy laughter." She leaned toward Hacon. "Robert isnae truly skilled in the use of sweet words. Now, dinnae think we make jest of the mon." She felt a need to clarify the reason for the laughter, knowing how easily it could be misunderstood. "'Tis but amusing that all Elizabeth has waited for so long came about so plainly and easily."

"Ah, aye." Hacon briefly clasped Elizabeth's hand. "Robert chose weel."

"Thank you most kindly, Sir Gillard." Elizabeth blushed faintly.

"And remember, Robert might be blunt and a wee bit dour, but he is also honest and steadfast."

"Oh, aye sir. I know well the worth of plain, blunt truth o'er the emptiness of sweet, pretty lies."

"Weel, tell your mon we head toward Liddesdale right after our noon respite." Hacon helped Jennet down from her pony, then lifted Murdoc from his sling.

Frowning slightly in confusion, Jennet asked Elizabeth, "Robert joins Hacon's men?"

"Aye, that was my other news. He and his brother Donald have taken up with Sir Hacon. I best hurry back to my man. We can talk later." Elizabeth strode away.

As Hacon led her to a clear, dry spot beneath a scraggly pine, Jennet regarded him in surprise. "Robert is a freedmon who can still choose to whom he will declare loyalty?" Sitting down, she took Murdoc into her arms.

Hacon nodded as he sat beside her. "Free and without landed kinsmen or a liege lord. He and young Donald asked if they might pledge themselves to my family. I agreed. Once they are settled at Dubheilrig, I believe the rest of their family will join them. New blood and a few more skillfully wielded swords will be welcome."

She nodded, biting back the question—Would *I* be welcome? At least now she would know where Elizabeth was. Her new friend would not be completely lost to her.

That thought did not lift her spirits as much as she would have liked, however. Her future was still unknown, even as to what *she* wished it to be. That some of the uncertainty was of her own making did not help her feel any better.

When Murdoc stumbled off her lap to practice his awkward walk, she half smiled. There was something good she would be left with no matter how things turned out between her and Hacon. She would have Murdoc. There was no doubt in her mind that she would be allowed to keep the child. As she quickly stopped Murdoc from munching on a pinecone, she decided it was time to hold in her mind all her blessings. Such as the fact that I am still alive, she thought, and inwardly sighed.

"Ye are looking very woeful, lass," Hacon murmured, slipping his arm about her shoulders and tugging her close.

"I am weary, 'tis all." She relaxed against him.

"Aye, we move fast and o'er hard ground. We seek to put the defense of rough land twixt us and the English."

"I ken it. They could yet cease their bickering, garner their courage, and set after us." She smiled faintly as she watched Murdoc toddle unsteadily over to some of Hacon's men, who lay sprawled lazily beneath a large tree. "The lad will soon be running about. His skill increases daily. 'Tis strange indeed, but he appears to thrive in this hard life."

"He will make a fine warrior."

"Mayhaps," she drawled, "he will make a fine priest."

She almost laughed at Hacon's look of utter dismay.

"Nay, 'twould be a sin to keep such a fine lad from breeding more of his ilk," he said.

A moment later men began to move, activity sweeping through their numbers from the front on back. Silently she and Hacon stood up and brushed themselves off. She did not look forward to three or four more days of travel. It would be a hard trek through the border uplands, through forests teeming with boar, wildcats, and wolves, with the twin dangers of deadly thieves or some vengeful English force. As Hacon put Murdoc back inside the sling on her back, she decided that going to her kinsmen might not be such a bad idea after all. At least there she would get some rest from the constant travel and the equally constant danger.

"Come, loving," Hacon murmured as he helped her onto her pony. "Soon we may rest for more than a few hours."

She forced a smile. "That is something to look forward to."

He gave her a brief kiss and strode off toward his own

mount. As Jennet waited for Ranald to join her, she watched the men start on their way. Instead of numbering in the thousands, they would now be a small party of only twenty or so. It would feel strange to travel without so many men about, but she knew there were some things she would not miss. She was weary of the mud, the dust, and the fighting.

"Ready?" Ranald's soft question brought her out of her reverie.

"Aye." As he nudged his horse forward, she gently kicked her pony into motion.

"Soon we will reach your village in Liddesdale and ye will ken your father's fate," Ranald said.

"Aye." She felt a pinch of guilt, for her father had not entered her thoughts for quite some time. "Soon I will ken it all," she murmured, and turned her attention to guiding her pony among the trees.


"Ahead lies your village, Jennet."

Shifting slightly in the saddle, she turned her gaze from the cluster of thatch-roofed cottages to look up at Hacon, who watched her closely from his mount. Knowing he expected it, she forced a smile.

"My aunt and uncle's cottage is the farthest, that one with the pair of twisted rowan trees by the door." Thinking of her aunt, Jennet felt her smile grow more honest. "She believes that since a branch hung o'er the door will protect against demons and witches, then a whole tree will be even more of a guard. 'Tis why another grows near the cowshed. She has been seen protecting her trees from raiders and others, sword in hand. Even a dog risks his life if he eyes one of those trees with interest." She laughed along with Hacon.

"'Tis verra quiet," said Ranald a moment later. "Are the villagers still there?"

"They may have seen us and run away to hide." Observing closely, Jennet realized Ranald was right. It looked empty.

"They *did* see us," Hacon said. "A few leagues back they kenned our approach. I espied their sentry in the woods, even caught sight of the laddie sent to warn the village. 'Tis why I slowed our pace. I wanted to ease their fear of attack. I wished no fight to start with your kinsmen." He looked at Ranald. "Tell the men to keep their swords sheathed and to make no threatening gestures." When Ranald left to do so, Hacon turned to Jennet. "Ye and I shall lead. Mayhaps one of the people will recognize you and this tense visit will grow more friendly."

Nodding, she turned her pony toward the village, glancing at the encircling common grazing grounds and idly noting that a protective wall was half constructed around it. Soon the village would be walled in as so many others were. She prayed the defense was born of caution and not the result of some tragedy. None of the cottages appeared to be damaged, not even the poorer carthen-walled ones. As the silence of the village surrounded her, her concern for her kinsmen grew. It was hard to keep her pace slow, not to race to her aunt's home. Then, suddenly, the priest stepped out of the tiny stone church they neared, two burly, armed men flanking him.

Hacon pulled his horse to a stop beside the common well directly in the center of the village, and she did the same. As the men approached, she studied them closely, searching their faces for familiar features. It was not until they stopped in front of her that she believed she recognized one.

"Malcolm?" she asked, causing the man on the priest's right to look her way. "Lame John's son?"

"Aye." He stepped closer, frowning up at her, then his eyes widened. "Wee Jennet? 'Tis you, Moira's bairn?"

"The verra same. Where is everyone?"

"Where they will stay until we are verra certain this braw knight is no foe." Malcolm looked at Hacon.

"No foe," Hacon murmured and held out his hand. "Sir Hacon Gillard of Dubheilrig." He shook each man's hand and dismounted. "We brought Jennet here to visit her kinsmen and mayhaps gain some word of her father's fate."

"That rogue Artair," grumbled Malcolm. "He was here for the planting time but left ere we could force him to help."

"He is alive?" Jennet felt weak with a mixture of relief and hope.

"Aye, lass. Didnae ye ken it?" When she shook her head, Malcolm smiled, revealing badly chipped teeth. "Oh, aye, the mon lives, though old Alaistair tried to end his wicked life ere he left. Old Alaistair has himself a fair young lass for a wife." He chuckled when Jennet grimaced. "Caught your father rolling about with her in the heather. Chased your father into your aunt's house. Your father was naked as the day he was born as he ran through the village at a fair pace, old Alaistair screaming vengeance right behind him all the way." Malcolm laughed. "Your aunt cursed him all the while she kept old Alaistair from using the sword on the rogue." He leaned toward Jennet and winked. "We dinnae mention it much now. Old Alaistair's wee wife is with bairn and the old fool struts about fair proud of himself, certain the bairn is his."

"Oh." Jennet was torn between amusement and annoyance. "Oh dear."

"Your father confessed his sinful ways, my child," the priest said, his round face solemn. "He sought and gained absolution."

Jennet opened her mouth to give her succinct opinion of her father's piety, then caught the grins on the men's faces. She decided it was an opinion that did not need saying. The priest was young. He would learn.

"Come," the priest said, smiling at Hacon. "'Tis evident ye have come as friend, not foe. Marcus," he said to the man on his left. "Go tell our people that all is weel." He looked at Hacon. "And ye may tell your men they are welcome to take their ease."

Malcolm helped Jennet down from her pony. "And that they will be treated as our own," he said.

"Which means," Jennet murmured as Hacon reached her side, "ye need not keep too close a watch on your goods." She smiled when Malcolm laughed, then asked him, "How are my aunt and uncle?"

"Your aunt is setting firm in her cottage, sword in hand, waiting to cut down any mon fool enough to threaten her home or her trees. Go right down there. She will ken who ye are ere ye reach her gate. Your uncle took the children into hiding, but he should join you soon."

Whatever nervousness Jennet felt faded the moment she reached her aunt's gate. Sorcha Armstrong raced out of her stone cottage to heartily embrace Jennet even before she could call out a greeting. The next hour was a confusing round of introductions as Sorcha's husband arrived with their large brood of children, and Hacon and his men were settled throughout the village. By the time a meal was set out, Jennet was exhausted. She let Hacon do most of the talking until she gained the strength to ask about her father again.

"My father is alive, so Malcolm tells me." Jennet smiled faintly when Sorcha rolled her hazel eyes and grimaced.

"Aye, though how that mon escapes killing, I dinnae ken. A sweet-talking rascal who is e'er in trouble, he is."

"Now, loving," murmured Sorcha's husband, Alain, "the lass seeks news."

"Aye, and Malcolm gave her an earful, no doubt of it."

"He did," Jennet agreed. "Old Alaistair's wife. I but asked if Father was alive. 'Tis clear he is as alive as he ever was."

"Verra alive. I ken ye have heard naught since ye were sent from Perth. Artair has come here every year since then, hoping to find that ye have returned to us. And a fair harvest of red-haired bairns is our gain."

"Sorcha!" Alain scolded, then placed his large, work-worn

hand over Jennet's. "He means no disrespect to your mother's—my sister's—memory, lass. I hope ye ken that."

"I do, uncle. I also ken that the mon deserves a scolding. Aunt is right to cluck her tongue o'er his ways." She grinned. "The mon is shameless." She briefly shared a laugh with the others. "But—he *is* weel?"

"Verra weel," answered Sorcha. "As all the village can attest to, having seen his wares weel displayed the day old Alaistair set after him. But, dinnae fear, he will return to look for you again. 'Twill warm his feckless heart to find you here."

"She will be at Dubheilrig," said Hacon, pushing aside his empty trencher and taking a long drink of wine from his wooden goblet. "We but stopped here so she might learn of her father."

Jennet stared at him, not sure how she felt about that blunt announcement. "Ah, we did, did we?"

"Aye, we did. After a visit and a rest, *we*—ye and I—travel on to Dubheilrig."

Before Jennet could say another word, Sorcha gave Alain a sharp look and he stood up. With a calm but firm invitation to join him in a walk, he neatly cleared the room of all but Sorcha and herself. Hacon even took Murdoc with him. Although Hacon spoke of seeing that his men were settled, Jennet recognized it as a retreat from the talk Sorcha so clearly intended to have. She turned to say as much to her aunt and frowned. Sorcha was staring at her with intense curiosity, idly twirling one thick strand of her golden brown hair on one finger. Jennet suddenly wished she had left with the others. She cast about for some subject of conversation with which to divert her aunt.

"Ye should have seen the house in which we quartered in Berwick," she began, and pointed at her aunt's central hearth, where the smoke curled up to slowly creep out the small venting hole in the thatched roof. "It didnae have a center hearth but one set against the wall. The smoke didnae go through a wee hole in the roof but through a stone—"

"Chimney. Aye, lass," Sorcha drawled. "I ken the things. Your uncle has promised to build me the like. Ye willnae divert me with that. Tell me how ye came to be with this fine, braw knight."

Sighing with resignation, Jennet gave her aunt a succinct account of all that had happened since she and her father had parted in Perth. Once finished, she saw only a touch of sympathy in her aunt's pretty round face, no hint of condemnation or anger. She also saw that the talking-to she had tried to avoid was still to come.

"So ye and that fair-haired lad have been lovers since Berwick." Sorcha collected up the wooden trenchers, spoons, and goblets. "Nay, sit," she ordered Jennet who had risen to help. "Pour us each some wine. We are going to talk."

"Oh, how nice," Jennet muttered as she refilled their goblets.

Sorcha sat down after tossing the dinnerware into a large cauldron of water. "Why did ye act so surprised when your mon said ye are to stay with him?"

"He ne'er told me that I was to stay with him." Jennet admitted to herself that she was highly annoyed about that.

"But he has kept you with him since Berwick. 'Tis clear he set ye in his bed then and means to keep ye there."

"Ah, weel, aunt, he didnae exactly set me in his bed at Berwick."

"Ye were his captive. Are ye saying he didnae take his pleasure of you right away?"

Blushing faintly, Jennet explained how and when she and Hacon had become lovers. She was not sure she liked the way Sorcha studied her so intently. Jennet suspected her aunt thought much like Elizabeth did.

"Weel, that news will please your uncle."

"Uncle will be happy that his niece was seduced?"

"Ye could have been taken the moment Hacon set hands upon you and weel ye ken it. Ye were spoils of war."

"I still am, it would seem. He hasnae wed me, has he, nor spoken of doing so."

"Nay, lass, ye mean more to him than plunder and I think ye ken it. That mon doesnae treat you as naught but some bed warmer. And what of marrying him? If he asks, what would you say?"

Jennet was unable to answer and looked away. "Weel, he hasnae asked, so what does it matter?"

Sorcha grasped Jennet's chin and made her face her squarely. "'Tis a simple question requiring but an aye or a nay. Why do ye hesitate? And if ye cannae answer, why did ye let him seduce you?"

"Because he makes me feel verra good," Jennet grumbled.

"Wheesht, any mon a wee bit fair of face, with a hint of skill and a pintle that works as it should, could do that lass."

"Aunt Sorcha!" Jennet was shocked by such blunt talk.

"'Tis true, and weel ye ken it. And 'tisnae enough to make your mother's daughter bed down with a mon."

"Do ye forget? I am my father's daughter too."

"Who could forget when those eyes and that beautiful skin bespeak it with each look? Yet, 'tis Moira's spirit ye hold in your heart. As she would, ye would ne'er let a mon bed you unless ye had some feelings for him. So, I ask ye again—why do ye hesitate?"

"He is a knight."

"Aye, and a good one—honorable and skilled, from what I can see."

"Can ye not see the rest? He is a mon who gains from the killing of others. War is his way of life."

"'Tis the way of life of nearly every mon, lass, and child in Scotland. Since Scotland decided to shake off the cursed English, we have been at war. Before that, we fought the English for other reasons, or the Norsemen. Aye, and if there is ever a lack of enemy from without, we turn upon each other. Do ye wait for peace in the land?"

Stung by the scorn in her aunt's voice, Jennet leapt to her feet. "And what is wrong with wishing for a little peace?"

"Not a thing. But one cannae stop living while doing so." She watched Jennet begin to pace the large main hall that made up nearly the whole lower floor of her home. "Do ye condemn the mon for his skill at arms?"

Stopping at the edge of the center hearth, Jennet folded her arms beneath her bosom and stared into the flames. "I cannae say I condemn him for it, but I cannae like it. I have lived my whole life amidst war and bloodshed."

Turning on the bench so that she faced Jennet, Sorcha shook her head. "So have we all. Is he cruel? Does he beat you? Mayhaps he turns mad in battle like some Norsemon, slaying all in his path. Is that it?"

"Nay, none of those. He battles soldiers, armed men only. While he cannae stop the murder of innocents or the wanton destruction, he makes no secret of his disapproval and ne'er takes a part in it. Neither do his men." She frowned, realizing that her aunt was cleverly prompting her to speak of all that was good about Hacon. "He lied to me," she said. "I asked him if he had been at Perth the day Bruce took it from the English and he said nay. 'Twas a lie."

"Ah, weel, if he took a part in the blackhearted murders done there—"

"Nay, he didnae. I have no call to think the mon who told me all this was lying either. He told me Hacon refused to take part in the executions the Bruce called for. Hacon and his men left to camp outside the city."

"And would ye have let the mon explain himself? Once he said he was at Perth, the place ye thought your father was murdered, would ye have let him tell you any more than that?" Sorcha asked softly. "Aye, or believed it if he did tell you?" When Jennet flushed slightly, Sorcha nodded. "Ye might weel have condemned him then and there. That is why he lied. He dared not chance it. Has he told you other lies?"

"Nay, I think not," Jennet mumbled. "I cannae seem to make anyone understand how I feel."

Sorcha walked over to her and hugged her. "I understand, but I fear ye arenae being too sensible, lass. I doubt ye could ever find a mon who would ne'er fight. Even the men of God peopling the abbeys and churches ken weel how to wield a sword. 'Tis the way of the world, and one wee pretty lass cannae change it."

Stepping back a little, Sorcha held Jennet by the shoulders and regarded her sternly. "Ye have set your heart against something and have become a wee bit blind. Try to look at the good in the mon, not only what ye dinnae like. He was born to be either a knight or a priest. A mon of his blood has little choice. As a priest," she drawled, "he wouldnae be making ye feel good, would he?"

Blushing, Jennet shook her head. "I suppose he is a good mon."

"Ye ken weel that he is." Sorcha gave her a little shake. "Look to that, lass. I have but just met the mon, but I ken the good outweighs all else. Ye will ne'er find a mon who is perfect. Here is one who is good, strong, and able to protect you and yours. Ye would be the greatest fool alive if ye didnae try to keep him."

"But to live kenning that each time he picks up his sword he could die? To ken that his life is bought by the blood of others? I am not sure I could bear such a life even if he offered it to me."

"Ye can. We all do. Your uncle is no knight, yet I am oft left here to worry about him. And as for 'the blood of others'—wheesht, lassie, do ye think the ones he faces dinnae mean to hold their lives or gain by his death? 'Tis all equal," she added in a soft voice when Jennet just stared at her, wide-eyed. "As ye say, he faces only those who are armed and ready to fight him. They are there for the same reason he is. Many are there, no doubt, for far less noble reasons."

"I ne'er thought on it that way," Jennet whispered.

"Weel, think on it now. Come along. We must find a place for ye and your braw knight to bed down."

"Aunt," she cried, a little shocked. "Hacon and I arenae wed."

"Aye, and I will probably do a penance for letting you share a bed, but 'tis foolish to part you now. And"—she winked at Jennet—"together beneath a blanket is the best place to get the mon to start talking of marriage. Besides, I greatly doubt that mon would let me put ye in separate beds," she added, laughing softly.

"'Tis glad I am your aunt didnae set herself against me about this," Hacon murmured as he slipped into bed that night and tugged Jennet into his arms. "In truth, I feared how your kinsmen would respond to your place beside me."

"My kinsmen arenae as proper as mayhaps they should be." She reached across him to make sure the blanket obscuring their small sleeping alcove was fully closed. "Did Murdoc settle in the loft without a fuss?"

"Weel enough. Having other children about has made him a wee bit excited, but your two girl cousins said he would be all right. He will be happy at Dubhielrig, for there are many children there." He pressed a kiss to her forehead. "So will you."

"I will, will I?" She was unable to see him clearly in the dark but knew he was studying her. "Ye might have told me sooner that I would be going with you."

"Ah, I see." He inwardly breathed a sigh of relief, realizing her reaction earlier had been one of surprise, undoubtedly tempered by some annoyance. "I thought ye already kenned it."

"Mayhaps, in future, ye will make certain I ken your plans for me ere ye set them in motion."

"Fair enough." He nuzzled his face against her neck. "Do ye ken my plans for you now?"

She hooked her leg over his, pressed close to him, and moved against him in open invitation. "I believe they may be similar to mine for you."

A soft laugh escaped her when he groaned. Slipping her arms about his neck, she kissed him. Her aunt was right, she decided with sudden conviction. She would be the greatest fool alive if she did not try to keep him.

# Chapter 12

"Hacon! Hacon!"

The welcoming cry was repeated again and again as they rode through the gates of the small walled village and down the wide cottage-lined street that led to the largest, finest house in the village. Jennet could see that Sir Hacon Gillard was well loved by those who gathered beneath his family's banner. Her aunt was proven right again. The good in Hacon far outweighed the bad. A man who ruled through brutality, cruelty, or dishonor would not receive such a warm, heartfelt greeting from his people. Sorcha had been wise to say that this was what Jennet had to look at if she was really to know Hacon.

It was too bad, Jennet mused as the women hurried to meet the men, that not everyone would find joy in the men's homecoming. Several women began to weep openly upon learning that the men they sought would never return. Glancing to where Elizabeth rode with Robert and his brother Donald, Jennet hoped her friend would not be made to suffer simply because she was English. Grief could too easily turn to hatred, a hatred that might be unfairly aimed at Elizabeth. Jennet promised herself she would keep a watch out for her friend.

"Dinnae worry about her," Hacon said, drawing Jennet's attention his way. "Robert and all the men she aided when they were wounded will see that she suffers no harm—by word or deed."

"Of course." Jennet smiled faintly. "'Tis just that Eizabeth is so happy, I didnae wish to see that diminished."

"Aye, ne'er saw a woman grab hold of a priest as swiftly as she did. We had barely dismounted in your village when she had hold of that holy mon. 'Twas as if she feared old Robert would change his mind." He chuckled along with Jennet, then suddenly tensed, his gaze fixed upon the couple walking toward them.

Jennet followed his gaze. It had to be his parents. The tall man's limp gave her one reason the son had gone to war and not the father. The closer they drew, the less she doubted that this was Hacon's father and mother who approached. Hacon's bearing and stature came from his father, but his fair hair was clearly a gift from his mother. Jennet's nervousness increased when Hacon dismounted and embraced the woman, then the man, leaving her sitting on her pony with an active Murdoc squirming in the sling on her back. Even though she told herself not to be a fool, Jennet felt as if she stood out as clearly as a wart on the end of a nose.

"M'lord." The woman smiled faintly, her blue eyes alight with laughter as she curtsied before her son. "Welcome home."

"M'lord?" Hacon laughed and, clasping his mother's hands, urged her to rise. "What jest is this?"

"No jest, my son." The man clapped Hacon on the back. "News came but a few days ago. Word was sent here, for no one was certain where you were. I accepted the honors in your name. Duhbeilrig, and all its land are again in the hands of a Gillard—you. Aye, and with it comes the title of baron. Dahheilrig is now a barony. Our fortune is secured."

"But surely the title would go to you, Father."

"Nay. When I let ye ride out to fight for the Bruce in my stead, I sent word to our king. I told him that any rewards, any honors or titles or lands won by you, must go to you. It pleases me beyond saying that my wishes were heeded. With this leg"—he lightly slapped his hand against his stiff right thigh—"and near all strength gone from my sword arm, I cannae take the lead. Since I must press you to do all the hard and dangerous work in my stead, then 'tis right ye gain all the honors." He smiled at Hacon. "I am proud of you." When Hacon whooped with joy and embraced him, the man laughed.

"As we all are." The woman kissed Hacon's cheek as he exuberantly hugged her.

"At last, masters of our own lands again." Hacon turned to those of his men who still lingered nearby. "Dubheilrig belongs to the Gillards again!" he announced, and grinned as they cheered.

When the noise eased, the woman touched Hacon's arm to draw his attention to Jennet. "Is this a friend?"

"Ah, Jennet." Hacon quickly turned to help her down from her pony, standing her between him and his curious parents. "Jennet, may I present to you my parents, Lady Serilda and Sir Lucais Gillard. Mother, Father, this is Jennet Graeme, daughter of Artair Graeme and Moira Armstrong. We, er, met at Berwick."

Jennet curtsied, watching how Hacon's mother's eyes narrowed. It took all her effort to subdue a blush. Mistress Gillard knew that Jennet was no mere acquaintance but plunder taken in battle. Jennet felt the sting of shame and fought to push it aside. The elder Gillards were all that was courteous. Until they treated her otherwise, Jennet knew she should not assume that they condemned her out of hand.

"And the bairn?" Hacon's mother glanced around Jennet to Murdoc. "Ye, er, met him as weel?"

"Ah, young Murdoc." As Hacon released the child from his

sling, he told his mother how Ranald had saved the child's life. "The laddie appears to thrive no matter how hard the life." Hacon settled the boy on his hip.

"Oh, your sister Katherine will be so proud of her son," Serilda exclaimed, smiling broadly at Ranald and ruffling Murdoc's thick curls.

"Where is my sister?" Hacon looked around, seeing that Ranald still stood with them.

Moving to slip her arm through Ranald's, Serilda kissed her grandson's cheek and shrugged. "Katherine feared to find that her son was one of those who would never see Dubheilrig again. She waits at home." She smiled a little sadly at Ranald. "She fears to lose you as she lost your father. It took all her courage to let you leave and join Hacon."

"I ken it." He kissed his grandmother's smooth cheek. "I will go now and soothe her fears."

As soon as Ranald started away, Serilda looked at Hacon and Jennet. "'Tis time we too made our way home."

Jennet took Murdoc from Hacon, allowing him to pick up the reins of their mounts. She walked a little behind him, his parents, and Dugald as well, who joined in the retelling of their adventures. Fight the feeling though she did, she began to feel lost, uncertain. She realized she should have given more thought as to how Hacon's family would see her. To them she was only a mistress, a bed warmer collected on a raid. They were courteous, but she knew that courtesy was not the same as acceptance.

They entered a large stone house with a slate roof. There was a two-story great hall encircled by heavy wooden doors which led to more private rooms. A curving stone stairway led to a railed walkway halfway up the thick stone walls of the great hall. More sturdy doors lined it, revealing that there were more private rooms on the upper floor.

Despite Hacon's talk of loss, Jennet could see that his family was still one of some wealth. There were fine tapestries on the walls, pewter jugs upon the tables, and large chairs mixed in with the more common benches. Each sign of wealth made her more painfully aware of her own poverty.

Hacon ushered her up the narrow stairs. As they made their way along the open hallway, Jennet glanced down into the great hall below. Lady Serilda was busily instructing her servants. It was clear that a celebratory feast was being planned.

Jennet frowned as Hacon opened a large, thick door banded with wide straps of iron. He nudged her inside the room and she inwardly sighed. His chambers had tapestries upon the walls, as well, thick sheepskin rugs upon the floors, and a huge, high bed, the headboard and posts elaborately carved. All more evidence that the Gillards had once been rich. Now that Hacon had regained all that they had lost, they were rich again.

Once settled with Hacon in his quarters, Jennet used the excuse of weariness and the need to tend Murdoc to remain there for a while. She watched Hacon wash, then hurry away to rejoin his family. Sighing, she sat down on the bed and watched Murdoc playing contentedly at her feet. Coming to Dubheilrig had been a mistake. She did not have the stomach to lodge in a man's family home as his mistress. Even if Hacon offered to make her his wife, she doubted his family would approve. He could do a great deal better than the penniless, landless daughter of a thief and a rogue. Her problem now was how to get back to her kinsmen. She had a strong feeling that Hacon would not be very cooperative.

"A verra quiet, modest lass."

Hacon looked at his mother across the vast table, startled from his thoughts by her remark. He had not been paying much attention to the talk swirling around him, despite the fact that it was a feast held to celebrate his return and success. Jennet—or, more exactly, the strange dark mood she had fallen into just before she had excused herself and retired to their chambers—filled his thoughts. It was clear from her words that his mother had misread that mood. A quick glance down the table at Ranald and Dugald told him they were curious to hear his reply. His sister Katherine watched him closely as well, but Hacon was not sure he trusted her interest in Jennet.

"I willnae say she isnae modest," Hacon answered. "But Jennet was, weel, not at her best today."

"Do ye think she is sick, uncle?" Ranald asked, briefly casting a worried glance toward the upper floor. "She didnae stay to table verra long and ate little."

"Troubled more like, though I cannae understand why."

Serilda nodded, smiling faintly. "I understand, but not kenning the lass, I dare not judge. Mayhaps, son, 'tis but fear and shyness. Ye have dragged the lass into a place filled with strangers."

"True, yet I wouldnae have thought Jennet prey to shyness." He told his mother how Jennet had come to be with him and briefly touched on the time between then and now. "Does that sound like a quiet, shy lass to you?" He frowned, suddenly realizing that both his father and his mother were staring at him in shock. "Why do ye look at me like that?"

"Ye dragged the lass from a nunnery?" Serilda's voice trembled with anger and disgust.

"Nay," he cried, then grimaced. "Weel, aye, but she wasnae a nun, nor planning to be one. I went to the nunnery hoping to stop Douglas's men from defiling it. That was not to be. Then I found Jennet." He shrugged and gave his mother a sheepish look. "I had to have her. And," he hastily added in his own defense, "to have left her there would have meant leaving her to Douglas's men."

"Aye, loving," Lucais murmured to his wife. "And that would have been a sad fate for the girl."

"I ken it." Serilda eyed her son closely as she sipped her

wine. "And ye dragged her along on a raid into England to save her from Douglas's men as weel, did ye?"

"In part, aye," Hacon agreed.

"And Douglas's men were a threat in her village too, were they? 'Tis why ye dragged her here, is it?"

Giving his mother a cross look, Hacon answered. "Nay, she is mine,"

"Ah, so ye are wed then."

"Nay."

"Not wed?" Hacon's sister Katherine regarded him with angry disgust. "Do ye mean ye have dragged your . . . your . . ."

"I should choose my words carefully, sister," Hacon said, his low voice heavy with unspoken warning.

"Weel, 'tisnae a proper way to act before those younger than you." She nodded toward Ranald. "He sees enough sin without his own uncle wallowing in it before his verra eyes."

"Oh, do be quiet, Katherine," Serilda ordered, then looked at Hacon. "So, ye havenae wed the girl. There is something wrong with her, or mayhaps she is highly unsuitable?"

"Neither. Poor but wellborn." He looked at his father. "I dinnae suppose ye can get her to leave it be?"

"Nay." Lucais smiled faintly. "I dinnae feel inclined to try either."

"Have your way then, Mother, but might we do it more privately?"

"Of course." She stood up. "Since we are all done with eating, we may retire to the solar with some wine." She started across the hall, pausing before a door at the far end to look over her shoulder. "Hacon? Lucais?" Without waiting for a reply, she went through the door.

Muttering to himself and ignoring his family's knowing grins, Hacon stood up. As his father grabbed a large jug of wine, Hacon gathered up three goblets. Together they followed Serilda into the solar.

The heavy shutters of the solar's three large windows were

closed, but the warmth of the day still lingered, and there were plenty of candles to light the room. Hacon smiled faintly when he espied his mother's tapestry frame in its usual place by the center window. He helped his father carry one of the chairs and a small table over to make a close seating arrangement. Serilda took her place on the padded window seat and signaled Lucais to sit next to her, leaving the chair facing them for Hacon.

Once the men were settled and the wine was served, Serilda asked Hacon, "Weel? Why havenae ye wed the girl?"

He leaned forward in his seat. "It may help if I tell you a few things about Jennet." As succinctly as possible he explained what he knew about her life and her opinion of knights. "She loathes what I am. How can I wed her?" He relaxed in the heavy, elaborately carved chair, certain that that would settle the matter.

"By saying the vows," his mother said, startling him. "I think, mayhaps, ye misjudge the girl."

"Ye havenae heard her."

"True, but what I see tells me a great deal. Hacon, the girl was a virgin of good birth. She became your leman. Would such a lass do so for a mon she loathed? She had the chance to stay with her own kinsmen, yet she left them to come here. Was that the way of a lass who hates you?"

Hacon frowned, rubbing his chin. "Nay, yet all she says . . ."

"Ye take too much to heart," Serilda finished. "I too spoke out against such things, yet I wed your father. No woman with any feeling can truly like her mon taking up his sword. What ye must do is heed her actions, not her words. Her words might condemn and scold, but all she has done has said she wants you. And ye want her. I saw it in the way ye looked at her as ye helped her down from the pony. Armor yourself against her words. They will soften in time." She smiled at Lucais. "Mine did, did they not, husband?"

"Aye, dearling, though many a day passed when I thought

ye all but hated me." He smiled at Hacon. "Sweet words came slowly to your mother, but 'twas worth the wait." His gray eyes soft with affection, he added, "And she is right to say that ye must look to how Jennet acts, not what she says. Therein lies the truth."

"Once ye are wed, I believe this dark mood of hers will fade," Serilda added.

"Aye, Mother? Why should that be?"

Serilda rolled her eyes. "Ye have raised a dim-witted son, Lucais."

"Mother." Hacon assumed an excessively mournful expression. "Ye and Jennet will be kindred souls when she shakes free of her odd humor."

"Ah, she calls you dim-witted too, does she?"

"She oft says I have been hit offside the head one too many times." He smiled crookedly as his mother laughed. "Now, tell me why ye think my wedding the lass will do aught to lighten her somber air."

"Because 'tis the lack of sanctioned marriage that troubles her. She was a wellborn virgin, not the sort of lass to welcome being made a mistress. Oh, aye, it may have been no great worry whilst ye were with the army. Nay, not even when ye stopped at her kinsmen's. But here? Amongst your kin? I wouldnae be surprised if she feels the bite of shame.

Hacon cursed. "Aye, I gave little thought to that, but ye may be right. I had hoped to clear away a few troubles between us first, but mayhaps 'twould be best to make her my wife. That would be one trouble set aside right away, even if it is one I didnae ken was there."

He stood and kissed his mother's cheek. "I believe I will seek my bed. As soon as I have gathered courage to ask Jennet to wed with me, I will tell you." He moved toward the door, paused, then looked back at his parents. "There is one thing ye should ken. 'Tis Jennet's father."

"Aye?" Serilda frowned when Hacon hesitated to reply. "Do ye think he will object to a marriage?"

"Nay. I but meant to warn you that he may weel appear at Duhheilrig. It could be in a year or as soon as a fortnight. His kinsmen by marriage have undoubtedly sent word that Jennet is alive and where she is. I say 'warn' because from all I have heard the mon is a rogue. A charming one, but a rogue nonetheless. Even Jennet, who loves the mon, freely calls him a thief, and he has an eye for the wenches. I but thought a warning would be wisest."

Lucais smiled. "Aye, but have no fear. Our lineage isnae free of that sort. We will manage him easily."

"Quite easily," agreed Serilda. "Now off to your bed. We can talk more on the morrow."


After quietly entering his quarters and silently securing the heavy wooden door behind him, Hacon looked toward the bed. He could see only the top of Jennet's head above the bed-covers. Instinct told him she feigned sleep. No longer bothering to be silent, he moved to disrobe and wash up. Murdoc, he noted with relief, had been placed in the nursery, so he and Jennet were completely alone

He climbed into the high, boxy bed and pulled Jennet into his arms, sighing over the tension in her body. "Have I angered you in some way, dearling?"

"Nay." She gave up all pretense at being asleep, knowing he had seen through her ploy. "Hacon," she began carefully, "mayhaps it would be best if I returned to my aunt and my kinsmen."

She gave a soft cry of surprise when he suddenly moved, pushing her onto her back and crouching over her. In the soft light of the candle by the bed she could see his expression as he scowled down at her. She had been right. He was not going to agree easily.

"What foolishness is this?"

"'Tisnae foolishness. Why is it that when a woman speaks of something a mon doesnae agree with, he quickly names it foolishness? I but think it best if I return home, to my kinsmen. Ye must see that."

"Nay, I dinnae." It annoyed him that her wish to leave should pain him so.

"Then ye are purposely closing your eyes. Ye have brought your leman into the verra heart of your faintly. 'Tis *not* right. 'Tis . . ." She muttered a curse against his lips when he kissed her, halting her words.

Hacon almost smiled. His mother was right. Jennet was upset to be his lover now that they were at his home. On the morrow he would take her to where he meant to build his tower house. Once he told her about the small L-shaped castle he planned for their safety and comfort, he would speak of marriage. There was still a lot to be settled between them, but marriage would keep her firmly tied to him until they could do so.

"We must talk about this," she said the moment the kiss ended, fighting to stop herself from being diverted by passion.

"Aye, but not now, not tonight." He began to unlace her chemise. "On the morrow."

"'Tis not wise to keep setting things aside until the morrow." She made a weak attempt to halt the removal of her clothes.

"It willnae hurt this time." He lowered his body onto hers and kissed the hollow in her throat. "It took us three full nights and days to travel here from your aunt's. Three nights of holding you close yet not being able to love you. Weel, we are alone now and in a fine, soft bed. And I"—he cupped her breasts in his hands, slowly rubbing the tips to hardness with his thumbs—"dinnae feel like talking. There will be time enough for that on the morrow."

She knew she ought to argue, that what she had to say was too important to be pushed aside like that. Then he replaced the caress of his thumbs with slow strokes of his tongue. Threading her fingers through his thick hair, she held him closer, silently urging him on in his seductive play. It really would not hurt, she decided, to wait until morning. In fact, she mused, it might be wise to grasp as much of the passion she so delighted in as she could before she had to leave him.

"On the morrow then," she murmured as she relaxed and let the desire they shared work its spell.

His lovemaking was gentle and tender yet had that delicious edge that only a fierce hunger can give it. He paid sweet homage to her body, stroking and kissing every inch of her until Jennet clung to him with near desperation and urged him to unite their bodies. Her soft cry as he filled her was one of delight and relief. As he brought them both toward completion, Jennet met and equaled his increasing ferocity. Their cries blended as they found passion's reward together. Jennet held him close when he collapsed in her arms. In her passion-drugged mind one question was repeated over and over again—did she have the strength to walk away from this man?

"Hacon, I thought ye brought me here so that we might talk."

Her arms crossed beneath her breasts, Jennet scowled at Hacon. It was difficult not to notice how good he looked. He wore a soft blue jupon, open at the neck, and snug gray hose. No sword was buckled at his waist, and he wore no armor at all. The light breeze tousled his thick, fair hair. With his hands on his trim hips, he surveyed his lands with open pride and pleasure. Jennet felt herself soften with appreciation, then quickly checked that feeling. She had every right to be annoyed with the man.

He had dragged her along a skinny, overgrown path through the bracken and heather to the top of a small rise. Half of it was encircled by a small loch. It was lovely. From any point atop the hill one could see for quite a distance, either out across the moors and fields, which nearly encircled the village, or across the bogs and moors that formed the banks of the loch. Jennet could see people working in the fields, cattle and sheep roaming freely, and even a group of ducks floating on the deep blue waters of the loch. In the village, a group of women were gathered in the center around the well. It all looked so peaceful. And that, she decided, was its greatest beauty. But she saw no reason to be there. She wanted to talk, and he was taking her or an idle walk over his lands.

"Aye, whatever ye desire, dearling." He draped his arm about her shoulders and kissed her cheek. "What do ye think of this spot?"

"'Tis verra lovely, but—"

"And a good defensive position."

"Aye, 'tis that too. Now—"

"Here is where I shall build my tower house."

"Oh." She looked around again, realized curiosity was diverting her from her purpose, and concentrated on what she wished to discuss. "The perfect place. Now, Hacon—"

"I dinnae plan to have some stark tower with no thought for the comfort of those who must live in it." He tugged her closer to the center of the hilltop. "I think ye can still see where I scratched out a rough plan ere I left on the raid."

Jennet stared down at the ground and almost smiled. The grass hid it a little, but there was a shallow trench scratched into the ground. She took Hacon's hand and followed the rough line all the way around, as he walked silently by her side. When they returned to their original place, she glanced up at him. Jennet found it rather touching that he would do such a thing. He had drawn his dream in the dirt, and he had let her see what he had done.

"'Twill be shaped like an ell?" she asked quietly.

"Aye, it will be defensible yet not as austere as many others." He smiled faintly. "I forsee it gracing this hill for many years to come." He gazed out over the loch. "Mayhaps even long enough to outlive the need for it."

He sounded very sincere. The way he looked now, she could easily envision him being content to stay at Dubheilrig tending his lands and watching out for his people. He truly cared for Dubheilrig, truly loved this land.

"That would be a pleasure beyond words," she whispered. "When do ye start to build it?"

"The men will break ground on the morrow." Hacon glanced at their still-clasped hands, then fixed his gaze upon her face. "Ye havenae said what ye think of it."

"I am certain it shall be the finest tower house between here and London." She smiled when he laughed and put his arm around her shoulders, then grew serious. She could not allow herself to be diverted any longer. "Hacon, ye said we would talk today."

He grimaced and rubbed his chin. "In truth, it was you who wished to talk."

"Aye, and I let ye distract me."

"I am willing to do so again." He began to tug her into his arms.

She neatly slipped free of his hold and moved to gaze blindly at the loch. "I cannae stay here, Hacon."

She cried out softly with surprise when he grasped her arms and abruptly turned her back to him. "Why?"

"I find I have too much pride to live here with your family, as your leman. The bite of shame is sharper than I can bear."

"Then stay as my wife."

"What?" She nearly gaped at him, for it was the very last thing she had expected him to say.

"Stay as my wife."

It took a full minute before Jennet could compose herself. She fought a brief, fierce struggle with the urge to give him an immediate and resounding aye. The few times she had imagined him asking her to be his wife there had been some tenderness and the exchange of a few sweet words. This sounded very much like a command. And it solved only one problem. She would no longer be a mistress, a possible object of scorn, but she would still be the daughter of a poor, landless thief. Hacon had not only regained his lands but had also been given a title. A match between them could be viewed only with displeasure by his family.

"Why do ye hesitate?" he asked, and smiled crookedly. "Am I so poor a choice?"

"Nay. Ye are too grand a choice for a lass like me."

"What do ye mean?"

"Hacon, think a moment. Aye, my blood is good. I am wellborn. Howbeit, that is all I can claim. I am the child of thieves. There is no land, no title, and no money. I dinnae even have the full set of linen expected of a lass about to be wed. I have no dowry at all."

He pulled her into his arms and heartily kissed her, not easing the embrace until they were both breathless. "There is your dowry, lass. 'Tis enough."

She frowned up at him, "I dinnae believe your parents, your kinsmen, or even your clan will be much impressed by that dowry."

"'Tis enough that I have chosen you."

"What arrogance."

"Come. I will prove it to you."

She was given no chance to argue or protest before he was dragging her back toward his parents' home. He pulled her along at such a brisk pace that speech was impossible. By the time they located his parents in the solar of the manor, Jennet needed a minute to catch her breath. She took a quick glance around the beautifully sunlit room as she did so.

Katherine sat curled up on one of the window benches doing some mending. The brief cool smile with which the woman greeted her brother was not extended to Jennet. Lady Serilda sat before another of the large windows. She paused in working on her tapestry to look at her son with affectionate curiosity. That expression was shared by Lucais, who sat at a small table writing letters. The man set down the quill and waited for Hacon to speak. Jennet told herself that she would try to understand their objections, that she would not take any of what they said to heart.

"I have asked Jennet to be my wife," Hacon announced. "She has accepted."

Jennet was stunned when both Lady Serilda and Sir Lucais moved to give her a hug. They appeared honestly sincere in welcoming her. She wondered if Hacon had told them much about her.

"I have no dowry," she was compelled to confess.

"None?" demanded Katherine, who had not moved from her seat in the window.

"A dowry is *not* important," Lady Serilda said, and gave Katherine a stern look. "Come and welcome your new sister."

Katherine strode over to Jennet and curtly shook her hand. "Welcome. Now, if ye will excuse me, I must find my son." She left the solar.

Lady Serilda grasped Hacon by the arm, stopping him from going after her. "I will speak to her later." She smiled at Jennet. "Pay our Katherine no heed. She feels God and fate have been unfair to her and wishes all of us to share in her unhappiness and ill humor. We dinnae need her to plan this wedding."

Sir Lucais tugged Hacon toward the door. "Weel, ye will have no need of our aid."

"Nay—not yet." Lady Serilda grinned when Hacon and his father quickly left, then she winked at Jennet. "We shall allow them this retreat." She led Jennet over to the window seat. "Now, let us begin to make a few plans."

It was not long before Jennet felt her fears ease. Hacon's mother truly did welcome her to the Gillard family. Jennet hoped she could win over Katherine as well. She did not wish to be the source of any contention within the family.

\* \* \*

The need to see that the evening meal was properly set out finally ended Lady Serilda's planning. Jennet slipped away and started up the stairs. She wanted to wash, change her clothes, and check on Murdoc before the meal was served. Just as she reached the sixth step someone called to her.

She turned to see Ranald bounding up the few steps and smiled when he halted just in front of her.

"Greetings—Aunt." He grinned and kissed her cheek. "I want to welcome you into the family."

"Thank ye, Ranald." She smiled briefly. "I hope I can soon bring your mother to my side."

Ranald grimaced. "Pay her no heed, Jennet. Ever since my father died, she has grown bitter, her temper sour. In the beginning we all tried to soothe her but it did no good." He shrugged. "So, we avoid her or shush her. Ye must do the same. Weel, I have to fetch my uncle and grandfather. They are helping Lame Walter get his cow and her calf out of the mire. They will need to clean up for the evening meal." He started down the stairs.

Jennet tried to picture Hacon struggling to get a cow out of a mudhole, then hurried to follow Ranald. "Wait. I will come along with you."

They found Hacon and his father in the field to the west of the village. Jennet did not even try to hide her laughter. A bare-chested, grime-covered Hacon stood knee-deep in mud as he cursed and pushed at a bawling calf. A skinny, gray-haired man stood on the edge of the quagmire swearing and yanking on the tether of the calf's dam. A grinning and mud-spattered Sir Lucais also stood nearby, ready to push.

Hacon looked Jennet's way, a grin curving his handsome mouth. "Unfair! I have one stubborn female who willnae move to save her own life and another who laughs at me."

Jennet couldn't contain her peals of laughter at the amusing sight. It was also a touching one. Hacon, Baron of Dubheilrig, cared enough for his people to help a poor herdsmen get his cow out of the mud. That he could tend to such a menial chore with such good humor told her a lot about the man she would soon marry. Perhaps he would be a simple farmer, would be perfectly happy to stay at Dubheilrig and manage his lands. Now that he was a baron and his fortunes were bound to increase, he did not need to go to war. He could send others, even pay mercenaries to fulfill his obligation to the king. She felt her hopes for a peaceful future begin to grow.

# Chapter 13

The sound of the door to the solar creaking open caused Jennet to look up from the shirt she was making for Murdoc. She grinned when she saw Hacon slip into the room. He had the air of a small boy planning some mischief. After being with him here for two weeks, she was not surprised to see the powerful knight Hacon acting this way. Since their arrival he had been carrying out duties that befitted a baron, hunting for game, meting out justice, and poring over the ledgers and estate accounts with his father. However, she had also seen him kicking a ball around with some of the village boys, teasing his mother, settling a squabble over a fat hen, and even lending a hand in the building of Robert, Elizabeth, and Donald's house. He rarely wore his sword unless he rode out beyond the village boundaries or required some symbol of his authority. Although she was delighted to see this lighter side of Hacon, it sometimes left her wondering just how well she knew him.

"Aha! Mother has left you alone and unguarded," Hacon said as he strode over to the window seat and sat down next to Jennet.

"Aye. There was some disagreement in the kitchens that

she needed to settle. I suspect she will return soon so that we might share our noon meal."

"She will have to eat alone." He stood up, and pulled her to her feet. "Ye are to dine with me."

Jennet tossed her sewing onto the pillowed seat and smiled. "I am, am I?"

"Aye, ye are. We shall enjoy a small repast and watch the men who labor to build my tower house."

"I have always been fond of watching others labor."

Hacon grinned, then urged her out the door. Jennet let him lead her along. He was acting so preposterously secretive that she found it difficult to completely smother her laughter. When they reached the hilltop where his tower house would one day loom above the village, she found a blanket spread out for them upon the ground and on it a small feast of bread, cheese, and wine. She shook her head and laughed as he sat down, gently pulling her down beside him.

"So, lassie, what do ye think of our grand home?" he asked as he cut them each a thick slice of bread.

Looking toward where the men worked at digging out the foundation pit, Jennet declared, "I have ne'er seen a grander hole in the ground. Truly, 'tis fine enough for the king himself."

"Impertinent wench. I thought ye might gain a better sense of the size of it now that 'tis more than a line in the dirt." He cut the square of cheese into smaller chunks. "Those shall be the storage chambers for the tithings, the grain, and the wine."

"And for the dungeon," she murmured, unable to ignore the dark use to which such underground chambers could be put.

"Aye, and one of those too. Howbeit, 'twill be no pit, no oubliette. I willnae have one of those dark holes in Dubheil-rig. Their only use is to throw a mon down into them and leave him there to rot."

"I am glad there willnae be one of those chilling places

here. And, aye, ye are right. Now that the ground is dug up, I do have a keener sense of how large it will be." She nibbled on a piece of cheese before daring to ask, "Hacon? Would it not have been less costly to simply better fortify your parents' manor?"

"Much less costly. Howbeit, no amount of fortifying would truly make it safe. We always planned to build a tower house up here once we had the funds. Sadly, just as we thought to begin, the land was taken from us. This construction will deplete our coffers, but I willnae wait another day. Though I wish it were not so, a fortress is absolutely necessary."

"'Twill be a fine haven for the people of Dubheilrig."

"And us." He pressed a kiss to her palm. "I intend to have a strong fortress, but I also intend to make a place of comfort and beauty."

Before Jennet could respond, someone called Hacon's name. They both turned to look toward the path which led up the hill. Jennet did not welcome the sight of Ranald. The youth looked disturbingly serious.

"Hacon, ye must come back," called Ranald as he hurried up to them. "A messenger has arrived from the king."

"Curse the king and his cur of a messenger!" Jennet snapped as Hacon stood and helped her to her feet "I pray their tongues will blacken and their manhoods will shrivel."

"Now, my sweet Jennet." Hacon scolded, but his voice shook with laughter. "Ye would feel sorely grieved if those curses took hold."

"Not now, I wouldnae," she grumbled as he led her back down to his parents' residence.

As they drew near home Jennet's anger began to fade, replaced by worry. Hacon's family and several of his men stood in the courtyard in front of the Bruce's messenger, gathered closely around the man. They all looked very serious, far too solemn for her peace of mind. She tensed when they faced the man, dreading his message.

"Our king embarks upon a campaign into Ireland," the man intoned. "He requests your aid and support, Sir Gillard, new lord of Dubheilrig."

"When?" Hacon felt Jennet tug her hand free of his but forced himself to pay heed to the Bruce's man.

"He means to set sail in a fortnight's time, so ye must return with me. Ye and as many men-at-arms as ye can muster."

Jennet did not wait to hear any more. She did not dare. The angry, treasonous words she ached to fling at the Bruce's messenger could easily pull her and anyone close to her into dire trouble. But her escape was halted at the door. Hacon caught her arm, and propelled her to his side. She looked ready to spit her fury at him, but he was not looking at her. Instead he was gazing out at the people gathered around them. He raised their clasped hands.

Hacon did not wish to go off and fight, but he was forced to obey the Bruce's summons. There was no possible way to have the wedding before he left, yet he did not wish to leave Jennet without the protection of his name and a claim to what was his if he did not return. In truth, he did not wish to leave her free at all, for he could be gone for months.

There was only one alternative. He would have to handfast with her. It would be enough to have her recognized as his wife. All he had to do was proclaim her his wife before witnesses and have her proclaim him as her husband. Glancing down at her angry little face, Hacon was not sure the latter part of the brief ceremony would be easily accomplished.

"Before all gathered here," he began in a loud, clear voice to draw everyone's attention his way. "Ye ken that I mean to have Jennet Graeme as my bride."

There was a murmur of agreement from the crowd.

"The king has bid us to fight for him," Hacon continued. "This means there can be no wedding ceremony. Howbeit, I willnae leave Jennet without the protection of my name and a rightful claim to all I own. Thus, I choose handfasting. I name Jennet Graeme my wife. Is that heard and accepted?"

"Aye!" cried the people.

For a moment Jennet could only gape at him. Handfast? He means to handfast with me now, then march off to war in some distant land? She was about to tell him he was mad when she realized someone was calling to her. Her mind whirling with a dizzying array of contradictory thoughts, she looked towards Lucais.

"And ye, Jennet Graeme," Lucais asked, "do ye call Hacon Gillard husband?"

A very sharp voice in her head, which sounded remarkably like her aunt, told her to say aye and worry about everything else later. Jennet stared at Hacon's father, fighting the urge, but that scolding, carping voice pressed her to agree. And so, she admitted with a silent curse over her own foolishness, did her heart.

"Aye. I call Hacon Gillard husband."

"Is that heard and accepted?" said Hacon.

"Aye," cried everyone without a moment's hesitation,

As the people offered their congratulations, Jennet yanked her hand free of Hacon's. "There. We are handfasted," she declared angrily. "Now, ye blood-hungry fool, ye may ride off and get yourself killed." She raced off to their chambers, desperate to get away and terrified of what else she might say.

Hacon sighed. After ordering Dugald to gather up their men, he started after Jennet, only to have his mother halt him. "I must prepare to ride, Mother."

"Now? Surely ye dinnae have to leave until the morning."

"Ye ken as weel as I that little time is needed. After so many years of war, we are always prepared to ride. Our horses are at hand. We but need to grab our blankets, our sacks of oats, and our arms. If more is needed, we may obtain it at the place chosen for the army to be mustered."

"So, ye will be gone within the hour."

"Aye, or near to. And I must try to soothe Jennet's fury in what little time I have left."

"There will ne'er be time enough to do that. Nay, not before ye are dragged off to war again by these fools." Her voice trembled with anger, and Hacon regarded her in some surprise. "Just recall what I said—heed her actions, not her words."

"I will try," he murmured, "though I find I face her with less courage than I can face armed men." With a faint smile for his mother, he added, "Tell Dugald that Ranald will stay behind," then strode off to his chambers.

When Hacon entered, Jennet remained seated on the bed. She wanted to scream at him, to hit him. He had claimed her as his wife before his family and village. While handfasting was not the best of arrangements, since it was not sanctified by the Church, it was enough to bring her happiness and hope. But she was not to be allowed that. The Bruce called, and Hacon answered without hesitation. Although fear for Hacon gnawed at her, her overriding emotions were fury and disgust with men and their ways. She knew some of her anger came from having her hopes crushed. After seeing Hacon so comfortable and content while working at Duhheilrig, she had deceived herself into thinking his days as a knight were over. When he sat on a stool to lace up his cuarans, she cursed and moved to help him. The maelstrom of emotion that seized her made continued stillness impossible.

Reaching out to smooth his hand over her hair as she knelt before him, Hacon said, "He asks payment for the honors given me, for the title and the barony." When she sat back on her heels, he rose to get his chain mail shirt.

Standing to help him don that armor, she snapped, "Ten years of your life wasnae enough?"

"The Bruce is my liege lord."

"And that gives him the right to keep ye constantly at war?

# Take A Trip Into A Timeless World of Passion and Adventure with Kensington Choice Historical Romances!
## —Absolutely FREE!

Enjoy the passion and adventure of another time with Kensington Choice Historical Romances. They are the finest novels of their kind, written by today's best-selling romance authors. Each Kensington Choice Historical Romance transports you to distant lands in a bygone age. Experience the adventure and share the delight as proud men and spirited women discover the wonder and passion of true love.

# Get 4 FREE Books!

We created our convenient Home Subscription Service so you'll be sure to have the hottest new romances delivered each month right to your doorstep—usually before they are available in book stores. Just to show you how convenient the Zebra Home Subscription Service is, we would like to send you 4 FREE Kensington Choice Historical Romances. The books are worth up to $24.96, but you only pay $1.99 for shipping and handling. There's no obligation to buy additional books—ever!

## *Save Up To 30% With Home Delivery!*

Accept your FREE books and each month we'll deliver 4 brand new titles as soon as they are published. They'll be yours to examine FREE for 10 days. Then if you decide to keep the books, you'll pay the preferred subscriber's price (up to 30% off the cover price!), plus shipping and handling. Remember, you are under no obligation to buy any of these books at any time! If you are not delighted with them, simply return them and owe nothing. But if you enjoy Kensington Choice Historical Romances as much as we think you will, pay the special preferred subscriber rate and save over $8.00 off the cover price!

We have 4 FREE BOOKS for you as your introduction to
**KENSINGTON CHOICE!**
To get your FREE BOOKS, worth up to $24.96, mail
the card below or call TOLL-FREE 1-800-770-1963.
Visit our website at www.kensingtonbooks.com.

## Get 4 FREE Kensington Choice Historical Romances!

♥**YES!** Please send me my 4 FREE KENSINGTON CHOICE HISTORICAL ROMANCES (without obligation to purchase other books). I only pay $1.99 for shipping and handling. Unless you hear from me after I receive my 4 FREE BOOKS, you may send me 4 new novels—as soon as they are published—to preview each month FREE for 10 days. If I am not satisfied, I may return them and owe nothing. Otherwise, I will pay the money-saving preferred subscriber's price (over $8.00 off the cover price), plus shipping and handling. I may return any shipment within 10 days and owe nothing, and I may cancel any time I wish. In any case, the 4 FREE books will be mine to keep.

NAME

ADDRESS _____ APT. _____

CITY _____ STATE _____ ZIP _____

TELEPHONE ( ____ ) _____

E-MAIL (OPTIONAL) _____

SIGNATURE _____

(If under 18, parent or guardian must sign)

Offer limited to one per household and not to current subscribers. Terms, offer and prices subject to change. Orders subject to acceptance by Kensington Choice Book Club. Offer Valid in the U.S. only.

KN116A

Zebra Book Club
P.O. Box 6314
Dover, DE 19905-6314

PLACE
STAMP
HERE

And Ireland? *Why* Ireland? Ye cannae tell me the English threaten Scotland there."

"His brother Edward was made king there. 'Tis clear that support is needed to hold the throne." Hacon grimaced when he saw the look on her face and quickly buckled on his sword.

"So," she hissed, "more Scots blood must run to keep a Bruce's arse on a throne. Ye cannae agree with this. Robert the Bruce was at least a contender to the throne of Scotland, but what claim does his brother have to Ireland's?"

Not sure of the answer, or even if there was a good one, Hacon repeated, "The Bruce is my liege lord. Honor demands that I answer the call to arms."

"Honor." She spat the word as if it was a curse. "Honor has drenched the earth from Stirling to London in the blood of good men. Mayhaps it is past time for honor to step aside so good sense can rule."

He ached to hold her, but she did not look very welcoming. "I have fought ten years to gain what I now hold. I cannae lose it now." Succumbing to his need, he reached out to touch her cheek, sighing when she pulled away. "My family will care for you and Murdoc. Ye ken weel that my parents have accepted both of you. Wait for me, dearling. I will return. I declared ye my wife "

"So ye could hurry away and make me a widow. Do ye expect me to thank you for that?"

"Nay," he whispered. "Wait for me. I will come back to you. It seems I can do naught else," he murmured, then hurried away.

Jennet stared at the empty doorway for a long time. She felt as if her heart had been torn from her body. Loving Hacon was all she had feared it would be, brief moments of delight broken by times of terror as he rode off to do battle again and again.

Then suddenly she realized she had sent him off to war with only harsh words. That thought banished all other considerations from her mind. She raced out to the courtyard, knowing only that she needed to rectify that slip in some way.

Hacon stood next to his mount, ending his farewells to his parents. Jennet hurled herself into his arms. She gave him a deep, searing kiss, one which expressed all her need for him, all her desperation and fear. Stepping back, ignoring the ribald remarks and laughter of his men, she pressed her rosary beads into his hand.

"Go with God, Hacon Gillard," she whispered, then fled back to her chambers, knowing she did not have the strength to watch him ride off.

# *Chapter 14*

"He has been gone for three months. He willnae be returning to you."

Jennet looked up from the woolen nightshirt she was
making for Murdoc to glance around the solar before
fixing her gaze upon Katherine. Lady Serilda and her maid
had gone. That did not surprise her. Katherine would never
have spoken so bluntly if her mother had still been in the
room.

"Ireland is verra far away," Jennet replied. "One cannae
expect Hacon to go there, fight a battle, and return in but a
fortnight."

"He should have returned by now. 'Twould be wise for you
to prepare your widow's weeds."

"Ye cannae wish your own brother dead."

"Nay, of course not, but I am not fool enough to cling to
false hopes."

"Until I am brought word of his death, I will believe that
he will come back as he promised."

"My husband also promised to come back, but he now rots
beneath English soil."

Katherine strode out of the solar, roughly shutting the door
behind her, and Jennet sighed. She wanted to ignore Katherine's

bitter words, but that was impossible. Hacon had been gone for a long time. Three long months had passed without a word from him or about him. She did not need Katherine's comments to make her fear she would be a widow before she had any chance to be a wife.

It puzzled her a little that Katherine seemed to want her to suffer the pain of widowhood. In wishing for that, Katherine was also wishing for her own brother's death. Jealousy seemed to spur Katherine on, and Jennet knew it was not simply a jealousy of her marriage. Katherine was beginning to feel the loss of her own mother's attention and affection. Lady Serilda had become a dear friend and, in some ways, a mother to Jennet. Jennet would not give that up to soothe Katherine, but she did wish there was some way to end the woman's unreasonable fears and irritation. Unfortunately, it was something that Lady Serilda and her daughter had to sort out by themselves,

"Jennet?"

She looked up to smile weakly at Ranald as he entered the solar and sat beside her on the window seat. "'Tis good to see you, Ranald."

"Ye dinnae look verra happy, but I shall lay the blame for that at my mother's feet. I saw her leave the solar, looking as sour as she ever has."

"Your mother is worried about Hacon."

"Mayhaps. Howbeit, ye most certainly are, so I have come to distract you."

"Have you now." She set aside her sewing. "What diversion have you planned for me?"

"'Tis past time ye had another inspection of the tower house. They have started work upon the wall."

"The wall?" she asked as she followed him from the room.

"Aye. The barmkin? That big stone wall encircling the tower house? The verra one ye asked for?"

"Ah. Pardon. I promise to fix my mind upon the building and naught else."

"Good. Now, fetch your cloak"

With a helping hand from Ranald, Jennet hefted herself up to sit on an unfinished section of the barmkin. Ranald was right. It had been her idea to add that encircling, protective wall around Hacon's tower house. Everyone assured her that Hacon would approve. She heartily wished he was there to do so himself. Instead, she and Ranald worked to build the tower house while Hacon fought for the Bruce in some faraway land. She cursed the Bruce, just as she had each day since Hacon had left.

"If the weather holds fine," Ranald said as he handed her an oatcake, "it could weel be done by next summer's end."

"Aye. I but pray Hacon will be pleased." She idly nibbled the oatcake.

"Of course he will. If naught else, we have followed his own plans."

"Weel, more or less." She exchanged a brief grin with Ranald. "Howbeit, I cannae believe he would have disagreed with what few additions we made. Aye, not when some were at the behest of his own mother and father."

She sighed, then gazed at the partly finished tower house. Building it had become important to her. Somehow it brought Hacon closer. And it had kept her from being overcome with fear and worry, at least during the day.

What surprised her was that she had finally come to accept Hacon's life as a knight. She did not like it, knew she would probably continue to complain, but she no longer condemned him for it. Although Hacon's mother and Elizabeth had both talked to her, she knew the change had come mostly from within her. She hated the waiting, the constant fear with which she must live until he returned, but she knew she would not run from it. It was the price she had to pay to be

with him. When he did return, she was sure she would consider it a small price. At least, she mused with an inner smile
over her own vagaries, until the next call to arms.

"Someone approaches," Ranald murmured, hopping off
the low wall and helping her down.

A sense of alarm rippled through Jennet as she watched a
group of three men march up the path, the middle one flanked
by two armed men. She tried not to fear that they brought
news of Hacon. Then, as they drew closer, her eyes widened.
The man who strode one step in the middle and slightly ahead
of the others had hair the color of a deer's hide. She began to
recognize other things—the cocky stride, the tall, elegantly
slim frame clothed in the finest linens and wools.

A glad hope-filled cry escaped her as she rushed down the
hill. The nearer she got the surer she was of the man's identity. Even as she flung herself forward he opened his arms to
hold her tight.

"Father? 'Tis truly you?" she finally whispered, and
stepped back to gaze up into eyes that matched hers to a
shade.

"Aye, lass, and 'twould please me if ye would tell these
men I am your verra own father, ere they spit me on their
swords." He glanced back at his guards, who had already relaxed their wary stances.

"Oh, Papa," she cried, and flung herself into his arms
again, feeling their slim strength encircle her as he held her
close.

Once in control of herself, she stepped back, holding his
hands in hers, and introduced him to Ranald and his former
guards. Those two men hurried away to inform Hacon's parents of their new guest. Growing calmer, Jennet more closely
eyed her father's attire.

He wore a well-fitted cotehardie of fine wool. His surcoat
was also of a rich material and lined with fur. Snug particolored hose covered his well-shaped legs, and he wore fine

leather boots belted beneath his knees. All in all, it was a fortune in clothing he wore, the shades of green perfectly complementing his coloring. She eyed him with suspicion.

"Where did ye steal these?" she demanded.

"Lass!" Artair Graeme clasped his hands over his heart and assumed a wounded expression. "How can ye accuse me so, me—the flesh of your flesh, the blood of your blood?"

"Verra easily. I ken ye too weel. We ne'er had the coin to afford such rich trappings."

"Weel, we do now." He hooked his arm through hers and, with a grinning Ranald following, urged her back down the newly widened path through the bracken. "Ye see, there was this rich widow—"

"Nay"—she held up her hand—"I think I can be pleased enough kenning only that ye didnae steal them."

"I didnae. I earned them through the sweat of my brow. Weel, mayhaps, 'tis more honest to say the sweat of my—"

"Papa!" She scowled at him and Ranald as they laughed. "Ye ought to be bent with shame."

"Why? For putting a smile on a lady's face and coin in my purse?" He winked at her. "And such a big smile it was too."

She had to bite the inside of her cheek to keep from laughing. Hugging his arm closer to her, she rested her cheek against it as they ambled down the path. He was a rogue, but she knew that only Hacon's return, hale and hearty from the war, could make her happier.

"Weel, there will be none of that while ye are here," she ordered. "Ye are to be on your best behavior whilst staying with my husband's family."

"Ah, so ye are wed to the rogue now."

"Weel, handfasted ere he was dragged off to war in Ireland."

"'Twill do. I hadnae liked the thought of coming to sword-points with the mon. I had heard he might even equal my skill," he drawled.

Rolling her eyes, she lightly punched his arm. "Boaster. And ye didnae promise ye would behave yourself."

"I shall be a saint," he vowed, and kissed her cheek.

Jennet doubted that but did not press him further. She was too happy to see him. Nevertheless, she promised herself she would keep a close watch on her charming, lovable, but errant father while he was at Dubheilrig.

Holding her woolen cloak snugly around her, Jennet made her way to the rear of the stables. An hysterical Katherine had demanded that she go to the stables and do something about her father. Poor Katherine had come to visit her pampered mare and had heard enough to know that Artair and Ranald were heartily misbehaving themselves. What Jennet did not understand was why Katherine had not simply tended to the matter herself. Ranald was Katherine's son, after all.

Jennet had no trouble finding the culprits. She scowled down at the two couples sprawled in the hay only a few feet away from each other, all oblivious to her presence. She grabbed a wooden pail hanging from a nail and threw it against the door of an empty stall. "Ye said ye would behave!" she shouted.

All four miscreants jumped and turned toward her, grabbing pieces of their scattered clothing and trying to cover themselves. She ought not to be surprised. Her father had been very good for eight long, dull, winter weeks. This, however, was no saint who lay sprawled on his back clutching a corner of the blanket over his privates.

"Ye said ye would behave!" she repeated.

"I have behaved, verra weel." He wriggled his auburn brows and grinned at the buxom woman kneeling by his side. "Havenae I, lassie?" He chuckled when the woman giggled.

Ignoring that, Jennet continued, "And to drag Ranald into sin as weel. Ye cannae tell me 'tis not your influence which has him rolling about in the hay with wanton abandon."

"Actually, Jennet," Ranald drawled, and patting the shoulder of the woman at his side, "her name is Fenella."

She gaped at her young friend and glared at her father. "Now he even has your impertinence."

"Aye." Moving to ruffle Ranald's thick hair, Artair laughed. "The lad's a fast learner. Lots of promise in the boy."

Turning her back on them, Jennet fought against laughing. She had to be stern. While she did not really see the harm in frolicking about with willing maids, it could lead to trouble. Katherine had taken to wailing about Ranald's slipping into "the depths of depravity," and she pinned the blame squarely on Artair Graeme. Jennet preferred such tirades to reminders of how long Hacon had been gone, but she knew she could not simply ignore Katherine's anger. Feeling in control again, Jennet turned to frown at the group.

"Weel, his mother doesnae like the lessons ye teach." She ignored Ranald's muttered complaints.

"The woman coddles the boy," Artair protested. "Boy? He is more a mon than a boy."

Although she agreed, Jennet was about to point out that it was not her father's place to interfere when someone called her name. Frowning in puzzlement, she turned just as a young man appeared in the doorway. It took her a moment to recognize Donald, Robert's brother. Her delight over how completely he had recovered from his wounds was brief, fading when she saw the concern in his expression.

"What is it, Donald?" she had to ask, for his attention was momentarily diverted by the four lovers.

"Oh"—he colored faintly—"there is a messenger."

"Weel, surely ye took him to his lordship's parents." Jennet told herself that her growing fear was absurd, that the messenger could have been sent by anyone, but still her anxiety grew.

"Aye, but he willnae give his message until ye are there to hear it as weel."

That sounded ominous to Jennet. Her heart pounding with increasing trepidation, she hurried out of the stables over the thawing ground and into the small manse. It took all her courage to step into the large hall, where the family was gathered and the messenger waited. She heartily wished she could be back within the stables scolding her father. The look on Serilda Gillard's face as the woman hurried over to greet her only added to Jennet's dread. It took all her strength to repress the childish and futile urge to cover her ears with her hands. She was glad to have Serilda's hand clasping hers as the woman spoke to the messenger.

"Ye may tell us your news now, Sir Bearnard."

The man sighed, twisted his fine liripipe hat in his hands and completely ruining the shape of the hood with its long conical tail. "I regret 'tisnae good news I must relate."

Lady Serilda smiled faintly, but her expression held only deep sadness. "I ken it. Go on."

"Sir Hacon Gillard, lord of Dubheilrig, fell in battle at Dundalk in Ireland. Our liege's brother fell in the same battle. Your son"—he looked at Jennet—"and your lord fought bravely and with honor."

Jennet felt cold, so very cold. She was only faintly aware of Lucais hastening to his wife's side and embracing her as she softly wept. Sir Bearnard's devastating words pounded into Jennet's mind, nearly deafening her to all around her. She felt a hand grip her arm, turning to the person who held her, and after a moment, realized it was her father at her side.

"M'lady?" Sir Bearnard called to her. "Lady Gillard?"

"Answer the man, lass," urged Artair, giving her a slight shake even as he watched her closely and with concern.

"Aye? What is it, sir?"

"I have brought something for you." When she held out her hand, he slowly placed her rosary beads in it. "His mon, a Sir Niall, believed ye would wish to have these returned."

Clenching her hand over the beads so tightly that they dug

into her skin, Jennet heard herself ask, "Sir Niall? He isnae Hacon's mon. Dugald is. Where is Dugald?"

"I dinnae ken this mon—Dugald? There were two men killed with your lord. Mayhaps one was this Dugald."

"There is no mayhaps about it," said Lucais, his voice thick and hoarse with emotion. "Dugald would ne'er leave my son's side. If any mon died with Hacon, 'twould be our Dugald. What of the other men from Dubheilrig?"

"I cannae say how many will return, but some will. They rest now at Stirling. The king wishes me to extend to you his heartfelt sorrow. Your son was one of his best soldiers. And if there is a kinsman ye wish named to the title and lands, or if ye will now take the honor yourself, ye need but speak it and 'tis done."

"My grandson, Ranald, will carry the weight of that honor now," said Lucais.

Unable to bear it any longer, desperately needing to get away, Jennet turned to leave. Even as she stepped toward the door she remembered she was not alone in her grief. Serilda and Lucais had lost their son. She struggled to think of something to say, wondering fleetingly why they were looking at her with such concern.

"I am so verra sorry," she whispered. "There are no words, are there?"

"Nay." Serilda lightly touched her arm. "Child, mayhaps ye should lie down."

"Aye, I was headed to my chambers."

Without another word, Jennet left. Clutching her rosary beads to her chest, she made her way slowly, numbly, to the room she had shared so briefly with Hacon. She stepped inside, closed the heavy door behind her, and started toward the bed. But inches from it, all the emotion on which she had kept such a tight rein broke free, bringing her to her knees.

\* \* \*

"I should go to her," murmured Serilda, but Artair blocked her path. "I dinnae think she should be left alone, Artair. The news dealt her a heavy blow. She was a sickly color and much too quiet."

"Aye, she was. I will give her a few moments, then I will go to her."

"But why wait?"

"I need to ken how her grief will turn her." Seeing the confusion in the Gillards's faces, he explained. "I have seen my wee lass through many such losses, from that of her mother to that of a wee friend. There are two ways she can act. She might push her pain aside, fight it, deny it. Or she might be ruled by it. Aye, it will tear at her so badly she will be ill with it for three, mayhaps four, days. I have seen my poor bairn through it all before. I will do so again. Aye, we kept each other from going mad with grief when my Moira was lost to us. Now, I will bring her through this black time."

"Ye will need help."

"Aye, but ye have your own sorrow." He briefly took her hand and kissed it. "That Sassanach lass, Elizabeth, will do. I best go to Jennet now. I grieve for your loss, mistress, sir." He bowed to the Gillards and strode off to Jennet's chambers.

Upon reaching the door to her rooms, he paused. He could hear her weeping, deep wrenching sobs that tore at his heart. Briefly he pressed his forehead against the door, closing his eyes. Here is yet another hurt ye cannae mend, he thought, wanting to weep with her, for her. Then, opening the door, he stepped inside. One look at her where she knelt on the floor rocking back and forth told him there would be long, painful days ahead.

Jennet slowly opened her eyes and winced. She felt battered and sore. Her eyes felt gritty and slightly swollen. For a moment she wondered if she had been ill. Then she remembered. Hacon was dead. She felt a spasm of pain and hastily placed her hand over her heart, surprised it could take such abuse yet continue to beat. When an elegant, long-fingered hand gently covered hers, she looked up to find her father at her bedside regarding her with concern

"Hacon is dead, Papa." Her voice sounded weak and raspy.

"Aye, lass. I fear he is." When she started to sit up, he quickly helped her, fluffing up the fine goose down pillows for her to lean against.

"And I have been a burden."

"Nay, no burden. The wound was deep and ye needed to wash it clean. 'Tis best this way."

"Aye, and your father was at your side the whole time." Elizabeth stepped up to the bed and helped Jennet drink some mead from an elaborately carved wooden goblet "There, that should soothe your poor throat."

"How long did I carry on? I cannae remember verra much."

"Three days," answered Artair.

"Oh, Papa, ye shouldnae have let me be so foolish, so . . . so selfish."

"Ye were neither. This was needed. Aye, and ye didnae carry on too long."

"Three days isnae too long?"

"Nay. I was planning to allow four, then I would shake or slap some sense into you."

She gave him a weak smile, then gasped. "Hacon's mother. His father. I should have been with them, tried to aid them in their grief. How could I be so thoughtless?"

"Be at ease, loving. No one considers you thoughtless. Aye, they too grieve, but they have each other to cling to."

Relaxing a little, she nodded. "True, but I shall try to make amends for my neglect. And to Murdoc. He is all right?"

"Fine," replied Elizabeth, "though he does fret some for you."

Nodding, she sighed and stared at her hands. "It hurts,

Papa, and what hurts most is kenning I sent him away with harsh words. I am not sure I can forgive myself for that."

He took her hands in his, silently urging her to look at him. "As has many another woman sent her mon away. Lass, he didnae go to his death with your sharp words ringing in his ears, if that is what ye fear. His mother had already given him the wisest advice any mother could give her son about a woman. Heed her acts, not her words, she told him. Your acts put the lie to all your words. Ye gave him a kiss that is still re-called by all those who witnessed it, and ye gave him your fine rosary beads. Now, as a mon I can tell ye what he re-called—that kiss. Ye could have chosen no better way to ease any sting caused by your words."

"Thank ye, although"—she frowned at him—"ye would-nae lie just to soothe me, would you?"

"Aye, I would, but I havenae. Not this time. Your mon would remember that kiss, which I hear tell was quite shameless."

"Aye, I think it was." Then she remembered that she would never kiss Hacon again and felt the sting of tears. "'Tis a pity that my long wallow in grief hasnae left me without pain. Will it ever leave me?"

"I cannae say, dearling. 'Twill lessen, soften with time. I can still feel the bite of it when I recall your mother. What ye will learn is to live with it, survive despite it, and aye, even find some joy in life again. I have."

"Ah, Papa." She briefly lifted his hands to her lips. "Ye are such a rogue, but no lass could have a finer father." She pretended not to see the glint of moisture in his eyes or the touch of color in his cheeks.

"Just ye remember that when next ye seek to scold me," he teased, his voice faintly unsteady. "Now, we should get ye some food. Ye have eaten little these last three days."

"My Robert is due to stop by," said Elizabeth. "We can send him for some."

"Robert is back? The men have already returned?" asked Jennet.

"Aye," answered her father. "Just a day behind the messenger. Elizabeth's fool mon steps by every hour to poke his gnarly head in the door. He fears I mean to seduce his wife. He sore tempts me to do just that." He winked at Elizabeth, who laughed. "Ah, I believe I hear him stomping this way even now."

An instant later Robert stood in the open doorway. He spoke with Elizabeth, offered his good wishes to Jennet for her continued recovery, and all the while he glared at her father. Artair simply grinned impudently. After Robert left, obeying Elizabeth's command to see that food was brought to the room, Elizabeth and Artair tittered like conspiratorial children. Jennet was able to laugh a little as well.

After struggling to eat enough to satisfy Elizabeth and Artair, Jennet found herself alone with her father. "I feel so verra tired," she confessed with a grimace of self-disgust.

"Then rest, dearling. Such black grief as struck you down can suck all the strength from a body. Aye, rest and once ye are strong again I will take you away from this place." He brushed a stray lock of hair from her face. "If it pleases you, that is."

Jennet took only a moment to decide. "Aye, there are too many memories here," she whispered. "I need to be free of them."


"Are ye certain ye willnae change your mind?" Ranald asked as, a fortnight after Jennet had collapsed with grief, she prepared to leave Dubheilrig with her father.

Jennet smiled at him. He wore his new honors as master uncomfortably. Standing with his family before the small manse, he looked painfully young. She was going to miss him, but knew he did not need her to stay. He but sought to hold close all those he liked and trusted during his time of uncertainty. She would feel guilty about leaving him except that she knew Hacon's parents would give him all the assistance in ruling Dubheilrig that he could need.

"Child," Lucais added, "ye ken ye are welcome to stay."

"Aye," Jennet replied as her father settled Murdoc in the sling she wore on her back, "but I cannae stay. Not now."

Moving to Jennet's side, Serilda briefly hugged her and kissed her cheek. "I understand. Return whenever ye wish. Ye and your rogue of a father," she added with a brief smile for Artair, "will always be welcome."

"Thank ye. I vow not to be such a burden next I stay."

"Ye were no burden. Ah, child, did ye think I did no weeping? I but face my pain in a different way. In truth, I cannae help but wonder if your way holds more sense. One large bloodletting instead of a slow one.

"Now, enough of such talk," she continued. "Please, return when ye can and when ye wish. Ye have many friends here." She kissed Murdoc's cheek. "As does this fine wee laddie." Serilda moved back to stand with Ranald and Lucais before asking, "Where will ye go?"

"South," replied Artair. "Mayhaps even into England. But first to Berwick. I still have friends there. We can abide with them for a time."

"God go with you," Lucais said.

The wish was repeated by all those who had gathered to say farewell. Jennet responded in kind as her father helped her onto her pony, then mounted his fine black gelding. She kicked her pony into motion to follow her father as he started down the path. As they passed the small chapel, Jennet paused, staring sadly at the gravestones. A moment later her father reined in at her side.

"This is a mournful place to linger, lassie," he murmured.

"Aye, I ken it. I just thought of how poor Hacon lies in Ireland, not here. He so loved Dubheilrig, Papa. He should be here."

"And he will be—in spirit. Come, loving, let us leave this place where too many memories haunt you."

"Do ye think I can outride the memories?"

"Ye can try." He winked at her and started on his way again as he added, "And a Graeme can do most anything he truly tries to do."

Nudging her pony to follow, she smiled faintly. "Then let us begin and leave the spirits for the graveyards."


"Spirits!" screamed a pale, sobbing Katherine as she burst into the great hall of the Gillard manse. "God help me, I have gone mad. I am seeing the specters of the dead."

Lucais Gillard barely stopped his chair from toppling over when his daughter hurled herself into his arms. He wondered if the August heat had affected her mind. He held her trembling form close and looked helplessly at Ranald and Serilda, who sat on either side of him at the large table. A sound at the doorway drew his attention, and the man standing there firmly held it. For a brief moment he felt as terrified as his daughter acted. They had been told Hacon was dead and had believed it for six long months. He faintly heard Ranald and Serilda gasp in shock as they too recognized the figure.

He finally spoke, his voice weak and unsteady. "Hacon? We were told ye were slain in Ireland." He wanted to join his wife and grandson in rushing to embrace Hacon, but a clinging Katherine kept him trapped in his chair. "Hush, woman," he snapped, giving her a slight shake.

It took several more minutes to calm Katherine down. By that time Hacon and Dugald were seated and provided with food and wine. Hacon struggled not to reveal his impatience, tried to understand the shock he had given his family. But, he grew increasingly tense as his thoughts centered on one person—Jennet.

"Son," Serilda said, reaching across the table to clasp his hand. "How is it we were told ye were dead?"

"I nearly was." Hacon resigned himself to explaining first. "The battle of Dundalk was lost, Lord Edward dead. We were fleeing for our lives, as was every other mon with the wit and strength to do so. We were set upon, but not by the Irish. Nay, 'twas by our own men. Young Alan was killed, Dugald and myself nearly so. The enemy was so close the rogues didnae wait to be certain of their filthy work." He gave his pale mother a reassuring smile.

"How did you escape alive?" pressed Ranald, clearly eager to hear the whole tale.

"We were able to hide until the enemy was gone. God smiled upon us, sending us a merciful mon who helped us. He tended our wounds and hid us until we had the strength to flee that accursed land. I regret it took so long."

"What does it matter," said Serilda. "Ye are alive. But who would wish to murder you?"

"Balreaves." He smiled grimly when his sister gasped, recognizing the name. "Aye, the same. 'Twas he who tried to murder me. The assassins he sent after me said as much, but 'twill do me no good. I am certain the Irish killed them. It seems it was also Balreaves who told everyone I was dead." He explained that he knew the man plotted against him yet he had no proof of it. "And so this deadly game continues."

"Ye must find the proof 'ere he wins," Lucais said, anger roughening his voice. "It cannae go on."

"Nay, and I *will* put an end to it," vowed Hacon. "But now I wish for only one thing, to see my wife. Where is Jennet?" Hacon grew alarmed as his family exchanged glances among themselves but failed to answer him. "*Where* is Jennet?"

"She thought you were dead," Serilda replied.

"I will need but a few moments with her to prove that a lie, *if* someone would just tell me where to find her,"

"She left here in the early spring."

"Left? Ye let her leave?"

"Not alone," Serilda hurried to assure him. "Her father arrived about two months before we were told ye were dead. Once that sad news came, she was no longer happy here and decided to travel with her father. They went south, into the borderlands and England."

"Aye," Ranald continued. "He did make mention of Berwick, but I was left with the feeling he didnae mean to linger there."

"He ne'er lingers at any place." Hacon cursed. "Weel, I will set out after her."

"Ye need to rest first," protested Serilda. "Ye have just arrived after a long and arduous journey."

"Aye, but only for a few days. The Douglas prepares for another raid into England. There has been word that the English king is raising an army and plans to retake Berwick. Douglas intends to harry England's northern counties in hopes of diverting or dividing Edward's army. I will join him. If I must search our enemies' lands for my wife, I had best do so with an army at my back."

# Chapter 15

"Lass, recall how ye claimed to dislike Berwick?" asked Artair as he hurried into the small cottage they shared.

"Aye, but ye paid me little heed." She frowned. "Why mention it now?"

She watched her father closely yet stayed seated by the central hearth, idly stirring a pot of venison stew. He seemed nervous as he crouched on the other side of the fire and needlessly warmed his hands.

After spending nearly a month with her aunt and uncle in Liddesdale, they had traveled on to Berwick. They had lived for almost five months in this small tenant cottage just beyond the city walls. It had been a poor but adequate life, which he had promised would change for the better. She began to fear now that whatever plan for gains he had devised had just gone awry.

"Are ye in trouble, Father?" she asked.

"Nay, but all of Berwick soon will be." He rubbed his eyes, then briefly glared up at the small chimney hole in the thatched roof, softly cursing its inability to properly vent the fire's smoke. "We are leaving this smoke-filled hovel."

"Leaving? Why? Ye *are* in trouble."

"Nay, nay. 'Tis the English, lass. They are gathering an army with the intention of marching this way."

"Oh." She sighed and filled a wooden bowl with stew and handed it to him. "Here. The benefit of your poaching."

"Ye dinnae seem too worried." He sat down more comfortably and began to eat.

After tying a rag around Murdoc's throat, she gave the child a bowl of stew, then helped herself to one. "Oh, I am verra worried, but it does no good to give o'er to it. That willnae stop the armies. I begin to believe nothing will."

"Weel, if they keep on like this for many more years, there will be naught but graves and rubble twixt York and Stirling. That might weel give them pause." He helped himself to another serving of stew.

"There is a dark thought." When Murdoc dropped a bit of meat on the dirt floor, she quickly tossed it into the fire before he could eat it. "Weel, what are the English about to do that makes ye wish to leave?"

"Word has come that that puppet, Edward the Second, is coming north intending to retake Berwick from our fine Walter the Steward."

"Regrettable, but it cannae be much of a surprise. I should think 'twas but a question of when it would happen."

"True. Weel, the when is now. An English army of thousands is assembling at Newcastle. They will march north any day now. 'Twill be a long summer for those caught within these walls."

"August has already begun. Aye, 'tis a week gone. Half the summer has already passed."

"The half that remains will seem verra long indeed, and I dinnae intend for us to spend it in Berwick."

Finished with her stew, Jennet set her empty bowl and spoon in a small pan of water on the narrow stone hearth. She took a drink from the wineskin, then handed it to her father. Her strongest emotion concerning this threat was one

of resignation, which troubled her. The last thing she wished
was to grow complacent about war. That hinted at a lack of
feeling, a numbness of the heart that worried her.

"I should prefer not to be caught up in yet another battle.
Howbeit, where can we flee?"

"I thought Boroughbridge."

"Boroughbridge? Why there?"

"I have friends there. Weel, Artos de Nullepart does." He
smiled, winked, then took a long swig of wine.

"How verra nice, but why go south into England, deeper
into the enemy's land? Why not go north into Scotland? We
have friends *and* kinsmen there."

Artair nodded and was briefly diverted into laughing when
Murdoc toddled over to play with the long tail of his liripipe cap. "We do, and I would travel that way except for one
wee trouble. Do ye think the Scots will just set back and let
the English regain Berwick?"

She grimaced and inwardly cursed. "Nay, they will rush to
aid Berwick or, if it's too late to do so, will fight to take it
back from the English."

"Aye, they will, though I cannae guess exactly what they
will do. They could ride straight here or engage in another of
those diversionary raids the Douglas so favors. Either way
would put us between two armies. I dinnae wish that."

"Nor I. We bear the colors of neither side, nor are we
wealthy enough to be held for ransom. 'Twould be but a race
to see which side would cut us down first."

"Which is just what I mean to avoid. So, on the morrow
we ride for Boroughbridge."

Jennet sighed and nodded. Although she disliked the idea
of moving yet again, she was not heartbroken to leave
Berwick. Since arriving, she had been surprised to find that
the town too held memories for her. She had not expected
that, for although she had met Hacon here, it had not been the
happiest of times. Her pain was clearly too fresh, any memory

able to stir it whether good or bad. What truly hurt was that now, when it was too late, she fully realized the difference between Hacon and too many another knight. While she would never have liked his going into battle, she knew now that she could have been less condemning. She could only pray that she had not wounded him in any way with her words.

"Away with that sad face, dearling," scolded her father, though his own face held only sympathy.

She had to smile. He and Murdoc were engaged in a tug of war with the liripipe cap. Her father's thick hair was now mussed by Murdoc's snatching of his cap. They were what kept her from sinking into black despair, what gave her a reason to live. Murdoc needed her, and although her father did not, he would be sorely grieved to lose her. Although she sometimes felt as if she had no purpose in life without Hacon, she knew it was not true. Life might no longer be so sweet, but it was far from over.

As she rescued her father's cap from a giggling Murdoc, she asked her father, "And if ye are Artos, who am I?"

"Ah, my daughter, of course."

"But I am not as skilled as you. I dinnae think I can sound French"

"No need to. I have always mentioned you if asked, claiming I took a wife during a brief stay in Scotland. Now I will say that ye, and your bairn, had need of me. Such things are easily explained."

"Mayhaps, but are not the French often the enemy of the English?"

"Not all of them. I always claim kinship to those in favor at the moment."

She shook her head and laughed softly. "One day ye shall trip o'er all these lies and half-truths." She picked Murdoc up in her arms. "Weel, we are to bed. I would assume ye mean to leave early and travel swiftly."

"Aye, I do. I wish to be weel away ere those armies clash."

* * *

Hacon scowled at the many small campfires that dotted the moor. He had been with the army for just a week, and already he was weary of it. A thin summer rain soaked him and the rest of Douglas's men. Only a few tents had been raised. Douglas's force traveled light, leaving such comforts behind. Huddled beneath his plaid, which Dugald had stretched over sticks to make a roof of sorts, Hacon wished they went as encumbered with such luxuries as the English. Instead he squatted next to Ranald and Dugald before a sputtering, smoky fire, feeling increasingly damp and gloomy. Only thoughts of Jennet kept him from racing back to Dubheilrig. He had to find her. He just wished he could he more confident of doing so while riding with Douglas.

"Why dinnae we travel to Berwick?" Ranald asked, breaking the heavy silence.

"To confront an army of twelve thousand or more?" Hacon shook his head. "Nay, though it angered me at first, the Douglas has a good plan. A diversionary raid into England. He means to sweep down the Swale Valley toward York. We will harry those lands as we did before, burning their fields and cottages and stealing all we can carry. Once news of our attack reaches Edward's forces at Berwick, many of his men will race home to protect their lands, wives, and bairns."

"But Jennet may still be in Berwick."

"I think not. If we kenned Edward's movements, the people in Berwick must have too. Many will have fled. One of those many will surely be Artair Graeme. That mon is a survivor. He was caught at Perth. He willnae be caught again."

"Oh, weel, if ye are sure."

A brief, sharp laugh escaped Hacon. "Nay, lad, I am sure of verra little. I have ne'er met Artair Graeme. My judg-

ments are born of all I have been told by Jennet and those at
Dubheilrig who met the mon. I feel none would question the
mon's bravery, but he is also one who kens weel how to protect his own. The cursed mon has been dancing freely twixt
England and Scotland for near as long as Jennet has lived.
Cunning allows him to do that, and I must believe that any
mon with cunning would swiftly leave a city upon which
thousands of the enemy are advancing."

"Aye, he would," agreed Dugald.

"Weel." Ranald hesitated an instant before asking, "We are
agreed he would flee, but where would he flee to?"

"I but wish I kenned," Hacon answered, weariness in his
voice. "Again I am left to make a decision with little knowledge. I believe the mon will go south into England. He will
ken that the Bruce willnae let Berwick fall. Not wishing to
be caught between two armies, he will move to the south. All
I can do is pray that the Douglas takes us on the same route."

"Which means Jennet could be caught in a town or village
under attack—again. She will be seen to be on the wrong
side—again."

"Aye." Hacon fought his own fears, not wishing to reveal
them to Ranald. "But we will reach them first."

"How can ye be sure of that?"

"We *will* reach her first."

Hacon was relieved when Ranald said no more. He was
sick with worry, and the youth's constant questions only
added to it. There was too much left to chance. Jennet could
be caught in the midst of another battle, swept up in another
raid. Despite his efforts not to, Hacon could not help thinking about all that could go wrong, all that she could so easily
suffer. She had her father, but that man could fall in an
attack, leaving her alone with young Murdoc to protect.

Over and over he reviewed his decision to join Douglas's
raiding force. What he ached to do was set out immediately
to hunt Jennet down, but he knew that was folly. He would

not be allowed to wander freely over England. Scotland and England were at war and he was the enemy. Nor did he have Artair Graeme's skill in changing his identity to suit his whereabouts. Traveling with the army was his only choice. He just wished he could be content with that.

The moment Ranald nodded off to sleep, Dugald gave Hacon a comforting slap on the back. "Ye must cease worrying."

"That isnae done easily, m'friend."

"Mayhaps not, but it steals your strength and resolve if ye let your thoughts prey on what could go wrong."

"All that could go wrong far outweighs what could go right. She willnae be standing upon the first hillock in England awaiting me with a smile."

"Nay, nor must she be spitted on a pike in the first village we chance upon. Ye would be a fool to think 'twill be easy, but 'tis just as foolish to think the journey doomed ere we begin it."

"Aye." Hacon sighed. "Why did she not stay safely at Dubheilrig?" he grumbled.

"Because she thought you were dead. She went with that rogue she calls a father. Aye, and I am thinking the lass is no weak, puling thing to fall so easily. Dinnae forget all she has survived thus far."

Hacon began to do just that, and his spirits lifted slightly. "Aye, she is a strong lass and a clever one."

"And no stranger to many of these men. Dinnae keep this search to yourself. Tell others. There is a host of men who would help you search her out. Aye, and if others ken we may meet her on this raid, they may be less swift to cut down all in their path. They may at least look first."

"Aye, they might at that. On the morrow I will spread the word. It cannae hurt." Suddenly thinking of Balreaves, Hacon qualified that. "I will also give a good description of her father. Not only might she be found with him, even in the

turmoil of battle, but I cannae risk him being killed by
my compatriots."

Grunting in agreement, Dugald scowled out at the rain.
"Weel, another night of sleeping squatting like a toad."

Chuckling softly, Hacon closed his eyes. Sleeping under
such conditions was never easy. Adding his deep concern
about Jennet's well-being made it nearly impossible. Nevertheless, he would struggle to get at least some sleep, for he
would need rest in order to face the days ahead. On the
morrow the raid into England would begin in earnest.

Wiping the sweat from his face with the sleeve of his
tunic, Hacon watched the Douglas and James Randolph, the
Earl of Moray, confer. The two leaders of the raid sat on their
mounts accepting the reports of their forward scouts, all the
while plotting their next move. He suspected they were discussing whether or not to attack York, which lay about thirty
miles to the south. Their armor glinted in the summer sun
from beneath their fine linen surcoats.

Hacon wondered how they could endure it in the heat.
September was now into its second week, but it had not
brought the cooler weather he had prayed for. He had discarded his helmet and his chain mail, keeping only his
lencroich, but even that padded, quilted garment was nearly
too hot to bear. A number of men had stripped to their shirts.
Since some did not wear braies, Hacon suspected many of
the English seeing them attack would be confirmed in their
opinion that the Scots were barbarians. While the urge to go
naked, or nearly so, was tempting, Hacon was not eager to
offer his unprotected nether regions to English swords and
arrows.

"Ah, Dugald." He greeted his cousin as that man set down
a bucket of cool water. "As always, ye find just what is

needed." Taking one of the rags out of the bucket, Hacon held it over his face.

"'Tis as hot as Satan's armpit," grumbled Dugald as he too took a rag from the bucket and slowly rubbed it over his face and neck. "No mon should have to fight in this."

"Nay, but we will, just as we have for the last month. There is a town ahead. Yet another cursed town," muttered Hacon as he dipped his own rag into the bucket of water and held the dripping cloth to his throat.

"She could be in this one."

"Ye have said that about every village, town, and crofter's hut we have chanced upon."

"Weel, she could have been there."

"Aye, and she could be in Oxford or even London. Do ye suggest we march on to those fine English towns?"

"So, ye wish to return to Dubheilrig, do ye?"

"Nay," snapped Hacon, then sighed. "I grow weary of finding no sign of her, and it shortens my temper."

"This cursed heat cannae help." Dugald dipped his rag into the bucket, then slapped it on his head, letting the cool water drip down over his face and neck.

"'Twill make the men sorely eager to clash swords with the English."

"I begin to think we will do little of that. We have ridden nearly the length of the Swale Valley and yet no English army confronts us. Douglas's plan to weaken the English army sieging Berwick by pulling some of their number after us isnae working. 'Tis clear the lordlings care little for these people or this land. They would rather squat before the walls of Berwick than halt Douglas's rampage. When we do fight, 'tis with peasants and merchants. All the English knights and soldiers have been dragged away to Berwick. There is no sign that even one of them rushes this way. This isnae war," he murmured, "but slaughter."

"'Ware, Hacon." Dugald glanced around a little nervously.

"There are too many ears about. What ye mean as a simple complaint could too easily be dressed in the colors of treason. One mon especially would be pleased to entrap you so."

Hacon nodded. "Aye, 'tis true. This heat and weariness dull my wits. Where is she, Dugald? Four weeks into England and there is no sign of her," Hacon whispered.

"She cannae be too far away. And if we dinnae find her whilst on this raid, all isnae lost. Ye ken where her kinsmen are. We can leave word with them."

"That could take months," Hacon grumbled, yet he was honestly glad he had that route to take if needed.

"Better late than never. Aye, the lass could even return to Dubheilrig. She was invited to, has friends there. So, there is no need to settle yourself into such a black humor if ye dinnae find her now."

"I *want* her now." Hacon knew that sounded childish and decided that months of celibacy were twisting his mood.

"Och, weel, I want a fine, cool breeze *now*," drawled Dugald, "but we dinnae always get what we want, do we?"

Deciding to let that moment of petulance and its reprimand pass, Hacon asked, "Where is Ranald?"

"Sprawled in a wee patch of shade with a few other of your men. A wee bit to the rear."

"The lad must be exhausted. I hadnae thought we would raid so deeply into England, o'er a hundred miles."

"Aye, a free clear run for the most of it." Dugald stared toward the southern horizon. "As I figure it, we arenae more than thirty miles from York itself. Do ye ken what lies ahead?"

"A village called Boroughbridge, God help it."

"Get dressed, lass," ordered Artair as he stepped into the small cottage they now called home.

Jennet opened one eye to regard her father with annoyance. She was sprawled on her small rope bed wearing only her chemise. A naked Murdoc slept on a floor pallet beside her. It was too hot to do anything. It was certainly too hot to get dressed. All of August had been hot, and September was not proving much better. She closed her eye. Her plan was to sleep until October, when the cooler weather would surely come.

"This is no time to play at sleeping, lass. Get up, put your clothes on, and gather together whatever ye value."

There was a tone to her father's voice that banished Jennet's stupor. Slowly, she sat up and watched him. He was putting on his heavily padded jupon, the only armor he possessed. Alarm seized her, thrusting away the last of her laziness.

"The English?" she whispered as she eased off her bed, careful not to nudge the sleeping Murdoc.

"I dinnae think so."

"Weel, it must be someone or why are ye arming yourself?"

"A young shephard crawled into town a short while ago. Someone had cut the lad and he didnae live long enough to say exactly who had done it. An army was all he could gasp out. An army gathers to the north of us."

"The Scots? Douglas's men?" She tugged on her undertunic and began to lace it up.

"If I dared a guess, I would say aye. The English are besieging Berwick. 'Twould be like the Douglas to push a raid into this beleaguered land, hoping to divert the English from Berwick." He began to buckle on his sword.

"Or, at least weaken the siege by drawing some men from it, those who would race to protect their lands here."

"Aye. It has worked before. Howbeit, I cannae say 'tis one or the other. The English could be riding this way, having lifted the siege or even taken Berwick. I dinnae want to see them either. Their arrival need not be a friendly one."

"What are we going to do?" She slipped on her overtunic and quickly did it up.

"*We* arenae doing anything. Not yet." He moved to stand in front of her, gently grasping her shoulders. "I am going to see exactly what is marching our way."

"Nay," she cried, suddenly afraid for him. "'Tis madness to walk toward an army."

"Lass, I ken weel what I am doing. I also ken that to run without being certain what we run from is foolishness. In truth, there may be no reason to flee. 'Twould please me if that proved true."

"Surely we can learn all we need to know by waiting here a wee bit longer."

"Once that army is in sight, 'twill be too late to act. None of the cowards or woodenheads living here understand that. So, I must do it myself. Now, ye are to stay here. Dinnae go anywhere, and, if anyone comes here, shoo them away."

When he strode toward the low, narrow doorway, she hurried after him. "This is too dangerous. Let us just leave here."

"Lass"—he kissed her cheek—"gather up your things and accept that your father does ken a thing or two, that he may go take a wee peek and return hale."

"I ken wool that ye have a fine skill, but I dinnae like this. I have an ill feeling about it all. Let us stay together, face whatever approaches together, or flee together."

Cupping her face in his hands, he quickly kissed her nose. "Set your fears and forebodings aside, sweeting. Now, obey your father."

"But—"

"Heed me, lass. 'Tis important. Get the wee laddie dressed and toss what ye most value in a sack. Then set right here. I will return. Howbeit, if I dinnae and something happens . . ."

"I will wait for you."

"Nay, ye willnae. Ye will grab the bairn and hide."

"And be parted from you for another eight years?"

"That willnae happen. Think of that wee laddie, child. He is the most important one. Take him and get away. If this is an attack, ye must not hesitate to save your own life and Murdoc's. I can take care of myself." He kissed her cheek again, and started out the door.

Jennet stood in the doorway and watched him leave, feeling terrified and alone. The sense of impending disaster she had tried to suppress grew stronger, choking her. She feared she was about to lose her father again.

A tug on her skirts drew her attention. She looked down to find Murdoc at her side, his sleepy-eyed gaze going from her departing father to her and back again. Sighing, she picked him up and gently hugged him as she watched her father disappear into the distance. She prayed that whatever army waited out there found him just as hard to see. The fact that they had killed the shepherd who had chanced upon them did not suggest they were friendly.

Turning back into the small cottage, she hurried to do exactly as her father had told her to. She knew he was right in all he had said. Murdoc was the one to think of now, not herself or her father. She had seen enough of war to know that even the babes were not safe. Using all her willpower, she kept her mind fixed upon the child.

It did not take long to gather up the belongings she considered important. The farther they had traveled from Dubheilrig, the poorer they had lived. There was little coin to be made in the war-ravaged land. Even her father, with all his guile and wit, had barely kept them housed and fed.

Finally, prepared to flee at any moment, she sat in the open doorway. Murdoc played happily in the dirt at her foot. She kept a close eye on him, but most of her attention was fixed upon the village. At any moment the quiet cluster of cottages could be beset by men eager to lay waste to it. The thatched roofs would begin to burn, women would scream, and the sound of deadly battle would rend the air. She dreaded it.

Foolishly, she had allowed herself to believe that, in leaving Berwick before the English army appeared, they had eluded the never-ending war.

Her dark thoughts were disrupted when a wagon appeared on the road before her tiny cottage. "Master Butcher, where do ye hie to?" she called out, frowning when she saw that his household goods and family filled the wagon. "Has trouble come?"

"Nay, but I do not mean to set still and wait for it." The barrel-chested man slowed his wagon. "We travel to my brother's farm, south of York. I will return when I am sure 'tis safe here."

"But why do ye believe it isnae safe now?"

"Child, that poor shepherd was not cut down out of mercy. I lost one family to war. I do not mean to lose another. Ye would be wise to flee as well," he added as he snapped the reins, urging his cart horse to a faster pace.

Jennet looked back toward the village. She tried to find comfort in the fact that no one else seemed to agree with Master Butcher. There was no sign of any other cart.

She took her rosary beads from her pocket. As she smoothed her fingers over them, she remembered Hacon and felt the sting of tears. The war had already stolen so much from her. How could it take more?

As if in answer, an alarm was suddenly sounded. The clanging bell startled her from her thoughts. Horrified, Jennet gaped toward the fields just beyond the village. Sweeping down on Boroughbridge was the Black Douglas. She recognized the banners at the fore of the rapidly moving army. The front line consisted of Douglas and his knights upon their fine horses, their armor glinting in the sun as they rode straight for the village. Behind that line came the mass of the raiding party. Hundreds of Scots on their sturdy ponies, the horde interspersed with an occasional knight on a larger mount, thundered down upon Boroughbridge.

The speed of their advance gave the villagers little time to prepare to defend themselves, little chance even to flee.

For just an instant she hesitated, thinking of all the men she had come to know while riding with the Douglas's raiding force. Then good sense returned to her. Even if she was lucky enough to meet up with one, he might not recognize her until it was too late. She grabbed Murdoc and ran for her life.

# *Chapter 16*

"She isnae here." Hacon stomped out of the ransacked inn and paused in the market street of Boroughbridge, Dugald and Ranald flanking him.

"Ye cannae be certain of that yet," Dugald protested. "We have searched but half the village."

"The other half burns. She wouldnae linger there."

"Uncle," Ranald began a little timidly, "I cannae feel she would linger in the village at all."

"Nay?" Hacon tugged off his helmet and ran a hand through his sweat-dampened hair.

"Nay. Though we fell upon this village as swiftly as we fall upon others, there was still some time when she could have seen us. Aye, there was even time for an alarum to be sounded. I believe she would have fled here as swiftly as she could."

"Aye," Dugald agreed, "the lad is right. Even if she *was* here, she willnae be here now. Now, I dinnae think we need to search the countryside all about us . . ."

"I am pleased to hear it," drawled Hacon.

"Howbeit," Dugald continued, ignoring the interruption, "it would be wise to speak to whatever hostages were taken, to those who survived. Once we find out if she and her father ever lived here, we will ken what to do next."

"'Tis exactly what I was thinking," agreed Hacon, then turned to Ranald. "Ye return to our horses. If Jennet is close by, she may try to find one amongst Douglas's men whom she kens would aid her." As soon as Ranald left, Hacon said to Dugald, "Weel, let us see if any of the villagers have survived."

"Or if any will speak to us," muttered Dugald as he followed Hacon in search of captives.

As Hacon strode through the smoldering village, he prayed Ranald was right. If Jennet had been in Boroughbridge and had not run at the first sign of attack, she could easily be one of the dead or dying now. He winced when he heard a woman's screams. Ah, lass, if ye had the wit to hide, he prayed, then stay there. Please, God, give her the wit to stay hidden until this bloodlust calms.

Jennet grimaced as one of the branches of the hedgerow stabbed her in the back. From her hiding place within the hedge's sharp tangles, she could see the village. Poor accursed Boroughbridge, she thought as she watched smoke curl up from the burning roofs. She recalled a similar scene from the raid she had been forced to join over a year ago, after Hacon had taken her from Berwick. It amazed her that the people had the strength to rebuild each time. Boroughbridge was a lovely place, yet it now seemed doomed.

Placing her fingers on Murdoc's lips, she silenced the boy's whimpers. She had spent long hours teaching him how to be still and quiet. At times she had wondered why she should try so hard, but the value of the lessons was now clear. Douglas's men trampled over the countryside looking for villagers to take captive and stock to steal. One thing she would not have to worry about was that Murdoc might reveal their hiding place.

But she also knew that did not mean they were safe, and

she tensed as a horse snorted close by. It was tempting to edge forward, to peek out of her uncomfortable thicket refuge. That, she knew, would be folly. She *might* be able to accomplish it unseen, but the risk was far too great

A strange noise drew her attention. Several yards away and drawing closer, the sound was difficult to recognize. Then she nearly gasped aloud, pressing her palm over her mouth to halt any noise's escape. Whoever was wandering outside the hedgerow was walking along slowly and prodding it with his sword. She had seen that done before. It never failed to flush out whatever or whoever tried to hide there. And, she thought with dismay as she looked at Murdoc, it would flush her out.

Holding the lad close, she carefully inched into a position which would allow her to bolt when the time was right. She kept her gaze fixed toward the sword, although it was several moments before it came into view, edging ever closer. She prayed the man would not think to mount the horse she could hear tethered nearby and simply run her down. When the sword plunged into the thicket but inches from her, she bolted.

The branches of the hedge tore at her clothing as she emerged. She immediately darted to the right, just in time to elude the grasp of the knight who waited there. She headed west, thinking to put so much distance between herself and the knight hot on her heels that he would stop pursuing her, would turn back to his companions, not wishing to plunge too deep into what could be enemy territory, alone and unaided.

But soon she realized that her pursuer was not one to give up quickly. So too, she was tiring fast, hindered by Murdoc's weight, her long skirts, and the heat. While she was still able she decided to make a stand. Quickly setting Murdoc down, she pulled out her dagger, turned, and gaped. The man who halted but a few feet from her, panting and sweat-soaked, was Sir Niall Chisholm. She started to relax, then tensed again as he aimed his sword at her. Whether he recognized her or not, he meant to kill her.

"Sir Niall!" she cried, desperate enough to plead, if only for Murdoc's sake. "Do ye not recognize me?"

"Aye. Sir Gillard's wee whore. Ye are with the enemy again."

He lunged and she nimbly eluded the deadly point of his sword. The ensuing battle was grossly unequal. She quickly realized that he was but toying with her. Her dagger was no defense against his sword. Within moments he tripped her, causing her to lose her dagger. He pinned her to the ground, sitting on her and holding his sword edge against her throat. Jennet could not understand why he should wish to kill her, which only added to her feeling of utter helplessness.

"Why?" she asked, her voice hoarse from her exertions and a fear that consumed her.

"Ye are with the English again. Need I have another reason?"

"Nay." She felt completely defeated, almost resigned to her fate. "Spare the bairn?" she asked as a softly sniffing Murdoc toddled over to sit by her head. "Ye could give him to any of the men from Dubheilrig and they would care for him."

"And why should I care a farthing about the brat's fate?"

His voice was low and sneering, but she sensed a softening in his demeanor. "He has done ye no harm." She felt an emerging spark of outrage. "Nor have I. I even tended your wounds."

"Aye, and your mon nearly cut my hand off."

When his gaze fell to her breasts, she stiffened. It was all too easy to read his thoughts, his changing plans for her. Having guessed the new threat, she was not surprised when he placed his gauntleted hand over her breast.

"Now that I think on it," he drawled, "he isnae here to stop me this time." He kneaded her breast. "I could take my fill of you right here. That would sorely cut at the mon's great pride," he muttered.

"Ye need to spite a dead mon?" she asked with ill-disguised disgust.

"Dead? Would that God deigned to give me such a gift."

"He died in Ireland, in Dundalk. Ye yourself sent my rosary beads back to me."

"A strange, fanciful gesture, was it not? Born of false hope too. The mon didnae die. Months later he had the cursed ill taste to return to Scotland. It quite soured my day."

Jennet was stunned. She forgot that her life was in danger, that the man sitting on her chest held a sword to her throat. Even the chilling threat of rape was banished from her thoughts. She finally moved, no longer keeping still out of an attempt to remain safe, and grasped the front of his jupon. She was only briefly aware of his look of utter astonishment.

"Sir Hacon Gillard is alive?" She could only whisper the question, afraid she had misheard him.

"Aye, curse his hide."

"Oh, praise God!" She closed her eyes, fighting the tumult of emotions raging inside of her until all that remained was the need to see him. "Ye must take me to him." When Niall did not move, she snapped, "Weel? Get off of me, ye great oaf."

"We have some unfinished business, wench."

"Ye cannae still mean to rape me! Sir Giliard and I were handfasted ere he left for Ireland. I am his wife."

"Then he will more keenly feel the bite of shame when he kens another mon has ridden you."

"And ye will keenly feel the bite of his sword."

"Let him challenge me. I dinnae suffer from a head wound as I did last time he and I fought o'er you."

Jennet wished she could give him a wound he would not soon forget, but she struggled to calm herself. She studied her captor for a moment. Deciding he suffered from bravado—

or, more likely, an inability to find a way of retreating from his threats without losing face—she tried to think of one. Praying her judgment was right, she went limp, lying beneath him with no sign of resistance, her eyes closed.

"Weel? Get on with it then. I wish to return to my husband."

She forced herself to remain limp when she felt him awkwardly run his hand over her breasts. When, a moment later, he stood up uttering a foul, vicious oath, she was strongly tempted to gape at him. She remained in the same position until he roughly grabbed her hand and yanked her to her feet.

"Changed your mind, Sir Niall?" she murmured, brushing herself off.

"'Twould be like rutting with a corpse," he grumbled. "I bet ye would have stirred had I continued."

"We will ne'er be sure, will we?" She held his gaze, thinking that he looked both sulky and surprisingly young. "Ye may escort me back to my husband now."

"Oh, aye, that I will do, and I will demand a verra dear price for you."

"Ye would ransom me?" She glared at him as he grabbed the reins of his mount. "Ye cannae do that."

"Nay? Why not?" Lightly slapping her on the backside with the flat of his sword, he ordered, "Start walking." He fell into step behind her when she picked up Murdoc, retrieved her dagger, and began to walk back toward Boroughbridge.

"Hacon is your ally, one of Douglas's men. Ye cannae demand ransom from one of your own."

"I can and I will. I will empty his purse. He lost you. I found you. That will cost him dearly indeed. Aye, and ye were on the wrong side of the border again. Sir Gillard should choose his wenches with more care."

Jennet swallowed her angry words. He had backed down. In truth, she began to think he had never been wholeheartedly serious about raping or killing her. She would allow him his swaggering to soothe his pride. Especially since, she mused with an inner smile, she doubted Hacon would pay the man a farthing.

As they neared the place where she had been hiding, Jennet remembered her small sack of belongings, still tucked inside the hedge. She turned to tell Sir Niall she was just going to retrieve it and gasped. Swiftly closing in on him were two armed men. Even as she quickly backed away, she cried out a warning.

Sir Niall reacted with speed and skill, turning neatly and cleanly blocking the forward attacker's sword swing. Jennet set Murdoc down and pulled out her dagger. She could see that Niall was a good fighter, that one of his assailants was timid and held back, but it was still two against one. At some point Niall might need help.

Briefly, she contemplated leaving Niall to his fate and running back to Boroughbridge alone. He had done little to deserve her help. Then she sighed, knowing that if he did not survive the attack, she would never forgive herself. She thanked God that neither of the men intent on killing Niall were ones she had come to know while in Boroughbridge. At least she did not have to face that moral dilemma.

The moment she had dreaded soon came. Seeing that Niall began to tire, the assailant who had held back grew bolder. The first few times the man flanked Niall, the Scot was able to counter the blows. But Jennet knew he could not continue to do so. As she edged closer, Niall cut down one of the men, but he did not turn fast enough to thwart the second man from neatly tripping him, sending him to the ground in a hard, awkward fall that left him gasping for air. Jennet did not wait to see if he would recover. She threw her dagger, and was both relieved and sickened when her aim proved true and the dagger pierced the assailant's chest.

After a brief hesitation to be sure both attackers were dead, Jennet moved toward Niall. He was breathing and she saw no wounds worthy of attention, yet he remained sprawled on his back, his eyes closed. Even his breathing was more or less normal as she knelt by his side.

"Sir Niall," she said, frowning down at him, "what ails you?" She tried and failed to keep all hint of impatience from her voice. The man could truly be hurt and the delay in reaching Hacon utterly necessary.

"Ye. Ye ail me, ye cursed woman," he grumbled, opening his eyes to glare at her as he raised himself up on his elbows. "Ye should have stayed back, cowering off to the side like any other woman would."

"Your display of gratitude is most humbling," she snapped, quickly getting to her feet.

"Gratitude? What have I got to be grateful for?" He hissed a curse, rubbing various aches as he got up.

"How about for saving your miserable life?"

"I could have defeated those two fools unaided. Aye, with one hand."

"Oh? How about whilst flat on your back unable to breathe?"

Niall cursed and resheathed his sword with abrupt, angry movements. "Aye, so be it. Ye saved my life."

"Ye still dinnae sound verra grateful." She wondered why it was so hard for him to admit that she had helped him.

"And why should I be? Ye have ruined everything," he muttered as he went to search the slain men, collecting what few valuables they had, and retrieved Jennet's dagger. "I cannae see much to be thankful for."

"'Tis clear ye value your life far less than I do, which, in truth, isnae verra much."

He wiped her dagger clean and handed it to her. "Sharptongued wench," he muttered. "I was told ye had some wit, but 'tis clear ye arenae using it now. By what ye just did here ye took away my chance to gain any coin from your husband. Now I owe my verra life to you. Honor demands I return ye safely to Sir Hacon. Aye, safely and without demanding ransom."

Shaking her head, she picked up Murdoc and started back the way they had come. "Weel, I cannae say I feel badly about that. Ye shouldnae have been planning such a thing anyway."

"I would have been a fool *not* to think of it. Where are you going?"

"To get my belongings. I left them behind when I had to run or be skewered by you."

She set Murdoc down and retrieved her sack of belongings. As she did so she mused on how swiftly her situation had changed. Only a short while ago she had been huddled in the hedge afraid for her life; now she was squabbling with the man who had threatened it. Niall no longer frightened her. He was certainly jealous of Hacon, but he was no longer truly a danger to her. In fact, she thought with an inner smile as she gathered up Murdoc, Sir Niall reminded her very much of a rather petulant little boy.

"I should let ye find your own way back to your mon," Niall snapped as he walked up to her, leading his mount. "I dinnae see any reason to do the work when I will gain no reward for it."

"Is that the way a knight should treat the one who saved his life?" She fell into step beside him as he began to walk back toward town.

"Do ye intend to remind me of that fact for the rest of my days?"

"Mayhaps." She had to bite back a smile when he cursed. "'Tis always good for a mon to feel a touch of humility." The scent of smoke reached her and she sighed. "Did many die?" she asked.

"Nay, few chose to fight us."

"Yet ye fired their roofs."

"Aye. Ye cannae be sure there will be little fighting until ye are actually there. 'Tis best to attack each time as if resistance will be fierce and bloody."

"Ye didnae perchance see a mon with eyes like mine and red-brown hair?"

"Nay. Why? Have ye lost more than your husband? Ye *are* a careless lass."

Ignoring his snide tone, she nodded. "Aye—my father."

"He has taken the side of the English, has he?"

"Nay. He takes no side in this war."

"Is he a Scotsmon?"

"Aye."

"Then if he isnae fighting with the English what is he doing in England?"

"There is more wealth here, more coin which may be earned or slyly tricked away from its owner. True, 'tis held tightly in but a few hands, most people being too poor even to feed their families. Howbeit, if the coin is there, Papa can find it."

"Ye became separated when the battle began?"

"Nay. He set off just before the attack." She told him about the shepherd. "Father wished to ken exactly which army marched our way. He didnae return ere the attack began."

"Weel, he willnae return now if he still lives. He can only be seen as an enemy if he approaches."

Jennet sighed and nodded. She prayed her father was alive, that they would simply be apart for a while. It would be a cruel twist of fate if, when she held such joy in one hand through the discovery that Hacon was alive, she should be delivered only sorrow in the other through the death of her father. She fought to push aside all thought of such a possibility. Her father was simply hiding for his own safety. Once it was safe, he would find her again. As they neared the village she struggled to believe that, to banish all doubt.


"They were here," Hacon muttered as he sat on the threshold of the stone cottage that Dugald had claimed for them. Leaning against the low, sturdy door frame, Dugald frowned. "'Twould appear they were, even though the name we were given isnae the right one."

"Ye have let your French lag sorely, cousin. Artos de Nullepart means Artair of Nowhere." He smiled faintly when Dugald cursed, then gave a reluctant laugh. "I have no doubt that Artos de Nullepart is Artair Graeme. Such a game would explain how he can move so freely from Scotland to England and back again. Such a rogue. I ache to meet him."

"So, they were here. Where, then, did they go?"

"I wish I could say. No one has seen him or Jennet since the alarum was sounded. One mon swore he saw Artair heading toward our army, but none of our men recalls seeing him. And why would he leave alone? What of Jennet?"

"Neither is amongst the dead."

"True. There is comfort in that. They must be hiding somewhere, waiting until we leave."

"Aye, but where to look?" Dugald ran a hand through his hair and scowled out at the quieting village.

"I dinnae ken where to start. They could be anywhere. I have our men looking, but the sun will soon set, ending the search."

"And come dawn, we march toward York."

Hacon nodded and muttered a curse. "And we must go with the Douglas. If naught else, 'twould be too dangerous to linger here once the strength of the army has been taken away."

"Then ye must leave word with the people here. They will tell Jennet ye are alive and searching for her."

"Which could cause her a wealth of trouble. After this they willnae look kindly upon one who is wed to one of us. They will turn their fury and hate upon her and her father. I am certain of it. I would make the mon who found her a verra wealthy mon," he vowed. "I would give him every farthing I have if it was needed."

"Weel, ready your purse," drawled Dugald.

"What? What say you?"

"Look there." Dugald pointed to a couple slowly walking toward them.

"Jennet," Hacon whispered, slowly standing up. "'Tis truly her."

"Aye, and with a mon who willnae hesitate to accept any coin ye mean to toss his way," Dugald said.

"I would willingly give him all I own," Hacon replied, not truly heeding his own words.

"Sweet lord, dinnae say so. That one would take it."

Only faintly aware of what Dugald was saying, Hacon fixed his gaze upon Jennet. He had searched so long and so unstintingly he dared not believe he had found her. The threat of painful disappointment kept him rooted to the spot, contradictory emotions knotting his insides. He ached to run to her, ached to scold her for entering the land of the enemy once again, and yet he feared that touching her would cause her to disappear like some chimera in a dream. So he stood and waited, hoping she would act.

She looked so good to him it hurt. Months of need for her swelled up within him. Her thick hair was tousled, and he wanted to comb away those tangles with his fingers. She was still slim but did not look as if life without him had treated her harshly. It was enough that she was alive. Hacon tensed, braced for the moment when she would finally see him.

As she and Niall walked down the main street of the village, Jennet sought out Hacon. When she finally saw him she dared not believe her eyes. But there was no denying the sight of him. She knew no other amongst Douglas's men who had such fair hair. So too did she easily recognize that tall form before she was close enough to see his face.

In her mind she rapidly envisioned the many ways she wished their reunion to unfold. Dignity played a large part in each swiftly changing scene, dignity and regal calm. She cast both aside with little hesitation. Thrusting Murdoc into

Niall's arms and ignoring his muttered oaths, she tossed aside her sack, lifted her skirts, and ran to her lover. He smiled and held his arms wide. She readily hurled herself into them.

His mouth was instantly on hers. The kiss he gave her was fierce, almost too fierce, but she heartily welcomed it. It was proof that he was alive. Though he finally raised his head, he did not ease his grip on her. Jennet kept her arms wrapped tightly around his neck, for her feet were several inches off the ground. Her cheek was pressed against his shoulder. He smelled of horses, smoke, and sweat. They were not scents she usually enjoyed, but this time she savored them.

"I cannae believe ye are alive!"

"Verra alive." He slowly loosened his grip on her until her feet were back on the ground and she could lean back a little to look up at him. "Ye are not an easy lass to find."

"If I had kenned ye had arisen from the dead to look for me, I would have left a clearer trail." She gave a shaky laugh and touched his beard-roughened cheek.

He took her hand in his, kissed her palm, and kept hold of it. "Your father should cease dragging ye off into the enemy's lands. Am I to meet the mon at last?"

Some of her relief and joy at Hacon's return faded a little. "I dinnae ken where he is." She felt Hacon's grip on her hands tighten slightly and knew he shared her sudden fear—that with his return, he could have brought death for her father.


"Pssst, Harold. Nay, do not turn. Just listen and try to answer without being seen."

Artair breathed a sigh of relief when the burly Harold quickly hid his surprise. It had not been easy to crawl up behind the captives who were being held at the edge of the village. The thick, gnarled growth of hawthorn and blackberry bushes offered a place to hide, but they were neither comfortable nor quiet. He was now too close to the well-armed Scots. There was a chance he would not be harmed, but at least until he knew Jennet's fate, he preferred not to take the gamble.

"Have you seen Jennet?" he asked his dice-playing friend when the guards moved away to share the contents of a wineskin.

"Aye. I see her right now. She is in the arms of a big, fairhaired Scot. If you dare a peek around me, you will see her too."

Cautiously, Artair edged forward until he could peek through the sheltering brambles more clearly. "By the saints, the man is alive! 'Twas said he had been slain in Ireland."

"Well, 'twas said you were a Frenchman," Harold countered.

"Ah, ye are no longer fooled." Artair immediately discarded the thick French accent he had been using.

"Nay. That great Scotsman has been asking after you and Jennet. 'Twas clear he sought no Frenchman. 'Twas also clear he sought no enemy. So, why do you hide?"

"He may not see me as an enemy, but he isnae the only one there nor the most powerful. I am a Scotsman in England. That will brand me a traitor in most eyes."

"Ah, aye. Well, there are not many in this village as forgiving as I, my friend. They too now know you have lied, and many guess you are as much a Scot as your daughter. They will not welcome you back after this. Not soon at least. So, how do you intend to get back with your Jennet?"

"I will meet up with her in Scotland."

"She will think you are dead."

"Aye, and I am sorry to cause her grief, but better that than the trouble I would bring her if I appeared now. 'Twould grieve her more if she couldnae save me from a traitor's fate. That braw knight can care for her."

"Shall I try to get word to them?"

"Nay, my friend. 'Twould put ye at too great a risk. Watch your own hide," he advised as he began to edge away.

"And watch yours, as if I need to tell you that," Harold said in a soft mutter. "God be with you, you rogue."

"And you."

After one last look toward Jennet, Artair began his retreat. It was time for him to make his way back to Scotland. He hated leaving Jennet uncertain of his fate but promised himself he would make amends when they met again at Dubheilrig.

# *Chapter 17*

"Ye willnae saddle me with this brat," Niall objected.

Jennet was startled enough by that harsh voice to turn. Suddenly Murdoc was thrust into her arms. She laughed softly when, an instant later, the child lunged toward Hacon with his small arms outstretched. Hacon quickly accepted the child and gave the boy a hug. She huddled closer to Hacon's side when he put his arm about her shoulder. He was talking to Niall.

"I owe you, Sir Niall, for safely returning my wife to me." When Dugald took Murdoc, Hacon extended his hand to Niall.

After hesitating only briefly, Niall shook his hand. "Ye owe me nothing."

"I must disagree. The return of my wife demands some reward."

"Ye owe me nothing." Niall glared at Jennet. "I leave ye to tell him why I act so nobly." Still leading his mount, he strode off down the street.

"What ails the mon?" Hacon watched Niall's abrupt departure with a frown of confusion.

"I fear 'tis my fault his mood is so sour. At least, more sour than it has been. I had the ill manners to save his life."

"Ye were attacked?" He hastily looked her over, searching for any hint of a wound.

That display of concern made Jennet feel decidedly warm. She wondered if her deep desire to drag Hacon off to the nearest private spot and make fierce love to him was obvious to all who looked at her. Then she decided she did not care if it was.

"Two men attacked us. Sir Niall did verra weel but"—she shrugged—"two against one can defeat even the greatest swordsmon."

"Ah, and ye decided to lend a hand. That must have sorely stung his pride."

"More like his purse. He had planned to ransom me back to you, the rogue. It didnae please him to owe me his life."

"He didnae hurt you, did he?"

"Nay." She decided that was not really a lie, for despite his dark threats, Sir Niall had done her no real harm. "Hacon, have ye seen my father or heard any news of him?"

He hugged her as he shook his head. "Nay, dearling, I fear not. We have asked everyone we could. None have seen him since the alarum sounded, although a few saw him walk toward us before that."

"Aye." She slipped her arms around his waist and rested her cheek against his chest as she yet again told of the shepherd. "My father wanted to ken what we might face ere we fled from it. He left me ready to run and hide at the first sign of trouble. I havenae seen him since. I cannae believe I have lost him again."

"Now, dearling, we have no proof that he is dead."

"But if he lives, why has he not returned?"

"If ye werenae so worried, I believe ye would think of the answer yourself. He is a Scot on the wrong side of the border. That could easily mark him as a traitor. He must hide. If he was captured, even I might not be able to save him. He will work his way back to Scotland and search us out at Dubheilrig."

"Aye, aye, he will. I must believe that, as ever, he has escaped death and I will see him soon." In an attempt to stop worrying, she asked, "Ye must tell me how it is ye are alive when we were told ye had fallen at Dundalk."

"Ah, now there is a long, complicated tale." He lifted her up in his embrace.

Jennet slipped her arms around his neck as he started to enter the cottage. "Does that mean ye willnae tell me?"

"Oh, aye, I will, but I think 'twill take me until dawn. Dugald, watch over Murdoc," he ordered before kicking the battered door shut behind him.

He set her on her feet and Jennet smiled faintly as he bolted the door. She easily recognized the look on his face, and she had no objection to satisfying it. His desire equaled her own. She simply wondered if they would make it even to the rude bed on the far wall before succumbing to their passion.

"It is still verra hard for me to believe ye are alive," she whispered.

"Weel, then," Hacon murmured, "mayhaps I had best ease *all* your doubts."

Her soft laughter was ended by his kiss. She lost all sense of where she was. Only Hacon existed, Hacon and her intense, desperate need to be one with him. She joined him in the frantic unlacing of their clothing. He paused only long enough to haphazardly throw a blanket onto the floor. When he urged her body down onto the blanket she made no protest, welcoming him as he covered her. She wrapped her limbs around him after assisting him in pushing up her skirts. A soft cry of delight and deep satisfaction escaped her when he thrust into her. It seemed as if it had been a lifetime since he had filled her body with his.

His urgent need made him a little rough, but her own need met his. In truth, she welcomed the slight roughness despite knowing she might find a bruise or two in the morning. It left her with no doubt about his continued good health. Nor could the man plunging into her body so vigorously be a mere dream.

Her release came swiftly, as did his. Jennet laughed with pure joy as she felt his seed flow into her. Trembling, she held him tightly when he sagged on top of her, holding him locked in an intimate embrace. She savored the impractical thought of holding him there forever.

"That was shameless," she murmured when she finally regained her breath.

"Aye." He winked as he kissed the tip of her nose. "Ye ken I am alive now, though, eh? My pretty plunder."

"Weel, I am a wee bit more certain of it."

"Wheesht, are ye ne'er to be satisfied?"

"Probably not," she murmured. Then, unable to hold his intent gaze, she wriggled slightly. "The floor grows hard."

"Not only that . . ." He grinned beneath her hand when she hastily covered his mouth with it.

Hacon chuckled softly as he gently ended the rich intimacy of their embrace. The water he had earlier set to heat on the circular central hearth was ready and he used it to bathe her, kissing each scrape and bruise that marred her fine skin. His passion already hot and fierce, she pushed it to new heights as she took the cloth from his hand and washed him. When he could stand no more he picked her up and took her to the bed. There, he loved her with a gentle ferocity born of their long separation and his fears for her safety. To his delight, she matched it with a fierce greed of her own.

"Did ye check the bed for vermin?" she asked when she could finally speak, frowning at the rope-slung bed on top of which they were so carelessly sprawled.

"Aye. I may have dreaded sleeping alone again, but that was company I was eager to forgo." He moved to lie on his back and tugged her into his arms.

"Hacon?" She idly smoothed her hand over his chest, finding

the need to keep touching him irresistible. "What happened in Ireland? Were ye hurt and left behind as the others fled?"

He sighed and idly kissed the top of her head. Their re-union was sweet, yet not all he had envisioned. Their love-making was more than he could ever want, yet they had shared no words of love. His urge to speak of what was in his heart was stifled by the memory of what she had said just before he rode away from Dubheilrig. The way she acted now gave him hope, yet he still faltered. How could he bare his soul, reveal his vulnerability, to someone who thought him blood-hungry? While he grew more confident that he had conquered more than her passion, he had no indication that he had gained her respect. How could he offer his heart to a woman who did not seem to understand what he was, *all* that he was—man *and* knight?

That was what he wished to talk about, not Ireland, not Balreaves. He wanted to delve into what she felt, what she thought, yet he admitted to cowardice. While he felt a need to know, he feared the knowledge. Soon, he promised himself even as he cursed his own timidity. Soon I will take the bit be-tween my teeth and have done with it. All could continue as it was for a while longer, but he knew that the questions and doubts, if left unsettled, would begin to destroy what they shared.

Now, however, she waited with increasing impatience to hear what had happened in Ireland. The story would worry her, frighten her. Briefly, but only briefly, he considered lying. One lie was all his conscience could bear.

"Aye, Dugald and I were wounded and left behind, but 'twas not the Irish who laid us low."

Jennet shivered and huddled closer to him. "Balreaves," she guessed.

Combing his fingers through her thick hair, he replied, "Aye, Balreaves. The men who attacked us didnae wear his colors, but I ken they were his hirelings. They certainly werenae Irish. And when they thought we would ne'er see another dawn, they boasted of being Balreaves's assassins."

"He used the confusion of a lost battle and retreat to hide his treachery. 'Twas most clever of him."

"Verra clever. Dugald and I should be as dead as young Alan. We were badly wounded."

Tracing the new scar along his left rib cage, Jennet nodded. "Ye could have bled to death."

"'Twas what Balreaves's hirelings prayed for. 'Twas our good fortune that the enemy was so close upon our heels. Those murderers didnae take time to make sure they had succeeded. Once Dugald and I fell, they paused only to steal what could be easily grasped and ran. We roused enough to drag ourselves into a ditch to hide from the Irish. I fear the rosary beads with which ye gifted me were lost."

"Nay. They were returned to me as proof that ye were dead. Somehow Sir Niall gained hold of them and sent them to me at Dubheilrig. He himself called it a fanciful gesture."

"Sir Niall has a reputation for such. Just as one decides he is all he appears—a sour, mean-spirited youth—he does something admirably chivalrous, something indisputably kind. Then he returns to grumbling and sneering. A strange lad." He brushed a kiss over her forehead, "Ye have many a bruise, lass. Are ye certain he did naught to harm you?"

"Naught worthy of trouble. He didnae recognize me at first and we had a brief tussle."

"I think ye arenae telling me the whole of it, but I willnae press you."

"Good, for all turned out weel. Now, finish your tale. How did ye escape? Was Dugald less injured than you and able to help?"

"Nay, Dugald was worse. He courted death more assiduously than I. We were fortunate. A godly mon discovered us. He cared nothing for who we were, who we fought for, only that we were fellow men in need of aid. He took us into his poor house, healed our wounds, and kept us safe. Fortunately, not all of my wealth had been stolen so I was able to repay him with some coin ere we left. Fate continued to favor us, allowing Dugald and me to escape that cursed land and find our way home."

"Only to be taken on another bloody raid," she observed.

"Ah, but that is your fault." He grinned when she lifted her head to stare at him. "'Tis."

"And just how did ye come to that conclusion?"

"Ye didnae stay at Dubheilrig. Now, if ye had stayed for a few months more, wailing and tearing out your hair over my death, all this would have been unnecessary. Instead, ye strolled off to England with your father."

"Ah, ye wished to return home to a bald lass with swollen eyes." She smiled faintly when he laughed.

Jennet realized no one had told him of how she had taken the report of his death, and she was glad of it. She found her behavior embarrassing to recall, especially now that she knew the report had been a lie. What it might tell him about the depth of her feelings for him was also something she was not eager to discuss. She was still too uncertain of *his* feelings for her.

"My father was at Dubheilrig," she went on to explain. "Since I thought myself a widow, it seemed wisest to go with him. Your family urged me to stay, assured me that I and Murdoc were welcome, but"—she shrugged—"I chose to be with my father. Howbeit, I dinnae see why that should cause you to go on a raid when ye had only just returned home."

"To find you. Artair had taken you into England. I couldnae march into the land of the enemy alone. I dinnae ken why your father continues to do so."

"The coin is here. And when he deals with the English he does so as a Frenchmon."

"Ah, aye, Artos de Nullepart. We discovered that guise

as we asked after him. I fear we revealed his trickery. He willnae be welcome back here, not for a while."

"He will realize that. Dinnae worry on it. Why did ye not just leave word with my kinsmen?"

"Then sit at Dubheilrig, waiting? Nay, I couldnae stomach that." He lightly rubbed his hands over her slim back. "I needed to act. 'Twas more difficult to find you than I had thought. I was resigning myself to sending word out through your kin, and to waiting, when I found you."

Resting her forearms on his broad chest, she lifted her head to look at him. "So now we shall return to Dubheilrig?"

"Soon." He grimaced when her eyes narrowed. "I am now bound to follow this march to the end."

"Does the Douglas mean to try and capture Edward's queen then?" she asked, her voice softened by trepidation.

"Is Edward's queen at York?" He idly traced the shape of her collarbone with his fingers.

"Rumor claims she is. She and Edward's royal judges." She thought of how Edward's father had treated Robert the Bruce's queen when she had been taken prisoner over ten years ago, how he had hung the woman in a cage from the walls of Berwick. "The Bruce might seek revenge for the barbarous treatment his own queen suffered long ago."

"He might, though I should like to believe the Bruce wouldnae act so cruelly. I have no doubt the Douglas would." He shook his head. "I cannae say what lies ahead. I have paid little heed. All I cared about was finding you." He slid his hands down her sides to caress her slender hips. "I had no time for, nor interest in, the plots and schemes of our leaders. I sought only you."

"Well, ye have found me." She brushed her lips over his. "At least I will suffer only through the end of this raid."

Cupping her buttocks in his hands, he moved her against him. "Then we shall hie back to Dubheilrig and find the priest."

"The priest?" She traced his firm jawline with soft, nibbling kisses. "We need a priest?"

"Aye." He murmured his approval when she began to kiss and caress his chest. "Handfast suited when there was no time left to us, but we have time now." An increasing hoarseness entered his voice as her kisses and the light, tantalizing strokes of her tongue went lower. "Now a priest can wed us."

Jennet was both delighted and surprised. "Ye still wish to keep me about?"

"Oh, aye, lass," he replied huskily as she stroked his inner thighs with her tongue. "There is none to equal you. Not in all of Scotland. Nay, nor in England."

"And in Ireland?" He had been gone a very long time, and she suddenly wondered if he had spent that time alone.

Easily guessing how her thoughts had turned, he half smiled. "Weel, there was this lass who cast an eye my way." He smiled more fully when she glanced at him. "Ah, but I wasnae tempted. Weel, not enough." He laughed at her look of disgust. "A mon can wait when he kens he waits for the best he will ever find."

Warmth raced through her body, for it was the nearest he had come to admitting he cared for her. "Weel," she managed to say, her own voice hoarse, "then this bold fellow must be rewarded for his fidelity."

Hacon groaned softly with delight when she curled her long, silken fingers around his erection. Fidelity was not difficult to keep when he had a woman like Jennet. Memories of her touch were more than enough to give him the strength to turn from any temptation. He wondered if and when she would ever guess that truth, then lost his ability for coherent thought as her mouth replaced her seductive fingers.

Jennet praised him with her lips, excited and honored him with her tongue, loved him with her mouth. His guttural cries of pleasure, his writhing movements beneath her, fired her desire to greater heights. When he abruptly grasped her beneath the arms, pulled her up his body, and set her upon him, she was ready and eager for the joining of their bodies. At first she sweetly taunted him, moving upon him slowly and gently, denying him the fierceness he craved. But soon her own need stole her control and she gave him what he called for, driving them both to the convulsive satisfaction of their hungers.

Once her sanity began to return, Jennet eased the lingering intimacy of their embrace. "'Tis too hot for this," she murmured as she flopped onto her back at his side and ignored his soft laughter.

"Mayhaps I shouldnae have heated that water," he mumbled as he turned and rested his head upon her breasts.

"Nay, I was glad of the wash even if ye did get me all asweat soon afterwards." She smiled sleepily when he responded with a drowsy chuckle. "So, we ride for York on the morrow?" she asked, idly tangling her fingers in his thick hair.

"Aye, at dawn's first light. Although I would rather spend each minute of this night making love to you, I fear we must get some rest." He briefly kissed the tip of each of her breasts before resettling there and closing his eyes. "When riding with the Douglas 'tis foolhardy to become too weary. So, good sleep, dearling."

"Good sleep, Hacon," she murmured.

It was not long before she knew he was asleep, but she did not soon join him in that blissful oblivion. Jennet needed to keep looking at him, to keep touching him, to reassure herself that he was really alive. She lay there for hours praying that nothing would steal him away from her again.

Trying not to wince, Jennet shifted in the saddle. Despite their best intentions, she and Hacon had made love several more times during the short night. She was tired and—she inwardly grimaced—in no condition to travel mile after mile on horseback. When Sir Niall rode up beside her, she silently cursed. She was in no humor to deal with him either.

"Enjoying your ride, Mistress Gillard?"

The way he grinned at her told her he knew exactly what discomfort she suffered, and its cause. She supposed it did not take any great wit to guess how she and Hacon, reunited after so long, would have spent the night. It was, however, very ill-mannered of Sir Niall to refer to it, and she glared at him.

"I meant to ask the same thing of you, Sir Niall. After all," she drawled, "'twasnae I who was knocked onto my backside by some puling Englishmon." To her astonishment he laughed.

"Ah, m'lady, if ye didnae already belong to Sir Gillard, I would gift him with you. I could ne'er plague him with the skill ye do, my tart wench." He saluted her and started to ride away.

"I shall plague you sorely if ye dinnae cease to call me wench," she called after him, then cursed when he only laughed harder.

A moment later Hacon rode up beside her. "Trouble?" He frowned after Sir Niall, who disappeared into the group of knights gathered around James Randolph, the Earl of Moray.

"Nay, he was but passing a greeting with me, with his usual skill and tact."

Hacon grinned briefly, then scowled. "Where is Ranald?"

"He had to answer nature's call. Aye, see? He returns even now." She smiled at Ranald as he rode up on her other side, "Are we nearing York?"

"Near enough," Hacon said. "Mayhaps fifteen miles distant. We will stop to sup within the next mile or so."

"Are we to attack the city then?" Ranald asked.

"I dinnae ken. 'Tis verra hard to gain any news, but"—he started toward their leaders—"I will try more earnestly. Stay with her, Ranald, for we draw too near a weel-fortified town." Then Hacon rode off.

It was another hour before the army halted. Jennet shivered a little as she dismounted. The end of September drew near, and the chill of fall was occasionally in the air. In the distance she could see the Swale River. It hurt to think of how soon the landscape's pristine beauty would be destroyed and that she rode with the men who would wreak that destruction.

Forcing herself to think only of her immediate needs, she turned her attention to feeding herself and Murdoc. She moved to find Dugald as Ranald saw to the care of their horses. Dugald, she mused with a half smile, would have already located the best, most comfortable place to camp.

Resting against the trunk of a tilted birch tree after washing clean Murdoc's food-smeared face, Jennet smiled at Hacon as he joined her. He sat down beside her, draping his arm across her shoulders, and she readily leaned against him. After a short respite from sitting in a saddle and with her stomach comfortably full, she felt quite content. She stared out over the moor dotted with so many campfires and wondered idly how something so threatening could look so pretty, even in the late afternoon. Just as she was about to remark upon the scene to Hacon, Balreaves approached with two thick-necked swordsmen, one on either side. Nothing else could have better served to destroy her good humor.

"So, ye found the wench," Balreaves drawled, giving Jennet a contemptuous glance.

"I found my wife—aye." Hacon ached to draw his sword but knew Jennet was right to hold him back, silently urging him not to succumb to Balreaves's goading.

"She appears to make a habit of living with our enemies."

Hacon tensed, all too aware of how bad it looked for Jennet to keep turning up on the English side of the border. "The lass thought herself a widow. Understandably, she put herself under the protection of her father again."

"Who brought her back into England. One can only wonder what reason a Scotsman would have to keep returning here."

"I shouldnae wonder on it too loudly, Balreaves."

Balreaves shrugged. "So now ye will desert the Douglas."

"Nay, I stay with him until the end." That hint of insult to his sense of loyalty, even his courage, made it almost impossible for Hacon to remain calm.

"Ah, there ye are, Sir Balreaves," called Sir Niall as he ambled over to them. "The Douglas looks for you." He half smiled as, after one sweeping glare at them all, Balreaves and his companions stalked away. "There." Niall looked at Jennet. "We are even now."

"What do ye mean—even?" she demanded, fighting to push aside the fear with which Balreaves always left her.

"Did I not just save your husband's life?"

"I didnae see any swords drawn."

"Balreaves wishes Hacon dead."

"I willnae argue that, but ye certainly didnae save anyone's life just now."

"If your husband had drawn his sword, as Balreaves would have soon goaded him to do, he would now be dead."

"Then mayhaps ye should have waited until that happened," snapped Jennet, "before proclaiming yourself a hero."

"I could have beaten Balreaves," Hacon protested before the argument between his wife and Sir Niall could continue.

"With two daggers between your shoulders?" Niall drawled. "I dinnae think even ye are that fine a swordsmon, m'lord." Niall glared at Jennet again. "I *will* see this debt paid. I cannae bear being indebted to some wee, green-eyed wench." He stomped away.

"And dinnae call me a wench," she cried after him, then

frowned when Hacon started to laugh. "And just what amuses you?"

"The two of you. Ye squabble like brother and sister." He tucked her back up against him and kissed her cheek.

"Brother and sister? I recall that ye once thought he wanted me."

"Oh, he still does, but it doesnae worry me any longer."

"I wish ye could honestly tell me that Balreaves himself shouldnae worry us any longer," she muttered, then tensed. "Hacon, Niall kens that Balreaves means to murder you. Others may see it too. Isnae that enough proof?" She could tell by the look on his face that it was not.

"Each and every mon here could ken it, but unless the mon is caught in the attempt, it serves us no good. Balreaves and his kinsmen are too powerful, too important. And *wanting* a mon dead isnae truly a crime. Ye ken that as weel as I." He briefly kissed her, then relaxed against the tree again. "Dinnae let Balreaves torment you. Come, ye were at ease ere he showed his ugly face. Be at ease again. 'Tis a fine cool evening and all is quiet. Nothing more will disturb our peace."

She doubted the truth of that but forced herself to relax. The moments when peace reigned were all too few. If the men were not on the move, they were at battle or caught up in the confusion of camp life. Jennet decided she would not allow Balreaves to spoil the brief, precious moments of quiet she and Hacon had found. She heartily wished it was a mood that would last for what remained of the raid and all the way back to Dubheilrig.

# Chapter 18

"Hacon!" cried Dugald as he and Ranald hurried up to the tree where Hacon and Jennet dozed.

Startled out of her comfortable half sleep, Jennet scowled at the pair. Murdoc, who had crawled onto her lap and fallen asleep just moments earlier, stirred slightly. She touched his tousled curls as the men's tense expressions dashed her hope that it was an idle interruption.

"I fear there is trouble approaching," Dugald reported, pointing one slightly stubby finger toward the southwest.

Hacon stood up, stretching a little. Jennet took the sleeping Murdoc and also rose to her feet. Growing worried, she stepped up beside the men and stared off in the same direction. Her heart sank. A force of some sort was approaching from the vicinity of York, marching toward the still-dining Scots. But it did not look to be a proper army. A mob of seven thousand or more followed behind men dressed in white robes. The standard of Saint Peter of York, patron saint of the city, was carried to the fore, which indicated that the archbishop of York himself was leading the group.

"Monks," Hacon said. "Cistercian monks and farmers. 'Tis a poor army."

"They might be a vanguard for a more reputable force," said Dugald.

"Mayhaps." Hacon turned to briefly kiss Jennet. "Stay here and—"

"I ken it." She sighed. "And run and hide if the battle turns against us."

"Aye. I would rather have to search for you again then bury you and the wee laddie. Howbeit, if this is all York can muster against us, I cannae believe there will be a battle. There would be no honor in it."

Even as the three men hurried away, a furious outcry arose amongst the men nearest the advancing force. Jennet shuddered as men but yards away from her rose to form schiltrons, bellowing their defiance at the English as the spear rings took shape. She held Murdoc a little closer as she watched Hacon and his loyal companions disappear into the now rousing Scots army.

She knew she should move, knew that she stood out a little too plainly in the late afternoon sun. Silently promising the unseen Hacon that she would run at the first hint of a threat, she sought out a better spot from which to watch and soon joined several men atop a small rise. The presence of a chronicler told her it was a good place even before she looked out to see for herself. The whole of the valley, all the way to the Swale Rivet, was laid out before her.

The lances of the Scots' schiltrons glinted in the fading sun. Their belligerent cries carried on the still air. The army from York immediately faltered, hesitation rippling through its motley ranks. It did not surprise her when the peasants immediately turned and fled. Few of them wore armor and their weapons consisted of crude farm implements for the most part. They were no soldiers. She began to relax, thinking that the threat was over, that the battle would involve only a few traded insults and shows of bravado. But then the men in the schiltrons began to move toward their hobbled horses. She

watched in growing shock as, beneath the colors of the Earl
of Moray, the Scotsmen began to ride out after the retreating
English.

Her brief hope that the Scots meant only to further frighten
the weak defenders of York quickly faded. A few of the English took a stand and were easily cut down. Still, Moray's
men did not halt there but continued to pursue the fleeing English. She watched in numb horror as clergy and peasant alike
were dispatched by swords, battle-axes, and spears. The Scots
left hundreds of dead in their wake.

Moray's men chased the English to the banks of the Swale,
then drove the terrified men back to where the River Swale
met the Ure. Even from where she stood Jennet could see the
slaughter taking place as men were ruthlessly butchered on
the banks of the river or were driven into the water, where
they drowned. She prayed no one she knew was taking part in
the carnage.

"I would ne'er have thought such a sight to your taste."

Slowly turning from the bloody scene, Jennet looked up to
see Sir Niall. The fact that he stood by her side unmarked by
blood gave her new confidence in her judgment. Beneath his
sour, sneering outside was a good man.

"They were fleeing. The threat was gone," she murmured.

"Aye. There is no need for this bloodshed," he whispered.

She wondered why he spoke so softly. Then he briefly
looked past her. Following his nervous glance, she saw Balreaves standing near the chronicler. The way Balreaves's head
was tilted ever so slightly in their direction made her certain
that the man was trying to hear them. As so many others did,
Niall feared his criticisms would be overheard and then used
against him. The gory state of Balreaves's surcoat told her
that, although he was not with Moray's men now, he recently
had been. She wondered if he was trying to get his name
mentioned prominently in the chronicler's accounts.

"Have ye seen Hacon?" she asked Niall as she turned her

attention back to him, much preferring his face to the sight of the murder being enacted below.

"Do ye truly feel he would take a hand in that?" Niall gave a short, bitter laugh. "Ye dinnae ken your mon verra weel, do ye?"

"I didnae say he was down there," she retorted. "I but asked if ye had seen him." The sting of guilt stirred her temper because for one brief minute she *had* wondered if Hacon ran with Moray's wolves.

"Weel, I have seen him. He and his men claim all they can lay hands upon as plunder or as captives for ransom. Aye, he is down there, but the fine lord of Dubheilrig doesnae take part in that slaughter. Not for him the taint of bloodlust. Nay, fool that he is, he is even trying to save a few. When they beg to surrender or cry for mercy, he heeds them. His gallantry could cost him dearly," Niall muttered, and shook his head.

Deciding she would gain nothing by asking him why he had spoken so sneeringly of Hacon's deeds, Jennet concentrated on his final words. "What do ye mean—'twill cost him?"

"He interferes. 'Tis never wise. 'Tis best to join in or quietly stand back, especially if ye are a mon who must keep fetching his wife out of England."

"Is my whereabouts mentioned often?"

"Sir Balreaves does his best to see that no one forgets it." He grasped her arm and tugged her along as he started down the small rise. "Ye shouldnae be here watching such slaughter."

"Why do they do it?" she demanded, her soft voice weighted with horror.

Niall shrugged. "Hate. Bloodlust. Who can say? It gains us little. In truth, we may come to rue this day."

"They are murdering men of the Church."

"Lass, with Scotland repeatedly placed under a papal edict

of excommunication, do ye really believe those men are worrying about their souls? The Pope himself has damned us
all. Why should we worry o'er a few monks and minor English priests? Not that they were so verra holy themselves,"
he muttered. "They marched on us with swords in hand. I
dinnae think they meant to bless us all, do ye? Weel, God allowed them to take up arms, but He neglected to give them
backbone. They are paying for that cowardice now."

"'Tis naught but murder to cut down hundreds of men as
they flee."

"More like thousands." He stopped and released his hold
on her. "And ye would be wise to keep such thoughts to yourself. The Earl of Moray himself leads this charge. Now, here
is where your mon left you, and here is where ye had best be
when he returns."

Jennet glanced around her and realized she was back by the
tree she and Hacon had dozed against earlier. Turning to say
something to Niall, she saw that he was already yards away,
disappearing into the group of milling soldiers. She was
briefly alarmed to see Balreaves close behind him. That awful
man had followed them. Jennet knew he had done his best to
hear all she and Niall had said. There was nothing she could
do about that, but she vowed to keep a closer watch on the
man. With a heavy sigh she slumped against the tree trunk.
Murdoc partly awoke, then settled himself more comfortably
against her breasts.

The slaughter went on until nightfall, when darkness put a
merciful end to it. Word came from the scouts and spies sent
to watch York that Edward's queen, his judges, and his ex-
chequer had all fled the city for Nottingham. Jennet was relieved. She had thought the Scots were not so cruel as
Edward's father had been, that they would never hang a
woman in a cage from a city's walls. Now, however, she was
not so sure. She was glad there would be no testing of their
cruelty. She did wonder if the pathetic army from York had

been sent out by Edward's queen, if those thousands of ill-prepared men had been sacrificed to give her a chance to flee. If that was true, and the possibility was there, Jennet hoped the English queen was punished in some way for that sad, careless waste of her own people.

By the time Jennet saw Hacon walking toward her, she knew only one thing—she wanted to return to Dubheilrig. She could not remain with the army for another day. While she conceded that such brutality had never happened before, not while she had traveled with them, she did not wish to chance experiencing it again.

Hacon sat down beside her, weary and heartsick. The look on Jennet's face told him she had seen more than he would have wished. He had been tempted to return to her still tainted by the blood from the field, to test her opinion of him and see if she would think him capable of taking part in the slaughter. But at the last moment he had lost the courage to do so and had paused to wash before seeking her out. If she had such thoughts about him, he did not have the stomach to know about them.

"Are you unhurt?" she finally asked when he simply sat there, slouched against the tree with his eyes closed.

"Aye. There was no fighting, was there." He inwardly grimaced over the harsh bitterness in his voice.

"Why, Hacon? Why would they do such a bloody, heartless thing?"

He finally looked at her, seeing from her expression that she shared his confusion and disgust. "Only God can say."

"I should like to believe God was napping, that He looked away for a wee while. Why else could He allow this? I cannae see the reason He would allow it. Can ye?"

"Lass, if I could answer that, I would be the Pope, not a mere knight."

"The Pope will surely excommunicate us all again for this sin. Weel, if we arenae under his edict even now."

"We may be. I dinnae ken. Since the Bruce stepped forward to claim the throne, we have been damned by the Pope, then not damned, then damned again so often I have lost count. I dinnae ken where we stand anymore."

"Weel, we dinnae need the Pope to damn us for this."

"Nay," he whispered, and shook his head. "This was slaughter. Between here and the river lie three thousand, mayhaps four thousand dead. The river itself is choked with bodies, the shore stained red with the blood of another thousand men. 'Tis a wonder any mon paused to take prisoners for ransom. Mayhaps we have been at war for too long. We no longer fight—we just kill. Mayhaps hatred and the need to spill all English blood is now stronger than honor or mercy. If that is true, and this wasnae but some brief madness, then I want no part of it."

He sounded so disappointed, so bitter, Jennet felt compelled to say, "Not every mon took part."

He slipped his arm about her shoulders and tugged her close. "True. There may be hope to be found there. Howbeit, I dinnae wish to linger here."

"Nay. I want to return to Dubheilrig."

"As do I." He kissed her cheek, stood up, and brushed himself off. "I shall take my men home ere they are infected by this bloodlust. Aye, ere *I* am," he muttered as he strode away.

Jennet sighed, She was glad they would be leaving, yet sorry at how heartsick Hacon had become. For the first time in her life she found herself looking for good things to say about the soldiers, even the war. Hacon had given too many years of his life to the Bruce, to the cause. She ached to convince him that they had not been wasted.

She was still puzzling over that thought when Dugald and Ranald arrived. Both men were somber and unusually quiet. Ranald, sickly pale with disillusionment, drew her greatest sympathy. It was, she mused, a hard lesson for a youth to learn.

"Where is Hacon?" Dugald asked as he sat down in front of her and offered her his wineskin.

After taking a sip and handing the skin to Ranald, who settled beside her, Jennet replied, "I believe he went to speak to one of the men who leads us. He wants to leave the army, to return to Dubheilrig."

"I would like nothing more, yet . . ." Dugald paused and frowned as he accepted the return of his wineskin.

When he fell silent, she pressed him to continue. "And yet what?"

"Weel, I cannae help but fear it may not be the wisest step to take."

"Ye cannae wish to stay for more of this."

"By all the saints—nay. I dinnae have the stomach for it. Howbeit, I think we drew enough attention to ourselves by claiming so many prisoners, espccially when many of them are too poor to bring any ransom. Our failure to follow Moray into the slaughter may be questioned."

"Surely such mercy can only be approved of."

"That should be the way of it, but I think ye ken weel that it might not be. It could also be seen as an act of defiance or a criticism of Moray. Neither would be good. Some enemy could easily turn it against Hacon and use it to bring him down."

There was a chilling truth to that, but she struggled to deny it. "Nay, Hacon has been loyal for too long."

"True, and that should be enough to shield him from all accusations, but in these troubled days mistrust hangs heavy in the air. No mon dares to step wrong or speak too freely."

"Weel" Hacon drawled as he walked up to them in time to hear Dugald's final comments, "ye need not fear that I spoke too freely. I didnae speak at all." He sat down next to Jennet and accepted Dugald's silent offer of a drink of wine, "I didnae need to."

"What do ye mean?" Jennet asked. "Are we returning to Dubheilrig or not?"

"Aye, we are, but"—he grimaced—"we will be marching with the army."

"But, Hacon—" She began to protest, not wishing to further plague him when he was so deeply troubled, yet dreading the possibility that she might live to see a repetition of the day's horror.

Hacon lightly kissed her, "If there is even the hint of such a black act being done again, we shall simply ride away. I swear it, lass. We saw today that ye cannae stop it nor can ye save many from such a mad bloodletting."

"How can ye be sure we will be returning home?" Dugald asked, breaking the heavy silence which followed Hacon's words.

"As I approached the Douglas and Moray, I realized they were discussing what steps to take next. I stood waiting for my turn to speak and heard them decide to march back to Scotland. So I left. They travel the way I wish them to. I ken weel the risks, m'friend," he added, smiling faintly at Dugald, "so I swallowed my words. I may not wish to ride with the army, but 'tis safer if we do. And they are going to be marching toward home."

He was right and Jennet knew it, but still she was discouraged. She wanted to distance herself from the army, wanted to pull Hacon and the others from Dubheilrig away before they were stained by the wanton killings. Instead she swallowed her disappointment and prayed they could get back to Scotland without more innocent blood being shed.

Jennet sighed with relief when Ranald took Murdoc from his sling. The child was growing too big for it, and too big for her to comfortably carry day in and day out. She stood rubbing the small of her back and watched Ranald lead their mounts away, Murdoc sitting easily on his hip. Looking at the scrub pine forest spread out before her, men wending through its depths to find a place to camp, she felt at ease. It had taken a month after the murders by the River Swale, but they were finally back in Scotland. Soon they would leave the Douglas and Moray behind. Soon they would leave the war behind, too, at least for a little while.

"'Tis Sir Gillard's wandering wife," murmured a voice from behind her that Jennet immediately recognized as Balreaves.

She turned to face the man, and was dismayed to see that Balreaves's companion was Sir James Douglas himself. She fought to calm her uneasiness. She smiled in greeting and briefly curtsied. Sir Douglas was gaining a power it was wise to acknowledge. He was one of the few men the Bruce trusted.

"Ye were found in Boroughbridge?" Sir Douglas asked.

"Aye, sir. My father took me there when the English advanced upon Berwick."

"Your kinsmon is verra fond of England," Balreaves said.

"My kinsmon is verra fond of England's money, sir."

Jennet did not like the way Balreaves kept telling everyone that she had been found in England. Sir Douglas's dark face was expressionless, and she could not tell how much weight he gave Balreaves's sly insinuations or how favorably he judged her defense.

"Of course." Balreaves smiled faintly. "Ye must have been weel pleased with Sir Gillard's miraculous resurrection and safe return from Ireland."

A chill went down Jennet's spine. Balreaves stressed those last six words in an ominous way, heavily weighting them with suspicion.

"Any wife would be pleased to have her mon back safe and hale from the war."

"And where is your mon now?" asked the Douglas.

"Actually, sir, he said he was to meet with you."

"Ah, the meeting I called for. I wish you well, m'lady."
Douglas nodded in lieu of a bow and strode away.

When Balreaves did not immediately follow the man,
Jennet frowned. "Is there something ye need, Sir Balreaves?"

He was frowning into her eyes. It made Jennet very uneasy.
Her father had always told her that the unusual green of their
eyes made people remember them. She prayed that this time
her father was wrong and that Balreaves would have no rec-
ollection of her.

"I still feel we have met before, m'lady," he said after a
long moment of silently staring at her.

"Nay, ye are wrong. I am certain of it."

"Are ye now? We shall see."

She watched until he disappeared into the crowd of soldiers. Then she saw Dugald waving her over to the spot he
had chosen for them. Jennet made a swift and firm decision
not to mention the confrontation with Balreaves to anyone,
especially not to Hacon. He was already aware of Balreaves's
sly campaign to blacken his name. There was no need to add
to his concerns. She would use the time until Hacon returned
to camp to put the chilling meeting with Balreaves out of
her mind.

It was late before Hacon joined her. She was just beginning
to think she might as well go to bed alone when he appeared
at their campfire. Ranald had bedded down near the fire,
Murdoc sleeping peacefully at his side. The other men from
Dubheilrig were scattered amongst the surrounding trees, not
easily seen yet close enough to answer if called to arms. Only
Dugald remained awake to greet Hacon with her.

"I begin to curse my title," Hacon murmured as he sat next
to Jennet and warmed his hands at the low fire. "Suddenly I
must attend all the huddled talks. It wouldnae be such a
burden if they always spoke of important matters, but I fear
they are oftimes given to repeating rumors and gossip."

"Some of that can be of interest." Jennet sidled closer, seeking his warmth, for the October night was chill.

"Aye, but they often chew it to death. England has raised the siege of Berwick. Scotland still holds the city."

"Mayhaps what happened by the Swale prompted England's retreat," suggested Dugald.

"Mayhaps." Hacon shook his head as he put his arm around Jennet. "Though I shouldnae like to believe any good was born of that shame. I but pray it doesnae taint Walter the Steward's fine work in holding fast to Berwick for the Bruce."

"I doubt it will. His driving back of the English is a prouder tale," murmured Dugald. "'Tis on to Dubheilrig on the morrow?"

"Aye, toward home." Hacon looked at Jennet. "Do ye wish to stop at Liddesdale to see your kinsmen on the way?"

"If it willnae cost ye many days of travel—aye. They may have gotten some word of my father's fate."

"'Tis but a day added, mayhaps less. It will be weel worth the effort if it can ease your worry."

"Thank ye, Hacon, 'Twill be good to see my aunt and uncle again too."

"Did the Douglas or Moray ask ye to stay with them?" Dugald asked,

"Nay. I didnae need to go against their wishes, if that is what troubles you."

"Aye, though it also troubles me that ye havenae been asked to join them at court."

"I was thought dead until this summer and was but newly made a baron when we took that fateful journey to Ireland. Scotland has more barons than it probably needs. 'Twill be a while until I am drawn to court."

"I ken it. I but think it would be for the best if ye were seen by the king from time to time."

"He saw me but a year and a half ago when we took Berwick. Aye, and he kens I answered his call to fight in Ireland."

"Robert the Bruce was in Berwick when ye found me?" Jennet asked.

"Briefly. Disappointed ye didnae get a wee peek at the mon?" Hacon teased.

"Aye, a wee bit. He is, after all, the reason for this war."

"I shouldnae worry on it, dearling. This king is not so special. Most kings are ne'er all one would believe them to be."

"What? Ye mean he isnae seven feet tall with hair like flame and a face to shame the gods?" She grinned when both men laughed, and realized that the thought of returning home had lightened all their hearts.

"He does have reddish hair at least." Hacon looked at Dugald. "Why are ye so eager for me to draw the king's notice?"

Dugald shrugged. "We all ken there are those who seek to murder you. They have thus far failed to do so by sword or dagger. They might yet try by word—a hint of treason scattered here and there. I but thought it would help if ye were a mon the king easily recalled. 'Twould steal the threat of such lies."

"I cannae spend all my days fearing whispers, cousin. Aye"—he held up a hand to halt Dugald's response—"I ken their threat. At the same time one must trust in justice and that truth has the strength to conquer lies. For each mon who tries to blacken my name, there is one who can attest to my loyalty to our king. Aye—and to Scotland. I must trust in that."

"As ye wish," Dugald mumbled, poking at the small fire with a thin stick.

"Which means," drawled Hacon, "that Dugald thinks me a great fool but has decided not to wear himself to the bone trying to convince me."

Jennet smiled but did not find much to laugh at. Dugald was right. Unfortunately, so was Hacon. What most worried her was the thought that someone was clearly already very busy trying to blacken Hacon's good name. And she knew exactly who that someone was—Balreaves. It both frightened and surprised her that the man could continue to get away with his treachery.

"Mayhaps," Dugald said, "'twould be easiest to cut out the lying tongue."

"Mayhaps, but we cannae lower ourselves to do as he does. Soon he will step wrong, grow too bold. We must wait."

The look on Dugald's face told Jennet he hated the thought of waiting as much as she did. She tried to find strength and hope in the knowledge that they would soon be back at Dubheilrig. Balreaves could not reach them there, nor, she prayed, could his lies.

"Enough of this dark talk," said Hacon. "We ride toward home on the morrow. Our spirits should be light. And I do have some good tidings. I hesitated to speak about it because nothing is certain, but there is talk of a truce."

"Ye mean an end to the war?" Jennet dared not believe it.

"Ah, weel, I dinnae think 'twill put a final end to all the troubles. There is still no sign that England's king or the Pope will recognize the Bruce as the king of Scotland. Howbeit, a truce will give us some respite. We can only be thankful for it."

"True, though a final peace would be much better. How long do ye think the truce would last?"

"Two years is what I have heard mentioned."

"It doesnae seem verra much time to me."

"Time enough for a harvest or two, to rebuild, to strengthen walls and tower houses. Aye, time for us to be wed by a priest and set our house in order."

"Can we be wed by a priest if the Pope has excommunicated us?"

"His Holiness usually sends his edict only to the Bruce, his closest allies, and our bishops. Not that I can be sure of that, but it hasnae stopped our priests from doing all they ought. I shouldnae worry o'er it. Whatever happens between popes and kings matters little to us. We will be wed, finish the building of our fine tower house, and mayhaps"—he winked at her—"have ourselves a bairn or two."

"A bairn?"

She stared at him—stunned. Mostly it was her own stupidity which so utterly astounded her. Not once, in all the time they had been together, had she given a thought to children— to Hacon's children. With her father scattering his bastards over England and Scotland, the possibility of a child should have occurred to her from the very start.

"Dinnae ye wish to have children?" Hacon was unable to read her expression and fought the urge to immediately assume the worst—that the thought of bearing his children appalled her. "Or are ye afraid? Come, tell me what has ye looking as if ye have been knocked senseless."

"'Tis neither of those things. I but just realized I ne'er even thought of the possibility." She frowned, trying to look stern when both men began to grin. "If ye mean to make jest of me, I should think again."

"Och, lass." Dugald's voice trembled with amusement. "And when ye have given us such a fine chance at it. 'Tis cruel of you to seal our lips."

"I already ken how foolish I was. I dinnae need bawdy jests to remind me." She looked toward Murdoc and suddenly realized there was something else she had given little thought to. "Hacon, what of Murdoc?" she asked, feeling uncertain, for she could not even begin to guess what he would say.

"He will stay with us, lass. The lad calls you Mother. I wouldnae part you. Did ye think I would?"

"I had no idea what ye might do. 'Tis a verra odd situation. The boy is born of neither of us."

"Aye, but he is the child of all of us. He will be my foster son."

Jennet hugged him. "Thank ye, Hacon. I think he will grow to do ye verra proud.

"I have little doubt of it. Mayhaps some day we can discover something of his kinsmen. When he is grown he may wonder on his true bloodline. 'Twould be useful if we know something to tell him."

She nodded, then grimaced. "And we shall have to be verra careful in telling him how he came to be an orphan."

Hacon gave an exaggerated shudder. "I dinnae even want to think on it now. In truth, what I want to think on is seeking out my bed. Where have ye spread it out, Dugald?" he asked as he stood up, tugging Jennet to her feet.

"Just behind you a few paces. Behind that tree and the tangle of shrub at its base."

Before she could bid Dugald good night, Hacon dragged her away. Within no time at all they were huddled beneath the blankets, Hacon wearing only his braies and she only her chemise. The bed was surprisingly comfortable, Hacon's plaid spread out over a padding of pine boughs and moss. She smiled, a little surprised when Hacon pulled her up against him, for he was clearly considering a little lovemaking before getting his rest.

"At last I have you alone," he murmured, nuzzling her neck.

Giggling softly, Jennet glanced around. "Alone? With all of Bruce's army snoring about us'?"

"Snoring, are they? Good. The noise will muffle your cries of passion."

He kissed her before she could protest his impudence, and soon she cared as little about the presence of Bruce's soldiers as he did.

# Chapter 19

Three weeks later, just as the sun crept over the horizon, Jennet, Hacon, and the rest of their group left the village of Liddesdale behind and headed toward Dubheilrig. Jennet had enjoyed a fortnight's visit with her aunt and uncle, resting and hoping her father would return, but finally she had had to leave a message for him instead.

Hacon set an easy pace that day, and the weather remained clear and warm. Late that afternoon Jennet and Hacon were sharing a teasing conversation when, just as Jennet leaned forward to murmur in his ear, a voice called, "'Ware your backs!"

She barely caught a glimpse of the armed men bursting out of the surrounding thickets before Ranald was hurrying her to the far side of the small clearing, out of the way of the erupting battle. Their peaceful ride through the forest had been ruined in the blink of an eye. Suddenly Jennet wished they had not parted from the Bruce's army three weeks ago. That large, battle-hardened force would have deterred this attack. Instead, Hacon's band was barely twenty men strong. With Ranald on one side and a youth named Thomas on the other, she waited and prayed that Hacon and his men could beat back the unexpected ambush. She also prayed that none of the thirty or more attackers were Armstrongs. They were but a day's ride from her kinsmen's lands, and it was possible that these were some of the thieves who controlled the area.

"Balreaves," Thomas hissed and spat on the ground.

"Are ye certain these are his men?" she demanded.

"Aye, I recognize some as his hirelings. Yet again he tries to kill Sir Hacon."

"Did ye think it was someone else?" asked Ranald.

Jennet managed a weak smile and shrugged. "I feared they might be my kinsmen. Some of them, leastwise. They run freely through this wood and set upon many an unwary traveler. The word that we have been promised safe passage might not have reached every mon living in wait through this thick forest."

"Weel, Thomas is right," Ranald assured her. "These are Balreaves's murderers. A few dinnae even try to hide the fact that they wear his colors."

Watching the fierce battle taking place, she cursed Balreaves. The man had to be mad. Bitterness and jealousy must have turned his mind. All she could do was hope he would fail and that this time Hacon would gain all the proof needed to come out boldly against the man. If they could just capture one man wearing Balreaves's colors, who was willing to admit that Balreaves had ordered Hacon's murder, they could finally put an end to this deadly game.

Hacon cursed as he turned aside yet another sword and kicked his foe square in the face, sending the man to the ground to die beneath the hooves of Dugald's mount. He had been alert for just such an attack but had hoped it would not come. It infuriated him that because of one man's jealousy and ambition several of his men might die within reach of Dubheilrig and their loved ones. He vowed he would make Balreaves pay dearly for that.

"I want one of these dogs collared alive," he bellowed, leaping from his mount to take up the battle on foot.

He saw that most of his men did the same. In the small clearing there was no room to maneuver on horseback. Nervous, riderless horses blundered through the fighting men, causing a brief moment of wild confusion. But the men of Dubheilrig recovered faster than their foes and used the short-lived advantage to ruthlessly cull the numbers of the opposition.

It took Hacon a while to work his way around until he and Dugald stood back to back. Each one of their ambushers was eager to be the one to cut him down. Even as he settled into the familiar battle stance, a new development made him curse. From within the surrounding forest came another battle cry, swiftly followed by more armed men bursting into the clearing with their swords and battle-axes at the ready. Hacon and his men would have turned back the first onslaught with little cost, but this added strength could prove to be too much for them.

"God curse Balreaves and his mother," swore Dugald. "They waited until we tired some."

"He doesnae mean to fail this time."

"But, Hacon, Balreaves's dogs seem as surprised to see these new men as we are."

"Aye, that they do."

Hacon gave a short, joyful laugh as the new men set to work attacking Balreaves's hirelings, fighting side by side with the men of Dubheilrig. He was certain he recognized the reddish brown jupon on one of the armored men. The final proof that these new arrivals were allies came an instant later when two of Balreaves's hirelings lunged at Hacon. He parried the first sword thrust, but could not elude the swing of the other man's battle-ax. As he braced for the blow and hoped it would not take Dugald as well, the man in the reddish brown jupon ended the threat by beheading Hacon's opponent with one clean swipe of his sword. His rescuer briefly lifted his helmet, and Hacon recognized the grinning face of Jennet's kinsman Malcolm.

"We thought ye might wish some assistance, m'lord," Malcolm yelled over the din of battle.

"Verra kind of you," was all Hacon had a chance to say before Malcolm dropped his helmet back into place and plunged back into the fighting.

In moments the attack became a rout. Hacon called again for one of the men to be taken alive, but his command went unheeded. Enraged by the treacherous assault, his own men fought on with murderous intent. Those who fled into the forest were loudly pursued, and Hacon found his attempts to capture someone alive quickly thwarted. Each man he cornered refused to surrender and fought to the death.

When it was finally over, none of the men from Dubheilrig lay dead, although a few were seriously injured and might yet succumb to their wounds. The men who had come to their aid calmly proceeded to strip the dead of all that was of any value. Hacon was about to thank Malcolm's companions when Jennet gave a glad cry.

"Malcolm?" she called out. "That *is* you beneath that battered helmet, isnae it?"

"Aye, wee Jennet." Malcolm stepped over to her as he removed the helmet. "None other."

Hacon quickly joined the group, pausing only to praise Ranald and Thomas for their steadfast guard of Jennet and Murdoc before asking Malcolm, "Why are ye here? We are nearly a full day's ride from your village."

"Aye, but someone was seen following you, flanking ye, in truth. They tried to slip past the village unseen, and we can allow none to do that, m'lord."

"As I weel learned," murmured Hacon as he moved to help Jennet dismount. "So, ye followed them?"

"Aye. We thought just to warn you but decided that might not be for the best. By warning you, we might have warned *them* and given them a chance to elude us. Not kenning your skills, m'lord, and not wanting them to fall upon you later at will, we followed them all day. I regret that our plan may have cost you some men."

"And," interrupted Jennet, "I had best set about seeing that they dinnae succumb to those wounds."

Ranald and Thomas dismounted to assist her. Hacon ordered his men to set up camp and invited Malcolm and his men to stay the night. Malcolm was quick to accept and had just finished ordering his men to rest and eat when Dugald called Hacon over to where he had found a survivor.

"This one lives," Dugald called from several yards away, squatting beside a severely wounded foot soldier. "But not, I think, for long."

Hacon hurried over, Malcolm at his heels. He waited a little impatiently as Jennet rushed to view the man's wounds. She took only a moment, then shook her head and left to tend to those she could help. Hacon quickly knelt. While some of the others wore Balreaves's colors, this man was dressed as many another poor peasant.

"Were ye sent by Balreaves?" Hacon demanded, seeing death in the man's face and fearing it would claim him before he could speak.

"And why should I tell you anything?" The man coughed, staining his lips with blood.

"Would it not be better to face your maker with the truth upon your lips?"

"Ah, I suppose so, though 'twill do ye little good. Aye, 'twas Balreaves who hired us and sent us after you."

"And ye were ordered to murder me?"

"If ye be Sir Hacon Gillard—aye."

The man struggled to make the sign of the cross and barely completed the gesture before he died. Hacon slowly stood up, as did Dugald. Staring down at the dead man, Hacon felt relieved. At last what he had long suspected had been confirmed aloud.

"Weel, now ye have your proof," said Dugald.

"Do I?" Hacon signaled his men to remove the body.

"The mon told you—'tis Balreaves."

"The mon is dead. He cannae tell anyone else, can he?"

"But 'tis the word of a dying mon. Malcolm and I heard it, we've witnesses to it."

"Dugald, ye are my mon and few men would question your honesty. Howbeit, ye ken as weel as I do that your echoing my claim in this willnae carry much weight, not for the accusation we mean to toss out."

"Weel, Malcolm isnae your mon."

"Nay, but he is my wife's kinsmon." Hacon knew there was a lot more that would lessen the power of Malcolm's word, but he could not think of a way to say so without possibly insulting the man.

"And"   Malcolm smiled at Hacon—"what his lordship is too good to say is that my word willnae be honored much. I am one of a family weel known as thieves and rogues. They would but say I was paid to lie, or the like."

"Some of the dead wear Balreaves's colors," said Dugald

"They could be stolen. Or they might have deserted their laird's service to take up the lives of thieves. They could indeed be his men still, but when they arenae called to arms, they might keep their purses full by emptying others—without Balreaves's knowledge or permission." He smiled faintly when Dugald cursed. "This isnae enough, Dugald."

"Then we have gained nothing at all here."

"Ah, weel, I shouldnae say that. *I* have proof now. My suspicions have been confirmed."

"But ye kenned it was that cur Balreaves. We all kenned it."

"Aye, aye, but now one of his own men has confirmed it. No longer is the dagger in the night held in an unseen hand. I ken exactly who points it. We put a name to the murderer.

Now even his own mon has done so. It makes my suspicions truth. Until that was done, I did at times glance in other directions. Ye did as weel, Dugald. But we willnae waver now. We have a name."

Dugald nodded. "Aye, but if this isnae proof enough, what must we wait for—Balreaves washing his hands in your blood? We could get one of the royal chroniclers to write it all down as it happens and set the king's seal to it. Then we could hang Balreaves on a gibbet built o'er your grave."

"Enough, cousin." Hacon exchanged a grin with Malcolm and draped his arm around Dugald's broad shoulders. "Balreaves willnae win. Am I not the better mon?"

"Aye, but the better mon has sometimes defeated his enemy only *after* he is set beneath the cold clay. His heirs are left to clear his name and seek justice. Ye dinnae even have any heirs yet."

"Then ye had best keep me above the ground until I can solve that wee problem. Ah, now there is something to cheer you, m'friend." He pointed to the campfire Ranald had prepared. "Ranald seems to have found some sort of fowl for our meal."

"Humph, the lad cannae cook. We will be crunching upon cinders if I leave it in his hands," Dugald muttered as he hurried over to nudge Ranald aside.

Hacon laughed softly and invited Malcolm to share their booty. He looked for Jennet, saw that she was nearly finished tending to his men, and went to sit by the campfire. They had won this battle, but the war with Balreaves was far from over. There had to be a solution. He just needed a chance to find it.

"I sorely miss Elizabeth," Jennet said as, replete from her meal, she took a drink from Hacon's wineskin.

"Aye, she is skilled at healing, which, I fear, is why she remains at Dubheilrig. That failure in Ireland left several of my men needing her care. 'Tis why I chose her mon Robert and his brother Donald to be part of the guard left behind." Accepting the return of his wineskin, he took a long drink. "My men will heal?"

"Oh, aye, I believe so. But we must travel slowly, Hacon. A hard journey can easily turn a small wound into a fatal one."

"We will move at a snail's crawl if need be. When the attack came, the one thing that truly enraged me was the thought that some of my men would die within reach of their home."

"And after they survived so much else," she murmured, sidling closer to him until he put his arm around her.

"Aye, but that tragedy was avoided and we have your kinsmen to thank." He smiled at Malcolm. "Ye must come to the wedding."

"The answer to that honorable invitation must still be nay. We cannae come. Jennet kens the why of it."

She frowned at Malcolm with widening eyes. "Is that old trouble still plaguing you?"

Malcolm nodded. "'Twould be worth our verra lives to ride much farther than here."

Suddenly understanding, Hacon cursed. "Ye have gotten on the wrong side of the Douglasses."

"Aye, we have, and their lands nearly encircle yours. There is no path to Dubheilrig we can safely travel."

"I could have my men ride with you as escort. The Douglasses have no quarrel with me."

"But they willnae like ye doing that, and weel ye ken it. 'Twould be a mark against you, and ye cannae afford one, from what I have heard. Nay, best we stay away. Jennet kens that our love and best wishes go with her."

"Thank ye, Malcolm," she murmured. "Howbeit, ye should try to mend this breach with the Douglasses. They gain more power each year. 'Tis ne'er wise to have such enemies."

"Oh, we ken that weel enough. We try, lassie. Dinnae worry over us. It hasnae been as long as ye think either."

"Weel, mayhaps not. It has been all of my life but, 'tis true, my life hasnae been so verra long."

"'Tis a verra short time when it comes to feuds."

"Ye should have told me of this before," Hacon said. "What led to the trouble?"

"We had the impudence to treat the Douglasses as we do all who travel through this rough land." When Hacon grimaced, Malcolm shrugged. "Aye, we robbed them. Spilled a wee bit of blood along the way, too, although no murder was done, I swear it. Sadly, one mon did get maimed, and I fear he feeds the hatred."

"Have ye ceased to attack the Douglasses' men?"

"Oh, aye. As Jennet says, they grow verra powerful. We are but a small group, not even a clan yet, and verra poor."

"I will see what I can do."

"That would please us, but ye should clear aside your troubles with Balreaves first, ere ye take on ours."

Jennet frowned. "Isnae the trouble with Balreaves over? We have proof now." When Hacon did not immediately respond, she pressed, "Weel, dinnae we?"

"Nay, we dinnae." He sighed and ran a hand through his hair.

"The mon said nothing before he died?"

"He did admit that he was one of Balreaves's hirelings." Hating to see her growing disappointment, he carefully related what little the man had said and exactly why it would not help to defeat Balreaves.

Jennet found it hard to hide her dismay. For a brief moment she had felt certain that Hacon could now end the threat posed by Balreaves. She hated to feel her fear for Hacon return. She did not know whether to curse or cry, knowing all the while that neither would help her feel better. Nor, she mused with a heavy sigh, would either help Hacon.

In truth, there was *nothing* she could do for him. That was what bothered her most.

"God curse Balreaves and his mother," she cried.

"Again?" Hacon briefly smiled at Dugald. "My cousin did the same. That poor woman may be completely innocent."

Giving him a disgusted look, Jennet shook her head. "So we continue to wait. The mon tries to murder you at each turning and we can do nothing. There is no justice in that. Justice would be served if that worm was suddenly struck down by lightning," she finished, savoring the thought of it.

"A fine idea." Hacon could not help laughing. "If a mon can be hurt by ill thoughts, Balreaves must be writhing in unendurable pain right now. Come, my sweet plunder, dinnae let the matter trouble you."

"This mon continuously tries to murder you and I shouldnae let it trouble me? Wouldnae ye be troubled if someone kept trying to murder me?"

Hacon frowned, not at all pleased with that question. "'Twould be different. 'Tis a mon's duty to protect his wife."

Jennet stared at him, wondering idly if she should hit him, then decided it would not help. "I may not be able to protect you, but I can worry as weel as you. If ye expect me to sit quietly and ply my needle day after day, not burdening my poor weak wits with any thought, mayhaps we should reconsider this marriage."

Hacon eyed her warily. "Are we having an argument?"

"If ye wish to call it that—aye."

Glancing at the others around the fire, who were watching them with amused interest, he said, "Weel, if we are to have one mayhaps we should do so in private."

"Fine." She stood up and started toward the place where she had seen Dugald spread out their bedding.

"Wheesht." Hacon grinned at the others as he stood up. "I wonder what I said to so rouse her ire?"

"Ye willnae find out by talking to us," drawled Dugald.

"Am I to have this quarrel all by myself?" Jennet called.

Quickly smothering a laugh, Hacon hurried after her. When he saw her standing by their poor bed, her hands on her hips, he almost smiled. She looked beautiful. He knew, however, that saying so would only add to her temper.

"Now, dearling, what have I said to make you so angry?"

"Why dinnae ye think I should feel desperately worried about you, as ye would if this danger was mine, not yours?"

*Because I love you,* he almost said, then swallowed the words. She was not ready to hear them. Nor was he ready to speak them. He was not sure of her full respect, and he needed that as much as he did her passion or her love. And now, he knew, was not the time to try to learn the extent of her respect.

"Loving"—he took her hands in his—"it pleases me that ye do worry. It does no good though, does it? Balreaves still stalks me and will continue to do so until I can find proof that cannot be denied or lied away. Who can say how long that will take? I but try to make you stop something that helps no one. Is it wrong of me to do that?"

"Nay." She felt her anger slip away and knew a lot of it had been born of her fears. "'Tis but the way ye spoke. Hacon, if ye seek a wife who will ne'er criticize or question . . ."

He laughed and kissed her. "I would ne'er have set ye at my side."

"I dinnae ken whether I should be flattered or nay," she murmured, half smiling. "I fear ye set spark to tinder when ye spoke of a mon's duty to his wife."

"I will be certain to avoid such ill-chosen words in the future." Cupping her face in his hands, he brushed her lips over hers. "Although there is one duty I truly look forward to fulfilling."

"And I will see that ye fulfil it—often. Hacon." She frowned, stepping out of his light hold. "Mayhaps ye should think again before wedding me. There is no bairn, so our handfast marriage can be ended in a year and a day. Ye are now a baron and could easily rise higher. I may not be the right wife to aid ye in that goal." Seeing the way he was scowling at her, she hurried to explain, "But think—my kinsmen even have a feud with the Douglasses."

"Lass, when we return to Dubheilrig we will be married by a priest. If who I wed makes any difference, then so be it. I have all I truly desire. If I gain more, aye, that would please me, but if I dinnae . . ." He shrugged.

"All right." She laughed softly when he pulled her into his arms and heartily kissed her.

"Weel, that wasnae so hard," he murmured as he held her close and rubbed his cheek against her hair.

"What wasnae so hard?" She sighed her enjoyment when he began to nibble her ear.

"Our first argument."

"I think there may be more."

"Oh, I ken it."

"I probably will ne'er be a peaceful wife, meek and obedient."

He chuckled. "I ken that verra weel indeed."

"I dinnae think," she managed to say as he picked her up, laid her down on their bedding, and sprawled on top of her, "ye are giving this confession of my faults the solemn attention it deserves."

"I treat every word ye utter as the jewel that it is," he drawled while kissing her throat.

Her laughter was abruptly cut off as an eerie, chilling howl echoed through the forest. "Hacon?"

He touched her lips with his finger to silence her and sat up listening intently. Aware of the sudden silence of the camp, he prayed he had misheard the sound. Then it was repeated and answered. The chill of fear seeped through his veins. Standing up, he tugged Jennet to her feet and began to collect their blankets.

Jennet looked all around her, fighting her growing fear. "'Tis wolves?"

"Aye. Mayhaps the stink of blood is strong around here and draws them."

"But the dead are buried."

"In only a shallow pit."

"Weel, surely they wouldnae attack so many men."

"I dinnae think so, lass. Not if we are all together." Grabbing her hand, he hurried back to the others. "We cannae tell how bold they may be. If they are driven hard by hunger . . ." He shrugged. "Even if they arenae, 'twould be best if we crowd together."

"Wolves?" a tense Dugald asked, seeking confirmation as Hacon reached the shared campfire.

"Aye, and by the sound of it they are near and drawing nearer. Everyone should gather closer together. Set the wounded in the middle. Build up the fires. Mayhaps a circle of them with us in the midst of it. And bring the horses in nearer."

"Do ye think there is much danger?" asked Malcolm as Dugald and Ranald hurried to carry out those orders. "There is a score and ten of us here, mayhaps more. So many men together should make the beasts hold back."

"Aye, if we are together. But at the moment we are scattered about in these trees. We also have wounded men, ponies, and horses. I should prefer to be too cautious than not cautious enough. If these beasts have suffered the bite of hunger as sharply as many of the people in this land, they could be verra dangerous indeed."

As Malcolm and Hacon moved to help secure man and animal against any possible attack, Jennet picked up a sleeping Murdoc from Ranald's blankets. She sat down close to the fire, rocking back and forth until the disturbed child fell asleep again. The sounds of the wolf pack seemed to encircle her. She prayed Hacon would hurry in drawing their camp into a tighter circle. Perhaps in the midst of so many closely

quartered men and horses she would feel safer. Wolves terrified her and she saw no reason to hide the fact. She noticed
few of the men tried either.

"There are a lot of them," she murmured when Hacon and
the others returned to sit around the fire.

"Aye, it sounds like a big pack." He put his arm around her.
"We will be safe now." Idly he smoothed his hand over
Murdoc's soft curls. "They willnae cross the fire. Our biggest
worry will be keeping the horses from growing too frightened. We may weel lose one or two of them."

Dugald nodded. "If they break free and run, the wolves
will have them."

Feeling Jennet shudder, Hacon kissed her cheek. "Even a
starving wolf would hesitate to enter this circle of men and
fire. Lie down." He patted his lap. "Rest your head here."
When she did so, he spread a blanket over her.

Settling Murdoc comfortably against her side, she asked,
"Are ye not planning to get some rest?"

"Mayhaps later. I wish to keep watch for a wee bit."

"Ye dinnae think they will just draw near then flee?"

"Nay. I think we will have the pleasure of their company
for most of the night."

"Then 'twill be a verra long night."

No one disagreed, and she closed her eyes. It would not be
easy to sleep with the cries of wolves breaking the night's silence. They frightened her more even than enemy soldiers, a
fact which puzzled her a little. Shrugging away that confusion, she tried to close her ears.

When Hacon began to idly rub her back, she felt herself
grow calmer. The soft murmur of deep male voices also
proved soothing. She was surrounded by strong, well-armed
men who had survived many a bloody battle, she reminded
herself. And, she thought with an inner smile as she felt the
touch of sleep, no mere pack of wolves would keep her from
her wedding.

# Chapter 20

A soft cry of fear escaped Jennet and she reached for Hacon, only to find herself alone in her bed. It took her a moment to assure herself that howling wolves were not encircling her bed at Dubheilrig, that she had escaped that chilling encounter unscathed two long months ago. The circle of fire and the armed men had kept the wolves at bay, and the animals had finally slinked away just before dawn.

She stared up at the ceiling of her chambers and worked to calm herself. Briefly she cursed Lady Serilda for insisting that she and Hacon sleep apart until they were properly wed, but immediately she felt guilty. It was only a temporary hardship, and if it made Lady Serilda happy, it should be borne without complaint. Jennet grimaced. She did wish she could have had some warning of Lady Serilda's sudden insistence upon propriety. Then she and Hacon would have taken better advantage of the last week of their journey back to Dubheilrig. Instead, because of possible dangers and the belief that they would be together once they got home, they had made love only once. She sorely regretted that now.

"Still abed?"

Startled by the soft voice, Jennet sat up and smiled at Lady

Serilda. "Aye, I needed to calm myself. I had a nightmare about those wolves. I hope that isnae some omen."

Lady Serilda laughed as she directed the maid to set a tray of food on the table next to Jennet's bed. "Nay, I dinnae believe so. Thank ye, Christine," she murmured as the maid left and she shut the door behind her. "Now, Jennet, eat your breakfast and then we shall prepare you for your wedding. Hacon is already awake and dressed."

Jennet paused in biting into a thick slice of bread. "Have I overslept?"

"Not at all." Lady Serilda sat on the edge of the bed. "My son is verra eager. Just as I had hoped he would be."

"Is that why ye kept us apart?" Jennet asked, and began to grin.

"But of course. A wedding night should be special. It cannae be verra special if ye but climb out of a shared bed, say a few vows, and climb back into that same bed. I should have thought of it before. It did the boy good. He has placed his great energies elsewhere."

"Into the building of his tower house."

"Aye, when this cursed winter weather allowed it." She smiled at Jennet. "Did ye begin to think he was avoiding you?"

"At times—aye. I told myself I was just spoiled. By traveling with him as I have been, I have become too accustomed to him always being at my side."

"And I have kept you verra busy as weel."

"'Twas good for me. I have ne'er had to plan such a large celebration before." She thought about all that would be expected of her as the wife of a baron and felt a shiver of uncertainty.

Lady Serilda smiled gently and patted Jennet's hand. "Ye will do my son proud, child. Now, finish your food and then we shall prepare you for this wedding."

\* \* \*

Jennet stared at herself in Serilda's mirror, her mouth slightly agape. She knew the reflection was hers, but she found the image a strange one. Her gown was a soft shade of green. From beneath its armless drape showed the tight, long-sleeved undertunic of a slightly darker shade of green. Ribbons of both shades decorated her hair, which hung long and loose. Her clothes were of the finest linen and wool, the ribbons of silk. She had never worn such rich, beautiful clothes. Even her shoes were of soft leather, elaborately embroidered. It could not be her she was looking at in the mirror, and yet it was.

"Ye are a lovely bride," murmured Serilda as she affixed another ribbon to Jennet's thick hair.

"'Tis the gown, Lady Gillard. I have ne'er worn such beautiful clothes."

"A gown is only as lovely as the woman who wears it. Now"—she linked her arm with Jennet's—"let us try walking a wee bit more. I think ye havenae had a train on your dress before."

"Nay." Jennet began to walk around the room with Serilda, gaining confidence. "They would have been a hazard for me most of the time."

"Aye, ye have been caught in the heart of this cursed war a great deal. Weel, we have yet to suffer much from the war at Dubheilrig. Ye will be allowed some peace here."

"That will be verra nice. 'Twould be even better," she muttered, "if all of Scotland could enjoy peace."

"We all pray to God that He will grant us such a precious gift. Jennet," Serilda began, but Katherine suddenly burst into the room, ending her question before she could begin it.

"Everyone is waiting for the wedding to begin," Katherine announced, her tone sharp.

Serilda frowned and Jennet, surmising that she meant to reprimand her daughter, quickly replied, "We will begin the ride to the church in but a few moments. Ye can tell Ranald we willnae make him wait much longer."

"Aye, I will tell him."

As soon as Katherine left, shutting the door behind her with a distinct snap, Serilda sighed and shook her head. "I am verra sorry, Jennet. I dinnae ken what ails the woman. She was a sweet child."

"'Tis no matter."

"Nay, 'tis a problem I mean to solve. In truth, I believe I ken what gnaws at her. Her husband was riding with Hacon's men when he met his death. She ne'er blamed Hacon for it, yet at times I sense a . . . weel, a resentment. I believe that is what sours her mood now. She is a widow still while Hacon is to be wed."

"Aye, that could weel be the way of it." Jennet was certain Katherine also resented the time and attention Lady Serilda gave her, but she hoped some of that would ease once she and Hacon went to live in the tower house.

"I shall ignore the problem for a few days. Her ill humors usually pass. Howbeit, if she continues to be so poor mannered to you, I *shall* speak to her."

"I dinnae wish to cause any disharmony."

"Ye dinnae. Katherine does." Taking Jennet's hand, Serilda led her to the door. "We best be on our way or my son shall come to fetch you. Hacon has many virtues, but patience was ne'er one of them."

Again, Hacon straightened the wide sleeves of his tunic and scowled toward the manse. He felt as if he had been waiting in front of the chapel for hours. Just as he was about to walk back to see what was causing the delay, he saw Jennet and his mother emerge through the door. Despite the distance that separated them, he could tell that Jennet was beautiful.

"Ah, look at her, Dugald. Am I not a most fortunate mon?"

Glancing toward Jennet as she was helped onto the pony's back, Dugald nervously tugged at his finery. "Aye, ye are. Ye may have been able to wed a lass of higher birth and greater fortune, but this one is your mate. She will give you strong sons and ever stand at your side."

Looking at his cousin with some surprise, Hacon asked, "Do ye truly mean those words?"

"Aye. I didnae just cough up what ye wished to hear. She willnae be a restful wife, but ye wouldnae be happy with any other. And what I believe is best of all, she can be the fine lady riding toward you now, but she can also endure a hard life. Ye may not always enjoy the good fortune ye do now."

"True, but I mean to cling tightly to what I have. Nay, no need to say more." He held up his hand to halt Dugald's words. "I ken how easily it can all be lost. I but felt a need to voice that vow. My Jennet has earned fine gowns and a strong lodging that she can feel safe in."

When Ranald halted the pony carrying Jennet in front of the chapel, Hacon slowly approached her. He did not think he had ever seen a lovelier woman. The colors of her gown made her eyes look an even richer green. A hundred sweet, flattering words crowded his tongue, but as he helped her down, he was unable to say any of them. Taking her hand, he lifted it to his lips and brushed a kiss over her knuckles, then led her to the chapel.

Jennet felt a knot begin to form in her stomach. She had always considered Hacon an extraordinarily handsome man, but dressed in his rich blue finery he was overwhelming. While his clothes were all that were fashionable, they lacked excessive decorative touches. His soft low boots with the button fastenings did have a pointed toe, but it was not extended. His dark blue hose was well-fitted but not particolored, as was increasingly popular. There were dagged edges on his open-sided overtunic, but they were softly cut. His undertunic was short. Its tight, long sleeves hugged his strong forearms in a flattering way. He wore no liripipe but a small hat with a shallow brim. Any rich courtier could approve Hacon's attire, yet he was far more subtle in his plumage. He was so elegant Jennet knew he would put many a court peacock to shame.

All of which made her feel suddenly inadequate. He could walk freely and proudly in any world, from a poor shepherd's bothy to the finest royal court. She was not sure she could do the same and felt a full renewal of her nervousness.

As Hacon stepped into the chapel, he took off his hat and handed it to Dugald, then looked at Jennet. "Come now, my wee plunder, this willnae be so verra hard."

She managed a smile for him and concentrated on the marriage ceremony itself. As they knelt before the plump priest, it became necessary to fix all her attention upon repeating the vows. She was glad of it, knowing that now, at the altar and before all Hacon's friends and kinsmen, was not the time to turn cowardly.

When the ceremony ended and Hacon kissed her, Jennet felt a brief desire to collapse. The idea of herself sprawled on the chapel floor made such a ludicrous picture in her mind that she was able to smile with ease as they walked into the fresh air, the congratulations of their friends and Hacon's family enfolding them. She spared an extra smile for Elizabeth, then blushed over her friend's somewhat ribald wishes for a lengthy and rowdy wedding night.

They walked back to the manse, the festive mood spreading. It was a moment before Jennet realized that a man was standing next to the studded doors. Her steps faltered as she slowly recognized that slim figure. With a glad cry she hiked up her skirts and raced toward him, then flung herself into his readily opened arms.

"Oh, Papa," she whispered, fighting back tears, "I was so afraid ye might have been hurt."

"Och, lassie." He eased his grip on her and gently grasped her shoulders. "Ye ken weel I have the gift for living. I will be about to bounce my grandchildren on my knee. Aye, and their children too." He smiled and held out his hand as Hacon arrived. "At last we meet," he murmured, looking Hacon over closely as they shook hands.

"I am glad ye survived Boroughbridge. Did someone there tell you where Jennet had gone?"

"No need. I saw you."

"Ye saw us?" Jennet asked, stunned by her father's apparently charmed life.

"Aye. I neared the army just as they began their attack. Once it grew quiet again, I slipped up to the prisoners and passed a few words with an old friend. I saw you and Hacon reunited and kenned ye would be safe. I am verra sorry ye were left to worry, not sure of my fate, but I ken ye have the wit to understand why I couldnae rejoin you then and there."

"Oh, aye, Papa. It doesnae matter. Ye are here now, for my wedding. Come and enjoy the feast."

Taking Jennet by the hand, Hacon reiterated the invitation, then led her into the great hall. He kept hold of her all through the various toasts and only released her when they sat down to eat. All the time that he watched Jennet's father Hacon struggled to hide his feelings, yet he suspected he was not successful.

It took him a while to admit it to himself, but he was jealous of the man. Artair Graeme was stunningly handsome and inordinately charming. He was a rogue and a thief, yet people liked him. Despite it all, Artair's word could be trusted, and if asked, he would do all he could to help someone in need. What really ate at Hacon was the knowledge that Jennet loved and respected the man, faults and all—loved him wholeheartedly. It was what he himself wanted from her.

Hacon also found himself wondering how he could live up to Artair. He himself was not so smooth of tongue. And while he knew he had an appearance women favored, he could not equal the near beauty with which Artair had been gifted. If Jennet was one of those women who weighed the worth of their husbands against their fathers, Hacon worried he would come up wanting. He was still worrying over it when his mother, Elizabeth, and Katherine escorted Jennet up to his chambers.

"I wouldnae hie away with the silver at my own daughter's wedding feast."

That smooth, rich voice startled Hacon out of his thoughts. As he looked at Artair, who had moved to sit next to him, Hacon felt color sting his cheeks. "I wasnae thinking that."

"Nay? Ye must have been thinking something, for ye have kept a close watch on me since I arrived."

"Do ye truly wish to ken what I was thinking?"

"Aye. I wouldnae ask you if I didnae."

"I was thinking ye will be a difficult mon to live up to."

Artair grinned. "Aye, I will be."

Hacon was startled into a laugh. "I see ye dinnae suffer the fetters of modesty."

"Nay, too troublesome. Laddie, ye dinnae truly believe my lass would judge your worth with me as her rule, do ye?"

"Women have been known to do such things."

"Weel, my lass isnae so foolish. She sees my faults more clearly than I would like. I am a fortunate mon in that she loves me despite them. Nor does she weigh any mon or woman against another. I have ne'er known her to do so. She certainly wouldnae do so with her own husband." He made a dismissive gesture with his hand. "Set aside your concerns, lad. She will trouble you more than enough through the years. There is no reason to take on needless worries. Save your strength. Ye will have need of it."

Hacon grinned. "Such comforting words for a father to give his daughter's new husband."

"If ye dinnae ken the truth of my words now, after being her mon for so long, it willnae matter what I say. My Moira was a sweet lass, not puling or weak, but sweet. There is some of her within Jennet, but, I fear, there is a fair piece of me there as weel." He lifted his goblet in a toast. "Ye will have an interesting life."

"Oh, aye, I guessed that months ago."

For a short while they discussed the truce that had been signed a month ago. Hacon had thought it a fine Christmas gift, signed as it was so soon before that holy day. He discovered, just before being dragged off to join his bride, that some of Jennet's cynicism came from her father. Artair showed as little faith in the truce's lasting the two years that had been agreed to as Jennet did. Hacon could only pray that they were both wrong. He now had all he could possibly want and ached for some peace in which to enjoy it.

After the rowdy group who had brought Hacon to their chambers was gone, Jennet watched her husband prepare to join her in their large bed. She felt nervous, almost shy, and thought it foolish. Although Serilda had insisted that they sleep apart until the wedding, she and Hacon had been lovers for a long time before then. It should not feel so new, so different to her. She had even had time to become accustomed to the idea of him as her husband, for they had been handfasted for months. Inwardly sighing, she decided that sometimes she simply suffered odd humors.

After shedding the last of his clothing and snuffing all the candles save the ones flanking the bed, Hacon slipped beneath the heavy coverlets and tugged Jennet into his arms. "Are ye pleased your father was able to attend your wedding?"

"Of course I am, Hacon," she protested halfheartedly when he quickly removed her lacy nightdress, "that was meant to entice you." She eyed the lovely gown longingly as he tossed it away.

"Lass, ye could entice me if ye were eyeball-deep in swine muck."

"What a horrible thought," she murmured, laughter making her voice unsteady.

"Weel, here is a more pleasing thought." He slid his hand down to her backside and pressed her loins close to his.

"That isnae a thought."

"'Tis all I have thought of since we returned to Dubheilrig. That and finding some suitable revenge to enact upon my mother for separating us. I dinnae ken what game she was playing."

"Mayhaps"—she slipped her arms about his neck—"she but meant to ensure ye had the appropriate ardor for a new husband." She hooked her leg around his and rubbed up against him.

"My ardor," he said, gently pushing her onto her back and easing his body on top of hers, "doesnae need starving to stay sharp."

"I am verra glad to hear that. Mayhaps ye should cease boasting about it and prove it."

She laughed when he growled, her amusement quickly turning to pleasure when he kissed her. His hunger was immediately evident and she savored it. With each caress she sought to strengthen his need, and her easy success made her feel heady and seductive. Soon she was too caught up in her own passion to know or care who was urging whom on.

She held nothing back, denied Hacon nothing. She writhed and panted beneath his kisses and caresses. He writhed and panted beneath hers. When he finally steadied her under him, she arched greedily to accept the joining thrust of his body. She encouraged his increasing ferocity with her body and her words, clinging to him as tightly as she could when they simultaneously reached the culmination of their desires. Still trembling from the strength of her release, she accepted his weight with lethargic welcome as he collapsed on top of her.

It was not until Hacon slipped free of her body and rolled onto his side that she roused from her drowsy satiation. She turned her head to look at him, smiling faintly when she saw

that he appeared as replete as she felt. When she brushed a
lock of his hair from his face, he did the same for her.

"So, did I prove my boast, wee Jennet?" he asked as he
tugged the tangled covers back over their cooling bodies.

"Ye will have to give me a wee bit of time to decide.
'Tisnae wise to rush a judgment."

When he tickled her to punish that impudence, she begged
him to stop. Still laughing, she curled up in his arms. Her passion had eased and she began to feel the chill with which
winter cursed their chambers. While she had Hacon's delightful warmth to curl up against, she intended to make good use
of it. "I recognize that impudence," he said, nuzzling her thick
hair. "Your father said ye are much like him."

"So, ye had time to have a wee talk with Papa?"

"Aye, a wee talk. And he didnae need to tell me ye have
some of his mischievous spirit. I quickly saw it."

"What am I to think of that? Do ye feel it a good or a bad
thing?"

"Ah, a good thing. Oh, the mon is a rogue and not above a
bit of thievery, but there is a lot of goodness in him."

"Thank ye, Hacon." She felt relief and realized she had
been concerned over how Hacon would judge her father.

"There is no need to thank me, dearling. 'Tis but the truth."
Idly smoothing his hand up and down her back, he mused
aloud, "Your father could rise verra high if he set his mind
to it. With his charm and fine looks, he could make great
gains. Aye, and he has wit and skill."

"All ye say is true, but, Hacon"—she patted his chest—"I
wouldnae try to change Papa's ways. There lies a sure road to
madness. He is what he is. If he wishes to change, he will. If
he doesnae, I think only God Himself could change his mind."

"Aye, and your father would probably argue with Him,"
Hacon drawled, laughing softly.

"I wouldnae be at all surprised. I just hope that while he

stays here he doesnae drag Ranald into his mischief with the lasses again. It doesnae make your sister happy."

"Verra little makes Katherine happy anymore. Dinnae worry about her. She coddles Ranald too much. A little mischief would do the lad good. Aye, especially when his duty now requires him to take up arms from time to time." He smiled down at her when she failed to fully smother a yawn. "Tired, lass?"

"I fear so. 'Tis puzzling. I lingered in bed this morning so that I wouldnae be."

He felt her cheeks and forehead, but there was no hint of fever. "Ye dinnae feel ill, do ye?"

"Nay, just weary. Mayhaps 'tis just the winter. 'Tis so cold and dark. That may tire me."

"Weel"—he kissed the top of her head—"get some rest. After such an arduous beginning to our wedded life, ye have earned it."

She yawned again and, giving in to the overwhelming urge to close her eyes, decided to ignore that impudence. "I am sorry. Sleeping on one's wedding night seems a poor thing to do."

"'Tis a long night. Ye may wake from time to time," he hinted. "In truth, I feel verra sure ye will."

Giving a sleepy laugh, she snuggled closer to his warmth. It felt good to be sharing his bed again. It felt good to be married to him, to have exchanged vows before a priest. There was a lot that was good, but there was also a shadow over her happiness. He had still spoken no words of love. She had spoken none either. That was sadly wrong, yet she could not bring herself to bare her soul unless he at least attempted to do the same. She suddenly wondered if Hacon suffered a similar fear. As she succumbed to the irresistible pull of sleep, she promised herself she would gain the courage to test that possibility—soon.

Jennet blinked, wondering why she was awake. She did not want to be. Several delightful interludes with Hacon during the night had left her tired. Hacon, she noted a little crossly, was not even restless. She closed her eyes, determined to sleep.

Her mouth filled with warm saliva. She swallowed with difficulty. A moment later it happened. Her stomach clenched and roiled. With a curse, she quickly bent over the edge of the bed and yanked out the privy bucket just in time.

Hacon woke with a start. It took a moment to realize the wretched sounds he heard came from Jennet. He leapt from the bed and hurried to give her what aid he could. When she was done he bathed her face, gave her some wine with which to rinse her mouth, and tucked her back into bed. Sitting on the edge of the bed, he held her hand and felt her cheeks and forehead. There was still no hint of a fever, but she felt unpleasantly cold and damp.

"Do ye think it was bad meat or the like?"

"I dinnae ken. If it was bad food, wouldnae ye be feeling sick as weel? Ye ate the same foods I did."

"Aye," he muttered, frowning down at her. "I but sought some reason."

Jennet was beginning to feel better when a new thought occurred to her. Last night had been her wedding night. It had also been the night her very regular menses should have begun. She had forgotten that. In fact, she had not thought about her menses for a very long time, since Hacon had found her in Boroughbridge. And the reason I havenae given them any thought is because I havenae had them, she realized, silently cursing her stupidity. Her last time had been shortly before Hacon had arrived to reclaim her. That meant she had conceived in Boroughbridge in mid-September, or shortly thereafter. By the time they had returned to Scotland she should certainly have had her woman's time again, but it had never arrived.

Still a little groggy, it took her another moment to rethink all the facts, reach a conclusion, and make a guess at how far along she was. The sleepiness, the sour stomach, and the remarkably hearty appetite she had acquired of late all made sense now. All the rich food, the drink, and the excitement of her wedding could explain why she had gotten ill now and not before. She hoped the lack of previous sickness meant she was one of those fortunate few who suffered little during pregnancy, but she knew it was still too soon to be sure. Again it irritated her beyond words that she could have been so blind to her condition.

"Mayhaps," Hacon said, interrupting her thoughts, "ye have some winter's augue."

She almost smiled, happy over her news yet at the same time a little nervous over how he might react to it. "Nay, 'tis not that."

"Nay? Mayhaps I should fetch Elizabeth. She has gained a wide knowledge of the healing arts."

"I dinnae need Elizabeth."

"Jennet, something ails you. This isnae right."

"Weel, sometimes it is." She smiled at his look of confusion.

"Do ye ken what ails you?" he asked, a slight hesitation in his voice.

"Aye, I think . . . nay, I *do* ken what ails me. I cannae believe I dinnae guess it before now but"—she took a deep breath to steady herself and then announced—"I am with child." When he just stared at her, she asked, "Hacon? Did ye hear what I just said? I am with child. In truth, I would guess I have been with child these last three, mayhaps four months. I wish I could say how long with more certainty."

"With child?" His voice was little more than a hoarse, unsteady whisper.

"Aye, with child."

He reached out one shaking hand to touch her cheek. "Are ye certain, Jennet?"

"Oh, aye, verra certain now." She gave a soft cry of surprise when he suddenly pulled her into his arms.

Hacon released her, gently settling her back against the pillows. "Did I hurt you? I am sorry. In my happiness I forgot how gently ye should be treated now. Ye must take care and I—"

She placed her fingers against his lips. "Hacon, I can bear a hug from my husband. I was with child last night too and no harm came to me. Neither of us was verra gentle and ye did a lot more than hug me."

His eyes widening in an expression of alarm, he asked, "Was that why ye were ill this morning?"

"I was ill because I ate a great deal of rich food, drank a lot of wine, and it was a verra busy day. And mayhaps 'tis just my time to start suffering the illness that so many other women do." When he kissed her, then leapt to his feet to start toward the door, she asked, "Where are ye going?"

"To tell my parents the glad tidings."

"They may still be abed."

He sent her a crooked smile. "But I feel a need to tell *someone*."

"Hacon," she called when he reached for the door latch, "I can understand that." She grinned when he looked her way. "Howbeit, dinnae ye think ye should at least put your braies on?" She giggled when, after a startled look at himself, he cursed and hurried to don his braies and undertunic.

Once he was modestly covered, he bent to give her a soft, tender kiss. "Ye couldnae have given me a dearer, more welcome gift," he whispered. "I willnae be verra long and I will bring ye something to eat. Nothing too rich," he added as he left.

Jennet laughed softly as the door shut behind him, then got snugly comfortable beneath the warm covers. She had no doubt that he was happy over her news, and that thought added to her own joy. For the moment all she could think of was what her aunt had told her the last time she had seen the woman. According to Sorcha, she was now in the perfect testing ground concerning Hacon and his feelings. Sorcha believed a man most revealed his heart when his wife was pregnant with his child. Often, he exposed his feelings in how he treated his wife. Now was when Jennet could settle her doubts and gain the courage to finally speak her heart. Sorcha had been right before. Jennet looked forward to seeing her aunt proven right again—hoped that as she and Hacon awaited the birth of their child, they would draw closer together and all that hung unsaid between them would finally be spoken aloud.

# Chapter 21

Sighing with exasperation, Jennet was torn between amusement and annoyance, as Hacon carefully spread out a blanket on the ground and helped seat her comfortably on it. She had been placed at a safe distance from the tower house and the workmen, beneath a wind-contorted pine so that she was shaded from the sun. Which, she thought, was barely shining. As her pregnancy grew more advanced, Hacon's coddling of her grew worse. She had now lived through four months of his occasionally excessive pampering. If she were not so pleased by what it said about his feelings for her, she could easily have found it beyond tolerating.

Sitting down beside her, Hacon briefly smoothed his hand over her well-rounded stomach. "Are ye certain ye are only seven months along?" He inwardly grimaced, knowing he asked her such questions far too often.

"As certain as any woman can be. I think 'tis nearer to eight, for May now draws to a close. Hacon, my last woman's time was shortly before ye arrived in Boroughbridge. Ye certainly proved ye were alive," she drawled as she patted her stomach.

He smiled. "Aye, I did that weel." He grew serious again. "'Tis just that, weel, ye appear large enough now."

"And I will grow larger." She had to laugh at his brief look of horrified concern. "Hacon, I believe I may look too large to you only because I was so small ere I got with child."

"I have to help ye rise from the bed."

"Ye dinnae truly *have* to help me. I could do it myself but, aye, it grows more difficult. Ye worry too much."

And that, she mused, warmed her deep inside, although it also annoyed her at times. Each day she grew more confident that he cared for her, cared deeply. The fetters of fear and doubt that held her declarations of love locked inside of her grew less binding day by day. While she still wanted to hear some words of love from him, it grew to be a less important requirement for her to speak her own heart. Often she found herself envisioning how and when she would tell him of her love for him.

"Aye, mayhaps I do worry too much," he murmured, and took her hand in his. "Our fine new tower house should be finished before the bairn is here. We will have our own place to live. That will get us away from Katherine's moods."

"She isnae so bad. She even apologized for being so sharp those days before and after our wedding. Actually, 'twas the day after my father left, so 'twas nearly a month after our wedding. His departure pleased her so that it put her in a generous humor. She fears he will corrupt young Ranald. She is just unhappy and afraid, Hacon."

"Which can be tiring to live with. Now, ye may wish to begin deciding who should serve us."

She nodded. "If ye agree, I should like Elizabeth as our nurse for this child. Her appointment to that place wouldnae displace anyone."

"A fine choice, especially when one thinks of her healing skills." He scowled and stood up, staring down into the village at the foot of the hill on which they sat. "Something is happening," he muttered, his hand going to his sword. "Stay there," he ordered when Jennet began to try to stand up.

"Hacon, if trouble approaches, 'twould be best if I am on my feet."

Muttering a curse as he reluctantly saw the sense of that, he took her by the hand and helped her up, then returned his full attention to the village. Something had caused a sudden flurry of activity and was drawing people from their work and homes. A force of armored men appeared on the road, riding toward the village; the red lion upon gold emblem, which decorated the banners they carried, marked them as the Bruce's men. But those banners also carried the markings of Sir Gilbert Hay, the Lord High Constable of Scotland. With their banners, full armor, and surcoats, the force entering Dubheilrig suddenly looked less than friendly. There was no need for the king to send such a well-armed force of nearly two dozen soldiers simply to call the men of Dubheilrig to arms again.

"Mayhaps ye should stay here whilst I go down and find out why our king sends a small army to my home."

"Nay, I will come too. These are the Bruce's men. It cannae be dangerous."

Even as he took her hand to lead her down the path, he murmured, "I shouldnae believe so, yet why send armed men? Why not just send a messenger?"

A chill went up Jennet's spine, and she tightened her grip on Hacon's hand. There were many reasons why the Bruce might send an armed force, and none of them were good. As they descended the hill into the village, she tried to strengthen her failing courage by remembering how loyal Hacon had been, faithfully answering every call to arms. Unfortunately, she could also all too easily recall the threat Balreaves still presented.

As they walked to where the Bruce's men had reined in and dismounted near the public well, Jennet saw how tense Hacon's own men were. They too sensed trouble. Women and children began to gather, cautiously remaining a few yards separate from the men, looking worried and frightened. She prayed there would be no fighting, no bloodshed.

"What is this about?" Hacon asked the man to the fore of the five men who had halted their horses before him.

"Ye are Sir Hacon Gillard, Baron of Dubheilrig?"

"Aye. Why does the king send armed men onto my lands?"

As he signaled to the men with him, he replied, "'Twas felt they would be needed to bring a traitor to justice."

The four men callously pushed Jennet out of the way as they grabbed Hacon, holding his arms behind his back and relieving him of his weapons before he recovered enough to ask, "Am I charged with treason against our king?" He could not believe it.

"Aye, and 'twould be best if ye would advise your people to surrender their arms and cause no trouble."

Jennet was pulled from her shock enough to see that Hacon's men were bristling, their hands on their swords. A few had already drawn them. Standing where she had been pushed aside by the Bruce's men, she wondered if she should do something, then wondered what she *could* do. She caught sight of Lucais and Serilda hurrying toward them from the manor and prayed they could help.

"Hold, men!" Hacon bellowed. "Take no stand. Ye cannae pull swords on the king's own men."

"Ye are no traitor!" Dugald cried, stepping forward, only to be blocked by one of the Bruce's men.

"Aye," cried Jennet, "this has to be some grave error." She also tried to move closer to Hacon, but was roughly shoved back.

"Dinnae touch her!" Hacon snapped, briefly and fruitlessly struggling against the men who held him and now bound his wrists with thick rope. "Ye fool, cannae ye see she is great with child?"

Although each man backed away from her, their leader replied, "So? What matter? 'Tis but a traitor's spawn."

"He is no traitor!" Jennet nearly screamed, but was once again firmly, if less forcefully, blocked from nearing Hacon. "Who would claim such a thing?" she demanded. "Ye cannae have plucked this mad lie out of the air. Someone must be the accuser."

"Aye," said Lucais as he and Serilda reached Jennet's side. "Who so falsely accuses my son?"

"Sir John Balreaves." Bruce's man frowned at the venomous reaction the name stirred. Hacon's men spat or loudly cursed, and many took threatening steps toward him. "He presented a great deal of proof."

"One mon's word is enough to bring such a heinous charge against my son, against a knight who has been loyal to the king for over ten years?"

"'Twas more than one mon's word."

"What proof? What charges? And who are you that we should heed what ye say?"

"I am Sir John Burnett." The man curtly bowed toward Lucais. "I act in the name of our king and the Lord High Constable of Scotland." He moved to extract a roll of parchment from his saddlebags and returned to stand before Lucais, Serilda, and Jennet. "Sir Hacon Gillard, Baron of Dubheilrig, is called before the king to answer charges of treason against the Crown and Scotland," he read, his homely dark face tight with outrage. "By word and by deed, Sir Gillard has betrayed his liege lord, Robert the Bruce, King of all Scotland."

"By word and by deed?" Lucais questioned. "He has done nothing and said nothing. These accusations are plucked from the air."

"At the battle of Perth in the year of our Lord 1311, Sir Gillard refused the honor of executing the traitors within the walls of that town. At the siege of Ripon in the year of our Lord 1318, Sir Gillard was heard to remark that our good king had no firm claim to the Crown, that he had seized it through murder. That same year he traveled to a village in

Liddesdale where there resided known enemies of the good Sir James Douglas. Sir Gillard betrayed his good king in Ireland, aiding in the defeat of our army and the grievous death of the king's own brother. On the twentieth day of September in the year of our Lord 1319, at the battle of Mytton, Sir Gillard was heard to demean that honored victory and did much to impede the king's men, led by the Earl of Moray, as they sought to slay our enemies, the English. In that same year Sir Gillard again visited the enemies of Sir Douglas and with their aid viciously slaughtered men in the service of the king. And, finally, Sir Gillard continues to hold close a woman known to dwell freely amongst our enemies, the English."

As Sir John ended the litany of accusations, all of Jennet's worst fears were confirmed. Balreaves was using *her* family and circumstances to accuse her husband. He was attributing *her* words to Hacon and using them to condemn him. It was she, not Hacon, who had scorned the king's claim to the throne and had decried aloud the massacre at York that they now called the battle at Mytton. She had given Balreaves a weapon to use, and he was wielding it with deadly skill. Guilt and fear consumed her.

Her father-in-law had not lost his combative spirit, however. "Hearing such lies is all I can stomach," he declared. "This is madness."

"I but carry out the king's orders. Mount Sir Gillard on a horse," Sir John ordered his men.

"Nay, ye cannae!" Jennet protested. But when she started after Hacon, both Lucais and Serilda held her back. "He isnae guilty, Sir Lucais, Lady Serilda," she begged. "There must be something we can do."

"Nay, ye mustnae endanger yourself," Lucais declared.

As Hacon was roughly thrown onto the back of a horse and the rope around his wrists was secured to the pommel of the saddle, several of his men bellowed their outrage and waved clenched fists. Those who had weapons gripped them tightly. Lucais hurried forward to try to calm the men and prevent a violent confrontation. The Bruce's men took quick advantage of the villager's uncertainty by encircling and disarming them.

Several women, including a wide-eyed Elizabeth, moved to close in around Jennet and Serilda, seeking to protect them. Jennet peered around them and was shocked by what she saw.

The men of Dubheilrig were being herded into one of the cottages, which was surrounded by several of the Bruce's men. The others proceeded to loot Dubheilrig, pushing their way into every building and dragging out all that was of value. They herded what horses and cattle they could swiftly round up into the middle of the road. Jennet saw her three goats, the ones she had dragged all the way from Berwick, pulled along with a few head of plump sheep. Other people, frightened and driven from their homes by the looters, gathered in the center of the village. Most clustered around the well, parents holding their children close.

"These men act as if Hacon has already been proven guilty!" Jennet cried, finally tearing her gaze from a tautly erect Hacon to look at a pale Serilda.

"The charge is treason, child." Serilda put her arm about Jennet's shoulders.

"It must still be proven."

"The Bruce would ne'er have sent men to take Hacon if he didnae already believe it or at least fear the truth of it."

"Nay, nay." Jennet brought her clenched hands to her lips. "They must let him speak in his defense. Nay, they *must* let him prove his innocence." But one look at Hacon told her that his was not a stance of fury or defiance but of a man prepared to meet his fate.

"I but pray they do. Yet, sweet God help us, I have ne'er heard that it made much difference."

"Which is why they are already treating us as outlaws," Jennet whispered.

"Aye. We are fortunate that they havenae murdered our people. Mayhaps that is a good sign." She tightened her hold on Jennet. "I ken that 'tis madness to ask ye this now, while this injustice is heaped upon our shoulders before our verra eyes, but ye must try to calm yourself. Think of the child, Jennet. Try to think only of Hacon's child now."

Jennet knew that was what she should do, but even as she fought to comply, she watched the rape of the place she now called home. She saw Hacon, bound securely to the back of a horse, waiting to be led away to what even his own mother saw as a certain death.

It was a long time before the Bruce's men were ready to depart. Jennet suddenly pushed a path through the women, ignoring Serilda's protests. Some of the Bruce's men tensed as she approached her husband and Sir John Burnett finally stepped in front of her, halting her progress inches from the horse on which Hacon sat.

"Jennet," Hacon said, his voice hoarse with emotion, "please go back. There is naught ye can do to aid me, and you will put yourself and our child in danger."

She ignored her husband's words, and held the hard gaze of the leader of the Bruce's men. "I will kiss my husband farewell. Ye have greedily helped yourself to all of value in Dubheilrig. I willnae let ye steal that too."

"He is a traitor," the man snapped.

"He is my husband and the father of my unborn child. I *will* kiss him farewell." She flicked a glance at the man's hand, which rested on the hilt of his sword. "If ye feel ye must draw your sword against a wee lass weighted and awkward with a full belly, then so be it."

He spit a curse and began to move away. "And am I to let every woman do the same?" He nodded to a point just behind Jennet.

Following his gaze, she was not surprised to see Serilda just behind her. "'Tis his mother."

She stepped over to Hacon and reached up to place her hand over his clenched, bound fists. She used her hold there to help stretch up on her toes even as Hacon bent toward her. The gently sweet kiss that they exchanged made her feel like weeping, but she clung to her strength. She refused to send Hacon off with tears of defeat on her cheeks.

"Ye are mad, lass," he murmured after briefly exchanging a kiss with his mother. "Ye should distance yourself from me—as swiftly and as completely as you can."

"Whilst ye are dragged down by these lies? Nay, I think not. I willnae let Balreaves win."

"Dearling, think of our child."

"I am. God go with you, Hacon," she whispered, and walked away, afraid her pose of calm was crumbling.

"Mother," Hacon called, halting Serilda from immediately following. "Watch over her."

"Ye ken verra weel that I will."

"She may try something. Aye, I *ken* she will. She must think of our child now—not me."

"Ye worry about yourself. I will take care of Jennet."

Hacon silently cursed as he watched his mother hurry after his wife. He was not sure his mother understood his warning. Or worse, he thought as he was led away, perhaps his mother completely understood, understood and was willing to aid Jennet. He prayed that they would not do anything dangerous, that common sense would finally prevail.

As soon as the Bruce's men were out of sight, Jennet ordered the men of Dubheilrig to be set free. She watched as they stumbled out of the cottage, among them Lucais, who immediately embraced his wife. Ranald and Dugald were both pale, a fury born of their own helplessness twisting their features.

"Sir Lucais," Jennet finally said when no one else spoke up, "I think some of Dubheilrig's men should follow."

"To try and free Hacon?" Lucais's voice revealed his doubts over such a plan.

"Nay, that would serve little purpose. 'Twould mark Hacon—and mayhaps all of Dubheilrig's people—as outlaws. That would also add strength to the false charges against him. Nay, I but thought some men should follow to ensure that Hacon reaches the Bruce's court alive. Remember who has placed the charges against him."

"Balreaves," Lucais spat, as if merely saying the name had soiled his mouth. "He failed to murder Hacon with his hirelings and twice-cursed curs. Now he seeks to get the king himself to do the deed."

"Aye, but he may not wish to give Hacon any chance to speak. Balreaves has been verra clever, but he kens his accusations are all lies. Despite having made the king believe these lies, Balreaves may not trust fully in his plan ending as he wishes."

"Child, once the charge is made—"

"'Tis considered truth. Serilda told me that. I understand and believe it. Howbeit, can Balreaves afford to believe it? What if by some sweet miracle, Hacon sheds this black charge? Then all eyes would turn to Balreaves, and people more powerful than he would begin to ask why. He has built a lie that must hold firm. His lie must work for him, gain him all he seeks, or 'twill turn against him."

Lucais stared at his son's wife, a little surprised at how astutely she reasoned. She was pale and clearly terrified for Hacon, yet she understood the situation with a clarity that had not yet come to him. Her understanding of Balreaves's deviousness, of the contorted politics involved, was very sound.

"Balreaves could find," he murmured, "that the sword he has placed at Hacon's throat is suddenly being held at his own."

"Exactly," Jennet agreed. "Balreaves cannae help but think of Hacon's long years of loyal service. He cannae help but fear that some of Hacon's friends may gain the courage to speak up in Hacon's favor. This lie *must* hold firm and one way, one sure way, to see that it does is to see Hacon dead while he is still marked as a traitor."

"Dugald," Lucais ordered, "find what horses or ponies ye can."

"There are some grazing on the far side of the loch," one man said. "Ponies mostly."

"Take a few men and gather them up." Then Lucais returned his attention to Dugald. "Ye arenae to draw too near to the Bruce's men. Make no threatening moves. Ye are only to watch to ensure that my son reaches Stirling, or wherever else they may take him, alive. Since ye are Hacon's men, 'twould be best if ye approach the court itself unarmed. Ye must not be seen to present any threat. Once at the king's court, ye are to stay there to watch o'er Hacon and send whatever news there might be back here to Dubheilrig."

"Aye. I may even be able to find men who will speak up for Hacon."

"I pray to God ye will. I have only one firm plan. I will-nae allow my son to die on the gallows" he whispered so that the others would not hear him, and Dugald nodded.

As Lucais continued to direct the men, Jennet made her way toward a rough bench near the door of the cottage in front of which they were crowded. She had only just sat down when Elizabeth and Serilda moved to either side of her. Fleetingly, seeing how concerned the women looked, Jennet wondered just how poorly she must appear to them.

"Mayhaps ye should seek your bed," suggested Serilda.

"Aye, mayhaps I should. I feel so weary. How could this have happened?"

"I demanded some answer to that same question from one of the Bruce's men," Elizabeth said, "when he was done robbing us."

"Did he give you an answer?" asked Serilda.

"Aye, he did. I got the feeling he knew Sir Hacon, though not well, and had some doubts about his guilt. When he spoke, it was as if he meant to reassure himself of the rightness of his actions."

"But what possible proof could there be?"

"None, judging by what he said. Not much more than what Sir John read to us, among them that Sir Hacon did not take part in the killing of the 'traitors' in Perth."

Seeing the fearful glance Serilda sent her way, Jennet managed a faint smile. "I learned he was there a short time after he told me he wasnae. I understand why he lied. Some day he will admit it."

"Aye, I was surprised when he confessed it to me. He is sore troubled by guilt over it," Serilda murmured.

"So he should be." Jennet's weak attempt at humor brought equally weak smiles in return. "Any more, Elizabeth?"

"Well, there was mention of Ranald's brief confrontation with the Douglas's men the day Hacon caught ye in Berwick. That should be easily talked away." Elizabeth hesitated before she added, "You heard the claim that Sir Gillard was scornful of the Bruce's claim to the throne."

"Aye, to my everlasting regret."

"They were *your* words," Serilda guessed, putting her arm around Jennet's slumped shoulders.

"Aye," Jennet choked out as she fought her tears. "'Tis my careless tongue that has condemned Hacon."

"Nay, no more than my son's goodness in not taking a sword to innocents or his good luck in returning from Ireland alive."

"I was told to watch my words. I finally did, but 'twas not soon enough. I put a dagger in Balreaves's hand, and he has buried it deep in Hacon's back."

"Enough of this!" Serilda cried. "Ye arenae to blame. Sharp words spoken by a woman should ne'er condemn my son, not when he has fought so loyally for ten years or more.

If what women said about wars and kings was heeded, then few men would escape the charge of treason. Balreaves is playing upon the fears and mistrust of the court. Weighting yourself with a guilt ye dinnae deserve isnae good for you or the bairn. I will hear no more of such nonsense."

"Ye may see it as nonsense. Aye, and I might convince myself that I need carry no guilt. Howbeit, when Hacon thinks over the charges and realizes what has been used to blacken his name, will he be so forgiving, so understanding?"

"Aye," Serilda replied without hesitation.

"I pray you are right, for if we cannae save him, if he goes to the gibbet, I shouldnae wish him thinking I helped to put the noose about his neck."

"We *will* save him. That is all ye need think of, all ye must believe."

Jennet silently vowed that she would do just that. She held a part of Hacon within her womb and did not want to risk losing it. However, she also vowed that she would not sit quietly by and do nothing. Her words had been used to hurt Hacon. It was her duty to mend that hurt.

As she watched Dugald lead a small force of men after Hacon, she decided to wait until some word came back from him. If his news offered no other hope, then she would act. Hacon would not go to his death thinking she had abandoned him.

"Your men are following us. If they try to help you, they will fail."

Looking up at Sir John Burnett, Hacon felt a brief shiver of alarm. Surely his father would know the folly of trying to rescue him by force. If Lucais had meant to stop his son's arrest, he would have done so at Dubheilrig, not waited until Burnett stopped to camp. Nor would a rescue be attempted the first night, while they were still on Gillard lands. That would certainly bring the king's wrath down upon his people. Whatever reason Dugald had for following him, it was not some gallant but mistaken attempt to save him—at least not yet.

"If my men were meaning to free me, ye would be dead by now."

"My men could easily fight off some traitor's hirelings."

Shrugging, Hacon returned to eating oatcakes and sipping wine, a task made difficult by his bound wrists. "If that is what ye wish to believe." Since he had not been released to eat his first meal, Hacon assumed he was to be kept bound until they reached the king's court.

"If they dinnae mean to try and free you, then why should they trail us?"

"Mayhaps they but wish to be sure I reach the king alive." Hacon strongly suspected that was indeed Dugald's intent.

Sir Burnett stiffened, his scarred face dark with outrage. "Of course ye will. I have been charged with delivering ye alive to face the court and our king. I *will* do so."

"We shall see. 'Tisnae only ye and me playing this deadly game. If the king truly wishes me brought before him alive, then dinnae waste all your strength watching my men. There could weel be others stalking you."

"What do ye mean?"

"There are those who willnae wish to give me any chance to speak the truth."

"The truth is that ye are a traitor. I begin to think ye are also mad."

Muttering a curse, Sir Burnett strode back to his campfire. Hacon sighed and wondered how much the man would consider his warning. He knew Dugald would keep a close watch for any attack by Balreaves's hirelings, but it would help if Sir Burnett would also keep watch. Hacon knew it would make him feel less as if he were already convicted and was merely being led to the gallows, that he would have no chance at all of proving his innocence.

He still felt stunned. Dugald had warned him of the danger of being called a traitor, but he suspected even his dour cousin had been shocked when their worst fears had come to pass. What little he had been told of the charges that had brought about the chilling arrest made it all the more unbelievable. Balreaves had taken innocence and mercy and twisted it into treachery.

Anger and a sense of betrayal also gnawed at him. He had given the Bruce over ten years of his life. Many a good man from Dubheilrig had died for the Bruce's cause. Despite all that, the lies of one man were enough to blacken his name, to taint him with the charge of treason. It made all he had done for the cause seem wasted, worthless. Even when he reminded himself of how often the Bruce had been betrayed by men he had thought loyal to him, Hacon's rage did not lessen. His life was at stake and he was innocent!

Hacon could not help but wonder how, if such a charge against him was believed despite all he had done, he could ever prove his innocence. His only weapons would be words. He doubted any man would step forward to vouch for him. The fear of also being tainted with treason would be too strong. As Hacon battled feelings of helplessness and defeat, he told himself again and again that his long years of loyalty would in the end, hold him in good stead, and that he would be exonerated.

His thoughts went to Jennet. She must realize that her own words had been used against him. He prayed she had the sense to believe that, despite the accusations, she had had no real hand in his trouble, that she carried no blame nor would he fault her in any way. If he was not able to return home and assure her of that himself, he vowed he would find a way to get word to her.

He had to smile as he recalled their farewell and the way she had faced the burly, battle-scarred Burnett. Poor Burnett had not known what to do with the tiny and very pregnant

Jennet. Although Hacon had been briefly terrified for her safety, he had to admire her spirit and was deeply touched by her effort.

Her parting words, however, preyed upon his mind. He had told her not to do anything rash, and her response contained no promise to behave herself or to stay safely at Dubheilrig. He was not sure what she might try, and he could only pray his parents could keep her in hand. His one comfort was that she had not also been accused of treason. His greatest fear was that in trying to aid him, she would misstep and join him on the gallows.

# Chapter 22

"He has been taken to Dunfermline in Fife." Jennet greeted Lucais's announcement with both resignation and dismay. She was sitting at the large table in the great hall with the rest of Hacon's family, including the ill-tempered Katherine. For the past two weeks they had eagerly awaited some news from Dugald, but she could see that the rest of the family was now as uncertain as she was. Dunfermline was a royal palace located only forty or fifty miles north of Dubheilrig. Had he been taken there so that he could declare his innocence before the king, or to be executed by royal command? Had a place so near at hand been chosen to allow those who knew Hacon to come to court and act as his advocates or because his enemies wished to have him tried and executed before the king even arrived to be swayed by Hacon's pleas of innocence? Only some relief came with the knowledge that Hacon had arrived at the court alive.

"There is more?" Jennet asked, seeing how Lucais frowned at the message Dugald had sent.

"Aye. They have thrown him into the pit, there to await trial before the king."

"Sweet mother of God." Serilda moaned, and Lucais paused to pat her shoulder in a helpless gesture of comfort.

"The king is already at Dunfermline?" Jennet asked, forcing aside the chilling memory of how Hacon had described the pit, as a place to toss a man and leave him to rot.

"Not yet, but he will arrive soon," Lucais replied. "He is said to be traveling there even now. Dugald works to gain advocates who will speak on Hacon's behalf. Aye, and he still keeps watch o'er Hacon, for Balreaves is riding with the king. Dugald feels certain some of the mon's hirelings are already at the castle."

"Ye say Dugald works to gain advocates? That must mean none are stepping forward of their own accord."

Lucais sighed and gave Jennet a mildly irritated look as he ran a hand through his still-thick hair. "Ye are annoyingly sharp-witted. Aye, it does mean that."

"No one will speak up for him?" Serilda looked at her husband with hurt dismay. "Not one mon?"

"Nay, at least not yet. Dugald is still trying. We must believe that he will succeed."

"I dinnae think we have the time to sit about and believe," Jennet murmured. "Hacon has been accused of treason. I dinnae think the king will delay long in judging him. Hacon needs an advocate as quickly as possible. Since no mon outside of Dubheilrig appears to have the courage to step forward, then a woman must—his wife."

"Jennet, by virtue of being his wife, your word as to his loyalty will carry little weight. As little as ours or that of our men."

"True, but mayhaps I can at least take away the damage done by my own ill-thought words."

"Ye cannae go," protested Serilda. "Sweet heaven, child, think of the bairn ye carry."

"I do, and each time I think of the bairn, I think of it growing up without a father, learning that his father was branded a traitor. I think how the name of Gillard could be forever stained with that crime."

"Ye cannae be certain that by going there ye can stop any of that," Lucais said.

"Nay, but I will be able to look my bairn in the eye and say I did all I could to stop it. I can tell him that I went and laid claim to my words, that I didnae allow them to be used against his father."

"But if ye lay claim to them too, weel, ye could join him on the gallows."

"That is a risk I must take."

"A risk ye would expose the child to as weel."

That was one of her greatest fears, but she refused to give in to it. "I will plead for the child. I cannae believe the king would slay an innocent for the faults of his parents. If the king wished all who claimed kinship with Hacon to pay, then it wouldnae have been only Hacon who was taken away. The Bruce's men didnae raise a sword against us, didnae even hit anyone. Nay, my child will be safe. If all else fails, I can always pledge him to the Church."

"There is naught we can say to change your mind, is there?"

"Nay, this is something I must do. I think ye ken it too."

"Aye, mayhaps I do, but there is one difficulty. 'Tis a three-day ride to Dunfermline, two days or less if one moves swiftly. The few horses and ponies left to us by the Bruce's men were taken by Dugald. We have no way to get ye to Dunfermline."

"'Tis a difficulty on which I have given some thought. At least at first, I must walk."

"This plan grows madder by the moment!" Serilda cried. "Ye cannae walk all the way to Dunfermline in your condition."

"I suspect I could, but I really dinnae think I will have to. 'Tis now June and summer draws nigh. Many will be on the road. I will ask for a ride. Papa and I were often forced to travel that way."

Ranald finally joined the discussion. "If enough coin can be found, a pony or horse, mayhaps even a cart, could be bought once she is beyond Dubheilrig's lands. It doesnae need to be the best stock. 'Tisnae needed for a battle or a race."

Lucais nodded, leaning back in his chair and rubbing his chin with one hand. "True, and I think we can find some coin. The Bruce's men didnae get everything of value. They but grabbed what they could see."

Serilda hit the table with her fist. "Lucais, ye cannae mean to allow this wild scheme!"

He patted her clenched fists. "I think whether I allow it or not, 'tis out of my hands." He looked at Jennet. "Ye mean to go no matter what I say, dinnae ye?"

"Aye. I am sorry to cause you any grief or concern," she added to Serilda.

"Hacon will be furious," Serilda muttered, but she reached out to clasp Jennet's hand.

"So, since there is no stopping you," said Lucais, meeting Jennet's look of determination, "then 'tis my duty to do all in my meager powers to help you. Ranald and that mon Robert will travel with you."

"Nay," Katherine protested, clutching Ranald's arm. "My son willnae take any part in this madness."

Ranald yanked free of her grip. "Aye, he will."

"Katherine!" Lucais spoke sharply to his daughter when she started to protest again. "'Tis Ranald's duty. He is a Gillard by blood. If Hacon falls, he takes the name with him. 'Twill be blackened for many years. Aye, this scheme may be madness, but it must be done." He sighed and shook his head when his daughter ran weeping from the room.

Feeling guilty to have brought about such a breach, Jennet said, "Ye need not send Ranald. I—"

"I will go," interrupted Ranald, slapping his hand on the table. "I will be eighteen soon. She must cease to treat me as a child. In truth, it grows painfully embarrassing."

"I will speak to her while ye are gone," Lucais promised.

"I wish I could go as weel, but that would mean Ranald must stay behind and he can better aid you. In truth, with this leg, I believe I would move more slowly than you, Jennet. This work is something that must be done by the younger and the stronger. Now, let us make what few plans we can."

Jennet breathed a sigh of relief. Her plan, mad as it seemed, had been accepted. Now, she thought, I have to make it work.

After kissing and hugging Murdoc farewell, Jennet and Ranald stepped outside of the manse into the damp early morning of the following day. Jennet's eyes widened with surprise when, instead of finding just Robert waiting for them, there stood Elizabeth as well. It was clear from the bundle she carried that she was not simply there to bid farewell to her husband.

"Ye are coming too?" Jennet finally asked her friend as she pulled up the hood of her cloak.

"Aye. Lady Serilda asked me, but I was set on it myself anyway when Robert told me what you were planning. I said you would be needing a woman along. Truth to tell," Elizabeth added as she linked her arm with Jennet's and they started on their way, "Robert was pleased of it, for as he said, he and young Ranald have no knowledge about a woman in your condition."

"Truth to tell"—Jennet exchanged a brief grin with Elizabeth—"'tis a comfort to have a woman along. I cannae foresee any great trouble, for I dinnae intend to risk my health, but . . ." She shrugged.

"Exactly—*but*. When it comes to carrying or bearing a child, *but* is a very important word to remember."

"Do ye think I risk the child?" Jennet asked in a muted voice, that constant fear making her momentarily waver.

"Ah, well, a little perhaps. Howbeit, you are healthy and strong. You have had no trouble yet. I think that, if we stay at an easy, steady pace and you do not allow yourself to grow too weary, you should be fine. If you can ride with a Douglas raiding party when the babe was still newly set in your womb, you ought to be able to walk a few miles now. Um, exactly how far away is Dunfermline?"

Jennet sent her a slightly apologetic look. "About forty miles, mayhaps fifty. Weel, if we can cross the Firth of Forth. If not, then we must go up to Stirling and turn east again. That would add a good many miles." Seeing the stunned look on Elizabeth's face, she asked, "Do ye wish to turn back? I will understand if you do."

"What? And have my Robert think me a puling weak woman? Never."

"Thank ye, Elizabeth."

"You are most welcome. Let us just pray that we find a horse, a pony, or some kindly cart driver ere my feet wear out beneath me."

Sighing with a weariness she could no longer hide, Jennet sat down beneath a large pine tree. It was the noon hour of their second day on the road, and they had not found even a crippled pony to buy. Neither had any rider or cart passed by. She smiled a little when Elizabeth sprawled on the moss-covered ground at her side. Robert and Ranald sat by the edge of the rutted drover's road, sharing a wineskin and talking in low voices.

"It doesnae make sense," Jennet murmured. "'Tis nearly summer. Ye would think someone would be traveling toward the larger towns like Stirling."

Without opening her eyes, Elizabeth replied, "Well, unless there was some great exodus, there is sure to be a time when the road is simply empty of people. We were just unfortunate enough to start out at one of those times."

"Misfortune has haunted me a wee bit too doggedly of late."

Lazily reaching out, Elizabeth took Jennet's hand in hers. "Do not lose heart. You must believe that all will be well."

"Oh, I am not losing heart. Even if I do lose heart in the chances of my success, I willnae cease to try. I willnae give up, turn back, or fall down into a heap of wailing."

"Nay." Elizabeth laughed softly. "You would never do that."

"'Tis just that my fear for Hacon weighs so heavily upon me at times. What he has been charged with is so grave a crime, it usually brings a swift and brutal punishment. This is the king he faces. 'Tis the king *I* must face. I am but a wee lass with no great wealth and no powerful family. How can I think I can change anything? Yet I must try. What I fear the most is failing and seeing Hacon die because of that failure.

"Although," she continued, "I begin to think Dugald and all the skilled soldiers of Dubheilrig are not in Dunfermline just to protect Hacon from Balreaves. I discovered that Dugald took Hacon's armor with him. I believe Lucais and Dugald have no intention of letting Hacon die."

"But Sir Lucais has said nothing."

"'Twould be treason. 'Tis best if he keeps their plans as silent as possible. Even if he is rescued, Hacon would be marked as a traitor and he would be hunted as an outlaw. That would slowly kill him. I pray I can prevent all that."

"You have finally accepted that you love the man," Elizabeth observed, turning on her side to look at her friend.

"I rather thought ye had kenned that already."

"Aye, but I mean *you* now accept that you love the whole man—the one who holds you in the night, the one who makes you smile, the one who fathered that babe you carry, *and* the one who must answer the king's call to arms."

"Oh—aye. I dinnae like what he must do, ne'er will, but I dinnae condemn him for it. Something my aunt Sorcha said brought that about. Weel, more or less. She made me see that he doesnae have much choice. She also said, 'Do ye think the ones he faces dinnae mean to hold their lives and gain by his death? 'Tis all equal. They are there for the same reason he is.' And she reminded me that many men fight for reasons that are far less noble than Hacon's."

"A very wise woman."

"Aye. Those words preyed upon my mind until I could no longer deny their truth. Oh, I will still complain, for I dinnae want him to go to war, but my condemnation is for those who lead, for those who feel it right to gain what they wish with the blood of others." She sighed. "I but pray I shall be given the chance to still complain."

"You will. Your husband is innocent. Surely the king knows how loyal Sir Hacon has been."

"The king, I fear, kens only that treachery dogs him. 'Tis the charge that Hacon may have been a traitor in Ireland that I most fear. The Bruce lost Edward, the last of his brothers, there. The other brothers were given over to the English by Scots who supported the English—traitors, according to the Bruce's followers. Nigel was hanged and drawn and quartered by the English in 1306. Thomas was killed at the same time, dragged through the streets of Carlisle by a team of horses before he was hanged. Alexander was caught by the Mac-Dowells the next year and given over to the English to be hanged in Carlisle. Even the hint that Hacon may have aided the Irish, may have done something that led to Edward Bruce's death, could be enough to hang him—or worse. That will be the hardest charge to argue."

"Sweet Mary." Elizabeth shuddered. "I should dread even trying to do so."

"I do. I wish my father hadnae left Dubheilrig, that he could be with me now. He would ken what to say. Howbeit, there wasnae even time to send word to him."

"Someone is coming," announced Ranald as he and Robert jumped to their feet.

"'Tis a cart," Elizabeth whispered with restrained excitement as she rose and helped Jennet up as well.

As Robert and Ranald halted the cart, Jennet hoped they had found what they needed. The old man driving it was wary, naturally fearing thieves, and it was several moments before a smiling Ranald waved for them to join him. Elizabeth picked up both their sacks, and they hurried over.

"He can help us?" Jennet asked, smiling at the old man but speaking to Ranald.

"Aye, Angus here travels to the court at Dunfermline just as we do. He brings some birds for the cockfights."

Glancing at the wooden cages in the cart, Jennet was relieved to see that the fighting gamecocks had their sharp beaks and talons properly sheathed. The old man quickly assured her that the birds would do her no harm. Ranald and Robert spread some blankets on the hard, dirty floor of the backless cart, then helped her and Elizabeth onto it. They made no move to join them.

"Ye arenae going to ride?" she asked even as the cart jerked to a start and Robert and Ranald fell into step behind it.

"Nay, not much," Ranald answered. "The mon's horse looks to be as old as his owner."

"And still as sprightly," Angus called back, causing everyone to grin.

"Angus says there is a farmer in a village three miles ahead who can sell us a pony or two."

"Then we need not impose upon his kindness for verra long," Jennet said, although she did not look forward to a long pony ride.

"Aye, we will still have need of him. Ye cannae ride in a saddle for so many miles," Robert said.

Ranald nodded his agreement. "Robert and I will try to get something to ride, but ye and Elizabeth will stay in the cart. That is best for you and the bairn ye carry. I think ye ken it too."

"Weel, mayhaps, but I dinnae wish to trouble Angus."

"No trouble, lassie," Angus said. "I like the companionship. Aye, and I get two fine swordsmen to guard me and my birds all the way to Dunfermline. As I see it, this is all in my favor. I will trundle you right into the inner bailey of the castle itself."

"Um, Angus," she said, "that may not be the wisest thing to do, though 'tis verra kind of you. Didnae Ranald tell you why we travel to Dunfermline?" She felt it only fair to warn the man of what trouble he might be courting.

"Aye, and I cannae believe it. I have been taking game-cocks to court for many a year. I ken who Sir Gillard is, and I ken that cur Sir Balreaves. The treachery done here is by that blackhearted Balreaves. I pray ye succeed, lassie, for Scotland needs men like your husband. 'Twould be a sad day if an adder like Balreaves won o'er a fine mon like Sir Gillard."

"Thank ye, Angus. I need to hear such things. 'Twill give me courage."

"Weel, how about a wee bit of advice from an old mon?"

"I would be a fool to turn aside any advice."

"The Bruce can be merciless, but he can also be merciful. Aye, he fears treachery, and weel he should, but he is a wise mon and can see a lie. Aye, and a pretty wee lass heavy with child could soften the mon's heart."

"Angus," she said with false outrage, "do ye suggest that I use my condition as some ploy, that I tug upon the king's sympathy in some underhanded manner?"

Looking over his bony shoulder, Angus gave her a nearly toothless grin when he saw the mischief in her eyes. "Och, ye need no advice of mine. Ye had already thought on that. Good, good. 'Tis a strong weapon ye have, and one that will work strongly on the heart of any mon who has one."

"I but hope I am in time to use that weapon."

Ranald helped Jennet out of Angus's wagon as soon as it halted several yards before the heavy gates of Dunfermline

Palace. "The king is already here, Jennet," Ranald said. "His banner waves above the palace."

"Then we had best make haste."

"I could let ye ride through the gates with me," offered Angus.

"Nay." Jennet smiled at the old man. "'Tis best if we part here. Ye go in before us, and with all my heart I thank you for your help."

Angus flushed slightly. "'Twasnae any bother, lass. Ye take care."

Jennet clasped her hands together and stood with Ranald, Elizabeth, and Robert as they watched Angus urge his horse toward the gates. The guards stopped him, then looked his goods and his person over carefully before letting him through. It was clear that the king's soldiers were being extremely selective about who they allowed inside. Since Hacon was charged with treason, Jennet began to fear that she would not even get within the gates.

She briefly surveyed the castle's position on a rise by a winding stream. The Bruce was even now busily rebuilding the castle, which the English had destroyed in 1303. Although it looked as if he planned this royal tower house to be as grand as it was strong, the abbey next to it was far grander. All Jennet truly cared about was that Hacon was somewhere within those thick walls and in danger of losing his life. Ranald took her hand and offered her a smile.

"Courage, Jennet," he murmured as he led them to the guards at the gates.

"Hold!" cried the shorter of the two guards who blocked their way. "Ye cannae go in bearing arms. Take their swords, Gilbert," he ordered his companion. "And search them weel for any hidden daggers," he added as the young, pimply-faced Gilbert moved to take Robert and Ranald's swords.

"The women too, Will?" asked Gilbert as he tossed Ranald's and Robert's arms on a pile behind the second guard.

"Ye willnae touch the lasses," snapped Robert, clenching his fists and glaring at Will.

Will took a step backward, then cuffed Gilbert offside the head. "Ye dinnae lay hands on the women, fool." He then scowled at Jennet and her small group. "What business do ye have within the castle?"

"We come to speak as advocates for Sir Hacon Gillard," replied Jennet.

"The traitor?"

"He is *no* traitor," she snapped.

Will shrugged his bulky shoulders. "Docsnac matter much to me. Howbeit, ye had best hurry along. He is being brought before the king even as we speak."

Ranald's sudden tug on her arm was unnecessary. Jennet was right in step with him as he strode through the gates into the crowded inner bailey, Robert and Elizabeth hurrying after them. Jennet paid little heed to the soldiers and courtiers strolling about, or to the merchants delivering and selling their goods. At the heavy, iron-studded doors leading into the palace, two more guards blocked their way.

"Hold!" commanded the one on the right. "What business do ye have within the palace?"

"I come to speak for Sir Hacon Gillard," Jennet replied. "Ye must let us pass."

"Are ye from his lands?"

"Aye—from Dubheilrig."

"No mon from Dubheilrig is allowed inside."

When Ranald and Robert began to protest loudly, Jennet silenced them with one curt gesture of her hand. "That order doesnae hold for women, does it?"

The man frowned. "Nay, I dinnae believe so."

"Good. Then let me and my maid pass." She met the guard's steady gaze without flinching, and he finally stepped aside. "Ranald, ye must find Dugald. Tell him that I am here and what I seek to do." She grasped Elizabeth's hand and started into the palace.

"I do not like this," Elizabeth muttered.

"We have no choice." Jennet gently squeezed her friend's hand, but it did little to ease Elizabeth's trembling. "Now, we must find where they are holding Hacon's trial. 'Twould probably be in the great hall just ahead." Seeing the guards standing before a pair of heavy, iron-banded doors, Jennet tried to prepare herself for yet another confrontation and delay.

Glaring at the soldier who barred her way, Jennet fought against letting her fear and impatience rule her tongue. Her condition did not seem to draw much sympathy from the man blocking her path. The guard was belligerently denying her entrance to the great hall, and nothing she said was proving strong enough to sway him. Nor did a terrified Elizabeth, standing wide-eyed just behind her, give her any aid. She was going to have to cross this barrier herself, and she was increasingly afraid that she was losing the chance to help Hacon.

"I have come to be an advocate for Sir Hacon Gillard," she said for what she felt must be the hundredth time.

"Aye, and what can ye say for that traitor? That his pintle works?" Smirking, he ran his gaze suggestively over her full belly.

"Sir Gillard is no traitor," she insisted. "And I mean to say so before the king and all his judges, earls, lords, and whoever else sits in judgment upon him in there."

"And who needs or wants to listen to a poor wench like you?"

She grimaced as he eyed her muddied attire with open scorn. Her finest gown was still packed away. The gown she wore now was a dull brown linsey-woolsey, loosely cut and hardly fashionable. It was also mud-stained, dusty, and badly wrinkled. She doubted her attire would give her next claim much weight.

"They will at least extend the courtesy to listen to Lady Jennet Gillard."

"Lady?" The guard gave a low, derisive laugh. "Ye must think I lack all wit."

"I begin to!" She immediately regretted the sharp words when his look of scorn quickly changed to sudden anger. "I *am* Lady Jennet, Sir Gillard's wife."

"Good God, wench, what are you doing here?"

Even if the voice had not been so familiar, the word *wench* would have told Jennet who spoke. She turned to glare at Sir Niall and his companion. It took a moment for her to recognize the other man as Sir Bearnard, the one who had delivered the premature news of Hacon's death. As she slowly recognized the possible use to which she could put Sir Niall, she struggled to calm her temper. With a cry of dismay she hurried over to grasp him by the arm.

"Oh, my dear Sir Niall, how relieved I am to see you!" She did not find it difficult to put a tearful waver in her voice, for the urge to weep had been strong since Hacon had been taken away from her. "I have come to be with my husband, to speak for him in this desperate hour, yet this brute willnae even believe I am Hacon's wife." She started to frown when the expression on his face became one of amusement.

"Ye play the part verra weel," he drawled.

"What part?" She straightened, knowing what he meant but hoping to bluff her way through.

"The pose of a poor, teary-eyed woman who cannae do aught without a mon's aid."

"Sir Niall," she cried in outrage, "I should ne'er do that, nor should I wish to."

"Weel, ye were making a verra good start. What goes on here?" he demanded of the guard.

"This wench demands to see the king."

"This 'wench' is Lady Jennet Gillard to you," Sir Niall said, his voice icy, then he turned from the flushing guard to look Jennet over. "Even though she looks a rather dirty wench from some poor bothy."

"Thank you," she snapped, yanking her hand from his arm. "Ye are as gallant as always." She glared at the guard, who did not look either cowed or mollified by the proof that she was who she had said she was. "So, ye must let me in."

"Nay, he doesnae," Sir Niall replied before the guard could speak. "This is no place for a woman."

"I am Hacon's wife, curse you. I must speak in Hacon's defense."

"The mon is a traitor." Sir Niall crossed his arms over his chest and leaned against the gray stone wall.

"He is no traitor and weel ye ken it!" She noticed that both Niall and Bearnard avoided her gaze for a moment.

"What can ye do, save watch him die, or is that why ye are here?" Sir Niall finally asked.

Jennet felt the blood drain from her face. She suspected she looked ill, for Elizabeth was suddenly at her side, and Sir Bearnard took a hesitant step toward her as well. Sir Niall cursed and looked fleetingly ashamed of himself.

"I came to try and bring him down from the gallows," Jennet insisted. "It was clear no *mon* would speak out for him." Both Sir Bearnard and Sir Niall briefly looked guilty again. "One of the things held against him are words *I* said. If I can lessen the sting of that accusation, mayhaps the others will be seen for the twisted lies that they are."

"And mayhaps ye will find yourself accused alongside your husband," Sir Bearnard said in a quiet voice.

"That is a chance I must take. Hacon is innocent. Ye both ken it." Watching Sir Niall closely when he frowned and hesitated to respond, she added, "If I am successful and Hacon is exonerated, the one who aids me in getting to the king could be seen as having saved Hacon's life. That would certainly clear away all and any debts, monetary—or otherwise."

Sir Niall abruptly straightened, cursed, and eyed her with annoyance. "I wondered when ye would begin to speak of debts."

She shrugged. "I thought ye might have forgotten."

"How I ache to. All right, I shall go and seek an audience with the king. I will try to get him to let you speak for your husband."

"Thank ye," she said, but he had already headed into the hall and used that as an excuse to ignore her.

"Lady Jennet?" Sir Bearnard gave her a look of guilt-tinged sympathy when she turned to face him. "I pray ye succeed, for I am sure Sir Gillard is innocent." He shrugged. "I fear that when charges of treason are flung, most men think only of standing clear of it."

"For all my harsh words, Sir Bearnard, I do understand. 'Tis just that I have no choice. I thank ye for your belief in my husband. I but pray I can convince others to share it."

It seemed like hours before Sir Niall returned, yet she knew that only a brief time had passed. She clasped her hands together and watched as he strode over to her. Although she wanted to present a calm facade, she knew her hope was clear to read on her face.

"Did ye plead my cause?" she asked when he stood before her.

"I should like to say aye so I could be sure ye couldnae hurl that matter of debt at me ever again. Howbeit, the king was calling for advocates for Sir Gillard when I entered the court. I said I knew someone who wished to speak in his favor, and the king ordered me to bring that person in." He took her by the arm. "Are ye going to swoon?" he asked sharply when she swayed a little.

Shaking away the brief light-headedness a symptom of her relief, she replied, "Nay. I would ne'er be so weak."

"Good." He started toward the doors to the great hall.

"Not unless it could serve some purpose," she added, and met his startled then angry look with a calm expression, until he cursed and dragged her along into the King's court.

# Chapter 23

Hacon had remained scowling after Sir Niall's departure. He could not think who his advocate could be. None of the men from Dubheilrig would be allowed to speak on his behalf, and from what little he had learned from Dugald, no one else had garnered the courage to stand for him. Glancing toward Balreaves, who sat at the white-linen-draped table with Robert the Bruce, Hacon saw that the man looked as surprised as he felt. He wondered idly how Balreaves could have been so sure that no one would come to his aid. Hacon also noticed that the man sat at the end of the table, nearest the doors. If the need arose, Balreaves could swiftly retreat from the great hall.

Balreaves was dressed in the finest green wool. He wore a surcoat ornately decorated with his coat of arms. It was clear that he felt himself a man of great importance and hoped the exposure of a traitor would add to that prestige. Dubheilrig would be forfeit if Hacon was found guilty, and he felt certain Balreaves would request the lands as a reward for his diligence in uncovering this betrayal. Hacon ached to wrap his hands around his enemy's throat, but the shackles at his wrists and ankles, both attached by short chains to an iron ring set in the wall, made that wish impossible to fulfill.

When the guards opened the door again, and Hacon saw who accompanied Sir Niall, he could not believe his eyes. Stunned, he took a step forward, only to be roughly yanked back against the wall by his two thick-necked guards even before he reached the end of his short chains. It was not until Jennet looked directly at him that he began to believe she was really there. His emotions wavered among dismay, fear, and anger. She could not understand the danger in which she had placed herself. He also hated having her see him now, chained and filthy as he was.

Jennet wanted to race to Hacon's side. Sir Niall's firm grasp upon her arm was all that stopped her. It was terrifying to see her husband manacled at wrist and ankle, with two large guards standing close watch over him. His stay in the pit of Dunfermline had left him filthy, his fair hair and new beard darkened by dirt. His clothes were stained and torn.

She briefly turned her gaze to Balreaves, glaring at the man with all her hate and fury. His eyes widened, and he went pale. And in that moment Jennet knew that he had finally recognized her as the small child with whom he had briefly locked gazes while standing over her mother's still-warm body. For the first time his recognition of her did not frighten her. She wanted him to know exactly who was going to destroy him. That old crime could do him little harm now, but this new one could end all his hopes of wealth and power, perhaps even end his life.

Sir Niall, stopping before the king and bowing, brought her to her senses. She pushed aside her anger and turned to Robert the Bruce. His reddish hair was shaggily cut and hung to his shoulders. His white surcoat was brilliantly decorated with the royal lion and the Bruce's own heraldic arms. A gold circlet crown rested upon his head. He was not as tall or as broad as she had thought he would be. Once, she suspected, he had been handsome enough, but now he looked very tired and older than the nearly fifty years he carried. Grief and constant war had taken a heavy toll.

Besides the Bruce and Balreaves, Jennet found herself facing the Douglas. That man's cool stare so unsettled her that she forced herself not to look his way. The Lord High Constable and the Abbot of Dunfermline sat to the left of the king. Of the twelve men on the dais, they were the only ones she recognized, though she knew the others must be powerful as well. She fought to conquer her sudden uncertainty.

Slowly, she lowered herself to her knees, startling Sir Niall into releasing his hold on her. She noticed that the Bruce looked surprised and curious. It was a good start, she decided. She clasped her hands together in a gesture of prayer.

"Will ye stand up?" hissed Sir Niall. "What game is this?"

"My liege," she began, twisting her voice with sorrow, something easily conjured up when she reminded herself of Hacon's fate if she should fail. "I am Lady Jennet Gillard, and I come to plead for my husband."

"Ye need not do that upon your knees," the Bruce said. "Rise. It cannot be good for you to kneel upon these cold, damp floors."

"Get up," snapped Sir Niall, but he kept his voice low so that the men on the dais could not hear him.

Jennet felt his grip on her arm and allowed him to pull her to her feet. Careful not to lose her balance, she nevertheless made the ascent awkwardly, doing all she could to stress the fact that she was heavy with child.

"Are ye fully aware of the crime with which your husband has been charged?" the king asked.

The sharp reply "Of course I am" rushed into her mouth, but she bit back the words. She decided that playing sweet and just a little dim-witted would be her best tactic. And to keep tugging hard on any reasonably good man's instinct to protect a pregnant woman, she made her face wince and, resting one hand on her large belly, rubbed the small of her back.

"Is something wrong?"

"Nay, my liege," she said. "I am but weary. As ye can see"—she gestured at her skirts—"I have but just arrived here from Dubheilrig. Since all the horses and ponies we own were taken with my husband, I was forced to walk for two days ere a kind mon gave me a ride in his poor cart."

"Sir Niall, ye may fetch the woman a stool so she may sit down," the king ordered.

"Thank you, my liege," she murmured as Sir Niall brought her a stool and set it behind her.

"I am sorry ye were so sorely pressed," the king said, "but you must realize that all goods of a traitor are forfeit."

Jennet sat down hard, placing a hand over her heart. "Then my husband has already been found guilty? I am too late? I had thought he had been but accused, that the accusations had yet to be proven. Am I still able to speak?" The look that fleetingly passed over the men's faces told her she had made her point.

"Aye, he has not been declared guilty or sentenced."

"Then let me begin by saying that one of the charges should ne'er have been directed at my husband but at me. This matter of words said, complaints made—"

"Nay, Jennet," yelled Hacon, but when he moved toward her, his guards hurled him back against the wall and drew their swords.

Jennet made no attempt to hide her terror this time. She feared she would see Hacon murdered before her eyes! Although they did not use their swords, the guards hit Hacon with their gauntleted fists. She cried out as they rapidly delivered several blows to his midsection.

"Hold!" the king yelled, hitting the table with his fist. The guards stopped immediately. "Would ye murder the man before his wife's very eyes?"

"Nay, but . . ." began one of the guards.

"Sheath your swords and cease this brutality." He looked at Jennet. "Are you all right, Lady Jennet?"

"Aye," she whispered. "I will be fine."

She struggled to quell the urge to run to Hacon. The hint of success for some of her plans aided her greatly in maintaining some restraint. The king and most of his companions at the table were regarding her with sympathy and concern. That they would react so increased her growing belief that the king was not fully convinced of Hacon's guilt.

"She doesnae ken what she is saying," Hacon managed to gasp out as he regained his poise.

Robert the Bruce looked at Jennet. "You realize that the words to which you mean to lay claim are treasonous?"

"Treasonous? Nay, merely angry. The harsh words of a wife who fears for her husband's weel-being and would try to hold him safe at home. As many women do, I can speak without thought to the consequences." She hated to say that, but could see from their reactions that the men felt it was true. Most nodded slightly in agreement.

"Some of the things were said ere you became Sir Gillard's wife." The king turned toward Balreaves. "Is that not true, Sir Balreaves?"

"Aye, my liege. She was still but a Scottish lass taken in Berwick when the town was rescued from the English."

When the Bruce looked back at her, Jennet hurried to dull the importance of Balreaves's words. "My heart was my husband's long before he honored me by wedding me." She ignored Sir Niall's mutters under his breath, knowing he had guessed her ploy but also knowing he would not expose her. "My liege, I cannae understand how a wife's cross words can carry any weight. In my fears for Sir Hacon and my anger over his many absences, I use my only weapon—words. Aye, I have cursed you and Scotland, but I have also cursed England and Edward. And, my liege, so too have I cursed my husband. I have cursed mud and ponies and rain and even the poor Scots whose wounds I tended.

"I have a quick, sharp tongue. I could fill this room with witnesses to attest to that. They are but words born of anger or fear, spat out and quickly forgotten. Mayhaps my husband should silence me more than he does. But should he die for that failure? Should his name be blackened because his wife cannae keep a still tongue in her head? If such was a crime worthy of death, I fear we would have few men left in the land."

It annoyed her a little to see the smirks on the men's faces. However, if she had to stoop to echoing their erroneous opinions about women in order to help Hacon, then she would. She kept her expression wide-eyed and slightly fearful. Sir Niall was starting to irritate her with his constant whispered asides, but she ignored him, promising herself she would save her retaliation for later. In an odd way, he gave her strength.

"Ye were captured in the English-held Berwick," Balreaves accused. "And when you thought your husband was dead, ye returned to England."

"That does put some weight behind your words," the king said.

"'Tis where my father took me. It pains me to admit it, my liege, but my father's honesty is not steadfast. He has been a thief, and he is verra good at parting foolish men from their coin. For many a year now England has been the best place in which to find coin. Even in the much harried northern counties of that country there is more chance of gain than can be found in this land."

"So, your father is English?"

"Nay, my liege, a Scot. A Graeme."

"He married an Armstrong from Liddesdale," Balreaves said, looking toward the Douglas. "Ye ken that group of rogues, do ye not, Sir Douglas?"

Douglas nodded, then flicked his hand toward Balreaves in a gesture of dismissal. "That is of little concern now."

"Aye, Balreaves." The Bruce kept his gaze fixed upon Jennet. "Continue."

After taking a deep breath to steady herself, she did as he commanded. "My father plays at being a Frenchmon when he enters England, one from the English-held parts of France. My husband has met Papa only once—at our wedding. Is he important?" She adopted a look of nervous confusion. "Papa has made no vows of allegiance."

"Your father goes freely from England to Scotland and back?" demanded the Bruce.

Jennet realized the king's interest had briefly veered from Hacon and talk of treason. "Somewhat freely, my liege. He is a mon who fights for coin. 'Tis verra hard to explain about Papa. He is a rogue and can make people believe he is what they wish him to be. He has no lands, no liege lord, so wanders about a great deal."

"Can you find him if you need to?"

"Aye, but, my liege, he is my father." Unsure of where the king's interest lay, Jennet was suddenly afraid for her father.

"Ease your fear. I do not ask you to betray the man. 'Tis just that one who moves so freely could be of use to me. Howbeit, back to these charges. Mayhaps the words can be discarded. There remains your husband's questionable actions at Perth, at Mytton outside of York, and in returning alive from Ireland, escaping with apparent ease from an enemy land."

Although tense and afraid, for these accusations would be hard to argue against without criticizing the orders given, she donned an expression of sweet confusion. "Questionable? I thought 'twas all weel kenned, with many a witness."

"Questionable in that he acted against orders at Perth and at Mytton. And how did he escape Ireland?"

"Oh, I fear the same thing that keeps Hacon from silencing me is what prompted his actions at Mytton and Perth."

Hacon tensed briefly as he realized she already knew he had been at Perth. Knew it, he thought, and had kept that knowledge to herself, clearly finding no fault with him.

"He has a . . . weel"—she shrugged—"a softness of heart. Mayhaps *too* strong a sense of mercy. I heard the good Sir James Douglas say so himself at Berwick." That man leaned closer to the king to briefly confer with the Bruce, and she prayed he was confirming her words.

When the king looked at her again, Jennet fleetingly wondered over the amusement in his expression, then continued, "My liege, when facing your foes, sword to sword, there can be few better than my husband. He is tireless, brave, and skilled. He would ne'er refuse to go to battle in your name. Howbeit, if those he faces hold no sword. . ." She shrugged. "He wasnae needed for the executions at Perth. There were swords aplenty to do the chore."

"Agreed."

That one word brought Jennet such a sense of hope she nearly cried out. She was winning them over to her side!

Balreaves's actions confirmed her opinion. After one hate-filled and fearful glance her way, he used the fact that all eyes were fixed upon her to slip out of the hall. He clearly did not want to be within reach if she was able to build upon this victory and continue to cut away at the net of lies he had built. She ached to stop him but knew it was not yet the time to fling her own accusations. It would also serve her better if he was not around to keep arguing her every statement.

"The battle of Mytton? Do you know much of that one?" the king asked.

"Aye, for I was there. 'Twas a ragged force of English peasants and monks that faced us. At the first bellow and shaking of fists from our men, they ran for their lives. There were many of your soldiers who didnae take part in the slaughter that followed," she felt compelled to say.

"My liege?" Sir Niall spoke, causing Jennet to stare at him in surprise.

"You wish to speak, Sir Niall? From all I have heard, you are no friend of Sir Gillard's."

"Nay, I am not, but neither am I his enemy. I didnae take part in the slaughter at Mytton either. The English ran with their tails between their legs, tossing aside their weapons. The fear of God was in them. I felt it was enough.

"As to Sir Gillard's bravery and skill," Sir Niall continued, "they are without question. So too his loyalty. I may not like the mon, but I wouldnae hesitate to fight at his side or have him guard my back. He is one of your finest knights."

"Ye have taken a long time to speak in his support."

"The charge against him is treason, my liege. I had no wish to chance that taint. Howbeit, as his time of death draws near, I realize he would be a grievous loss to your cause. Sir Gillard's only fault is that he willnae raise his sword against those who arenae fighting him equally armed and ready to die."

"Which many would not see as a fault," murmured the king. "What of Ireland?"

When Sir Niall looked to Jennet for an answer, she quickly explained, "He was guilty only of being very lucky. 'Twas no enemy soldiers who cut down Hacon and his mon, but hired murderers. They confessed as much when they thought my husband was past saving. Howbeit, a man of God chanced upon him and his mon, Dugald. Once healed of the wounds, which no Irishmon had inflicted upon them, they made their way home. Coin aided that journey, and only coin."

She noticed that the king's eyes had narrowed at her accusation of treachery, but he did not ask about her claim. "I fear the only witnesses to all of that are my accused husband, his mon Dugald, and that godly Irishmon. They are the only ones who can truly say what happened that day."

"You have most eloquently dulled the keen edge of each charge, Lady Jennet. How is it you can make what tasted of treason seem so innocent?"

"Mayhaps, my liege, one should ask how someone could make such innocent acts sound like treason—and why."

After briefly glancing toward Balreaves's empty seat, the king looked back at Jennet. "It appears your husband's accuser has left us."

"Aye," agreed the Douglas. "I saw him slink out of the doors earlier."

"Yet ye said nothing?" The king frowned at his friend.

"I believed it more important that Lady Gillard be allowed to speak uninterrupted. By leaving, Balreaves may weel have said more than enough."

"Quite true," murmured the Bruce, and ordered several guards to go and find Balreaves. "We will wait."

Hacon slumped against the wall, his gaze fixed upon Jennet, as it had been since she had entered the great hall. At first he had felt compelled to look his fill of her beauty, certain that it would be his last sight of her. Then, as the trial began to turn his way, he had watched her with a pride that swelled his chest and straightened his weary, battered body.

She cleverly used her beauty and her pregnancy, but mostly it was her words that held him transfixed. Somehow, unseen by him, she had come to understand the man he was. The respect he had ached for lay behind her every word. Her continued scorn of war and battle had ceased to be directed at him personally. He had taken her angry words to heart even when she had no longer aimed them at him.

That she would risk so much to come and plead for him now also told him a lot. She loved him. Her actions cried it to the world. Jennet loved him enough to put her own life in danger, perhaps even their child's. It infuriated him that she would do so even while he exulted over what it told him about the state of her heart.

He ached to go to her, but made no move. Although the trial appeared to be turning in his favor, he had not yet been openly exonerated. Until he was, his wisest choice was to stand silent unless directly questioned.

Jennet kept glancing at Hacon as they waited. He looked weary, but she could read no other emotion in his steady gaze. They were too far apart, and she could not go to him. Neither could she get close enough to the dais to hear what the men there were saying. She had to simply sit and wait, and she hated it.

Sir Niall was just serving her a goblet of wine when some of the men the Bruce had sent after Balreaves returned. She tensed, briefly thinking that waiting had felt a little better than the taut fear that gripped her now. She knew Hacon's fate could well depend on what action Balreaves had taken.

"Where is Sir Balreaves?" the king demanded.

"He and his men have fled," responded the guard. "We came upon them just beyond the castle gates. When we told him you wished to speak with him, he fought us, killing two of our men and badly wounding three more."

For a moment there was complete silence in the great hall. The king stared down at the papers on the table before him. The only outward sign of anger he made was to pick up those papers, slowly crumble them into a ball in one white-knuckled fist and, with his back turned to the room, throw them against the wall. While still turned away, he took several deep breaths. By the time he swiveled back, his face was calm. Two small slashes of color high on his cheeks were the only hint that his feelings were still running high.

Looking at Jennet, the king drawled, "It would appear that your husband's accuser does not wish to stand behind these grave charges." He looked at Hacon. "Mayhaps, Sir Gillard, 'tis time you stepped forward and spoke."

His heart beating fast with hope and the fear that all could yet fail, Hacon shuffled forward. The guards gave him no aid, and it took several awkward moments before he stood in front of the king. Finally he had the chance to speak against Balreaves, to put the guilt where it belonged. He dared not look at Jennet. His feelings were running so strongly, he knew he could be dangerously distracted and confused by her.

"I have ever declared my innocence, my liege."

"Aye, you have. But the accusations against you appeared strong and were presented by a man of high birth. However badly I wished to believe in you, I had little reason to doubt Sir Balreaves."

"Aye, Balreaves is of high birth, but he has little honor. He took the truth and twisted it. He has long wanted my death." Hacon told of how and when the feud between him and Balreaves had begun, and of Balreaves's many attempts upon his life. "This was but another attempt."

"It would appear we have been ill used. Howbeit, why have you not mentioned these murderous attacks before now?"

"I had no proof. Even when I had the word of one of his dying hirelings, my only witnesses were my friends and kinsmen. Although I ached to kill the mon, I needed unquestionable proof of his guilt. Without it, I knew it could bring my family grief, for as ye say, Balreaves is of high birth and part of your court. Howbeit, I believe there are those who have always shared my suspicions. They may be prompted to speak now."

"I believe Balreaves himself has spoken loud enough." There was a grunting murmur of agreement from the other men on the dais. "'Tis time this charade was ended. We have been made game of, tricked into becoming an instrument of murder. You are exonerated of all charges of treason, Sir Gillard. In an attempt to make amends, this court will see that the clearing of your name is widely told. All that was yours is restored. Including," he added with a faint smile toward Jennet, "your horses and ponies."

Jennet leapt to her feet and would have raced to Hacon, but Sir Niall grabbed her arm, halting her.

"Let go!" she demanded.

"Nay, though I crave witnessing your tender reunion." His tone of voice said just the opposite. "Your health must be my greatest concern. Your mon has more than dirt upon him. I cannae believe the wildlife he crawls with would do ye much good."

"He is right, Jennet," Hacon said as he faced her. "Let me shed the filth and shackles first. Then we may celebrate my freedom and"—he tried to look stern—"discuss the problem of wives who dinnae stay home as they are told to."

Jennet eyed him with a touch of wariness, wondering just how angry he was with her for the risks she had taken. "As you wish, my husband."

"Such meekness," he murmured, knowing she was already planning a way to talk him out of an anger he did not really feel.

"Lady Jennet," the king said, "ere Sir Niall escorts you to chambers where you might rest, I should like to know more about your father."

"My father?"

"I give you my word that I mean him no harm, whether he agrees or nay to a plan I have."

"I can tell you what ye need to know," Hacon said.

"So be it then. Lady Jennet, may I say no man has ever had a better advocate."

"Thank you, my liege." She barely had time to curtsy before Sir Niall began towing her to the door.

"I will send Sir Bearnard to aid you until your men are found, Sir Gillard," Sir Niall called over his shoulder.

"My thanks, Sir Niall," Hacon said, chuckling softly after the door shut behind them.

"Fetch a man to remove his shackles," ordered the king. "You may sit, if it pleases you, Sir Gillard."

"It would be welcome." Hacon sat on the stool Jennet had vacated. "I wish to request the right to pursue Balreaves."

"You have it. No man deserves such a right more than you. Sir John Balreaves will be declared an outlaw. He is yours. Do with him as you will. His death is decreed from this moment."

"Thank you, my liege."

"And I have something to give you," Sir Douglas interjected. "Consider it an apology for my failure to see what Balreaves was plotting.

"Ye may tell your wife's kinsmen that they no longer need fear the Douglasses. I declare a peace."

"Thank ye, Sir Douglas."

"Now, about your wife's father," the king said. "If he has but part of the wit and guile his daughter possesses, he could be very useful to me."

"Guile, my liege?" Hacon murmured, relaxing when the king smiled.

"Aye. Oh, I do not question her honesty, and her loyalty to you is inspiring. Howbeit, she lacked no grace once you were freed, and no woman so wide-eyed and sweet could speak as well as she did. Gifts of her father?"

"Aye. My liege, if you get that mon to swear allegiance to you, none will be more loyal. Howbeit, I would ne'er play dice with the mon," he added.

He knew everything would be fine when the king and his men laughed.


Hacon grimaced as he entered his chambers, shut the door, and carefully wended his way among the bodies scattered on the floor. The king had kept him longer than he might have wished, then insisted that he sup with him after he had bathed and changed his clothes. It had also taken him a while to find the chambers assigned to him in the crowded palace. Everyone from Dubheilrig slept in the room or kept guard at the door. It was good that Jennet was so far gone with child. Even if he was achingly tempted to try to make love to her, despite all their company, her well-rounded stomach would bring him to his senses.

Shedding all but his braies, he slid into bed beside her and pulled her into his arms, not wishing to disturb her much needed sleep but desperately wanting to hold her. She murmured his name, and he pressed a kiss to the top of her head, promising himself that, although he had woken her up, he would not keep her awake long.

"Do ye have any injuries that need tending?" Jennet asked, huddling as close to him as her extended stomach allowed.

"Nay, bruises only."

"Are ye verra angry with me?"

"Nay and aye. The risks ye took . . ." he murmured, and nuzzled her hair. "Yet no other would stand for me."

"Weel, Sir Niall finally did."

"Only after ye shamed him into it with your courage."

"Mayhaps."

"And he owed you his life."

"True. I suppose I should concede that debt paid now."

"Ye had to remind him of it again, did you? Ye sorely plague that mon."

"I begin to believe he enjoys it." She shivered as she recalled how close Hacon had come to experiencing a traitor's death. "I was so afraid for you. So terrified that Balreaves would win this time and not even have to bloody his hands."

"Aye, he nearly did. Howbeit, he didnae take into consideration the bonnie Lady of Dubheilrig. Ye did me proud, lass." He lightly massaged her back. "As for Balreaves, he stepped wrong this time, verra wrong."

"In fleeing as he did?"

"It declared his guilt loudly and clearly."

"Hacon, there is something I must tell you about Balreaves." She told him about Balreaves's part in the murder of her mother.

"Why didnae ye tell me before?" He found it hard to control his fury at the man.

"I feared it would make a verra bad situation worse. Each time he saw me, he said, 'Twill come to me.' Weel, he finally recognized me today. He went verra pale. Mayhaps that helped push him into making the mistake of running."

"Aye, I have no doubt of it."

"Are ye verra angry about my lying?"

"Weel, if ye can forgive my lie about Perth, I can forgive yours. When did ye find out the truth?"

"Shortly after ye told the falsehood."

"And so all those times ye asked me if what I said was the truth—Jennet, I was afraid ye would condemn me just for being there, ne'er let me explain or believe me if I did."

"I might have. Let us forget the past and start anew. No more lies."

He gave her a brief kiss. "No more."

"What is to happen to Balreaves now?"

"I have been given leave to hunt him down. And ye have just given me even more reason to do so. As the Bruce himself said, Sir John Balreaves's death was decreed from the moment he left the great hall. The good of that is twofold."

"How so?"

"'Twill allow me to end the threat that has dogged me for so long. And the knowledge of Balreaves's fate may weel make others hesitate before crying traitor or trying to lay false charges."

"I pray ye are right. I should ne'er wish this fearful agony we endured visited upon another. Hacon?" She looked up at him and was sorry she could not see him clearly in the shadows. "Why was the king so interested in my father?"

"Dinnae fear for the mon, dearling. 'Tis his skills the king is intrigued by and the chance to make use of them for Scotland. He has even said he willnae condemn the mon if he refuses the king's suggestion. 'Tisnae vanity, I think, to believe that unusual concession is meant as some salve for me, a gesture of gracious apology."

"And so the king should apologize. I dinnae ken how he could even think ye guilty of treason or treachery."

"Ah, loving, 'tis a troubled time. The mon cannae be too cautious. Balreaves had the power to bring such accusations, and the king has been betrayed often enough to listen. I believe the king was willing to listen to what ye had to say with an open heart because he had a doubt or two. He was willing to have me proven innocent."

"Mayhaps."

"Even the Douglas gave me a small gift."

"Oh, aye? What?"

"The end of this squabble with your kinsmen."

"Oh!" She hugged him. "That is good to hear." She fought to subdue a huge yawn and failed. "I am sorry. All of this has left me verra tired."

Tugging the covers up more securely around her shoulders, he kissed her forehead. "Then sleep, dearling."

"When do we return to Dubheilrig?"

"I should like to return on the morrow, but we shall wait until ye are rested."

"I shall be rested enough on the morrow. But should ye not get back all the property that was taken from Dubheilrig ere ye leave here?"

"'Tis all returned. Most of it was near at hand. Since the barony of Dubheilrig was held in the king's name, then all was forfeit to the king, so 'twas right here in the palace. What little was not, Dugald soon found."

"Then we shall return to Dubheilrig, starting on our way on the morrow."

"Jennet, ye have had a tiring journey and—"

"And I wish this child born at Dubheilrig." She gave in to the overwhelming urge to close her eyes.

Hacon tensed and slid one hand down to rest on her abdomen. "Does your time draw so near? Mayhaps we should linger here until after the bairn is born."

"Nay, that could mean a month or more of idle waiting. Aye, 'tis June now and the bairn is due in about a fortnight. Howbeit, ye can ne'er expect a bairn to come at a time to suit you. And if I wait and have the child here, then we will have to wait until the bairn and I can travel as weel. Let us hie back to Dubheilrig. I can rest all I wish to once we are there."

"All right. Now, go to sleep."

"I already am," she murmured.

He laughed, not really surprised, when a moment later her body went lax and her breathing fell into the light, easy cadence of sleep. Despite what he had said, he would delay the journey if she still looked deeply tired on the morrow. Now that their tribulations were over, even Balreaves facing utter defeat, he dared not take the slightest risk. She and the child she carried were all-important to him. That had become all too clear to him while he had sat in the dank pit of Dunfermline facing death for a crime he had not committed.

"And," he whispered, brushing a kiss over her forehead, "once we are comfortably back at Dubheilrig, my sweet wee plunder, we will talk about all we both know in our hearts yet cannae seem to say aloud."

# Chapter 24

"Was it truly necessary to buy a gamecock?" Jennet complained without any real rancor as, having stopped for a noon rest, Hacon helped her out of the cart she and Elizabeth shared. "He is a verra ill-tempered bird."

"I told you, Angus wouldnae take a reward for giving ye a ride to Dunfermline so I bought one of his birds at a verra high cost. I also bought a cart from his son, despite having been supplied with more than enough carts by the king himself. And," Hacon added as he led her to a shady spot at the edge of the road, "the bird might grow sweeter of temper if ye would cease glaring at it. Sit here and I will get something for us to eat."

Relaxing against the gnarled trunk of a hawthorn tree, she watched Hacon's dozen or so men-at-arms scatter amongst the trees on either side of the road. Dugald, Ranald, and Robert escorted Elizabeth to a shady place. They would be in Dubheilrig long before nightfall, and Jennet was certain the village would heartily welcome back its soldiers.

She looked forward to her soft bed. Although the journey had been made slowly over nearly four days, with extraordinary consideration given to her every ache and yawn, she was weary of it all. She really did ache now, all over, but she did not dare reveal her discomfort. They were so close to home she wanted no more delays. If she even rubbed her back too often, she was sure Hacon would have them halt where they were until the next day. She forced a smile for him when he returned.

"Here," he murmured as he sat down beside her and handed her some oatcakes. "Plain fare but filling." He set a wineskin between them. "Some of Dunfermline's best."

"Oh, that will be verra nice," she said even as she helped herself to a drink. "The trip is a wee bit dusty."

"We could pause here, wait until morning to finish the journey."

"Nay, let us continue right after the noon rest. I wish to get back to Dubheilrig and our bed."

He smiled and put an arm around her. "I can weel understand that. Kenning how soon we will be there, I feel a strong need to travel on. Howbeit, if ye feel tired . . ."

"I dinnae feel tired!" She realized she had come close to shouting and sighed, regretting her sharpness. "I am verra sorry. 'Tis just that I think I have heard that question a thousand times since we left Dunfermline. Hacon"—she covered his hand on her shoulder with hers—"I traveled to Dunfermline in far less comfort than this, and with far more speed, yet I didnae suffer. I will be all right. And if I do feel poorly, ye will be the first to be told."

"Agreed." He kissed her cheek.

"I will believe that when I reach Dubheilrig without having heard it once more."

"Best eat up then. The sooner we get there, the less chance there is that I will ask it."

When she was finally helped back into the cart, Jennet almost asked for a longer rest. She dreaded even another bumpy, jarring mile. Telling herself not to be such a complainer, she settled herself on the blankets spread thickly on the floor of the cart. When Elizabeth climbed in with her,

Jennet tried to smile. The look Elizabeth gave her made Jennet think it might have been better to make no effort at all.

"You are not feeling well, are you?" Elizabeth demanded as they started on their way.

"Dinnae say that too loudly or I will have half these fools o'er here peering at me."

"So, you *are* feeling poorly." Elizabeth clutched the side of the cart and swore when they hit a deep rut.

"And these bumps are one reason why I feel poorly, if *poorly* is the right word."

"By the look of you, I would say *poorly* is a very good word. Mayhaps we should stop."

"Ye even suggest it and I shall kick ye right out of the cart. We are but a few hours from Dubheilrig. I want this journey to end. I think when I get home I shall ne'er travel again."

"Humph." Elizabeth crossed her arms beneath her ample bosom and gave Jennet a knowing look. "You will change your mind the first time your man asks you to go with him on some journey."

"Mayhaps, but not if I am with child. Travel is ne'er comfortable, but this reaches beyond endurance."

"Ah, there goes young Ranald."

"Where goes young Ranald?" Jennet closed her eyes, hoping she could sleep for the rest of the journey.

"Your husband has sent him on ahead to tell those at Dubheilrig of our impending arrival."

"Ah, good. I hope he tells Serilda to ready my bed."


Ranald was already starting down the main road of Dubheilrig before he realized that something was wrong. His gaze lifted to Hacon's nearly finished tower house and he gasped. An army of almost two score surrounded it. Archers fired steadily at the tower and the wall encircling its bailey, while one large catapult was employed to doggedly pummel those same walls. The thick door leading into the inner bailey smoldered, but had clearly been soaked with water to thwart the power of fiery arrows. Ranald doubted that the door would last much longer, however. When it was breached, the defenders would be forced to retire to the tower house itself.

Suddenly realizing how easily he could be seen, he urged his horse toward one of the cottages. Once hidden by the low stone building, he dismounted and, clutching the reins of his mount, peered around the corner of the tiny house, trying to see what was happening. He decided the fact that none of the thatched roofs in the village had been fired was one reason it had taken him so long to sense trouble.

"I wondered when ye would gain the wit to hide, laddie."

Although he immediately recognized the voice behind him, he was so startled that he partly drew his sword as he turned. "God's beard, Artair, ye could warn a mon! I could have stuck my sword in you."

"Weel, ye didnae. It doesnae look good, laddie," Artair commented after a quick peek toward the tower house.

"When did ye arrive?"

"But an hour ago. I came to visit with Jennet. What are ye doing on this side of the battle?"

"Oh, ye wouldnae have heard yet." Ranald quickly told him all that had happened since he had departed shortly after the wedding. "We are just returning from Dunfermline. I was sent ahead to tell everyone. 'Tis strange that these dogs set out no rear guard."

"They had set one in the wood. He is dead," Artair muttered, then shook his head. "Wheesht, ye leave people for but a few months and they stumble knee-deep into trouble. Aye, and my Jennet wading right into it up to her pretty neck."

"I dinnae think ye could have been much help."

"Ye cannae be sure, son."

"Weel, at least she isnae huddled in the tower house."

"There is some truth in that. And where are ye off to?" Artair asked when Ranald started to remount.

"I am going to tell Hacon what is happening here."

"And what else?"

"What do ye mean?"

"Can ye tell him how many men? How weel armed they are? Do they hold any of the people of Dubheilrig?"

"I dinnae ken all that. How can I find such things out?"

"Not you—me. Ye wait here a wee while."

"And what do you plan to do—march up there and ask? How can you find out all that?"

"Laddie, I could get up there, tweak their leader's nose, and be gone ere the mon felt the pain of it."

Ranald was just preparing to tartly respond to that boast when he realized Artair was gone. Cursing softly, he returned to peering up at the tower house. He saw no sign of Artair and wondered how long he should wait for the man. The battle did not appear to be going in Dubheilrig's favor. Considering that many of the better skilled men-at-arms were with Hacon, he decided that was not surprising.

Just as Ranald began to fear Artair was not returning, the man's rich voice came from behind him. "Weel, it doesnae look good, laddie."

"We are losing," Ranald muttered as he turned to face Artair.

"Aye, but they arenae winning yet. 'Tis that low dog— Balreaves."

"Curse him and his mother!" Ranald slammed his fist against the stone wall. "He must have ridden here direct from Dunfermline."

"He has a goodly number of men, weel armed and hard-eyed. They have a few siege weapons as weel. Aye, a trebuchet and a mangonel. They mean to knock down the walls. Old Lucais must have something to equal those because some of the rocks that are going inside the barmkin are being hurled back out, but I couldnae see exactly what the weapon was."

"Can he keep that up verra long?"

"Nay, I shouldnae think so. Balreaves will be o'er that outer wall soon, and all your people will have to retreat to the keep itself."

"I wish there was some way to let my family ken that Hacon and the men are near at hand."

"It might ease their minds, but it cannae make them fight any harder than they already are. Best we cease talking and hie back to Hacon with the news."

"Do ye have a mount?"

"Aye, beyond the trees o'er there." He pointed to the line of trees west of the village. "I was a wee bit curious when I got so near to the village and no one hailed me. That didnae seem right to me."

Ranald slapped his forehead with the palm of his left hand. "I should have noticed that. What has happened to my wits?"

"I imagine they've gotten a bit rattled, if ye hit yourself verra often," teased Artair. "I will meet ye on the road to Stirling. Dinnae worry about being seen once ye get out of sight of the village. As I said, I closed the eyes of their rear guard and they havenae replaced him yet."

"Where on the road?" Ranald asked as he mounted.

"I will find you, laddie. Dinnae fear."

Artair slipped away, disappearing with a swiftness that Ranald envied. As carefully as he could, keeping a close watch on Balreaves and his men to be sure he had not been seen, Ranald resisted the urge to spur his horse into a faster pace, only to find Artair waiting for him about a half mile down the road.

"Where have ye been?" Artair demanded as Ranald trotted up beside him.

"How did ye get here so quickly?"

"I didnae have to worry about keeping a horse hidden from the curs on the hill. How far away is Hacon?"

"By now? Five, mayhaps ten miles."

"Let us hie to it then, son. Your people need aid as soon as possible," Artair said even as he spurred his horse into a gallop, Ranald quickly doing the same.

"Would ye like a sip of wine?" Hacon asked Jennet as he rode up beside the cart.

"Aye. That would be nice."

Keeping her face averted as she hefted herself into a sitting position, Jennet hoped to hide her discomfort from Hacon. She gave a soft cry of surprise when he neatly hopped from his mount into the cart. Flashing him an annoyed look as he sat down beside her, she accepted the wineskin he held out.

"We are but a few miles from home, loving," he murmured, lightly brushing a few strands of hair from her sweat-dampened forehead. "It willnae be much longer. That thought should improve your humor."

"I hadnae realized my humor was so in need of improvement." She suspected her mood *had* been increasingly sour but did not appreciate its being commented upon.

Hacon eyed Jennet a little warily. She was very close to being shrewish, something she had never been. He strongly suspected she did not feel well. There was a pinched look to her face as if she was, if not in pain, at least highly uncomfortable. She was also looking a little pale and sweating a bit more than was warranted by the warmth of the day. He dearly wished to ask her if she felt all right but suspected her reply would be neither the truth nor very welcome.

For a brief moment he contemplated halting the journey, then decided against it. They were so close to Dubheilrig, it had to be wiser to continue on. If she was ill or growing too weary, it would be better if she was taken to their warm, dry, and comfortable bed in the manse.

"I but meant that ye must be as weary of this journey as I am. Thus, kenning how soon it will be at an end will cheer you." He brushed a kiss over her cheek.

"Aye, as will having a verra good wash and lying down on our soft bed." She frowned as she caught sight of two horsemen rapidly approaching. "Hacon, isnae that Ranald? Why should he return? And, mercy on us, he has my father with him!" She suddenly remembered the secret she had recently told Hacon about their mutual enemy Balreaves. "Hacon," she said in a soft, hurried voice, "I dinnae think we ought to tell my father about Balreaves's part in my mother's death."

"Nay, dinnae worry. Satan's toes!" he cursed as he realized what their approach could mean. "Stop the cart," he ordered even as Dugald began to pull all the animals to a halt.

"Uncle!" cried Ranald as he and Artair reined in. "Dubheilrig is under attack."

With one sharp slicing movement of his hand Hacon ended the sudden rush of questions from the men of Dubheilrig, who had been riding behind the cart to spare Jennet the dust raised by their mounts. Now they gathered around the cart, all of them staring at Ranald and Artair.

"Who attacks us?" Hacon demanded, but he was already sure of the answer.

"'Tis Balreaves, uncle. He and his men must have ridden here straight from Dunfermline."

"So this battle is still newly begun," Hacon murmured even as he leapt from the cart and Dugald began to help him don his armor.

"Aye," replied Artair, "and your family holds out weel enough in your tower house. They have kept Balreaves out of the bailey yard thus far. Howbeit . . ."

"Howbeit," finished Hacon, "they are undermanned. The bastard fights mostly women and children, boys and old men."

"Those boys, old men, and the rest are making a fine stand. The village hasnae been fired either."

"Why fight? Why did he not just ride in and hold it until I returned?"

Although the questions were not really directed at him, Artair replied, "As to why your people fight when they must ken they can only lose, many dying, 'tis because Balreaves bears a banner with a dragon." Nodding at the horrified looks upon everyone's faces, Artair continued. "When the mon riding against you so openly declares no mercy for mon, woman, or child, fighting becomes your only choice. At least ye can make your murder cost him dearly."

"He has raised the dragon? Ye are sure?" Artair nodded.

Hacon cursed viciously and slammed his gauntleted fist against the side of the cart, splitting one of the rough boards. To carry a banner with the dragon upon it, and not simply as part of some coat of arms, was equal to crying havoc. Balreaves had given his men leave to kill everyone at Dubheilrig— to rape, slaughter, and pillage at will.

"Now he turns his hatred on my people." He fought down his fury, knowing it would only hinder him. "Weel, now that he is declared an outlaw and his life is forfeit, he feels he may as weel do his worst." When Jennet covered his hand, clenched on the side of the cart, he raised it to his lips.

"Uncle?" Ranald frowned. "How could Balreaves ken all that? He left the court ere his sentence was pronounced."

"The moment he ran, he confirmed that all he had said was lies. He knew what his fate would be. The mon kenned weel that he would either succeed or sign his own death warrant. Now he but strikes out in an act of blind vengence. Ranald, ye and"—glancing around, he named the four other youngest men in his band—"will stay with the carts."

"But, uncle, we too can fight. Aye, we have an equal right to defend our homes and families." Ranald's protest was loudly seconded by the other young men.

"Aye, ye do, but guarding what few riches Dubheilrig has is nearly as important. In those carts lies the wealth of every family. Aye, and in this one too." He nodded toward Jennet. "My wealth and the future of the Gillards. There may weel be some of Balreaves's men fleeing through here. Or they could attempt some rear guard action. Shall we leave all that we hold dear unguarded for them to steal or destroy at will?" When all five youths shook their heads, he nodded. "Good. I expect it to be guarded weel.

"Robert, I also ask ye to stay with them. I leave it to you to decide when or if they may best serve by joining in the fight at some time. Or by chasing down any of Balreaves's men."

Robert nodded and moved to take Dugald's place in driving the cart which Elizabeth and Jennet shared. "Shall I bring us nearer to Dubheilrig?"

"As near as ye dare, and then hide them weel in the wood."

"And if we see any of Balreaves's curs—do ye want them captured or slain?"

"I dinnae think, after this, any will wish to be taken alive." He turned and, leaning into the cart, gave Jennet a brief kiss. "Ye do as Robert commands."

"Aye. Take care," she added in a soft voice as he donned his helmet.

While Hacon moved to remount, Artair rode up beside the cart. "Dinnae do anything foolish, lass. Ye have two lives to consider now."

"I ken it, Papa." She raised herself up on her knees so that they could exchange a brief kiss. "Ye do have a skill for appearing at just the right moment."

"Ye are kind enough to save these troubles for the right times."

"Take care. And," she hastily added as he started to move away, "ye can better do that by donning your helmet."

"I think ye often forget who is the parent," Artair muttered, but took a moment to don his helmet. He paused by Hacon to say, "I took a close look at number and strength. Your kinsmen will be pushed into the tower house itself soon."

"Are there any men set on watch to warn Balreaves if we ride up?"

"There was one, but he willnae be warning anyone in this life, though I cannae promise they willnae have found his body by now and set out a new guard."

"And thus we could ride into a force ready and waiting for us." Eyeing Artair as he rubbed his chin, Hacon thought out loud. "If we draw close, can ye slip ahead unseen and determine our chances of surprising Balreaves?"

"Oh, aye. God has blessed me with a light tread. I can also take a wee peek to see if matters have changed in the battle."

"Good. Then we shall delay making set plans until we have that information. Men?" There was a muted bellow from his men, indicating their readiness to ride, and Hacon quickly spurred his horse to lead them.

Jennet watched them gallop away and tried to calm her fears. One look from Robert told her to sit down. The moment she was seated as comfortably and safely as possible, he started them on their way. Ranald rode ahead to ensure they did not draw closer to Dubheilrig than was safe. Jennet turned to Elizabeth.

"Why would Balreaves do this? What can he gain?"

When Elizabeth remained silent, shrugging her inability to reply, Robert spoke up. "He means to steal your husband's victory. Sir Gillard has won the game, but that low cur means to leave him only ashes and graves."

There was much truth in that explanation. Jennet grew even more afraid for Hacon, for their family and their friends. Balreaves was doomed, and in his bitterness he meant to destroy all he could before he was brought to justice. For a little while the fear and worry that thought caused, took her mind off of her own discomfort. She prayed Balreaves would receive his just punishment without too high a cost to Dubheilrig.

Hacon paced the ground in front of his men, who waited impatiently on the road but yards away from where it cleared the woods to begin its winding way through the village. He knew Artair had not been gone long, but he was eager, even desperate, to act. Each moment lost could mean another life forfeit. Balreaves wanted to make Dubheilrig bleed. The longer he held siege to the tower house, the more chance he would have to quench that dark thirst.

Hacon was also concerned about Artair. The man had an enviable skill, but that did not guarantee his continued safety. Hacon dreaded the possibility of having to tell Jennet that something had befallen her father. When he finally saw the man trotting leisurely toward him through the pine trees on their left, he was both relieved and tensed for battle.

"Weel, the fools are so caught up in their bloody work that they havenae realized they no longer have a rear guard," Artair reported as he halted before Hacon.

"So we are free to ride in as we please."

"Aye, though, as clear as it is all 'round the village, ye might be spotted ere ye reach him. Ye will have to be verra cautious in your approach. A direct assault willnae do. He has at least two men, nearer three, to your every one."

Using a stick he had picked up earlier, Hacon quickly sketched the plan of Dubheilrig in the dirt and handed the stick to Artair. "Show me how he is placed. We need to strike hard and swiftly. We need to pin him between us and those in the tower house. Only then will we finally lance this boil from our lives."

With the men encircling them, Artair, Hacon, and Dugald laid out their plan of attack. Once clear of the trees, they would spread out and slip up to the tower house from three sides. The oats and the grass in the fields were long enough to provide partial cover if they were careful. A few men would sneak up on Balreaves through the village. If they used all natural camouflage wisely and approached singly instead of as a solid force, they could get within yards of the outer wall of the tower house, directly behind the attackers. Hacon felt a lessening of his fears. If all went as smoothly as planned, victory would be assured.

Signaling his men to begin their stealthy approach on Dubheilrig, Hacon promised himself that he would not let any softness of heart deter him this time. The king had decreed Balreaves's death, and for once Hacon did not have any qualms about acting as the Bruce's executioner.

By the time everyone was in position, Hacon felt so taut he ached. Each sight of Balreaves's men pummeling the walls of the tower house or firing their deadly arrows added to Hacon's fury, to his need to strike the man down. His men suffered the same urges, and Hacon had been hard-pressed to hold them back, especially when Balreaves's men broke through into the inner bailey. Only their trust in his ability to gain them a victory with the least cost kept them from charging the tower house, from screaming out their fury and hatred. Now that they had Balreaves and his men encircled, Hacon could give the signal his men all craved. With a cold smile he did so, standing up with his sword raised and savoring the shock and fear that momentarily gripped Balreaves and his men as Dubheilrig's fighting force appeared from all sides, their cries for battle drowning out all other sounds. Hacon and his men swiftly scaled the crumbling, broken outer wall of the bailey and fell upon their enemies.

Lucais had paused in readying his people for a final stand when a new roar of fury was added to the cacophony of battle. He pushed a man aside to stare out one of the slender arrow slits of the keep tower. The sight that greeted his eyes made him hoot his relief and delight in a well-executed battle strategy.

"What is it, Lucais?" demanded Serilda as she came up behind him. "Not more of Balreaves's men?"

"Nay, *our* men." He slipped a strong arm around her shoulders and gave her a brief, hearty hug. "Our men are back from Dunfermline. That many-voiced bellow was theirs."

"Our men? Can ye see Hacon? Does he lead them?"

"Oh, aye. Big and bold and verra much alive. The lass has done it. Somehow she freed our son and he is here to make Balreaves suffer."

She hugged him back tightly and shed a few tears. "So, 'tis over at last. We are saved."

"Ah, weel, not yet. Our lads have caught Balreaves by surprise and surrounded him, but they will need help."

"Ye mean to go out there, to join that fierce battle."

"Dinnae look so fearful, dearling. I dinnae mean to charge out sword in hand. Howbeit, I am certain Hacon's plan includes our support and, though my arm is too weak to swing a weapon, my mind is still strong and quick. I need to direct these people."

"Can ye not just shoot arrows at the enemy from here and lessen their numbers?"

"Ye ken as weel as I that we could easily slay our own men, for 'tis a confused melee now." He started to signal the men to gather around him.

Serilda watched her husband quickly deliver his orders. Robert's brother Donald was the most battle-hardened, and she was pleased to see that Lucais kept the youth at his side. The men he would lead were mostly young and untried or past their youth. It was not the most impressive of armies. Their need to join in the battle was obvious, however. They wanted to strike a blow against the man who had kept them afraid and hurt, and had killed nearly a half dozen of their loved ones during three long, exhausting days of battle. She sighed and moved to organize the women as Lucais led the men out to join what was fast becoming a melee. There would undoubtedly be a great many wounds, large and small, to tend to when it was finally all over.

\* \* \*

Hacon kept his gaze fixed upon Balreaves as he moved through the tangle of fighting men and the rubble of his partially ruined tower house. Each time he was delayed by the need to defend himself he was infuriated. Balreaves was clearly trying to flee, even using his own men as shields as he struggled to reach his mount. Hacon was determined not to let the man escape.

Suddenly, armed men rushed out of the tower house, breaking what little control Balreaves still held over his men. Now they no longer fought to repel an attack but to clear a way for retreat. Hacon smiled, recognizing it was a decisive step toward victory. The confusion of men, hobbled mounts, siege weapons, and rubble within the encircling barmkin wall hindered them greatly. Hacon just prayed it would hinder Balreaves as well.

Just as Balreaves came within reach of his mount, Hacon came within reach of him. As Balreaves swung to face him, Lucais and Donald arrived to pull the nervous horse farther away and stand, swords in hand, as a deadly barrier. All chance of escape was taken from Balreaves now. Hacon smiled coldly at his enemy as the man swiftly readied his sword and shield to defend himself.

"And now, Balreaves, 'tis as it always should have been—ye and I face to face, sword to sword."

The man smiled back, but it was a weak, nervous expression. Fresh sweat glistened on Balreaves's pale, grime-smeared face. Then his look changed to a grimace of fury, and Hacon braced for the attack.

"Aye. Your whore of a wife will make a lovely widow. I shall enjoy her as I did her mother," he shouted out, and attacked.

Hacon easily blocked the fierce swing of Balreaves's sword. "Nay, ye shall now pay for that innocent blood."

"Will I?" Balreaves nimbly turned aside Hacon's sword thrust. "I am not without skill, Gillard."

"Ye have kept it weel hidden behind hired murderers."

Hacon danced out of reach of Balreaves's sword, but his own blow resounded fruitlessly off the man's shield.

"I saw no need to waste my strength. Howbeit, now ye shall discover that I am your better in this as I am in all else. Ye may have persuaded the king to let ye live, but your reprieve will be short-lived."

There was enough skill and strength in the man's next attack for Hacon to believe Balreaves made no idle boast. He ceased to taunt the man and concentrated on winning the battle, determined not to let Balreaves escape justice again.

# Chapter 25

"Robert, ye cannae mean to put me in this ditch?"

Jennet stared in dismay at the rut strewn with leaves and pine needles. The carts had been driven into the woods that stood between the road to Stirling and the open fields and moors that encircled Dubheilrig. She could hear the dull echo of battle, but no one would let her draw near enough to look. They also prepared for any possible attack or trouble from Balreaves's men if and when they fled this way. Jennet did not, however, believe she needed to be hidden to the extent of being tucked into a ditch. She scowled at Robert as he and Ranald lined the trench with blankets.

"Those dinnae make it any more welcoming. Why cannae I stay in the cart?"

"'Tis the first place ye would be seen," answered Ranald. "We cannae be seen weel from the road or from the fields of Dubheilrig, but Balreaves's men arenae apt to take such an open route if they break free of our men. Ye will be much safer here, better hidden and at a distance from the carts, which could too easily draw their attention."

"I may not draw *their* attention, but what of the interest of whatever might lurk in that hole?"

"There is nothing lurking in there. Please, Jennet, get in. 'Tis for the best."

With a sigh, she allowed Ranald and Robert to help her into the ditch, but to Elizabeth she said, "Why didnae you speak up? I was of the belief that one of these men is your husband."

"Aye, he is, but"—Elizabeth adopted an expression of meek piety—"I would ne'er argue with my dear husband."

Trying to get comfortable, Jennet noticed that Robert greeted that claim with the same scorn she did. She found the ditch no more comfortable than the cart, but no worse either. Left sitting there, able to hear only the muted sounds of the fight to save Dubheilrig, Jennet found her discomfort demanding more of her attention.

She frowned. Her aches and pains were slightly different from what they had been all day long. It no longer felt as if her whole body was sore. All the little pains were becoming one, uniting and centering around her abdomen. She required only a moment to understand what that meant, and cursed.

"Is something wrong?" Elizabeth asked, her attention immediately drawn to Jennet.

"Mayhaps." She looked up to see that Ranald and Robert were standing several yards away at the very edge of the wood, watching what was happening on the hill in Dubheilrig, and added, "Something could be verra wrong indeed."

"With the babe?" Elizabeth edged closer to Jennet.

"I believe it may have decided to arrive now."

"Now? In a ditch? With men fighting so near at hand that we can hear them?"

"Aye, now. I thought I was but bone weary of travel. Howbeit, what was an uncomfortable feeling with no purpose save to make me miserable now has a purpose. I had wondered why my verra active bairn was so still."

"Preparing to journey into the world. Robert!" Elizabeth called, bringing him and Ranald hurrying over.

"Keep your voice down, Lizbet," Robert scolded. "Do ye want the enemy kenning where we are? We cannae be certain that they are all trapped upon that hill."

"Well"—Elizabeth looked at Jennet—"mayhaps you had best find something she can clench her teeth on then."

"What?" Robert's eyes widened briefly before he cursed. "Not now."

"Aye, I fear so," Jennet murmured, then gasped softly as she felt her first recognizable contraction.

"Is something wrong? Do ye feel ill, Jennet?" Ranald frowned down at her.

"I am going to have the bairn now, Ranald," she explained, and had to smile at his look of pure horror. "'Tis not as terrible as all that."

"But—ye are in a ditch."

"True, I would prefer my chambers at Dubheilrig, but at least 'tis June and not December."

"Weel, mayhaps we can get you there. This fight might not take verra long."

"I shouldnae place a wager on that. I believe this bairn has been trying to get out all day. 'Tis just that I only realized it now."

"What can we do?"

"Get me more blankets, water, and some rags," Elizabeth replied. As both men hurried away to do just that, she turned to smile at Jennet. "A few more blankets and this hole in the ground will not be such a poor bed."

"Nay, 'twill do. If all had not gone so weel at Dunfermline, I would have been having this bairn in the castle dungeons."

"Sweet Mary, do not even think of it." Elizabeth gave an exaggerated shudder and quickly held Jennet's hand as she suffered another contraction. "Are they very strong yet?" she asked in a soft voice as Jennet's panting eased.

"Strong enough. Elizabeth, do ye think Hacon is all right?"

"Aye, of a certain. He is a fine, skilled fighter. His plan was to surprise Balreaves, and my Robert says he did just that. Come, 'tis time to think of yourself and this child. Your man is fine," she reiterated. "Why ask now?"

"Have ye ever heard it said that when one person dies another is born? I just wondered if—"

"Nay! Cease that talk right this minute. Such dark thoughts could mar the child in some way."

Recovering from another contraction, Jennet was still able to smile. "I think that belief must be as foolish as the one I just mentioned. No need to look so fretful. I will only think of having this bairn and of how surprised Hacon will be when he returns victorious. He will have saved Dubheilrig and become a father in the same day."

Hacon smiled despite his increasing exhaustion. Balreaves had indeed proved to be a skilled fighter, but he was not skilled enough. Hacon was tiring, but Balreaves was tiring faster. The man's skin was gray and dripping with sweat. Despite the cover of Balreaves's thick jupon and mail shirt, Hacon could see the man's chest heaving as he labored for breath. Soon he would falter, make a fatal mistake. He allowed a pause in their constant parry and thrust, watching as Balreaves struggled to gather some strength.

"Ye have a choice, Balreaves," he said, wanting to be sure he was not going to kill a man who would willingly give up.

"Choice? What choice? Death for trying to use the king to kill you, death for killing your little whore's mother, or death for trying to kill you."

"Ye could surrender. I would send ye to the king."

"Oh, aye, there is mercy. Either I die at your hands or at his."

"Ye could plead mercy. He may grant it. Ye may be but banished, exiled."

"Without a farthing to my name? Nay, I think not. Let us end it here."

"Where is the gain for you in that?"

"I dinnae intend to die, if that is what ye think."

"Ye cannae win. Aye, ye have skill, but ye have let others fight your battles for too long. Ye have lost the strength and endurance ye need to beat me. Surrender, Balreaves, or die now."

"If I die, I will take ye to hell with me." He lunged toward Hacon.

For a few more moments they battled each other fiercely, but Balreaves's renewed strength was born of desperation and faded fast. Hacon knocked back a savage sword swing, and Balreaves did not have the stamina left to absorb the blow. He staggered and lost his shield. Although he needed two hands to hold his weapon, he would not yield. Hacon's next strike was blocked and the man fell to his knees. Balreaves raised his sword again and Hacon knew the man would force him to be his executioner.

The end came but a moment later. Hacon felt no real exultation as his sword pierced Balreaves's heart. He had not felt the depth of hate nor the twisted bitterness that Balreaves had. The only real emotion he experienced was relief. Now there would be no more daggers slipping out of the shadows. He also had a sense of justice done, justice for Jennet's murdered mother.

He glanced around and saw that the battle was won. A few of Balreaves's men were secured as captives, the rest lay dead or nearly so. Hacon sat atop a battered-down section of the barmkin, thinking idly that the wall could be repaired, and smiled as his father approached. When his father returned the smile, Hacon knew that his mother, Murdoc, and Katherine were unhurt.

"Ye are free?" Lucais asked immediately.

"Aye, free and the Gillard name cleared of any taint. My wee wife could talk the devil into drinking holy water." He smiled faintly when Lucais chuckled. "I will tell ye the whole of it later."

"I am eager to hear it, as will be your mother."

"Did we lose many?" he asked, as Lucais sat down beside him.

"Ere ye arrived—aye, five. Three men, a woman, and a child. Some may yet die, for they suffered some grievous injuries. Howbeit, in this last melee—nay. Not yet, leastwise. Again, some are sorely wounded."

"Elizabeth is with us," Hacon said. "Her skills and Jennet's might stop the cost of this fight from growing."

"They do have the healing touch. I grieve for those who died, dinnae mistake me. Howbeit, I also thank God they werenae kinsmen or old friends. They were some of the new folk who had joined with us and claimed our protection in these troubled times."

"I understand. I am but sorry they didnae get all the protection they needed," he murmured.

"Nay, dinnae feel guilty. They were weel fought for, but we were sorely pressed. Your fine tower house proved its worth, though I fear it was battered some."

Hacon grimaced as he looked around. "'Tis not a pretty sight, but not beyond repair. If the weather holds good, we could still move in by fall or early winter. Dugald," he called when he saw the man looking for him.

Dugald hurried over, sparing a brief glance for Balreaves's body. "'Tis done then."

"Aye, done. He chose this end, though I offered him a chance to surrender." He shook his head. "He forced me to be his executioner, to carry out the king's decree."

"And to gain a swifter, cleaner death than many another would have granted. Most of his men chose the same."

"Most?" Hacon tensed, eyeing Dugald with wary suspicion. "I see some were captured."

"Aye, and some slipped free. They are being hunted down now."

"Then we had best hie back to Jennet and the others. Where is her father?"

"I believe he is probably there already," replied Dugald as Hacon stood.

"Surely ye left men to guard her?" said Lucais.

"Aye, Robert, Ranald, and four boys," Hacon said. "Tell Mother that, if she can tend to it in the midst of this confusion, Jennet would be deeply grateful for a fine, soft bed. The journey has tired her."

"There will be one readied. I dinnae believe our home was much damaged. Ye just go and get the poor lass and bring her back here safely," he added even as Hacon and Dugald left, loping toward the wood where they knew Robert would have concealed the carts.


"Push, Jennet," ordered Elizabeth as she crouched between Jennet's legs.

"I thought I was," Jennet snapped, the bite of her angry words lessened by her need to pant.

"Are ye sure I should be a part of this?" Ranald asked as he wiped the sweat from Jennet's brow with a cool, damp cloth.

Jennet was almost able to smile, but the increasing frequency and strength of the contractions made it impossible. Poor Ranald sat at her back. She was cradled between his long legs, her back and head resting against his chest, and she gripped his knees as each contraction ripped through her. That had to hurt him at times, but he made no complaint, acting as her support even as he tried to ease her discomfort by bathing her face. The few glances she had taken had told her he was feeling sorely embarrassed yet fascinated. She supposed she ought to feel embarrassed too, but she was too grateful for his aid to care what he saw.

"If ye keep rolling about in the hay with the lasses, acting like my wicked father, ye will see a lot more of this," she said.

"What a disrespectful lass ye are."

There was no mistaking that drawling voice, and Jennet looked up to see her father crouched at the rim of the ditch. He was smiling, but she could see the concern on his face. She wanted to say something to ease it, but knew there were no adequate words. The only way to put an end to his worry would be to bear the child and recover quickly.

"It doesnae hurt for the lad to ken the consequences of that sort of thing. I dinnae suppose ye brought a bed."

"Nay, lass. Ah, weel, your mother bore ye in a place much akin to this. Ye follow in her footsteps."

"Why couldnae I pick a footstep set in a sweet, enjoyable place with big, soft pillows?" She gave herself over to her contractions for a moment, then frowned as they briefly eased, and a sound besides her own panting reached her ears. "Is something wrong? I thought I heard shouting. It is Hacon?"

"Nay, though he should be along soon. And ere ye ask— his family and Murdoc are unharmed. Howbeit, I fear some of Balreaves's dogs have escaped and run this way."

"Where is Robert?" Elizabeth demanded.

"He is with the lads guarding the carts and will stay there. Ranald, I think ye had best get up here."

"Go," Jennet ordered when Ranald hesitated. "Elizabeth, hold me up so he can move."

Once Ranald climbed out of the rut, Jennet started to edge back. Elizabeth quickly aided her until her back was against the sloping end of the ditch. It was not as comfortable a support as Ranald had been but it would serve, she decided as she struggled through another contraction. She silently cursed when, as her head cleared, she heard the first clash of swords. She forced herself forward a little to yank at Elizabeth's skirt. The woman was quickly recalled to the need to keep down and stopped peering out at the men fighting a mere few feet away.

"This is the time," Elizabeth whispered, "when we are usually told to run away."

"Now there would be a sight to make folk gape, if I could run at all. I think it will be soon."

"Aye." Elizabeth checked her progress. "I can see the head."

"'Tis big and fat like his father's, eh?"

"'Tis covered with black hair like his mother's."

"Oh. I had rather hoped for a fair-haired bairn."

It was the last thing she could say, at least coherently. Elizabeth forced a thick square of leather between Jennet's teeth so that her cries would not draw attention to them. They had no way of knowing how many of Balreaves's men were out there or how much of a threat they posed. At the moment silence was their only and best means of defense if her father and the others failed.

Jennet wondered at the strangeness of it all. Here she was, crouched in the narrow, blanket-lined hollow with Elizabeth, struggling to bear her child, while all around her were the sounds of men locked in fierce combat. Through the increasing roar in her ears she heard the clash of swords, the yells and screams of men struggling to kill each other. She prayed she was not giving her child life only to have one of Balreaves's men end it. Then she lost all awareness of anything besides helping her child break free of her body.

There was a wrenching, all-encompassing pain. Jennet knew she screamed but heard only a low, soft moan. She felt her teeth dig into the square of leather. For a moment she was aware of nothing. Then she heard a muffled cry.

She spat out the leather and looked at Elizabeth. The woman held a birth-stained child and was gently wiping it clean. Still, Jennet could not hear anything. She felt the touch of icy fear.

"Elizabeth?" she whispered, briefly surprised at the hoarseness of her voice.

Elizabeth crept closer. She set the child in the crook of Jennet's arm and handed her a dampened rag.

"A fine boy," she said in a whisper. "You must put him to your breast to keep him quiet. I washed his head and face. Do the rest as you suckle him. I will clean you up."

With a weary sigh, Jennet did as she was told. She ached to look closely at her son, to hear his cry and count all his fingers and toes, but knew that would have to wait. Although no longer so close at hand, the sounds of fighting were still not far off.

Jennet held her child close and savored the feel of him in her arms while she prayed that the enemy threatening them would be defeated. In cautious silence, she tried to clean her child yet keep him from making any noise. His breath was hot against her skin, and that sign of life gave her joy enough for the moment.

It was several minutes before Elizabeth squeezed in beside her. Carefully they wrapped the baby in a blanket. He was awake but quiet, and Elizabeth took a minute to bathe Jennet's face and neck. Then they waited, silent and fearful, to see if they would be safe or might yet have to fight for their lives.

Hacon wiped his sword clean and looked around. He and Dugald had arrived in the woods in time to help dispatch the last of Balreaves's men. Only one of the youths he had left to guard the carts was injured, and the wound did not look serious. What troubled him was that he did not see Jennet, nor Artair, although the man had been at his side just a moment ago.

"Where is Jennet?" he demanded, stepping over to Ranald and Robert.

"She is unhurt," replied Ranald, tossing aside his helmet and splashing his face with water from a bucket near one of the carts.

"Aye, but *where* is she?" Hacon frowned, feeling a pinch of fear when both Robert and Ranald hesitated to answer. "Are ye telling the truth? She *is* unhurt?"

"Oh, aye, aye. I expect Artair had gone to her even now."

"Then why dinnae ye take me to her?"

"I ought to tell you something first," began Ranald.

"Ye can tell me after ye take me to Jennet and I can see for myself that she is all right."

"She is just o'er here." Ranald headed through the underbrush, Hacon at his heels. "And there is Artair," he said as they wended their way through the thick undergrowth and spotted Artair crouched by the ditch.

"Who is he talking to?" demanded Hacon, yanking his leg free of a clutching briar.

"Jennet. She and Elizabeth are in a ditch just there."

Muttering a curse, Hacon tried to hurry, but the briars impeded him. He knew that hiding Jennet had been the best thing to do, but he was anxious to get her home. A ditch in the forest was no place for a woman heavy with child.

"Ah, lassie," murmured Artair as he smiled down at his daughter, "ye did your father proud. Not a sound from you."

"It wasnae easy. I bit clean through the leather." She eased the blanket away from her son's face so that her father could see him. "'Tis a boy. That should please Hacon."

"I dinnae think the mon was particularly concerned whether he had a son or a daughter. But, aye"—he winked—"a mon in his place can only welcome a son. Got all his parts, does he?"

Jennet made a weary grimace of irritation. "Aye. Ye can judge the worth of his parts later. Do ye think Hacon will be along soon?" she asked as Elizabeth eased away from her to sit by her feet.

"Oh, aye, he is stumbling this way even now. The brambles are giving him a wee bit of trouble." He looked toward Hacon as the younger man finally broke free of the undergrowth. "Where have ye been, lad?" asked Artair.

Pausing to glare at his father-in-law, Hacon grumbled, "How did ye get through that tangle so cleanly? Fly o'er it?" He did not wait for an answer from the grinning man but looked down at Jennet and gaped. "My God!" he whispered in shock.

"Nay, only your son," drawled Artair.

"Papa," Jennet scolded, then joined Elizabeth in giggling over her father's nonsense. "We have a son, Hacon."

"A son," he muttered, kneeling at the edge of the ditch and continuing to stare at her. "Ye had the bairn."

"Aye." She glanced at her father. "I told ye I wed a mon with a wit as keen as any blade."

"I can see that." Artair nudged Hacon. "Wake up, lad. We need to get her home."

Hacon shook free of his shock long enough to help Artair, Ranald, and Robert lift Jennet out of the ditch. He yanked off his battle-stained gauntlets and tucked them into his sword belt before taking her into his arms. All the way back to the cart he kept looking from her to the baby, which Artair carried with an enviable ease. Hacon was barely aware of the interest and congratulations of Dugald and the youths waiting by the carts. It was not until he realized Dugald was laughing softly that he really began to regain his scattered wits.

"What are ye cackling about?" he grumbled as Dugald helped him settle Jennet and the baby in the cart.

"Just wondering how many times ye got cracked offside the head today." Dugald winked at Jennet, who smiled in response.

"Get up there and drive the cart," Hacon ordered as he climbed in next to his wife.

As they started on their way, Jennet eyed Hacon with increasing concern. She had expected him to be surprised, even shocked by the baby's birth, but he should have said something more than he had so far. Aside from that brief exchange with Dugald, he had been silent, simply staring at her and their new son. She told herself not to be foolish, that silence did not necessarily mean disapproval or disappointment. The time and place were not suitable for indulging in the sometimes foolish joy of new parenthood. Nevertheless, as Hacon's silence lengthened, her fears grew until she felt compelled to speak.

"Hacon?" She tensed when he raised his steady gaze from the child to look at her. "Are ye pleased?" She gave a soft gasp of surprise when he abruptly kissed her.

"Ye can be a foolish wee lass," he murmured, and gently trailed a finger down her cheek.

"Such flattery." She gave him a tired smiled. "'Tis just that I expected ye to say something and ye didnae, not a word."

"I couldnae think of one." He laughed softly. "Lass, I left ye heavy with child and returned from the battle to find myself a father. It has taken me this long just to believe it. I am so verra sorry ye had to bear our son in such a poor place."

"It couldnae be helped. Ye won? Balreaves is a threat no longer?"

"He will ne'er trouble us again. We lost a few people, but it could have been far worse."

"Aye." She smiled when he moved, sitting so that she could rest her head in his lap. "How is the tower house?"

"It has some damage, but it can be mended. It proved its worth, as did your wall. We shall have a fine, strong home."

"There is some comfort in that. Hacon, we need a name for our son."

"Ye have no ideas?"

"Nay, I ne'er did settle on one."

"Weel, I ended up with two." He idly stroked her hair. "Ninian or Pendair."

"Ah, I understand your trouble. Both are fine, strong

*Hannah Howell*

names. Mayhaps we should ask our friends and see which is chosen more often. I will be happy with either. Aye, and so will your son."

"My son," he whispered. "'Tis as sweet as the words *my wife*."

She blushed. There was an expression in his eyes that briefly took away all thought of how tired she was, that soothed her every ache and pain. Without words he was telling her something very important, but she did not trust her own judgment. She was about to say those words herself to him, when a sudden cry told her that they had been spotted by the people of Dubheilrig. Inwardly, she cursed, knowing the moment was lost, and swore she would seize the very next opportunity to open her heart to him.

Their arrival became a confusing round of greetings and congratulations. To Jennet's relief, Serilda quickly took matters in hand. In an admirably short time, she had Jennet in bed, washed, and attired in a clean nightdress. Her baby was also thoroughly cleaned, wrapped in fresh swaddling clothes, and placed in a cradle nearby. As she nestled against the pillows, Jennet realized how tired she was. She managed only a faint smile for Serilda when the woman helped her drink some mead.

"I think, child," Serilda said, "ye have done more than anyone to renew the spirits of the people of Dubheilrig."

"By having a bairn in a ditch?" she jested, smothering a large yawn.

"The lad will be delighted with the tale when he is old enough to be told. Now, ye rest."

"Where is Hacon?" she asked, wondering why he was taking so long to join her.

"Cleaning himself. He was slow to reach the bath we readied for him, so occupied with boasting was he," Serilda said, smiling when Jennet gave a tired laugh. "Men do tend to think they deserve more credit than they do." She tucked the covers more securely around Jennet. "Go to sleep. He will surely be here when ye next open your eyes."

Hacon slipped into the room as quietly as he could, easing the heavy door shut behind him. He had experienced so many different emotions in the last few hours he felt worn out. Walking with the same silent tread he used to sneak up on the enemy, he crossed the room and crouched by the cradle where his son slept. He ached to touch the child but did not want to wake him, if only because it would disturb Jennet.

"Tiny, isnae he," whispered Jennet, smiling sleepily when Hacon moved to sit on the edge of the bed and took her hand in his. "'Tis always a surprise to see how small and helpless a bairn is."

"Aye. I hope I can learn to hold him with the ease and skill your father does."

"Ye will. And he will grow sturdier verra quickly. Aye, especially if he means to be as large as his father."

Smiling, Hacon kissed her cheek. "How do ye feel? Mother assures me ye are hale and strong, simply weary."

"She is right." She yawned again and softly laughed. "As ye can see." She frowned when he stood up and began to shed his clothes. "Do ye mean to share this bed with me?"

"Aye. Why not? Would ye rather I didnae?"

"Nay, I should like it. I but wondered if it was . . . weel, allowed."

"Ah." He slipped beneath the covers and, lying on his back, gently tucked her up to his side. "I suspect someone somewhere will think it worth complaining about, but . . ." He shrugged. "On the morrow I begin work on the tower house again. Ye may see little of me for a while."

Snuggling up to him, she closed her eyes. "I can help too, as soon as I am done resting."

He smiled when she quickly went lax, her breathing falling

into the soft, slow cadence of sleep. Pressing a kiss on the top of her head, he stared up at the ceiling.

He had two months to ready their home. If the weather stayed fair he could do it. Then, he vowed, he and Jennet would spend some time alone. They would secure themselves in the tower house, away from the demands of Dubheilrig, of Murdoc, and of all the other demands that intruded on their lives. Finally they would really be alone, if only for a little while, and he would make sure they really talked to each other. It was past time, he decided, for them to stop hiding behind their work, friends, and family and be fully honest with each other. He could not bear to drift along anymore.

# Chapter 26

"Elizabeth, I asked you a question. Where is my husband?"

Not looking up from her chore of placing the newly cleaned linen in the chest, Elizabeth shrugged. "At the tower house. Is this chemise not the loveliest you have ever seen?"

"Aye," Jennet muttered with complete indifference as she sprawled on her back on the bed and scowled up at the ceiling. "He is avoiding me."

"Nonsense." After placing the fine, lace-trimmed chemise in the chest, Elizabeth closed the lid and stood up.

"'Tis *not* nonsense. I have barely caught a glimpse of the mon since I birthed Ninian nearly ten weeks ago."

"He was at the christening."

"Aye, but not there before it and gone soon after. 'Tis as if he fears I might speak to him."

"He is here each night sleeping at your side." Elizabeth moved to sit on the edge of the bed.

"Aye, sleeping. He sneaks in after I am asleep and sneaks out ere I wake up. I have seen him a few times when he came in whilst I was feeding Ninian, but ere I put the bairn back in his cradle, Hacon is snoring merrily and quite loudly." She frowned. "I ne'er realized before that he snores."

"'Tis for the best. You needed to heal from the birth. 'Tis no time to have a randy man pestering you."

"I have been healed for nearly a fortnight." She sighed. "He doesnae want me anymore."

"Oh, now you are talking nonsense. You are trying to find a reason for this odd humor of yours. Now, I know you got a message from your father. Is he well?"

"Aye, he is weel and he swore allegiance to Robert the Bruce. He is already off on some commission for the king. It sounds verra risky. I dinnae like it much. And dinnae try to turn my mind from the problem of Hacon."

"There is no problem. But I can see you mean to fret and sulk, so I shall leave you to it."

Turning onto her stomach, Jennet grumbled, "I should have realized I would get no sympathy from you. Ye are near to petitioning the Pope to make Hacon a living saint. Weel, I will tell ye what I think. Every mon wants a son. Hacon has his now, so he doesnae want me. He just hasnae found a way to tell me yet."

"I am not even going to reply to that. You can just lie here and wallow in your misery. 'Tis clear you want to."

Jennet winced as the door shut behind Elizabeth with far more force than was necessary. She supposed Elizabeth was right in a way. She did want to wallow in her misery. For days she had been trying to push aside her hurt and sadness, her sense of defeat. She was tired of doing that. It could not hurt to let those feelings flow for a while; it could even help a little.

That Elizabeth would call her fears nonsense did sting somewhat. They ran too deep, were too strong, to be so callously ignored. There was also a good reason for them. Hacon was showing signs of being tired of her. What else could she think when her usually lusty man turned his back to her night after night? She had made her eagerness to renew their lovemaking as clear as she could without boldly demanding he do his duty by her as her husband. The memory of that attempt still caused her to wince. He had muttered something about being too tired and had started snoring. What else could it mean other than he did not desire her any longer? She sighed heavily, close to tears. If matters did not improve very soon, she would not fear it or worry about it—she would know it.

Humming quietly to himself, Hacon strode into his parents' home and headed for the stairs, then came to an abrupt halt. Elizabeth and his mother were standing at the foot of the stairs and the looks they were giving him told him he was not in their good graces.

"Is something wrong?" he asked, eager to get to Jennet but not wanting any problem left unsettled which might later disturb them.

"I thought ye had some plan for Jennet," said his mother. "A few days alone or the like."

"Aye, I do. Now, if ye will tell me what troubles you, I can get to her all the sooner."

"But ye arenae getting to her. That is the problem. The poor child begins to think ye are purposely avoiding her."

"Ah, I see. Weel, if you sweet ladies would but step inside"—he gently shooed them out of his way—"I will immediately solve that problem. And," he added as he started up the stairs, "no one had better bring me any more problems until at least three days have passed." He winked at them over his shoulder, grinning when they both laughed.

He stepped into his chambers and frowned. Jennet was sprawled on her stomach on the bed. She did not even look to see who had entered. He did not need to see her face to know her mood. Her whole pose spoke of feelings of dejection. He had not considered that possible consequence of his subterfuge. Then again, he mused, the fact that she would react so strongly gave him hope. If she did not care for him, his lack of attention would not trouble her so much.

"Come along, Jennet," he said as, after striding over to the bed, he picked her up in his arms.

"What are ye doing?" she cried, quickly putting her arms around his neck as he marched out the door.

"Carrying you." He started down the stairs, briefly sending his mother and Elizabeth a look that made them hurry out of sight.

"I had guessed that for myself. Hacon!" She blushed, embarrassed when he stepped outside. Several people paused in their work and grinned at them. "Will ye put me down? I am able to walk for myself."

"A mon should always carry away his plunder. I think it might even be a law."

"I think ye have finally had one knock offside the head too many," she retorted. "Where are we going?"

"To the tower house."

"Is it finished then?"

"Finished enough."

That answer did not make any sense to her. She decided to simply play along. Hacon was clearly suffering from some brain fever. As soon as she could get him to lie down or stay put in one place, she would send for Serilda and Elizabeth. Together they would be certain to concoct some potion to bring him back to his senses.

Her concern over the state of Hacon's mind was briefly diverted as they entered the tower house. It looked nearer completion than it had even before Hacon had been dragged off to Dunfermline. They made their way up the stairs, built so that any attacker climbing them would find his sword arm against the wall. Jennet knew what a fatal disadvantage that could be. It reminded her that, despite the elegant tapestries and warm carpets, the keep had been built for defense.

When he finally stopped, she took a good look around. They were in a large chamber with a huge bed. A large fireplace filled one wall. Animal skins covered the stone floor.

She was just about to ask him where he had gotten the fine wool tapestries on the walls when he walked over to the bed and dropped her onto it. Once over her surprise, she eyed him warily as he sat on the edge of the bed and began to untie his cuarans.

"'Tis verra nice," she murmured. "Ye have done a lot of work."

"I told you I was working hard." He unlaced and took off his tunic.

"Aye, ye did." As he shed his undertunic, she demanded, "What are you doing?"

"Taking my clothes off."

"I can see that," she snapped.

"And it might be wise if ye took yours off too."

Trying hard not to be diverted by his increasingly naked form, she asked, "And why should I do that?"

"Because I wouldnae wish to tear them in my eagerness," he replied even as he tossed aside his braies and sprawled on top of her. "And I am feeling verra eager indeed."

Suddenly she was angry, despite how his nakedness and soft words stirred her desire. He had ignored her, even pushed her aside. Now he decided he wanted her. She deeply resented being used in such a way.

"Mayhaps I am too tired."

"Then I had best rouse you." He started to unlace her tunic.

"Oh, I see how it is." She unsuccessfully tried to halt his slow but dogged removal of her clothes. "Ye have suddenly decided ye want a wee tussle, so up and grab the wife. Weel, I willnae be treated like—"

He kissed her, interrupting her tirade. She tried not to let her needs rule her, tried to fight her desire for him, but it was impossible. By the time he ended the slow, hungry kiss, she had a less than firm hold on her righteous anger.

"Hacon, ye arenae listening to me."

"Can we have this argument later?" He nibbled on her ear as he finished unlacing her clothing.

"I shouldnae give in." She heard the huskiness in her voice and knew she had already given in.

"Oh, aye, give in. Ye can scold me later."

With a sigh of both pleasure and resignation, she decided he was right. She could make her displeasure with him known later. It might not be the best, right, or even wisest thing to do, but she needed what he offered. She ached for it.

When he removed the last of her clothing and they were finally flesh to flesh, she lost the last of her reluctance. She reveled in what he made her feel. Each stroke of his hand and tongue fed her passion until it took command of her. A soft cry of urgency and satisfaction escaped her when he finally joined their bodies. She used her arms and legs to hold him close as they worked as one to find release. The sound of their cries blending, the proof of how their passion was matched and shared, only added to the richness of her pleasure. She willingly accepted his weight when he collapsed on top of her, his sated body as limp as hers.

"Jennet?" Hacon eased the deep intimacy of their embrace but remained sprawled on top of her, lazily nuzzling her breasts.

"Mmmm?" Idly she moved her hand down his side and caressed his smooth hip.

"Do ye love me?"

"Aye."

It took a moment for Jennet to realize what she had just so blithely admitted. She was faintly aware of Hacon turning onto his back and hugging her tightly. In her mind that brief whispered conversation was repeated and repeated. Realizing she had been tricked, she gave a cry of outrage and hit Hacon, pulling free of his hold so that she could hit him again.

"Ye wretch! Ye sneaking, wretched mon!" she cried as she tried to keep hitting him.

Laughing and occasionally grunting as her small fists struck his flesh, Hacon wrestled with her until he got her pinned beneath him. His laughter faded as their eyes met. Before she was able to avert her gaze, he saw the glint of tears in her lovely eyes. That sweet confession which so delighted him had clearly left her very upset. He was not sure he understood why.

"Come, loving." He brushed a kiss over her mouth and gently smoothed a few strands of hair from her face. "Why are you so troubled?" He continued to toy with her hair, idly trying to recall when during their impassioned lovemaking he had undone her braid.

"Ye tricked me into speaking." She covertly studied him, slowly realizing that her confession had pleased him.

"Weel, it seemed to be the only way to get you to say what ye felt. I needed to ken what was in your heart."

"And what about what *I* need to hear? Ye pull the words from me yet give me none. Ye now ken all, and I ken naught."

"Naught?" He regarded her in surprise, propping himself up on his forearms. "Of course ye ken how I feel. Women always ken such things. 'Tis as plain as the nose upon my face. Everyone kens how I feel. 'Tis almost embarrassing," he grumbled. "Ye are making jest with me."

Jennet was filled with a mixture of emotions. He was, yet was not, telling her all she ached to hear. That brought her a pleasure so deep and all-encompassing she felt very close to tears.

But she also felt deeply annoyed, thoroughly disgusted with what she saw as a common male thickheadedness. He was honestly surprised that she did not simply know. Because he knew why he did what he did, he assumed that she would too. With the trick he had just played on her, she had proved that he needed to hear the words, yet he could not seem to understand that she did too. She still had a strong urge to hit him.

"Could ye explain *how* I was supposed to ken something ye ne'er saw fit to tell me?" she asked.

"Weel, there is this pas—"

"If," she quickly interrupted, "ye mean to say the fact that ye bedded me was some great sign, I should think again, husband."

He rubbed his chin and eyed her warily. "That doesnae say much to you?"

"Hacon, many a mon can bed most any woman or lass as long as she is still breathing. Aye, even if they have to put a sack o'er her head." She could see that he wanted to laugh, but he wisely repressed that urge. "A mon's passion doesnae tell a woman much. She doesnae ken if he feels or doesnae feel the same way with others. 'Tis clear my passion told you verra little about what was in my heart, even though I had ne'er been with a mon before. Why should your passion tell me anything about what is in your heart?"

"Fair enough. Weel, there is the way I have always treated you. Have I not behaved toward you in a manner that told you how I felt? Have I not protected you, even to the point of putting myself and my men at risk?"

"Ye have done the same for Murdoc."

He muttered a curse and regarded her with mild annoyance. "I took ye as my wife. Was that so unimportant too?"

"Nay, none of what ye have done was ever unimportant. Certainly not your wedding me. Howbeit, it doesnae tell me anything, not positively. Not even that ye took me for your wife, as ye are an honorable mon and I was a virgin of respectable birth."

Groaning softly, he pressed his forehead to hers. "We have been a fine pair of fools, havenae we?"

"We?" she murmured, slipping her arms about his neck. "Ye certainly have. I wouldnae say *I* have."

"Oh? Ye have been so verra honest and forthcoming then, have you? I cannae recall you speaking verra freely."

"Weel, mayhaps not. Oh, fair enough then," she said when

he lifted his head to give her a stern look. "*We* have been a fine pair of fools. 'Tisnae easy to speak so of what is in my heart."

"Nay," he agreed heartily, "'tisnae."

She started to laugh. "Listen to us. We commiserate with each other o'er how difficult it all is and yet say nothing. We but talk all around it."

Hacon grinned and laughed again, turning onto his back and gently tugging her into his arms. "We each ken what we ache to be told, yet still havenae said it."

"I told you."

"Nay, ye said aye after I asked you."

"'Tis much the same. So, 'tis your turn now."

There was a look in Hacon's eyes that told her he was playing a game with her. Settling herself more comfortably on top of him, she felt the quick response of his body and inwardly smiled. That suggested how he wished the game to be played. Kissing his chin, she peered at him from beneath her lowered lashes.

"And I say 'tis your turn. I may have only said aye, but ye havenae even said that yet." As she spoke she brushed soft, teasing kisses over his face. "So, ye have to say it this time. Three little words. It cannae be so verra difficult."

Murmuring his pleasure as she nibbled at his mouth, he said in an increasingly husky voice, "Ah, weel, I dinnae think I can say it . . . weel, just like that. I need some inspiration." He tried to take her tongue into his mouth, but she neatly eluded him.

"I see how it is. Ye tricked me into saying it, so now I must persuade *you* to say it."

"I didnae trick you. I but asked you a simple question. *And* ye didnae say it—not yet."

"Near enough. Nearer than you. *And* ye did trick me. Now, my great blond conqueror, I mean to *persuade* you until ye fair deafen me with the words."

"Have ye just thrown down a gauntlet, m'lady of Dubheilrig?"

"Aye, I believe I have, m'lord."

"Weel, I pick it up and readily accept this challenge. Persuade on."

Hacon knew he would lose the challenge within moments after she began to work her sweet magic on him, and he did not mind at all. He burrowed his fingers into her thick hair as she slowly covered his chest with soft, nibbling kisses and the warm strokes of her tongue. She moved her hands over his body in a way that robbed him of breath. He gave a groan of tense frustration when she dotted his thighs with kisses, drawing near but never reaching the place where he ached to feel her mouth. When she finally answered his silent pleas, eloquently voiced by his shifting body, he fought valiantly to maintain some control.

Finally, needing to feel her warmth surround him, he pulled her up his body. Sitting on top of him, she neatly eluded his attempt to make them one. He stared at her and suddenly recalled the game he had started.

"Unfair," he said, his voice thick.

"I ken it." She was a little surprised she had held on to her wits long enough to remember what she had intended to do when she begun. "Weel? Are ye persuaded yet?" She began to slowly ease their bodies together.

"Aye." He grasped her slim hips and pushed her down, driving himself home. "I love you. God help me, how I love you."

Bending forward, she placed her mouth against his and, in a voice that was soft and unsteady, said, "God best help me as weel, for I love you too." She kissed him then, their tongues mimicking the rhythm of their bodies as they sought and found the nectar their hunger demanded.


Jennet lazily moved her hand over Hacon's taut stomach. They had slept, eaten, and made love again. Even after Elizabeth briefly stopped by to bring Ninian, his demands to be fed had not interrupted them, for they had doted on him as Jennet nursed him. Once their son was back in his cradle, sleeping blissfully, she and Hacon had made love yet again. She decided this one day and night made up for all that had gone before, soothed all the hurts, doubts, and fears she had suffered.

"Hacon, when did ye ken that ye loved me?"

"'Tis hard to say, lass. I believe it was there long before I had the wit to see it."

"Did ye ken it when ye wed me?"

"Aye."

"Then why did ye ne'er say it, even on our wedding night?"

"Ye were waiting for me to speak even then?"

"Aye. I just couldnae get past my own fears and pride."

"Weel, I had much the same trouble. I was waiting for ye to respect me."

Raising up on her elbows, Jennet stared at him with a mixture of shock and confusion. "Ye were what?"

"Waiting for ye to respect me. I just couldnae bare my soul to a woman who didnae respect me. As ye can see, I couldnae set ye aside either. I kept thinking I could change the way ye felt."

"Hacon, when did I ever make ye think I didnae respect you?"

"Often. Ye made your feelings about knights and soldiers verra clear. I was sure ye accepted me without the armor. Howbeit, the moment I donned it and took up my sword to do what I *must* do, ye would turn from me. Then ye saw me only as blood hungry."

Wincing at her thoughtlessness, she bent forward and kissed him.

"What was that for?" he asked, lightly wrapping his arms around her.

"To try and ease the sting of those careless words. I gave

no thought to how they might hurt you. I was afraid for you and the men. And, I fear, I *still* dinnae believe the campaign in Ireland was right."

"Nay, it wasnae. We barely have a grip on our own lands, yet lost good men trying to take someone else's." He sighed as he idly smoothed his hands over her back. "I had no stomach for it but . . ." He shrugged.

"Aye—*but*. The king beckons and ye *must* answer. Ye must keep proving your loyalty. That was certainly shown when Balreaves so easily brought you before the king in chains with his lies. 'Twas your history of loyalty that eventually set you free."

"'Twas you who freed me by speaking so weel on my behalf."

"I had the weight of truth behind my words. Even Sir Niall could only agree. And I believe the king was troubled by the charges, held a seed of doubt about them in his mind. I could have talked until my tongue fell out at the king's feet, but it would have done no good if ye were not the mon ye are. That was why ye were set free and your name was cleared."

"When I heard you speak for me, heard the belief ye had in all ye said, I kenned I had won the respect I so badly needed. It was then I decided we would find time to be alone to speak our hearts, that this silence we kept between us must end."

"And that is why ye have avoided me these last two months?"

"Aye, I wanted us to have a place to go where we could be alone for a few days with no disruptions. We couldnae have had that at my parents' home. I wanted us to begin anew." He kissed her. "Did ye think I had lost interest in ye?"

"Aye."

"Weel, I am sorry for that. I ne'er meant to hurt ye. I just feared that if we began to be lovers again, without speaking on this first, we would simply fall back into our old ways."

"Aye, that could weel have happened. And I am sorry I gave

ye such hurt with my confusion, with my inability to understand what I felt or even, at times, what I believed. But, Hacon,
I always had respect for you. In truth, that was what caused
some of my confusion. For a long time my heart and all I
could see, all I kenned about you, warred with what I believed
about war and the soldiers who fought in it."

He brushed her cheek with his knuckles. "I ken it. At times,
I sensed the inner battle ye fought, but 'twas a battle ye had
to fight for yourself. I couldnae give you the answers ye
sought. Ye had to find them by yourself, within yourself."
He smiled faintly. "Although 'twas verra hard at times to
stand back and not defend myself."

"My confusion began that first night when ye didnae just
take me. Aye, and when ye went and got those foolish goats
so wee Murdoc could have milk." She smiled. "Ye were a
verra confusing mon."

"When did the confusion end?"

"Ere we were wed. I would ne'er have said those things,
ne'er have called you blood hungry, if I had thought ye would
take them to heart. I was so afraid for you and so verra angry
at the Bruce for asking you to risk your life for him again.
That shameless kiss"—she ignored his wide grin—"and the
gift of my rosary were my poor attempts to take back my
angry words.

"Dinnae ever take them to heart again," she continued. "I
should so like to vow I would ne'er say such things again, but
I cannae. Just remember, I dinnae like war and fighting, but
I ken ye have no choice. I also ken that ye are all a knight
should be. Ye do what ye must but with mercy, ne'er burning
the poor cottages or killing those who arenae trying to kill
you. I wish it would all stop, but we havenae the power to end
it so . . ." She sighed. "Just understand, and ne'er forget, I feel
only pride that my husband truly lives by the codes of
chivalry, that when ye answer your liege's call to arms, ye go
to fight only those who are ready and able to fight you."

His hands unsteady, emotion choking him, Hacon cupped her face in his hands and kissed her. As he ended the kiss and studied the small face he so loved, he whispered, "Those words mean nearly as much to me as those three little ones ye took so long to say."

"Ye mean—I love you."

"Aye." He hugged her, rubbing his cheek against her soft hair. "Ah, I do love you. Ye are the richest plunder I ever took. Ye have given me so much—yourself, our son. I can ne'er hope to repay it."

"Ye already have—by loving me, by being the mon ye are." She lifted her head, gave him a brief kiss, and slowly smiled. "I have ne'er been conquered by a finer knight."

"Ye have been conquered, have ye?" He neatly moved her so that she was sprawled on top of him.

"Aye, completely—heart and mind and soul."

"Then your conqueror has a command for you."

"And he expects complete obedience, does he?"

"Aye—in this. He commands you to love him, always, as he will love you," he ordered in a soft voice made faintly husky by the depth of his emotion.

"Aye—always." She touched her lips to his. "'Tis the sweetest command any woman has ever been given—and the easiest to obey."

Please turn the page for an
exciting sneak peek of

Hannah Howell's

HIGHLAND BARBARIAN

coming in December 2006!

*Scotland—Summer 1480*

"Ye dinnae look dead, though I think ye might be trying to smell like ye are."

Angus MacReith scowled at the young man towering over his bed. Artan Murray was big, strongly built, and handsome. His cousin had done well, he thought. Far better than all his nearer kin who had born no children at all or left him with ones like young Malcolm. Angus scowled even more fiercely as he thought about that man. Untrustworthy, greedy, and cowardly, he thought. Artan had the blood of the MacReiths in him and it showed, just as it did in his twin Lucas. It was only then that Angus realized Artan stood there alone.

"Where is the other one?" he asked.

"Lucas had his leg broken," Artan replied.

"Bad?"

"Could be. I was looking for the ones who did it when ye sent word."

"Ye dinnae ken who did it?"

"I have a good idea who did it. A verra good idea." Artan shrugged. "I will find them."

Angus nodded. "Aye, ye will, lad. Suspicion they will be hiding now, eh?"

"Aye. As time passes and I dinnae come to take my reckoning they will begin to feel themselves safe. 'Twill be most enjoyable to show them how mistaken they are."

"Ye have a devious mind, Artan," Angus said in obvious admiration.

"Thank ye." Artan moved to lean against the bedpost at the head of the bed. "I dinnae think ye are dying, Angus."

"I am nay weel!"

"Och, nay, ye arenae, but ye arenae dying."

"What do ye ken about it?" grumbled Angus, pushing himself upright enough to collapse against the pillows Artan quickly set behind him.

"Dinnae ye recall that I am a Murray? I have spent near all my life surrounded by healers. Aye, ye are ailing, but I dinnae think ye will die if ye are careful. Ye dinnae have the odor of a mon with one foot in the grave. And, for all ye do stink some, 'tisnae really the smell of death."

"Death has a smell ere it e'en takes hold of a mon's soul?"

"Aye, I think it does. And, since ye are nay dying, I will return to hunting the men who hurt Lucas."

Angus grabbed Artan by the arm, halting the younger man as he started to move away. "Nay! I could die and ye ken it weel. I hold three score years. E'en the smallest chill could set me firm in the grave."

That was true enough, Artan thought as he studied the man who had fostered him and Lucas for nearly ten years. Angus was still a big strong man, but age sometimes weakened a body in ways one could not see. The fact that Angus was in bed in the middle of the day was proof enough that whatever ailed him was serious. Artan wondered if he was just refusing to accept the fact that Angus was old and would die soon.

"So, ye have brought me here to stand watch o'er your

deathbed?" he asked, frowning for he doubted Angus would ask such a thing of him.

"Nay, I need ye to do something for me. This ague, or whate'er it is that ails me, has made me face the hard fact that, e'en if I recover from this, I dinnae have many years left to me. 'Tis past time I start thinking on what must be done to ensure the well-being of Glascreag and the clan when I am nay longer here."

"Then ye should be speaking with Malcolm."

"Bah, that craven whelp is naught but a stain upon the name MacReith. Sly, whining little wretch. I wouldnae trust him to care for my dogs let alone these lands and the people living here. He couldnae hold fast to this place for a fortnight. Nay, I willnae have him as my heir."

"Ye dinnae have another one that I ken of."

"Aye, I do, although I have kept it quiet. Glad of that now. My youngest sister bore a child two and twenty years ago. Poor Moira died a few years later bearing another child," he murmured, the shadow of old memories briefly darkening his eyes.

"Then where is he? Why wasnae he sent here to train to be the laird? Why isnae he kicking that wee timid mousie named Malcolm out of Glascreag?"

"'Tis a lass."

Artan opened his mouth to loudly decry naming a lass the heir to Glascreag and then quickly shut it. He resisted the temptation to look behind him to see if his kinswomen were bearing down on him, well armed and ready to beat some sense into him. They would all be sorely aggrieved if they knew what thoughts were whirling about in his head. Words like too weak, too sentimental, too trusting, and made to have bairns not lead armies were the sort of thoughts that would have his kinswomen grinding their teeth in fury.

But, Glascreag was no Donncoill, he thought. Deep in the Highlands, it was surrounded by rough lands and even rougher men. In the years he and Lucas had trained with Angus they had fought reivers, other clans, and some who wanted Angus's lands. Glascreag required constant vigilance and a strong sword arm. Murray women were strong and clever, but they were healers not warriors, not deep in their hearts. Artan also considered his kinswomen unique and doubted Angus's niece was of their ilk.

"If ye name a lass as your heir, Angus, every mon who has e'er coveted your lands will come kicking down your gates." Artan crossed his arms over his chest and scowled at the man. "Malcolm is a spineless weasel, but a mon, more or less. Naming him your heir would at least make men pause as they girded themselves for battle. Aye, and your men would heed his orders far more quickly than they would those of a lass and ye ken it weel."

Angus nodded and ran one scarred hand through his black hair, which was still thick and long but was now well threaded with white. "I ken it, but I have a plan."

A tickle of unease passed through Artan. Angus's plans could often mean trouble. At the very least, they meant hard work for him. The way the man's eyes, a silvery blue like his own, were shielded by his half-lowered lids warned Artan that even Angus knew he was not going to like this particular plan.

"I want ye to go and fetch my niece for me and bring her here to Glascreag where she belongs. I wish to see her once more before I die." Angus sighed, slumped heavily against the pillows, and closed his eyes.

Artan grunted, making his disgust with such a pitiful play for sympathy very clear. "Then send word and have her people bring her here."

Sitting up straight, Angus glared at him. "I did. I have been writing to the lass for years, e'en sent for her when her father and brother died ten, nay, twelve years ago. Her father's kinsmen refused to give her into my care e'en though nary a one of them is as close in blood to her as I am."

"Why didnae ye just go and get her? Ye are a laird. Ye could have claimed her as your legal heir and taken her. 'Tis easy to refuse letters and emissaries, but nay so easy to refuse a mon to his face. Ye could have saved yourself the misery of dealing with Malcolm."

"I wanted the lass to want to come to Glascreag, didnae I."

"'Tis past time ye ceased trying to coax her or her father's kinsmen."

"Exactly! That is why I want *ye* to go and fetch her here. Ach, laddie, I am sure ye can do it. Ye can charm and threaten with equal skill. Aye, and ye can do it without making them all hot for your blood. I would surely start a feud I dinnae need. Ye have a way with folk that I dinnae, that ye do."

Artan listened to Angus's flattery and grew even more uneasy. Angus was not only a little desperate to have his niece brought home to Glascreag, but also he knew Artan would probably refuse to do him this favor. The question was why would Angus think Artan would refuse to go and get the woman. It could not be because it was dangerous, for the man knew well that only something foolishly suicidal would cause Artan to, perhaps, hesitate. Although his mind was quickly crowded with possibilities ranging from illegal to just plain disgusting, Artan decided he had played this game long enough.

"Shut it, Angus," he said, standing up straighter and putting his hands on his hips. "*Why* havenae ye gone after the woman yourself and *why* do ye think I will refuse to go?"

"Ye would refuse to help a mon on his deathbed?"

"Just spit it out, Angus, or I will leave right now and ye will ne'er ken which I might have said—aye or nay."

"Och, ye will say nay," Angus mumbled. "Cecily lives near Kirkfalls."

"In Kirkfalls? Kirkfalls?" Artan muttered and then he swore. "That is in the Lowlands." Artan's voice was soft yet sharp with loathing.

"Weel, just a few miles into the Lowlands."

"Now I ken why ye ne'er went after the lass yourself. Ye couldnae stomach the thought of going there. Yet ye would send *me* into that hellhole?"

"'Tisnae as bad as all that."

"'Tis as bad as if ye wanted me to ride to London. I willnae do it," Artan said and started to leave.

"I need an heir of my own blood!"

"Then ye should ne'er have let your sister marry a Lowlander. 'Tis near as bad as if ye had let her run off with a Sassanach. Best ye leave the lass where she is. She is weel ruined by now."

"Wait! Ye havenae heard the whole of my plan!"

Artan opened the door and stared at Malcolm who was crouched on the floor, obviously having had his large ear pressed against the door. The thin, pale young man grew even paler and stood up. He staggered back a few steps and then bolted down the hall. Artan sighed. He did not need such a stark reminder of the pathetic choice Angus had for an heir now.

Curiosity also halted him at the door. Every instinct he had told him to keep on moving, that he would be a fool to listen to anything else Angus had to say. A voice in his head whispered that his next step could change his life forever. Artan wished that voice would tell him if that change would be for the better. Praying he was not about to make a very bad choice, he slowly turned to look at Angus, but he did not move away from the door.

Angus looked a little smug and Artan inwardly cursed. The old man had judged his victim well. Curiosity had always been Artan's weakness. It had caused him trouble and several injuries more times than he cared to recall. He wished Lucas were with him for his brother was the cautious one. Then Artan quickly shook that thought aside. He was a grown man now, not a reckless child, and he had wit enough to make his own decisions with care and wisdom.

"What is the rest of your plan?" he asked Angus.

"Weel, 'tis verra simple. I need a strong mon to take my place as laird once I die or decide 'tis time I rested. Malcolm isnae it and neither is Cecily. Howbeit, there has to be someone of MacReith blood to step into my place, the closer to me the better."

"Aye, 'tis the way it should be."

"So, e'en though ye have MacReith blood, 'tis but from a distant cousin. Howbeit, if ye marry Cecily—"

"Marry!?"

"Wheesht, what are ye looking so horrified about, eh? Ye arenae getting any younger, laddie. Past time ye were wed."

"I have naught against marriage. I fully intend to *choose* a bride some day."

Angus grunted. "*Some day* can sneak up on a body, laddie. I ken it weel. Now, cease your fretting for a moment and let me finish. If ye were to marry my niece, ye could be laird here. I would name ye my heir and nary a one of my men would protest it. E'en better, Malcolm couldnae get anyone to heed him if he cried foul. Cecily is my closest blood kin and ye are nearly as close to me as Malcolm is. So, ye marry the lass and, one day, Glascreag is yours."

Artan stepped back into the room and slowly closed the door. Angus was offering him something he had never thought to have—the chance to be a laird, to hold lands of his own. As the second born of the twins, his future had always been as Lucas's second, or as the next in line to be the laird of Donncoill if anything happened to Lucas, something he never cared to think about. There had always been only one possibility of changing that future—marriage to a woman with lands as part of her dowry.

Which was exactly what Angus was offering him, he mused, and felt temptation tease at his mind and heart. Marry

Cecily and become heir to Glascreag, a place he truly loved as much as he did his own homelands. Any man with wit enough to recall his own name would grab at this chance with both hands, yet, despite the strong temptation of it all, he hesitated. Since Artan considered his wits sound and sharp, he had to wonder why.

Because he wanted a marriage like his parents had, like his grandparents had, and like so many of his clan had, he realized. He wanted a marriage of choice, of passion, of a bonding that held firm for life. When it was land, coin, or alliances that tied a couple together the chances of such a good marriage were sadly dimmed. He had been offered the favors of too many unhappy wives to doubt that conclusion. If the thought of taking part in committing adultery did not trouble him so much, he would now be a very experienced lover, he mused and hastily shook aside a pinch of regret. He certainly did not want his wife to become one of those women and he did not want to be one of those men who felt so little bond with his wife that he repeatedly broke his vows. Or, worse, find himself trapped in a cold marriage and, bound tightly by his own beliefs, unable to find passion elsewhere.

He looked at Angus who was waiting for an answer with an ill-concealed impatience. Although he could not agree to marry a woman he had never met, no matter how tempting her dowry, there was no harm in agreeing to consider it. He could go and get the woman and decide on marrying her once he saw her. As they traveled back to Glascreag together he would have ample time to decide if she was a woman he could share the rest of his life with.

Then he recalled where she lived and how long she had lived there. "She is a Lowlander."

"She is a MacReith," Angus snapped.

Angus was looking smug again. Artan ignored it for the man was right in thinking he might get what he wanted. In many ways, it was what Artan wanted as well. It all depended upon what this woman Cecily was like.

"Cecily," he murmured. "Sounds like a Sassanach name." He almost smiled when Angus glared at him, the old man's pale cheeks now flushed with anger.

"'Tis no an English name! 'Tis the name of a martyr, ye great heathen, and weel ye ken it. My sister was a pious lass. She didnae change the child's christening name as some folk do. Kept the saint's name. I call the lass Sile. Use the Gaelic, ye ken."

"Because ye think Cecily sounds English." Artan ignored Angus's stuttering denial. "When did ye last see this lass?"

"Her father brought her and her wee brother here just before he and the lad died."

"How did they die?"

"Killed whilst traveling back home from visiting me. Thieves. Poor wee lass saw it all. Old Meg, her maid, got her to safety, though. Some of their escort survived, chased away the thieves, and then got Cecily, Old Meg, and the dead back to their home. The moment I heard I sent for the lass, but the cousins had already taken hold of her and wouldnae let go."

"Was her father a mon of wealth or property?"

"Aye, he was. He had both, and the cousins now control it all. For the lass's sake they say. And, aye, I wonder on the killing. His kinsmen could have had a hand in it."

"Yet they havenae rid themselves of the lass."

"She made it home and has ne'er left there again. They also have control of all that she has since she is a woman, aye?"

"Aye, and it probably helps muzzle any suspicions about the other deaths."

Angus nodded. "'Tis what I think. So, will ye go to Kirkfalls and fetch my niece?"

"Aye, I will fetch her, but I make no promises about marrying her."

"Not e'en to become my heir?"

"Nay, not e'en for that, tempting as it is. I willnae tie myself to a woman for that alone. There has to be more."

"She is a bonnie wee lass with dark red hair and big green eyes."

That sounded promising, but Artan fixed a stern gaze upon the old man. "Ye havenae set eyes on her since she was a child and ye dinnae ken what sort of woman she has become. A lass can be so bonnie on the outside she makes a mon's innards clench. But then the blind lust clears away, and he finds himself with a bonnie lass who is as cold as ice, or mean of spirit, or any of a dozen things that would make living with her a pure misery. Nay, I willnae promise to wed your niece now. I will only promise to consider it. There will be time to come to know the lass as we travel here from Kirkfalls."

"Fair enough, but, ye will see. Ye will be wanting to marry her. She is a sweet, gentle, biddable lass. A true lady raised to be a mon's comfort."

Artan wondered just how much of that effusive praise was true, then shrugged and began to plan his journey.

# About the Author

Hannah Howell is an award-winning author who lives with her family in Massachusetts. She is the author of twenty-two Zebra historical romances and is currently working on a new Highland historical romance, HIGHLAND SAVAGE (the second of a two book series focusing on twin brothers. Look for the first book, HIGHLAND BARBARIAN in December 2006!). Hannah loves hearing from readers and you may visit her website: www.hannahhowell.com.